Leisure Books is proud to present two novels of life and love in one special volume, by one of romance's most beloved authors . . . .

JOAN HOHL
writing as Amii Lorin

In **Breeze Off the Ocean,** beautiful young Micki had to keep from getting her heart broken yet again by Wolf Renninger. He had abandoned her once, but she longed to lose herself in his hard embrace.

In **Morgan Wade's Woman,** Samantha's marriage to devastatingly handsome Morgan had started as a business deal, but he wanted more from her—much more.

THE BEST OF JOAN HOHL

BREEZE OFF THE OCEAN
MORGAN WADE'S WOMAN

LEISURE BOOKS   NEW YORK CITY

A LEISURE BOOK®

May 1990

Published by

Dorchester Publishing Co., Inc.
276 Fifth Avenue
New York, NY 10001

BREEZE OFF THE OCEAN Copyright©MCMLXXXI by Amii Lorin

MORGAN WADE'S WOMAN Copyright©MCMLXXXI by Joan M. Hohl

Printed in the United States of America.

BREEZE OFF THE OCEAN

CHAPTER 1

Micki's foot eased off the gas pedal as she drew alongside the toll booth of the Delaware Memorial Bridge. After tossing her coins into the exact-change catchall, she pressed down on the pedal to begin the climb over the high-girdered twin span. Even though she had actually just begun her journey, as soon as she'd left the bridge and had driven onto Route 40 she had the feeling of coming home.

In her mind she ticked off the names of the towns she'd drive through. Woodstown, Elmer, Malaga, Buena, Mays Landing.

"Mays Landing."

The softly murmured name brought a curl of excitement simply because from there it was a relatively short hop on Atlantic Route 559 to Sommers Point, then home. At the thought of the Point a small smile tugged at her soft, full lips. She had had fun at the Point, she and the group of kids she'd palled around with all those years ago.

One particular memory wiggled into her mind and her smile deepened. They had been playing a game of tag, she and seven other kids, when one of the boys—Benny Trent —had let out a loud yelp of pain and began hopping around on one foot. They had all laughed and jeered at him until they saw his great toe become scarlet with blood. As they crowded around him, Benny had dropped onto the sand, twisting his foot to get a closer look at the wound. A deep gash, inflicted by a jagged, half-buried clam shell, ran diagonally across the pad of his toe, bleeding profusely.

One of the other boys, a college student a few years older than the rest, had taken a Red Cross first aid course and, after examining the gash, declared that it would definitely need stitches.

Off to the hospital they went, en masse, laughing and joking to keep the pale Benny's spirits up.

"Boy, Benny," Cindy Langdon, Micki's best friend, had jeered. "How dumb can you get? Didn't your mother ever tell you you can get hurt if you go jumping up and down on a stupid clam shell?"

At the hospital Benny was led away to have the wound cleaned and stitched, and the rest of the children had camped, noisily, in the waiting room, much to the obvious exasperation of the hospital personnel.

When Benny returned, his toe almost twice its size from bandaging, the taunts and jokes began again.

Micki shook her head ruefully at how callous they'd all been, then brought her attention sharply alert as she drove through Woodstown's early afternoon traffic. After she left the town behind, the traffic was sparse and Micki allowed memory to have its way again.

She and the other kids hadn't been altogether heartless, she thought with amusement. For two weeks they had slavishly waited on Benny hand and foot and that bonehead, as Cindy called him, loved every minute of it.

That memory triggered off others and Micki laughed aloud on realizing Benny had usually been the target of their banter. In the case of Cindy, well, her gibes had been downright insulting. If, at that time, anyone would have told them that eventually Cindy would be married to Benny, they would all, Cindy included, have become hysterical. But, two years ago, that was exactly what had happened.

Micki had not been able to attend the wedding, as she'd been on the West Coast on a buying trip, but she had sent a lavish wedding gift, along with her surprised congratulations.

It would be good to see Cindy and Benny again, Micki mused, as she headed the little silver car straight as its namesake—Arrow—toward the coast. How many, Micki wondered, besides Cindy and Benny, had made their home there? Except for Cindy, Micki had completely lost touch with the rest of her gang.

There had been eight of them that traveled around together regularly. At intervals their number swelled, for beach parties and dances and the like, but the eight had remained constant from grade through high school. They were all of the same age, with one exception, Tony Menella, who had been two years their senior. It had been Tony who had advised Benny to have his toe stitched. Where was Tony now? Micki sighed. She simply didn't know. A small smile curved her lips at the thought that she'd probably find out where they all were before too long. Cindy would know not only where they were but what they were doing, as Cindy had always kept tabs on all of them.

Memories, one after the other, kept Micki company as she made her way steadily toward the coast. Growing-up memories, many happy, a few sad, invaded her mind. Only one did she push away, refuse to recognize. That one particular memory she had not looked at for a long time; she had no intention of doing so now.

The miles sped by, even more quickly after she'd turned onto Atlantic Route 559, and as she drove through Sommers Point she switched off the car's air-conditioner and wound down the window beside her. Excitement mounting, Micki passed the sign reading WELCOME TO OCEAN

CITY and at that instant a breeze off the ocean told her she was home.

Just getting across the Ninth Street Bridge was a project. In mid-July the influx of tourists added to the going-home-from-work crowd to make traffic a late afternoon nightmare. Undaunted, Micki inched along serenely. She loved the sound, the smells, everything about her hometown, and the traffic, compared to the suppertime crush around Wilmington, didn't bother her a bit.

Drinking in the sights avidly, Micki observed the number of people, mostly families, on the sidewalks, obviously coming from the beach, lugging beach chairs, umbrellas, and other beach paraphernalia, and shepherding youngsters. Micki knew that most were headed to apartments or motels, some to prepare dinner, others to bathe and dress before going out again to dine at one of the city's many fine restaurants or fast-food shops.

There were changes, of course, as there always were in a resort city, and Micki noted them automatically. At one place several well-remembered buildings had disappeared and at another a very classy new restaurant now presided. The changes did not fill her with dismay. On the contrary, she had grown up with changes and through it all the city basically remained the same. It was still a clean city. A city full of churches. A family-oriented resort city that was lovely to vacation in and equally lovely to grow up in. To Micki it would always be the same. Except for one brief visit, she had been away for six years, and yet it was the same. Home.

She turned off Ninth onto Wesley and after several blocks the traffic thinned out considerably. Two more turns and there was hardly any traffic at all. And then there was the house she was brought to four days after her birth.

How achingly familiar it was, with the lacy-leafed mimosa in the middle of the front lawn and the profuse banks of fuchsia and white azalea bushes on either side of the front steps. Although she could see that the awnings were new, they were of exactly the same pattern as those that had always shaded the windows and large front porch.

With an emotional lump closing her throat, Micki turned the car onto the short driveway that ran along the side of the house and parked the car in front of the one-car garage at the end of the drive a short distance behind the house.

The soft whooshing sound of the kitchen screen door being pushed open came as she pulled on the hand brake.

"Micki!" Micki's father, Bruce Durrant, called as he strode along the flagstone path that led from the house to the garage. "Welcome home."

"Oh, Dad!" Micki flung the car door open and slid out into her father's arms. "It's so good to see you."

"Let me get a look at you." Grasping her arms, he leaned back, his eyes roving lovingly over her face. "You look more like your mother every time I see you," he murmured. "You've grown into a beautiful young woman, Micki."

"You wouldn't be just a tiny bit prejudiced, would you?" Micki laughed tremulously, blinking against the sudden hot sting in her eyes.

"Not in the least," Bruce denied firmly. "Your mother was an exceptionally lovely woman and you do look like her, maybe you're even more lovely."

Micki's eyes had been busy also and she noted the gray that now sprinkled her father's dark hair, the lines that radiated from his eyes, and the grooves from his nose to the corners of his mouth. Rather than distracting from his good looks, the signs of full maturity added character to his face and the silver among the dark strands of his hair lent a touch of distinction. Pleased with her perusal of him, Micki felt her smile widen.

"You look pretty good yourself, Mr. Durrant." Somehow the smile stayed in place. "How are you feeling?"

11

The hands grasping her shoulders gave her a little shake. "What a little worrywart you are." He chided softly. "I'm fine. Dr. Bassi assures me the ulcer is completely healed. I swear I haven't had a twinge of pain in months."

Micki's startlingly bright blue eyes gazed deeply into her father's dark brown ones. A sigh of relief escaped her lips at the happiness and contentment she found there. Happily Micki banished the memory of the panic and fear she'd experienced the night Regina had called her. God! What a horrible night that had been. Regina's voice, tight with fear, waking her with the news of her father's collapse with a perforated ulcer. Fighting the terror of the unknown, Micki had driven through the silent pre-dawn hours with a strangely icy composure. Thankfully, for Regina had been on the verge of falling apart, Micki's composure had lasted through the following nerve-racking two days, but after Dr. Bassi had told them that her father was out of danger, Micki had gone to her old room and relieved her anxiety by sobbing into her pillow.

Now, satisfied with the obvious signs of his glowing good looks and well-being, Micki gave him another quick hug. With her absorption in the most important man in her life, Micki didn't hear the repeated whoosh of the kitchen screen door.

"Are you two going to stand here in the driveway the whole two weeks of Micki's vacation?" Micki's stepmother, Regina, teased.

Micki's entire body tensed at the sound of Regina's velvety, throaty voice, then she made herself relax. What was past was past, she admonished herself sharply, and best forgotten. With unstudied grace, she swung her small slim frame out of her father's embrace, one hand reaching out to take the pale one Regina had extended.

"Hello, Regina." Micki was slightly amazed at the even tenor of her voice. "No need to ask how you are; you look fantastic, as ever."

It was true. At thirty-nine Regina was as exotically

12

beautiful as she had been when she had married Bruce Durrant at twenty-five, the exact same age that Micki was now. Her glossy black hair, worn smoothed back off her face in an intricately curved twist, was completely free of silver. Her pale-complexioned, unbelievably beautiful face was completely free of any sign of encroaching age. And her tall frame was still willowy, completely free of any unsightly bulges. And that voice! Oh, the hours a very young, twelve-year-old Micki had spent trying, unsuccessfully, to emulate that voice. Even today, as then, Micki had no idea of how pleasing to the ear her own soft, somewhat husky, voice was.

"You do not look the same," Regina returned easily. Then, to Micki's surprise, she echoed her husband's words of a few minutes ago. "You grow more like your mother every time I see you, and everyone knows how lovely she was."

Micki managed to hide her startled reaction to Regina's compliment in the general confusion of collecting her suitcases and getting them into the house.

Regina trailed behind Micki and her father as they lugged the valises to her bedroom and lingered after Bruce left the room with a promise of a pre-dinner drink for Micki as soon as she'd settled in.

"Micki?"

Micki's hand stilled in the act of unlocking her largest suitcase at the hesitant, uncertain note in her stepmother's voice. Features composed, Micki turned to gaze at Regina.

"Yes?"

"Do you suppose we could possibly be friends now?"

Regina's tone had smoothed out, but an anxious expression still clouded her beautiful black eyes.

"Do you?"

As soon as they were out of her mouth Micki wished the words unspoken. Why, she chided herself, hadn't she simply said yes and let the whole sorry business remain buried?

13

"I would like to try," Regina answered quietly. "I have always liked you." At Micki's slightly raised eyebrows, Regina stated firmly, "Yes, I have. And there is no reason now why we shouldn't be friends. I think you'll find I'm not quite the same person since your father's near brush with death. It's sad, but I nearly had to lose him to realize —well—just exactly how foolishly I was behaving."

"Regina, you do not have to—" Micki began, but Regina seemed determined to have her say.

"You were very patient with and kind to me while your father was so very ill, even though you were nearly out of your mind with worry yourself. I have not forgotten that and I never will." Regina paused, as if uncertain how to continue, and then, with a light shrug of her elegant shoulders, she plunged on forcefully. "I love your father very much, I always have. Yes, really," she vowed as Micki's brows rose again. "The only explanation, or excuse, I have for my previous behavior is his neglect of me—due solely to business pressures, I admit—after our marriage and my selfish reaction to that neglect."

"Regina, please—"

"No, Micki, let me finish," Regina insisted. "When we married, your father was a very handsome and charming man, as indeed he still is, and I wanted to be the only important thing in his life, even to the exclusion of an eleven-year-old child."

"I remember," Micki inserted, then felt petty at Regina's wince. And yet, she defended herself silently, she *did* remember, painfully.

"Yes, of course you remember," Regina went on doggedly. "That's why I must say all this, clear the air between us." Again she paused, wet her lips nervously. "From the time I was fourteen I was aware of my attraction to the opposite sex and I used that attraction to punish your father. It was foolish and immature, I know, but I realize now that at the time I *was* foolish and imma- ture. I—I had to almost lose Bruce before I woke up to

14

my own stupidity." She closed her eyes briefly and when she opened them again her lashes glistened with teardrops.

For several long moments the two women stared at each other. Micki's eyes, carefully veiled, revealed nothing of what she was feeling. Regina's eyes held mute appeal. Slowly, as if gathering strength, Regina drew a deep breath.

"And now, about that incident six years ago," Regina said softly.

No! No! a voice screamed inside Micki's head. What came out of her parched lips was a strangled whisper.

"No, Regina. I do not want to talk about that."

Regina's eyes flickered with alarm and her tone dropped to a murmur of self-reproachment.

"Oh, God, it still hurts you." One pale hand was extended, as if in supplication. "Oh, my dear, I had no idea the pain went so deep. How can you ever forgive me?"

Micki was saved from answering by the sound of her father's strong, impatient call from the bottom of the stairway.

"What in the world are you two women doing up there?" His tone took on a mock petulant edge. "I'm getting very lonely down here all by myself."

Regina's head snapped around to the bedroom's open doorway, then swung back to Micki.

"I'm sorry," she whispered. "Please believe that. I—I—" She shook her head and cleared her throat. "We better go down. Leave the unpacking, I'll help you with it later."

Forcing her stiff facial muscles into relaxation, Micki left the room, and Regina's line of conversation, gratefully, silently determined that that particular subject would not be brought up again during her visit.

Surprisingly, or maybe not too surprisingly, with the air between the two women somewhat cleared, the evening passed pleasantly.

During dinner Micki brought her father and Regina up

15

to date on her activities, saving the most important detail for last. They had carried their coffee into the living room and as Micki sipped at her creamy brew with a contented sigh, the only indication she gave as to the import of her news was an added sparkle in her usually bright blue eyes.

"Oh, by the way," Micki drawled diffidently. "Just before I left the shop for this vacation I was informed I was being promoted to head buyer."

A short silence followed her casually tossed statement, a silence that revealed to Micki exactly how aware her father and Regina were of the importance of her announcement.

After leaving the small college, where she had been studying business merchandising, so precipitously only six weeks into her second year, Micki had considered herself fortunate in acquiring the job of salesclerk in a very exclusive ladies' boutique, which was located in the lobby of one of the largest, most prestigious hotels in Wilmington. It was not the job of salesclerk that excited Micki, but the knowledge that the boutique was just one of a large chain of similar shops that ranged along the entire East Coast. When she had been interviewed for the job by the shop's manager, a tall, slim woman in her mid-forties, Micki had been informed that due to the size of the independently owned chain, the chance for advancement was excellent for anyone who did not object to relocating. Micki had been quick to assure the somewhat aristocratic woman that she had no objections at all to relocating, as Wilmington was not her hometown.

It had taken time and much hard work on Micki's part, but eventually the promotions did come and for the last eighteen months she had been assistant buyer for the Wilmington shop. And now—could it have been only yesterday?—this latest promotion.

"Micki, that's wonderful!" her father exclaimed, jumping out of his chair to come across the room and bestow a huge hug on her. "Congratulations."

"And you haven't heard the best part yet," Micki gasped laughingly when he'd released his crushing hold. "The position is for the Atlantic City store."

"Atlantic City?" Bruce repeated softly, then he nearly shouted. "Honey, that means you can move home."

Still laughing, Micki nodded her head. Totally absorbed in each other, both Micki and her father had completely forgotten Regina. In the old days Regina would have made her presence known forcefully, now the voice that penetrated their euphoria was soft, hesitant.

"May I add my congratulations to your father's, Micki?"

"Oh, Regina, I'm sorry," Micki murmured contritely. "Of course you may."

"Yes, darling," Bruce inserted, one arm encircling his wife's waist to draw her close. "Of course you may. We're a family." He paused an instant before adding, "Aren't we?"

A quick glance of understanding and truce passed between the two women.

"Yes, Dad," Micki agreed firmly. "We are a family."

Regina's black eyes spoke eloquently of her relief and thanks and Micki was amazed at the feeling of peace that washed over her. For the most part the fourteen years of her father's second marriage had been turbulent and Micki greeted the cessation of hostilities with a silent prayer of thanks. Still, she didn't want to strain the ties of this newfound accord, so she tacked on with equal firmness, "But I'll be looking for my own apartment."

"In Atlantic City?"

Bruce and Regina spoke in astonished unison and Micki fully understood the reason for their astonishment. It was a well-known fact that living accommodations in Atlantic City were almost as hard to find as brontosaurus teeth since the influx of the big hotels with their gambling casinos. The added fact that the shop Micki would be working in was located in one of those hotels lent a sprinkling of spice to her excitement. Now she hastened to correct their impression.

"No, not in Atlantic City, here in Ocean City. Atlantic City's such a short run up the coast I doubt it will take me any longer to get to work from here than it did in the early morning crush in Wilmington."

"The way I understand it," Bruce said quietly, "there are already quite a few people that are employed by the hotels making their home here." He hesitated, his eyes mirroring his sadness. "But why do you want to look for an apartment? Why can't you stay here at home?"

"Oh, Dad." Micki smiled weakly. "I've been on my own for almost six years now. I'm used to having my own place. I've got an apartment full of furniture and things I've acquired over those six years." Her smile deepened, became impish. "But I have made arrangements to have my stuff packed and sent here in the interim—if you don't mind?"

"Mind?" Bruce echoed. "Of course we don't mind."

"Not at all." Regina seconded her husband's words.

"Oh, sure." Micki's laughter rippled through the comfortable room. "But wait until you have all my stuff dumped onto your doorstep. You may wish you'd given a very firm no."

Regina made fresh coffee and the three of them settled around the kitchen table to make plans and discuss the pros and cons of various areas in which Micki might be interested in apartment hunting. During the course of the discussion the section of the city in which Cindy and Benny lived came up and at the mention of the young couple's name the topic of the conversation veered to them.

"I haven't seen either of them since they made final settlement on the house," Bruce told Micki. "But Cindy did call me at the office after they'd moved in, to again thank me for finding the property for them and inform me that they were absolutely thrilled with it." He grinned

18

broadly. "Those last words are an exact quote from Cindy."

"Sounds so much like her I can almost hear her voice," Micki grinned back. Her father owned a flourishing real estate business and it pleased her to know Cindy had gone to him when she was ready to buy a home. "It will be wonderful to see Cindy and Benny again."

"Did they know you were coming home?" Regina asked. "And that you'll be staying?"

Micki was shaking her head before Regina had finished speaking. "No, I wanted to surprise them," Micki answered. Then her eyes shifted to rest lovingly on her father. "Besides which, I wanted my first evening at home to be free of interruptions."

The answering look of love in her father's eyes and the understanding smile on Regina's lips deepened the feeling of well-being inside Micki. Stifling a yawn behind her hand, she pushed her chair away from the table and stood up.

"I'm going to have a shower then go to bed." Another yawn was unsuccessfully hidden. When Regina moved to get up, Micki shook her head at her. "You don't have to come up, Regina. I can finish my unpacking in the morning." After kissing her father lightly on the cheek, she wished them both a good night and swung out of the room.

Alone in her bedroom Micki stood still just inside the door and let her eyes roam slowly over familiar things. Everything was the same as she'd left it. Even the paint on the walls, though fresh, was the same bright daffodil yellow as it had always been. When her eyes touched the double, leather-bound picture frame sitting on the night-stand by the bed, they stopped. Her gaze unwavering, Micki walked across the room and picked up the frame.

The picture on one side was an enlargement of a snapshot that had been taken on the front lawn. Three figures stood under a mimosa tree. Micki's mother was turned slightly from the camera as she smiled up at her husband, and between them Micki, at age six, her favorite doll clutched in her arms, grinned impishly at the camera. The picture had been snapped by a close friend of her mother's the summer before her mother's death in a fiery highway accident.

Micki blinked over hot tears before shifting her gaze to the other side of the frame. It had been years since she'd really looked at the studio portrait of her mother and now, remembering her father's words when she arrived, she studied the color shot carefully before lifting her eyes to her own reflection in the dressing-table mirror opposite the bed. Yes, the well-defined features were very similar: a slim, straight nose; high, though not prominent, cheek-bones; softly rounded chin, although Micki's did have a more determined cast. If the color in the photo was true, they shared the same bright blue eyes and fair skin tone. But her mother's hair, worn long and smooth at the time, was a gleaming auburn with deep red highlights, whereas Micki's, which she wore short in an attempt to control her loose, unruly curls, was a dark chestnut. Yes, there were similarities, but her mother had been beautiful, and in Micki's own opinion, she was not.

With a brief, what-does-it-matter shrug, Micki replaced the frame, then stood eyeing her suitcases dispassionately. Sighing softly, she flicked the clasps of the largest case and opened the valise. Do it now, she told herself firmly, or everything will be crushed beyond wearing.

Micki kicked off her sandals and moved silently over the plush, gold wall-to-wall carpeting as she placed her clothes in the closet and drawers. When the bags were empty, Micki placed them against the wall beside the bedroom door for storage in the large hall closet in the morning, then turned back to the room, a tiny smile of satisfaction tugging at her lips. Everything about the room satisfied her.

Her father had given her carte blanche in decorating it

when she was sixteen, and now, nine years later, every-thing about the room still pleased her. Micki's eyes spar-kled as they skimmed the white wicker headboard, chair, low table, and clothes hamper. A stroke of genius that, she thought smugly. Who would have thought, nine years ago, that wicker would become so popular, not to mention expensive.

Humming softly she slipped out of her white denim slacks and pulled her blue-and-white striped shirt over her head. Her lacy bra and filmy bikini briefs followed her slacks and shirt into the hamper. She put on a terry robe, pulled the belt tight, scooped up a short, sheer nightie, and made for the bathroom for a quick shower.

Micki was patting her five-foot-two frame dry when she heard her father and Regina come up the stairs and go into their room. Gritting her teeth, she mentally clamped a lid on the flash of remembered pain and resentment the sound of their bedroom door closing sent through her. Always that sound, by the very intimate connotations it conjured, had had the power to hurt her, make her feel cut off from her father, bereft. Now she pushed those feelings away. You're a full-grown woman, she told herself sternly, with a full, rich life of your own. Go to bed, go to sleep, what's done is done and can't be changed. Forget it.

Minutes after she'd returned to her room, there was a soft tap on her door. Thinking it was her father coming to wish her a second good night, Micki called, "Come in," without hesitation, then wished she hadn't when she saw it was Regina. Fearing a repeat of their earlier conversa-tion, Micki tried to forestall the older woman.

"Whatever it is, Regina"—Micki faked a huge yawn—"could it wait until morning? I can hardly keep my eyes open."

Regina bit her bottom lip nervously, hesitated, then drew a deep, courage-gathering breath.

"Micki, I don't want to upset you, please believe that,

21

but"—she drew another, shorter breath before rushing on—"we must talk about Wolf."

"No!"

The one word escaped through Micki's lips like a muffled explosion and she flinched as if the other woman had actually struck her.

"But you don't understand." Regina's tone held a pleading note. "We must discuss this, he's—"

"Regina." Micki's voice was low, intense with warning. "This is still my room. I'm asking you to please leave it so I can go to bed."

"But Wolf—"

"Regina." Micki's teeth were clenched in an effort to control her voice. "You asked me earlier if we can be friends. Well, I'm willing to try, but there is one condition. I cannot, *will* not, discuss that person. Not now, not ever."

"Oh, Micki," Regina sighed. "You don't understand."

"And I don't want to," Micki snapped. "Do you want me to leave this house in the morning? Find a motel room until I can get an apartment?"

"No!" Regina exclaimed in alarm. "Of course not. Your father would—"

"Well, then." Micki didn't wait to hear what her father would do. "The subject will remain closed and forgotten. As long as Dad looks as well and happy as he does now, I'm content to meet you halfway toward friendship. I fully expect you to do the same. Do you get my meaning?"

Regina's eyes closed briefly in defeat and she nodded. Before staring directly into Micki's eyes, she murmured, "But please don't say I didn't try."

Micki wondered over those parting words several minutes after Regina left the room. What in the world could she have meant? With a shrug of her shoulders she turned toward the bed, then stopped and became very still, the echo of that name searing through her mind.

Wolf.

Wolf—a predatory animal's name that suited perfectly the predatory human male. A mental picture formed and, her face twisted with pain, Micki pushed it from her mind.

Damn, damn, damn Regina, for saying that name out loud.

Memories crowded in threatening to overwhelm her. Shaking herself like a wet dog, Micki moved jerkily to the bed. No, she would not allow the memories to gather, collect in her mind. Forcing herself to stand very still beside the bed, she breathed deeply. In. Out. In. Out.

"I must call Cindy."

In. Out. In. Out.

"I must go apartment hunting."

In. Out. In. Out.

"I must run up to Atlantic City and check out the shop, introduce myself."

In. Out. In. Out.

"I've controlled these emotions before, I will tonight."

Doing the breathing exercise, speaking softly, Micki felt the pain recede, the trembling leave her body. After what seemed a very long time she slipped between the bed-sheets, closed her eyes, and cried as if her heart were broken.

CHAPTER 2

The next morning Micki woke early, refreshed and ready to face a new day. Surprisingly, after her violent crying bout, she had slept deeply. The realization that she had once again won the battle against her memories added to the feeling of well-being her uninterrupted rest had instilled.

Glancing at the bedside clock, she sat up quickly and slipped off the bed; if she hurried she could have breakfast with her father. She thrust her arms into her robe and left her room at a near run, dashed into the bathroom to splash cold water on her face and brush her teeth, then hurried back along the hall and down the stairs.

"Morning." Micki breezed into the kitchen and planted a kiss on her father's smooth, freshly shaven cheek before seating herself at the old-fashioned wooden table.

"Morning, princess."

Micki's perfect white teeth flashed in a grin of delight at her father's use of the pet name. It had been years since he'd called her that, and she loved the sound of it.

"I thought you'd sleep in this morning." Bruce grinned back before adding, "What got you awake so early? Regina and I didn't wake you, did we?"

"No." Micki shook her head emphatically. "I must have been slept out." She smiled her thanks as Regina placed a glass of juice in front of her. "I'm used to getting up early, you know."

"All the more reason to sleep in when you get the chance," Bruce replied placidly. "Regina's scrambling eggs—would you like some?"

"No, thank you." Micki's mild grimace drew a chuckle from her dad.

"Kids!" The soft exclamation took the sting from his word. "Who can figure them out? You always loved eggs for breakfast until that last year you were in college."

Micki's stomach seemed to turn over and for a moment she felt trapped while she raked her mind for a reply. Thankfully neither her father nor Regina noticed the way her face had paled, as their attention was occupied by Regina serving the eggs.

"I guess I just got tired of them," Micki finally managed weakly, eyeing the creamy yellow mound on the plates.

"Just like that." Bruce snapped his fingers. "It doesn't make sense."

"Stop teasing, Bruce." Unknowingly, Regina saved Micki from the effort of finding a more plausible excuse. "As youngsters mature, their tastes change." As she sat down at the table, Regina offered Micki a tentative smile. "Don't mind your father, Micki. He's in a very good but devilish mood this morning, due, I'm sure, to your being home again."

The grin her father flashed at her confirmed Regina's words. A slow, silent sigh fluttered through Micki's lips as she returned Regina's smile.

"I can see"—Micki deliberately lowered her voice conspiratorially—"you and I are going to have to stick together to keep this feisty man in line."

Bruce's head snapped up from his plate, his glance sharp between the two women. The spark of hope that had entered his eyes seemed to grow into wonderment as he studied first his daughter's then his wife's friendly expressions.

Micki fully understood the almost breathless stillness that seemed to grip him. The two women had been opponents, at first silent and then very vocal, since the day Bruce married Regina. He had coaxed, cajoled, and even ordered Micki to make more of an effort at getting along with her stepmother. The only thing he'd achieved was to fill Micki with a deeper sense of resentment. She had made an attempt at friendship with Regina. At the very vulnerable age of eleven she had welcomed the idea of a mother. Regina, a younger, beautiful Regina, had quickly disabused her of that idea. Without actually saying the words, Regina had left little doubt in Micki's young mind of exactly where she stood. If Micki wanted her father's attention, she would have to fight for it. Micki had fought silently but bitterly, and until last night, she had thought it was a battle she could never win.

Now the gentle smile Micki gave her father erased the doubt lingering around the edges of his expression. She saw him swallow with difficulty and the action brought a corresponding lump to her throat. Shifting her eyes, she caught the quick flutter of Regina's lashes and the lump grew in size.

"Princess," Bruce murmured solemnly, "I wonder if you realize how happy I am to have you home." The slight emphasis he placed on the word *home* told the full story.

"And you can have no idea how happy it makes me to be home." Micki let her own emphasis reflect his before she laughed a little shakily. "And if you don't eat your breakfast, you are going to be late for work."

"Oh, but you see"—Bruce followed her lead in lightening the mood—"that's the fun part of being the boss. I can breeze in and out of the office whenever I please." He paused, a mock frown creasing his forehead. "The only thing is, as I have a very important client coming this morning, I damned well better please to get moving."

27

After her father had left for the office and Regina had refused her offer to help with the dishes, Micki went to the phone in the living room to call Cindy.

"Hello." Cindy's bubbly voice sang across the wire after the fourth ring.

"Hi, Cindy, how are you?"

"Micki!" The exclamation was like a small explosion. "Where are you? Are you here in Ocean City? How are you? When did you get home? Are you home?" The questions followed each other in such rapid succession Micki laughingly shouted to get a word in.

"Cindy, if you will take time to breathe, I'll explain the wheres and whys." The small silence that followed these words allowed Micki to continue briefly. "I am home, yes, and—"

"Then don't bother to go any further," Cindy broke in. "Jump in your car and come to the house, I'm dying to see you." She hesitated, then asked apologetically, "Or did you have other plans for this morning?"

"As a matter of fact," Micki laughed, "my only plans for today were to come and see you, if you had no other plans. Does that make any sense at all?"

"Perfect sense," Cindy declared happily. "So why are you still on the phone? Get truckin'." She hung up before Micki could even tell her she would.

Still smiling, Micki went to the kitchen to tell Regina where she was going, adding she had no idea when she'd be back.

"Oh, that will work out perfectly." Regina's smile was still somewhat tentative. "I have a lunch date with Betty Grant and we'd planned to do some shopping after lunch. How is Cindy feeling now?"

The question startled Micki, wiped the smile off her face.

"She sounded fine," she answered slowly, then asked anxiously, "Why? Has she been ill?"

"No, no," Regina soothed. "Not ill, but she did have a

28

few bad moments at the beginning of her pregnancy, you know."

Everything inside Micki seemed to freeze with an emotion she couldn't begin to put a name to. Cindy pregnant? Why hadn't she told her?

Regina glanced up from the dish she was drying; her face grew puzzled at Micki's stillness. "Is something wrong?" she asked with concern.

"No." Micki shook her head and forced the smile back to her stiff lips. "I—I didn't know Cindy was pregnant."

"Didn't know?" For a second Regina's eyes were totally blank, then they widened with dismay. "Oh, damn," she groaned. "Cindy must have wanted to surprise you and now I've ruined it for her."

"You couldn't know, and I'll play dumb when she tells me." Micki wet her parched lips as she turned toward the doorway. "Cindy will have her surprise." Moving swiftly through the doorway, she added, "I'll see you when I see you."

Inside her room Micki leaned back against the door and closed her eyes, a soft moan catching at her throat. Hugging her midriff tightly as if to contain the pain inside, she dug her teeth into her lower lip. For a few moments the remembered torment was so real she wanted to cry out against it. Oh, God, she thought sickly, would the hurt never go away? Breathing deeply, exactly as she had the night before, she forced herself to a measure of calmness. She had to get dressed, go see Cindy, and act surprised and happy about her pregnancy. She was happy for Cindy.

By the time Micki backed her car out of the driveway, she had her emotions under control. Driving slowly through the mid-morning traffic, she glanced around quickly. The tourist season was in full swing. People of all ages, shapes, and sizes were on their way to the beach. Cyclists pedaled their way toward their destination. The streets were crowded with cars; people coming into the city, people going out of the city, and some just driving

29

around the city pursuing their business, and over all, the gulls soared and dipped and sang their raucous songs. Micki loved it. She always had and as she drove through it she felt the stiffness ease out of her body.

It was not a very long drive, as the house Cindy and Benny had bought was located just south of where the long boardwalk ended. From Cindy's letters Micki knew it was a double unit building fronting the beach and ocean. The reason the young couple decided to buy a double unit was the obvious one: the increasing cost of real estate. The summer rental on the apartment made up half of the yearly mortgage payments. The cost of the building had been exorbitant but, Cindy had written, for a place of their own, it had been worth it.

Cindy was waiting at the door, and as soon as Micki drove onto the crushed-stone driveway, she pushed the car door open and ran to meet her.

After incoherent greetings and fierce hugs were exchanged, the two women stood back to examine each other, identical smiles of pleasure on their faces. Extending a slim hand, Micki placed it gently on the bulge that was Cindy's belly.

"I'm so happy for you," she said softly. "But, why didn't you tell me?"

"I wanted to surprise you." Cindy laughed. "If you remember, you wrote that you were thinking of spending your vacation at home this year and, well, I just wanted to see your face when you saw me."

"You nit." Micki shook her head in mock reproach. "Was my expression worth keeping the secret all this time?"

"Well worth it," Cindy affirmed, taking her arm and leading her to the house. "You looked absolutely stunned."

A mental picture of how she'd reacted to the news a short time ago allowed Micki to answer with complete honesty. "I assure you I was. When is the big event slated to happen?"

"Around Christmastime," Cindy replied happily. "Oh, Micki, don't you think that's exciting? I mean, a baby for Christmas."

"Very exciting," Micki murmured. She stepped over the threshold directly into a large, airy living room, resplendent with plants of all kinds, a half dozen of which hung from the ceiling.

The apartment was larger than Micki would have expected. In addition to the living room there was a tiny dining room, a roomy kitchen, one and a half baths, and three bedrooms, one of which was in the process of redecoration.

"The baby's room," Cindy explained needlessly.

"I love it," Micki enthused honestly. "All of it. And the fact that it's practically right on the beach makes it worth whatever you paid for it."

"That's what we thought," Cindy nodded. "Of course we don't know what it will be like in the winter, but we're delighted with it just the same."

They wandered back into the kitchen and from there onto the wide, awning-covered deck.

"I thought since it's so hot already this morning, we'd have lunch out here."

"Wonderful." Micki stared entranced at the view of the beach and sun-sparkled ocean the deck afforded. "Oh, Cindy," she breathed softly, "this place was worth almost any amount of money, just for the view."

"I know—it's super." Cindy laughed. "Benny and I have breakfast out here every nice morning."

"How is Benny?" Micki asked belatedly. "And how does he feel about becoming a father?"

"He's fine." Cindy smiled softly. "And he's so excited about the baby he can hardly wait." The smile grew into a grin. "We were shopping last week and would you believe I had to drag him out of the sports department? He wanted to buy the baby a football, for heaven's sake."

"Knowing Benny, I can believe it." Micki grinned back. "Do you think most men get a little soft in the head about their first child?"

Micki didn't even hear Cindy's answer, for suddenly she felt like a large hand was squeezing all the air from her chest. Dear God, why did the most innocent remarks still have the power to hurt her like this?

Cindy laughed and pulling herself together, Micki managed to laugh with her. The sudden explosion of air eased the constriction of her lungs, and as the conversation switched to the more immediate subject of lunch, Micki felt her emotional gear shift back into normal.

By the time they had finished their melon and gone on to small salads and cold chicken sandwiches Micki was glad she'd decided on a spaghetti-strapped sundress that morning. The July sun was brassy in a cloud-free blue sky. Even with the sea breeze wafting under the awning, by one o'clock the heat drove them indoors.

By the time Cindy had filled Micki in on the comings and goings of their friends and Micki had imparted her own news about her job and her plans to make her home permanently in Ocean City, most of the afternoon was gone.

After agreeing to have dinner with Cindy and Benny one evening, Micki left, cautioning Cindy to get plenty of rest to combat the enervating effects of the heat.

Driving through the shimmery heat waves that rose from the street, Micki reflected on what Cindy had told her about their mutual friends. They had really scattered —one as far away as Alaska. But Tony Menella was back. After finishing college, he had gone to work for a large advertising firm in Trenton, but a little over a year ago he'd packed it in and come home. He was working in Atlantic City, but he was living in Ocean City, much the same as Micki herself would now be doing.

32

Into her own thoughts, she stopped at an intersection when a car cut in front of her and, glancing up, let her gaze skim over the area. Idly she studied a new motel on the opposite corner. Very classy, she was thinking when she was startled alert by the opening of her passenger side door.

"What in the—!" Micki began, head swinging around. The words shriveled on her lips as she saw a long, lean frame settle into the seat next to her and felt the impact of the odd, silver-gray eyes of Wolf Renninger.

"It's safe to drive on now."

The soft, taunting words broke through the shock gripping her mind and by reflex Micki started the car.

Her mental process was set into motion at the same time. Anger searing her mind, she glanced around sharply for a parking space. She wasn't hauling his carcass anywhere.

"Pull into this lot here." The taunting edge to his tone was more pronounced, as if he'd read her thoughts and was amused by them.

Gritting her teeth, Micki glanced in the direction he'd indicated and saw it was the parking lot belonging to the motel she'd been looking at.

"But I can't park on that lot it's—"

"It's all right," Wolf interrupted, "I work there."

Angrily Micki spun the wheel and drove the car onto the lot, following his terse directions to a section marked EMPLOYEES PARKING—PRIVATE. The moment the car was stationary Micki turned to face him, blue eyes shooting bright sparks of anger.

"Now just what do you think you're doing?"

"Hello, Micki." Wolf's soft voice laughed at her. "It's been a long time."

"Not nearly long enough," Micki snapped acidly. "Why did you get into the car? What do you want?"

The smile that curved his sometimes hard, always sensuous lips sent a shiver racing along Micki's spine and she

33

gripped the steering wheel to keep her hands from trembling.

"I want to talk to you," Wolf replied smoothly. "And look at you."

"You've had your look," she said sharply. It was true. From the minute he'd entered the car his eyes had clung to her face like a beauty mask and it was making her very edgy. "So talk."

"Not here, it's too hot and I'd hate to see you melt all over the upholstery." That unnerving smile touched his mouth briefly. "Come with me, I have an apartment in the complex." The taunting laugh came back into his tone. "Or are you afraid?"

"Afraid of you?" Micki knew it was foolish to accept his challenge, but she also knew she had to prove something to him—and herself. Swinging open her car door with a flourish, she quipped, "Lead the way to your lair, Wolf. Or is it den?"

His soft laughter did strange things to her equilibrium, and for that reason only she allowed him the liberty of taking her arm.

He led her through a side entrance into the motel lobby, which was lavishly decorated in a south-seas motif, past the curious stares of the two men behind the reception desk, and up the curving stairway. As she mounted the last step, Micki barely had time to register the fact that the stairs opened onto what appeared to be a short crosswalk that connected two sections of the motel for, without pausing, Wolf turned right along the short crosswalk to where it connected with a long hallway. At the junction he turned left and strode along the hallway to the very end. The only difference between the door he unlocked and all the others that faced each other along the hall was the absence of a number.

The door opened into a fair-sized living room, but what caught Micki's attention, and her breath, was a large picture window on the far wall. From that height the window gave a panoramic view of beachfront and ocean. Without a word Micki entered the deliciously cool room and crossed the plush bronze carpeting to stare out the window. Micki was not unlike numerous other people as to the hypnotic effect the movement of the ocean had on the emotions. But Wolf's quiet voice jerked her out of her mesmeric state.

"Would you like a drink?"

The arched look she threw him drew his soft mocking laughter.

"A soft drink?" he chided. "Iced tea? Perrier?"

"Do you have lime?"

"Yes."

"Perrier with lime then, please."

Micki watched him as he went around the waist-high wooden bookshelves that divided the living room from the kitchen. While he went about the business of getting the drinks, she made a quick inventory of him. He had changed, matured, as she had herself and the change was heart stopping. He had been good-looking at thirty. Now, at thirty-six, life had left its stamp on him.

The square, determined jawline now proclaimed iron control. His golden tan skin stretched shiny and smooth over his long straight nose, his high cheekbones, and the angular planes of his face. The silver-gray eyes, arched over by thick, dark brows, now held a calculating sharpness. He wore his dark brown hair short in back, but its wavy thickness was completely intact. And his six-foot-plus frame, never thick, had pared down to the lean, sinewy look of the predator whose name he bore. One would not call him merely good-looking now. There were any number of adjectives one might apply, ranging from devastating to dangerous. One might even add slightly cruel-looking, but never merely good-looking.

Micki caught herself following his every move, a breathless sort of excitement clutching her throat at the sheer masculine look of him. *Don't be an idiot,* she told herself

35

harshly. *Play it cool. Play it safe. He's trouble, pure un-adulterated trouble, and no one knows it better than you.*

Casting her eyes away in search of something more worthy of her appraisal, she fastened on the living room. Masculine to the point of Spartan, Micki was surprised to find she really liked the effect the warm earth tones of bronze, brown, and gold, with a splash of green here and there lent the room. He probably didn't have a thing to do with the decor, she decided disparagingly. *I'll bet every room in the motel is decorated in the same way.*

"Like it?"

His quiet voice, startlingly close to her ear, made her jump. His next words brought a tinge of pink to her cheeks. "I decorated it myself." He cocked his head to one side as his eyes roamed the room. "Personally, I think I did a damned good job."

"Oh, I'm sure it's perfectly suitable"—Micki waved her hand carelessly—"for a man."

"You've grown up." The simple statement was issued as he handed her her drink. "Grown more beautiful too." The rider was accompanied by that disquieting, sensuous smile. He lifted his glass to her in a mock salute and Micki's brows arched at the amber-colored liquid it contained.

"A little too hot for the hard stuff in the middle of the day, isn't it?" she asked bitingly.

"I've yet to be flattened by a single glass of bourbon and water." His silvery eyes roamed insolently over her face and body. "It takes something a little more heady to put me flat."

She was perfectly well aware of what that something was. A warm female body, any warm female body. She lifted her chin and stared him straight in the eye. "You said you wanted to talk to me," she elucidated clearly. "What about?"

"About how you are." Wolf's voice had dropped an octave. He moved closer to her and she didn't like having to tilt her head back to look up into his face. His voice went lower.

"About what you've been doing."

"I'm fine." Micki's throat felt parched and she took several deep swallows of her lime-flavored water before adding, "I've been working."

Long, hard-looking fingers began teasing the bow on her dress straps and a remembered chill of pleasure feathered her arms. Micki opened her mouth to tell Wolf to stop as she lifted her head. The words and her breath dried up in her mouth. He had lowered his head and his face was so close she could smell the pungent aroma of bourbon. Now his voice was so low she wasn't sure for a moment that she heard him correctly.

"About who you're sleeping with."

For a full five seconds she stood stunned, then indignation kicked fury through her veins and retaliation from her mouth.

"That's none of your business!" She spun away from him, setting her drink down on a glass-topped table as she headed for the door. Hand on the knob, she turned back to him, eyes glittering with anger.

"But of one thing you may be sure—he's not already tied, legally, to another."

Micki turned the knob and pulled the door open. The palm of Wolf's hand hit the solid wood forcefully, slamming it shut again. Micki stood perfectly still, almost afraid to breathe. The quietness of his tone unnerved rather than calmed her.

"What, exactly, is that last dig supposed to mean?"

While he spoke he turned her around and forced her face up to look at him. Micki flattened herself against the door, hating the havoc the look of him and the scent of him created within her. His hard, taunting mouth was too close. Alarm vied with a sudden, urgent need to feel the touch of that mouth. Alarm won, sending her tone to sub-zero.

"I'm not a fool, Wolf." With effort she managed to not only meet but hold his intent gaze. "I never was the complete fool you thought I was."

"I never thought you were a fool," Wolf denied sternly. He loomed over her, his head lowering until his mouth was no more than a sigh away. "Baby, baby," he murmured hoarsely. "Why did you run from me?"

"Why?" Somehow she pushed a dry laugh from her throat. "Because this fool suddenly smartened up and realized what she didn't want."

His lips caught, played with hers. "Tell me now you didn't want this." His hands came up to grasp her hips, arch her close to him. Moving slowly, caressingly, they reached over her waist, settled possessively over her breasts. "Or this," he groaned into her mouth. When he felt her shudder, his hands moved again, long fingers encircling her throat while his thumbs stroked her collarbones. His breathing ragged, he rasped, "Or this," as his mouth crushed hers.

For one blinding instant everything inside Micki urged her to surrender. Then reason, plus a dash of self-preservation, took over and she went as cold and unresponsive as a stone.

Wolf didn't force the issue. Within seconds of her withdrawal he lifted his head and stepped back.

"I haven't the vaguest idea what you've been talking about." His silvery eyes had a dangerous, calculating gleam. "But I intend to find out."

"Don't waste your time beating a dead horse," Micki choked out. She wet her lips and felt her heart thump when his eyes dropped to her mouth. Pushing her words a little, she went on. "When something's dead, it's dead. And what happened between us died a long time ago."

"Prove it."

He rapped the words at her so fast she blinked in confusion.

"Prove it?" she repeated indignantly. "It doesn't have to be proven. It's evident."

"Not to me." His tone was hard and unyielding. "You have to prove it to me, if you dare."

"How?"

Micki eyed him warily, somehow certain she was walking into a trap, yet unable to resist flinging his challenge back at him.

"In no way that's frightening, so stop looking like a startled doe ready to bolt for the bushes." His soft, reasoning tone made her more wary still. She didn't trust him and it showed on her expression. His sigh was elaborately exaggerated. "Simply agree to see me occasionally, talk to me."

"And that's all?" In no way could she keep the blatant surprise from her face. His soft laughter skipped along her nerve endings.

"That's all."

It was too simple. Micki knew it was too simple, yet she had accepted his dare. Momentarily she had a very uneasy feeling she'd been had. Well, so be it, she shrugged mentally. If things got sticky she could always find an excuse for not seeing him. And maybe, just maybe, she could finally banish the pain, consign the memories to oblivion forever. Self-confidence won.

"All right." If she was so sure of herself, why was her voice so whispery? "I must go now," she lied. "I'm expected for dinner."

"Not so fast." His hand came up to catch her chin, lifting her face so he could see her eyes. "When can I see you?"

"I—I don't know." Her tongue stumbled over her words. "I have a lot to do and—"

"Friday," he cut in. "For dinner. I'll pick you up at seven thirty."

"All right, Friday." Micki tried to ignore her sudden leap of anticipation. "I'll be ready."

"Good." His hand dropped to her arm and he moved back, away from the door, drawing her with him. Ignoring her insistence that he needn't walk her to her car, he ushered her through the doorway and along the hall.

The heat hit her like a physical blow when they stepped out of the building. And like some blow to the head it seemed to knock her thinking back onto dead center. Was she out of her mind agreeing to have dinner with him? It sounded innocent enough, but Micki had the sinking sensation that Wolf hadn't had an innocent urge since puberty. She waited until he had opened the car door for her and she had slid onto the seat before glancing up with a hesitant, "Wolf, about Friday."

"What about it?" They were the first words he'd uttered since leaving the apartment and Micki feared the hard sound of his tone.

"Where are we going?" she sighed in defeat. "How should I dress?"

The sardonic curve of his mouth left her in little doubt that he'd been perfectly aware that she'd been about to make a stab at getting out of the date.

"Nothing fancy." Wolf's grin was pure animal. Wolf animal. "We'll take a run down the coast to Wildwood. The restaurant's quiet and the food's good. I hope you like Greek food."

"I do."

Micki turned the key and the motor sprang to life. Wolf closed the door gently but firmly. Knowing there was no possible way out of it now, Micki backed the car around and drove off the lot.

By the time Micki parked her car in the driveway of her father's house she had a nervous stomach and a sick headache. Moving listlessly, she followed the flagstone path to the back door. Before entering, she straightened her spine and composed her features. The scene that met her eyes was so homey and domestic that for a brief moment she felt like an interloper. Regina stood at the kitchen counter grating cheese to top the salad Bruce was tossing in a large wooden bowl.

"Hi, princess, you're just in time for dinner." Her father's warm tone sent the alien feeling packing. "How's Cindy?"

"Blossoming." Micki grinned. Stealing a slim wedge of tomato from the bowl, she added, "I love the house."

"Did she have the fun of surprising you?" Regina turned from the cheese, an uncertain smile on her lips.

"Mmm," Micki nodded, finishing the tomato. "I was properly stunned."

"I'm glad." Regina transferred the grated cheese to the table. "Run into anyone else you know?"

Micki felt her face go stiff. Had her seemingly accidental meeting with Wolf been planned? Could his desire to see her, talk to her, be part of Regina's campaign to cement a friendship between herself and Micki? Micki stared at Regina's mildly inquiring expression as her mind went over those few fantastic minutes she spent in Wolf's apartment. No, she decided firmly. If the meeting had been part of a let's-be-friends play, Wolf would not have made his own play. Her father rescued her from the need to answer Regina's question.

"What's all this about a surprise from Cindy?"

"I didn't know she was pregnant," Micki answered quickly.

"And I inadvertently let the cat out of the bag before Micki left this morning," Regina supplied contritely.

"But all went well." Micki finished the tale dramatically. "Boy, was I surprised."

During the dinner Bruce glanced at Micki and asked, "Are you going with us tonight, honey?"

"Oh, dear, I forgot," Regina moaned, her face stricken. "I was so busy telling Micki something I wasn't supposed to, I failed to tell her what I was supposed to."

Totally confused, Micki begged, "Do you think you

could untangle that for me, Dad? I'm afraid I must have missed something."

"Nothing very earth-shattering," Bruce chuckled. "We've been invited to watch the Night in Venice from the Gallagers' deck. When Dolly and Mike heard you'd be home, they asked me to tell you to come along, as they'd love to see you."

"The Night in Venice," Micki replied faintly. "I—I don't know—I—"

"You don't have other plans, do you?" Her father's face wore a confused question mark.

"No, but," Micki hedged, then offered lamely, "but I don't want to intrude."

"Intrude!" Now his face reflected sheer disbelief. "Dolly and Mike were at your christening. How could you possibly intrude?"

"All right." For the second time in less than two hours, Micki sighed in defeat. "I'd like to come."

It was a bare-faced lie. The last thing Micki wanted was to sit on that particular deck. It was on that deck she had been introduced to one Wolfgang Karl Renninger.

CHAPTER 3

As soon as the dishes were rinsed and stacked in the dishwasher, Micki escaped to her room with a murmured, "I'll be ready," when her father said they would be leaving around eight.

After stripping off her clothes, she headed for the shower. She felt half sick to her stomach and there was a throbbing in her temples that grew stronger with each passing minute. Standing under the tepid spray, water cascading over her head and down her body, Micki decided her acceptance of Wolf's taunting challenge had not been too bright. She knew what he wanted. What he'd always wanted from any woman hapless enough to wander into his orbit. And he thought she'd under persuasion be willing to answer his wants.

About who you're sleeping with.

His words echoed in her mind so clearly she jerked her head around to see if he hadn't somehow slipped into the shower with her. Knowing she was being silly, yet unable to control her reaction, she turned the water off and stepped out of the stall. Raking her memory, she tried to recall his exact tone as well as his words. Once again his words, complete with his shading, came sharp and clear.

Had he sounded derisive? Mocking? Angry? Micki shook her head, she couldn't pinpoint it. The word jealousy leaped into her mind, but with a snort she rejected it. Wolf jealous? Never.

Another thought slithered into her mind and she felt herself go hot then cold. That he'd asked the question in the first place must mean he'd taken for granted that she was sleeping with someone. The vaguely sick feeling in her stomach deepened. She had not denied it. Quite the opposite. The reply she'd flung at him could easily be taken as confirmation.

Her thoughts tormented her as she dressed. Damn him. Whenever she considered herself, her life-style, at all, it was along the lines of independent, self-sufficient, and confident. In less than one hour Wolf had managed to undermine her self-image. Suddenly she felt vulnerable, confused, and much younger than her twenty-five years. Damn him. Her last thoughts before leaving her room were *He's going to give me trouble, I know it, and I don't know what to do about it.*

They walked to the bay, enjoying the sweetness of the early evening ocean breeze. The Gallager house was full of people, as it always was the evening of Night in Venice. As it was still early, most of the people were milling about, laughing, talking, helping themselves to the large array of snacks Dolly had set out.

Micki had always enjoyed the Gallagers' company. About her father's age, they were a warm, friendly couple who liked having people around. When she was a little girl, Micki had loved visiting them.

After exchanging greetings and hugs and a few moments of small talk, Micki wandered out onto the nearly empty deck. She knew that before too long both the deck she was on and the one above her would be crowded with people, but for now, for just a few minutes, she could savor the near solitude.

As she crossed the deck toward the railing, Micki

44

glanced around. As far as she could see on either side, on the docks at street endings, on the porches and wide decks of apartment houses and private homes, people were gathered for the once-a-year show.

Making her way to a chair placed in a corner of the deck, Micki gazed out over the bay, affected, as she'd always been, by the molten gold sheen cast on the water by the fiery ball of westering sun.

She sat down and looked around idly, then froze in the chair, her hands gripping the armrests. Closing her eyes, she stifled a groan against the memory that would no longer stay locked away.

She had been sitting very near this spot when she'd first seen him. He had had one broad shoulder propped against a support beam and was half sitting on the rail when she'd felt his eyes on her and glanced up. She'd frozen then too, held fast to the chair by the bold stare from his silvery eyes. Micki experienced again the breathlessness she'd felt that night, the sensation that although six feet of deck separated them he was actually touching her. The shortness of breath had lasted until Mike had strolled up to talk to him and drew his eyes away from her.

Micki had studied his profile covertly while the two men talked. In his late twenties or early thirties, she'd judged, and was, without question, the most sexy, exciting-looking male she'd ever seen.

She'd been positive her heart had stopped when at Mike's quick, smiling nod, he'd lazily pushed himself away from the rail and followed Mike over the deck to her.

She had been amused at his name when Mike made the introductions and she'd made no attempt to hide it when she raised her eyes to his.

"Wolfgang?" she'd repeated in a laughing tone.

"Pitiful, isn't it?" he'd drawled. "It's a traditional name in my family. I, unfortunately, got tagged with it, being the firstborn male child." His eyes seemed to absorb her as he added, "Call me Wolf."

"And *are* you?" Micki had been amazed at the insolent sound of her voice. "A wolf, I mean."

"Of course," he'd returned smoothly, a wicked grin flashing on his tan face. "Isn't everyone who is single and unattached on the prowl?" He'd cocked his head to one side and those bold, silver eyes roamed over her, from head to foot to head again. "If you weren't so young, I may have decided to stalk you." His eyes laughed at the sudden pinkness in her face. His voice dropped to a low caress. "I still might."

Struck speechless, Micki had stared at him, praying for some bright, crushing words to pop into her head. None did, and then it didn't matter, for someone—that throaty voice could only have belonged to Regina—inside called to him and he turned away from her. He took one step, then glanced back at her, the wicked grin flashing again.

"A pleasure meeting you"—he paused—"young Micki."

Micki had gone all hot and flushed, first with embarrassment, then with anger. *He spoke to me as if I was a little girl,* she'd thought furiously, *and I'm not. I'm nineteen, for heaven's sake and I hope I never see that bigheaded, overbearing Wolf again.*

Even so, her anger and hope notwithstanding, his image filled her mind the rest of the night and she saw very little of the evening's entertainment.

"Well, honey, I see you've found a good seat for the show."

Micki blinked away the past and glanced up at her father, a shaky smile on her lips.

"Yes," she answered vaguely, noticing, for the first time, that it was nearly dark. "Shouldn't it be getting under way soon?"

"How far away were you?" Bruce laughed. "If you'll merely look to your right, you'll see it's nearly on top of us."

Micki's eyes followed the direction of his casually

waved hand. Then she whispered a surprised, "Oh!" Sure enough, the procession of gaily decorated, brightly lighted boats of all sizes was indeed nearly on top of them.

For several minutes Micki watched the parade of boats, enjoying the reflection of the lights on the water, laughing at the clowning antics of the men in the smaller boats, and waving at the people of all ages aboard the cleverly festooned crafts.

But her eyes soon drifted to that one spot at the rail, clouding over with the rush of memories.

She had not seen him again for almost a week. Then, when she was finally beginning to get his image out of her mind, she felt the touch of his silvery eyes again. At the time she'd thought it was very strange. She'd been walking near the far end of the boardwalk with Cindy and two other girls, all of them laughing as they munched on slices of pizza, when she felt an eerie shiver skip down her spine. What had made her lift her head, glance around, she didn't know, but she'd just felt compelled to look. This time he was propped against the boardwalk's pipelike railing, his eyes fastened on her. He didn't call to her or even wave, but the grin flashed white and wicked and his eyes seemed to speak of things beyond her wildest imaginings. She had caught herself just in time from choking on her pizza and had hurried on, but after a dozen steps she'd glanced back to find his eyes still on her.

Early in August she'd seen him again. That time she'd been leaving the theater after the early evening showing of a controversial R-rated movie. She had been with her gang and the comments, both pro and con on the film, were flying hot and heavy. Wolf, with a beautiful, high-fashion-type redhead clinging to his arm, was going in to the late evening showing. Micki nearly bumped into him. There was no grin this time, but as he passed her one eyelid came down in a slow, suggestive wink.

And then, in late August, there was a cookout at a

47

friend's beachfront house and all the unbelievable events that followed it.

There must have been twenty of them, not counting her friend's parents and the people they'd invited. After they'd eaten, they'd split up into two-man teams for a sand-sculpting contest, which, the adults vowed, they'd judge impartially. Micki had been teamed with Tony Menella, and even with all the horseplay and general craziness, their sculpture of a reclining nude had won hands down.

As twilight settled gently on the beach, Cindy had suggested they go hunting in the sand. They'd started out as a group, but their ranks thinned as some quit to go back to the house and others roamed farther along the beach.

Toting a brown bag to hold her dubious treasures, Micki found herself alone with a boy she'd met that night for the first time. Searching her mind, she came up with the name David Bender. She crossed her fingers in hope it was the right one.

"What happened to all the other kids?" Micki's fingers twined behind her back. "David?"

"Beats me." He glanced around scanning the beach. "I guess most of them got bored." His still boyishly slim shoulders lifted in a shrug. "Did you find anything worth keeping?"

"No." Micki laughed.

"Me either." David laughed with her. "Want to sit and rest awhile before heading back?" He shot her a shy look. "We've come down the beach pretty far."

"Okay," Micki answered flippantly, plopping down at the base of a low sand dune. "You're from up near Margate, aren't you?" she asked after he'd dropped onto the sand less than a foot away from her.

"Yeah," David nodded, not looking at her, his eyes fixed on the darkening ocean.

Sighing softly, Micki leaned back against the gentle slope of the dune, her eyes studying him with mild interest. About her own age, she thought, maybe even a little younger. He still had the look of the high-school boy, she mused from the exalted distance of one completed year of college. Unbidden, a picture of Wolfgang Renninger rose in her mind. Micki had to compress her lips to keep from laughing out loud at the comparison. Unfair, she chided herself sternly. Wolf's a mature man, while David's still in the throes of adolescence. She should have remembered how hot the blood can flow in teenaged boys.

"You're a very pretty girl." David's voice came softly close to her ear. During her perusal of him, he'd settled back into the dune, turned onto his side to face her. "Are you going steady with anyone?"

Startled out of her contemplation, Micki turned her head to find his face close to hers. Surprised, she smiled nervously. "No, not steady. I'm too busy with college and—David, what—?"

His soft, moist lips silenced her. With an inward sigh, Micki lay perfectly still, his inexperienced kiss drawing no response from her. It was a mistake. Her lack of interest seemed to spur a determination in him to make her feel something. The pressure on her lips increased painfully. Suddenly his hands pushed her beach wrap open, tore at the skimpy top of her bikini as his body rolled on top of her.

Her first reaction was sharp anger. Who did this jerk think he was, pawing at her? Bringing her hands up, she pushed at his shoulders, fully expecting him to move off her at once and apologize sheepishly. Fear began when she couldn't dislodge him. He was a lot stronger than he looked. With all her twisting and turning she could not escape his lips. She couldn't breathe and she felt sure that if he didn't lift his head soon she'd faint from lack of air. Panic shot through her when his fingers dug into her now-exposed breasts and one bony knee attempted to pry her legs apart. This couldn't be happening. Not to her.

Blackness was stealing into her mind when his lips slid

from hers, moved to fasten, hurtfully, on the soft skin on the side of her neck.

"David, stop," Micki gasped between huge gulps of consciousness-saving breaths. Fear lent inspiration as, struggling frantically, she lied. "I've got to get back, my father will be coming to pick me up."

"You don't have to go anywhere," David panted, his fingers digging viciously into her breasts. "I heard you tell Cindy you'd be alone all weekend because your folks are out of town."

His lips moved in a sucking action, drawing a cry of pain from her. Nausea filled her throat when his knee succeeded in pushing her legs apart and his slender frame pressed her deeper into the gritty sand.

"David, please stop." She was crying openly, her sobs catching at her throat when she felt his hand move down her body, tug at her bikini bottom. "No!" Her voice rose in a muffled scream of pure desperation.

"Hey!" David yelped loudly, then suddenly his weight was removed, yanked away from her violently.

"You stupid crumb." The enraged, unfamiliar growl was followed by the stinging sound of a hard, open-handed blow and a loud cry of pain from David. "Get the hell out of here or I'll break you in half."

Still crying, blinking against the tears that blurred her vision, Micki cringed back when big hands grasped her shoulders, lifted her from the sand.

"It's all right, youngster, he's gone." The soft tone that had replaced the enraged growl was recognizable now as belonging to Wolf Renninger.

"He—he—he tried to—"

"I know," Wolf snapped, preventing her from saying the word *rape*. "But it's over now." He went on in a softer tone. He pulled her impersonally, protectively against his broad, hard chest, brushed the sand from her back with his big hand. "I'll see that you get home safely."

50

"Oh, no," Micki moaned, rubbing her forehead back and forth over the smooth material of his shirt.

"No?" Wolf repeated impatiently. "What do you mean, no?"

"You don't understand," she wailed. "Dad and Regina are away for the weekend. I'll be alone in the house and David knows it. What if he—?" Micki paused to swallow a fresh lump of fear. "I don't want to go home."

He cursed softly, then was very still for long seconds before, moving away from her, he said decisively, "Okay, you can come with me for a while, then I'm taking you home."

The harshness of his voice confused and frightened her. Meekly, after hurriedly tugging her suit top into place and fastening her beach coat at the neck, she followed in his wake as he walked around the sand dune and strode toward the road where a low-slung car was parked.

"Come on," Wolf gritted irritably at her slow progress through the tall grass.

As she slid onto the seat of the sports car, Micki slanted a quick look at him through her long lashes, wondering what she'd said, or done, to make him so angry. Surely he didn't think she had encouraged David in any way? She jumped when the door slammed beside her, and again when his own slammed, after he'd folded his long frame onto the seat behind the wheel. Opening her mouth to ask him what was wrong, Micki glanced at him and closed her lips quickly at the hard, rigid set of his face. Wolf started the car and made a U-turn on Ocean Drive, heading away from the city.

"Where are we going?" Micki asked hesitantly.

"I've got my boat docked not far from here," he replied tersely. "I have to move it."

They drove a short distance beyond the city limits, then Wolf turned off the drive toward the bay where he parked the car on a small lot in front of a rather rundown building with a red neon sign that read BAR & GRILL.

51

"Where were you?"

The question was punctuated by his hard tug on the hand brake. For a second Micki blinked at him in confusion, then his meaning registered.

"At a cookout beach party, at a friend's home."

"Did you go dressed like that?" he snapped.

"No, of course not," Micki snapped back, beginning to feel a little steadier as the shock from her experience receded. "My clothes are at the house."

"What's this friend's name and phone number?"

"You're not going to call her?" Micki cried.

"Yes, I am," Wolf sighed in exasperation. "When you don't come back they're liable to call the police. If they haven't already."

Micki hadn't thought of the furor her absence might cause. Chastised, she murmured the name and number.

"Okay, I've got it." He opened the car door and stepped out. "Stay here, I'll be back in a minute."

The door swung closed with a loud bang. Biting her lip, Micki wondered again why he was so angry. As the minute stretched into five and then ten, Micki's temper flared. What was he doing all this time? Probably having a drink with the boys, while she sat alone in a dark parking lot. And who did he think he was anyway? He had no right to snap and snarl at her like some untamed beast of the wild. By the time he returned, she talked herself into a fury.

"What were you doing all this time?" she demanded the minute he'd opened the door beside her. "Making time with the barmaid?"

"Don't take that tone with me, youngster." Wolf's soft voice held a definite warning. "What I do, who I make time with, is no concern of yours. If you've got any sense at all, you'll guard that nasty little tongue. You couldn't even handle Joe College back there. I'd crush you like an annoying little gnat. Now get out of the car, I'm taking you home."

"But—" she began.

"Out," he cut in harshly.

Micki bit her lip, feeling very young, and very inexperienced, and very, very stupid. He was right, of course, she had no right to question him. If it hadn't been for him . . . She shuddered. Belatedly she remembered she hadn't even thanked him. No wonder he was angry. Knowing what she had to do, she drew a deep breath, slid off the seat, and stood before him, her head bent.

"I'm—I'm sorry, Mr. Renninger," she whispered contritely. "I know you must think I'm a stupid little ingrate." Wetting her dry lips, Micki lifted her head to look at him, her eyes made even brighter by the shimmer of tears. "I—I haven't even thanked you for helping me. But I am grateful, truly, and—and—" She had to pause to swallow against the tightness in her throat. "I wanted you to know I didn't invite that attack."

"I didn't think you had." Wolf's much gentler tone brought a fresh rush of tears to her eyes. "Don't cry, young Micki." His hand came up to cradle her face, one long finger brushed at her tears. "I know it was a bad experience, but you're unhurt and—" He broke off and leaned toward her. "He didn't hurt you, did he?"

"No, not really." Micki shook her head, drawing a deep breath to combat the increase in heartbeat his nearness caused. "The only thing hurt is my dignity."

"It will heal," he murmured, lowering his head closer to hers. His fingers shook as if he'd had a sudden chill, then he snatched his hand away as though her skin had burned him. "Come on, kid, I've got to get you home." The gentleness had gone, replaced by an edgy roughness Micki didn't understand, as she didn't understand the hard emphasis he'd placed on the word *kid*.

"But what about your car?"

"It isn't mine. It belongs to the guy that owns this place."

Grasping her arm, he hurried her around the building

53

and onto a rickety pier. Secured to the pier, bathed dimly in the glow from the building's side windows, was a cabin cruiser that brought a small gasp from Micki.

"Is that beautiful thing yours?" she asked in an awed tone.

"Yes," Wolf replied shortly. "Go aboard, I want to cast off."

"Please." Micki's hand caught his arm as he turned away. "Could I have a quick tour of her before we go?"

The muscles in his arm tensed under her fingers and Micki was sure he was about to refuse. Then with a soft sigh of resignation, he said crisply, "All right, a very quick tour."

He helped her to board the shadowy craft, then, one hand at her waist to guide her, he led her across the deck and down a short flight of stairs with a murmured, "Careful." There was the sound of a switch being flicked and Micki blinked against the sudden light that filled the small salon she was standing in. Glancing around at the sparse, masculine furnishings, she breathed, "How many does she sleep?"

"Ten," Wolf replied curtly, indicating a narrow portal across the room. Micki stepped through the portal into an equally narrow passageway, which had two doors on each side. When she hesitated at the first door on her left, Wolf grated, "Get on with it."

Biting back the retort that sprang to her lips, Micki pushed the door open. The cabin contained a small fitted dresser and four fitted bunks. The cabin next to it was exactly the same. As she withdrew from the second cabin, Wolf opened the door directly across the passage, with a terse, "The head."

The small, but adequate-sized bathroom was equipped with a stainless steel toilet, shower stall, and fitted wash-bowl. Wolf was standing at the open door of the last cabin when she emerged from the head. He made a half bow as she approached him. "The captain's quarters," he drawled mockingly.

Feeling herself grow warm under his mocking glance, Micki unfastened her beach coat and preceded him into the cabin. It was larger than the other two cabins. Instead of fitted bunks it contained a built-in bed, not quite as wide as a regular double bed.

At sight of the bed, Micki's body was suddenly suffused with warmth. Feeling constricted, she pulled her beach coat open. Casting about in her mind for something to say to the silent man standing just inside the cabin, she turned slowly.

"Is—is this where you sle—" The words died on her lips at the sudden, fierce look on his face. Her breathing stopped as he walked to her, his silvery eyes gleaming dangerously behind narrowed lids.

"What's wrong?" she gasped, terrified by the look of him.

"That creep bastard marked you," he snarled softly, bending over her to examine her throat and the smooth skin below her shoulders.

"Oh, no," she groaned, her hand flying to her neck. "Is it very bad?"

"Bad enough," he clipped, straightening. "Sit down, I'll get some antiseptic to put on it."

Disregarding his order, she walked to the small mirror above the dresser and leaned toward it to peer closely at the red marks.

"I told you to sit." The hard sound of his voice set her teeth on edge.

"I'm not a dog," Micki flared, close to tears.

"You're telling me," he drawled, holding his hand out to her. "Come on, infant, let me dab this stuff on you."

Ignoring his hand, Micki walked by him stiffly, miffed at the term *infant*. Sitting down gingerly on the very edge of the bed, she lifted her head to expose her neck, and closed her eyes. When the antiseptic touched the abrasion, she drew her breath in sharply and shut her eyes more tightly to stem the corresponding sting in her eyes.

"Sorry," he muttered softly. He was so close, his warm breath feathered her skin, setting off a clamoring inside her that ended in a visible shiver. "I could beat him up for doing this to you." The soft intensity of his tone increased her shivering. Keeping her eyes tightly closed, holding her breath, Micki sat immobile. Something strange was happening to her. Something strange, and a little scary, and almost unbearably exciting.

The feather light touch of his lips on her skin felt like a touch from an exposed electrical wire. Trembling, Micki moaned deep in her throat. She heard his raspy, indrawn breath an instant before he sighed softly, groaned, "Dear God, Micki."

His mouth touched hers gently, experimentally. When she didn't flinch away, the pressure increased and his hands grasped her upper arms. Her heart beating wildly, Micki returned the kiss. She gasped against his mouth when the hard tip of his tongue moved slowly across her lips, but she obeyed the silent command to part them. His mouth still gentle, exploring, he straightened, drawing her to her feet in front of him.

Micki didn't know what was happening to her. She had been kissed before, many times, but never had she felt this sweet joy zinging through her veins, this light-headed, intoxicating sensation. When she swayed toward him, touched his body with her own, he lifted his head, held her away from him.

"I've got to take you home," he rasped unevenly.

"Why?" Micki asked huskily.

"Don't you know?" Wolf groaned. "Have you really no idea of the effect you're having on me?"

Elation shot through her, gave her the courage to lean toward him, slide the tip of her tongue across his mouth. He went stone still, then gritted. "Where the hell did you learn that trick?"

Micki's eyes went wide at his rough tone. "From you, just now. I've never—never—"

"Why did you do it?" His growl had lost its bite.

"Because"—Micki wet her lips, felt a curl of excitement when his eyes dropped to her mouth—"because I was afraid you weren't going to kiss me again—and I wanted you to."

"You're too young to know what you want." Micki's head was shaking a denial before he'd finished speaking, but he didn't give her time to voice it. "If I kissed you, I mean really kissed you, you'd be fighting me in a cold panic within seconds, exactly like you were fighting that teenage Don Juan back at the beach."

"No, I wouldn't," Micki denied softly. "I didn't want him to kiss me. I do want you to."

His silvery eyes stared hard into hers, then dropped to her mouth, then lifted to her eyes again. "I must be out of my mind," he muttered. "I never should have brought you here after the jealousy I felt of that punk."

"You felt jealous of David!" Micki exclaimed. "But why?"

"Because"—Wolf's voice was very low as he drew her slowly against his long frame—"I wanted to be in exactly the same position he was in, you beautiful fool."

This time there was very little gentleness. His lips crushed hers, forcing them apart roughly. His tongue probed hungrily. Flaring lights actually seemed to explode behind her eyes. Raising her arms, she curled them around his neck, needing suddenly to be closer to him. He half groaned, half growled into her mouth, then his hands moved across her shoulders, down her back, molding her to his hard body. Responding to the demands of her body, Micki arched her hips against him. At once lips pulled away from hers, moved in a fiery path over her cheek to her ear.

"Micki, stop me while you still can." His voice held half plea, half command.

"I don't want you to stop." The moment the words were out she knew she spoke the truth. She had never behaved like this before in her life, yet she knew she wanted to, had to, belong to this man.

Although his hands still held her tightly to him, he lifted his head, gave her another of those hard stares. "You've been with a man before?"

Micki hesitated, knowing somehow that if she told him the truth he'd put her from him, take her home. Praying that in the dim light her flush would look like guilt, she lowered her lashes, whispered, "Yes."

A flash of something—pain, disgust—twisted his face. He gave an almost imperceptible shake of his head, then lowered his mouth to within a whisper of hers. Again she heard that half groan, half growl.

"I don't care." His hands spread over her hips, pulling her tightly against him. "Oh, God, baby, I want you."

Her beach coat and her bikini were removed gently but swiftly. For the first time in her life Micki stood naked before a man, amazed that she felt no shame or fear. As he undressed, his eyes, gleaming like liquid silver, moved slowly over her body, the burning, naked hunger in them igniting an eagerness in her to be in his arms, be part of him.

Slowly, expertly, his mouth and hands an exquisite torture, he fanned the flame inside her to a roaring blaze. Gasping, moaning softly deep in her throat, her lips leaving tiny, urgent kisses on his neck, his shoulders, she welcomed him when, finally, his body covered hers. Moments later he cursed her.

"Damn you!" Wolf's tone held anger, but an odd note of satisfaction as well. "You lied to me."

"Yes," she admitted into the curve of his shoulder, her arms tightening around his waist, refusing to let go.

"Oh, baby, baby." He kissed her mouth tenderly. "I'm sorry."

"I'm not," Micki replied honestly. "I wanted this as badly as you did, Wolf."

"Sweet Lord, I've found myself a sexy teenage vixen," Wolf muttered huskily, his body moving excitingly.

"You'd better enjoy it while you can," Micki laughed teasingly. "I'll only be a teenager two more months."

"A vixen and a tease," Wolf moaned between short, quick breaths, then, "Oh, God, honey, kiss me."

Micki's initiation into the world of serious lovemaking lasted until three o'clock the following morning. Wolf was a master tutor, and under his ardent guidance she caught a glimpse of the wondrous things his eyes had seemed to speak of that time on the boardwalk. Exhausted, she curled still closer to him, heard him laugh softly as his arms tightened around her.

"That was just the first chapter of the text," he teased. "Do you think you'll graduate?"

"Cum laude," she murmured sleepily and was rewarded by a light kiss on the corner of her mouth.

"Go to sleep, honey," Wolf whispered into her ear.

CHAPTER 4

"Wake up, honey."

Micki jumped at the sound of her father's quiet voice, the gentle touch of his hand on her arm.

"Is it over?"

Sitting up straight, she winced at the twinge of pain at the base of her spine and brought her hand up to massage the stiffness in her neck caused by the hard rim of the aluminum chair. Glancing around, she saw the deck was empty of all the other people. What time was it?

"Over an hour ago." Bruce laughed softly. "The party's breaking up. It's time to go home."

"I'm ready."

Moving carefully, Micki lifted her cramped body out of the chair, one hand going to her mouth to cover a wide yawn. In a young-girl, sleepy voice, she apologized, thanked, and said good night to her indulgently smiling host and hostess, then followed her father and Regina out to the hushed sidewalk.

Trailing a few steps behind the couple, she watched as her father's arm slid around his wife's waist, heard his low voice murmur something close to her ear. Regina apparently disagreed with what her father had said, for her head

61

moved slowly in a negative shake. The argument, if that's what it was, was obviously not over anything very serious. With a sigh of relief, Micki heard Regina laugh softly.

Dropping a few steps farther behind in order to give them complete privacy, Micki's fingers curled tightly into the palm of her hand. Well, she'd missed it again. It had been six years since she'd gone to watch the Night in Venice and she'd seen practically none of it. And for exactly the same reason—thoughts of Wolf had absorbed her attention, her senses.

Angrily rejecting the image of him that rose in her mind, Micki centered her thoughts on the couple a few feet ahead of her, wondering if she could be the bone of contention between them. She hoped not, but had the sinking sensation that she was. For all Regina's declared wish that they be friends, Micki was still very unsure of her. Their past relationship had been fraught with so much jealousy, so much resentment, that Micki was un-convinced of the permanency of their truce.

The minute Micki entered the house, Bruce ended her conjecturing.

"There is only one way to find out," he stated in a tone of amused exasperation. "And that's ask her."

"Bruce, please," Regina pleaded softly. "Not tonight, she's tired and—"

"She's wide awake now," Bruce insisted, studying his daughter closely. "Princess, I'm going to ask you something and I want you to answer honestly. Will you?"

"Yes, of course." Micki's gaze flew from her father's laughing eyes to Regina's worried ones. What was this all about? Her father answered her silent question.

"I want to take Regina on a second honeymoon," he said quietly, his suddenly serious, love-filled eyes resting on his wife's face.

"And?" Micki prompted, confused as to what a proposed second honeymoon had to do with her.

"Regina insists that it would be selfish of us to go away at this time."

"Selfish?" Micki repeated blankly. "I don't understand. In what way would it be selfish?"

A satisfied grin spread over her father's face. "You see?" he asked Regina before turning back to Micki. "Regina is afraid you'll feel, well, deserted, if we went away so soon after your return home."

"But that's ridiculous!" Micki cried. "When were you thinking of going?"

"Not till the end of the month." Bruce's eyes filled with pride and tenderness as he studied Micki's face. "It will take me until then to tie up some loose ends at the office."

Micki looked directly at Regina. "By the end of the month I expect the majority of my time will be spent in learning my new job." Her eyes swung back to her father. "I think a second honeymoon is a lovely idea, especially as I don't remember your ever having a first."

"It was impossible for me to leave the office at that time," Bruce defended himself. "And since then the time just didn't seem right." Bruce paused, then went on softly. "With one thing and another."

"Well, then," Micki spoke quickly, knowing too well that she was the one thing and Regina's behavior the other. "If you feel the time is now right, then go, and don't worry about me. I'm a big girl now and quite used to taking care of myself." At the contrite expression that crossed her father's face at her last words, Micki willed a sparkle into her eyes and shaded her voice with teasing excitement. "Where were you thinking of going, or is that a secret?"

"No secret." Micki felt relief rush through her at the way her father's face lit up. "I had thought San Francisco, I've always wanted to see it." His voice grew eager. "We could rent a car, drive through the Redwoods, along the coast, Carmel, Big Sur."

Watching Regina's face, Micki could see her father's

eagerness reflected there. Although she had been arguing against the trip, it was obvious Regina wanted to go.

"Sounds super." Micki spoke directly to Regina. "So do it. Make your arrangements and take off. I promise you I will be fine."

Grabbing Regina up in a bear hug, Bruce spun her around, laughing. "What did I tell you, darling? Is my girl something special or not?"

"Very special." Regina spoke for the first time. When he turned back to Micki, Regina mouthed a silent thank you at her.

Wide awake now, Micki murmured, "I think I'll sit on the porch a few minutes," when her father and Regina moved toward the stairs. "You two go on up, I'll lock up."

Micki stepped out onto the porch, then turned back to get a sweater from the hall closet. A mist rolling in off the ocean had turned the air cool and clammy. Settling back on the porch lounger, she watched the mist swirl and thicken, turn the light from the street lamp into an eerie orangish glow.

The mist had been like this that morning.

Shifting irritably on the thickly padded cushion, Micki tried to push the thought away. She didn't want to think about it. Didn't want to remember. Her shifting, her silent protests, were in vain. The floodgate of memory, which had sprung a leak earlier, now burst completely, swamping her, carrying her helplessly back through time.

Micki stirred when the warmth of Wolf's body was removed from hers. Through eyelids heavy with sleep, she watched him, his form barely discernible in the gray, pre-dawn half light. Moving noiselessly, he stepped into his jeans, fastened them, then pulled a battered sweat shirt over his head. Fear shot through her as he moved across the floor to the door.

"Wolf?" Micki's voice betrayed her fear. "Where are you going?"

At the sound of his name Wolf turned, the fear in her tone brought him back to the bed in a few long strides. Bending, he dropped a soft kiss on her lips.

"I have to move the boat," he explained quietly, one long finger outlining her mouth. "Go back to sleep. As soon as I have her docked at the marina I'll come back to bed." His lips touched hers again, lingered, then he was moving across the cabin, out the door.

Micki closed her eyes tightly, but it was no good; she couldn't sleep with him gone. Slipping out of the bed, and a moment later out of the cabin, she hurried into the tiny bathroom. She was stepping under the shower spray when she heard the boat's engine flare into life. Bracing herself with one hand, she washed her body with the other while Wolf backed the boat away from the pier and swung it around. When the craft was relatively steady, she stepped out of the shower stall, grabbed for the towel, probably Wolf's, that hung on a small fitted bar, and rubbed herself down briskly.

Back in the cabin, she stretched languorously. The tautening of her breasts brought the remembered feel of Wolf's hands, and her nipples set into diamond-hard points. Oh, Wolf. Just to think his name sent her blood racing through her veins, set her pulses hammering out of control. She couldn't wait until he'd docked the boat, she had to see him now.

Glancing around, she grimaced as her eyes settled on her bikini and beach coat, laying in an untidy heap where Wolf had tossed them. Shaking her head in rejection of the beachwear, she went to the cabin's one small closet and rummaged through shirts and jackets—obviously too short to cover the bare necessities—until her hand clutched and withdrew a bright yellow rain slicker. Pulling it on hastily, uncaring how incongruous she looked, she left the cabin, fastening the buckle closings as she went.

Not once did she pause to ask herself why she was

where she was, with a man she knew practically nothing about. Not once did she wonder about how suddenly it had happened. She was there. It had happened. Never before had she felt so tinglingly alive, so totally happy. But she didn't even pause to think of that. The only thought that filled her mind was that she had to be near him, see him. The whys and how of it would torment her later.

When she stepped onto the deck she came to an abrupt halt, her hand groping for something solid to steady herself with. An off-white mist lay over everything, muffling sound, obscuring visibility. The deck was beaded and slick with moisture. Placing her bare feet carefully, Micki moved cautiously toward the canopied section that housed the wheel, and the man who stood at that wheel, alert tenseness in every line of his tall, muscular frame.

She thought her progress was silent, yet the moment she stepped under the canopy, his left arm was extended backward.

"Come stand by me." Wolf's hushed tone blended with the cotton blanket that surrounded the boat.

Without a word Micki moved to his side, sighed with contentment when his arm closed around her, drew her close to his hard strength.

"Why didn't you go back to sleep?" Still the same hushed tone, not scolding, a simple question. He did not look at her, and her eyes following the direction of his intent gaze, she answered as simply.

"I wanted to be with you."

She saw his hand tighten on the wheel at the same instant the muscles in his arm tautened. He slanted her a quick glance and an amused smile curved his firmly etched mouth.

"I see you've made free with my shower and bath soap." The smile deepened. "Bedecked yourself with the latest yachting creations from Paris also."

"But of course," Micki teased back. "This particular

number was labeled MORNING SUNLIGHT THROUGH HEAVY GAUZE CURTAINS. Does my lord approve?"

Wolf's soft laughter was an exciting, provocative attack on her senses.

"But of course," he mimicked her seriously. "Still, I think I prefer the, er, more basic ensemble you were wearing earlier."

Flushed with pleasure, Micki rubbed her warm cheek against his cool, mist-dampened sweat shirt. Misunderstanding her action and the pink glow on her face, he chided her softly.

"You're a beautiful woman, babe." Wolf's soft tone brooked no argument. "Every soft, satiny inch of you. There's no reason for embarrassment." He paused, then slanted another, harder look at her. "Do you feel shame?"

"No!" Micki's denial was fast, emphatic. "Or embarrassment either." Rising on tiptoe, she placed her lips on the strong column of his throat. "I'm—I'm pleased that you find me attractive."

"Attractive?" Micki could feel the tension ease out of him. "I don't think that adjective quite makes it." Leaning forward, he peered, narrow-eyed, through the moisture-beaded window. "If I ever get this damned boat docked I'll try to come up with the right one. Now be still and let me get on with it."

Micki obeyed him explicably. Barely breathing, she watched as he inched the craft along through the mist-shrouded water, and sighed with relief when he murmured, "There's the marina." When he removed his arm, she stepped back ready to follow any order he might issue.

"Have you ever driven a boat?" Wolf asked tersely as he backed the vessel into the slip.

"Yes," Micki answered quietly, then qualified, "But never one this large."

"Good enough." Their voyage through the mist completed safely, all his intent tenseness fled. His silvery eyes glittered teasingly. "You hold her down and I'll tie her up."

Suiting action to words, he drew her to the wheel, gave a few brief instructions, and then he was gone, swallowed up in the gray-white mist. A moment later she heard the dull thud as the securing line landed on the pier, and then another as he followed it.

When the craft was secured, its engine silent, Wolf slid his arms around the bulky slicker at her waist and held her loosely.

"You hungry, baby?" His low tone, the way his eyes caressed her face, drove all thoughts but one from her mind. "Do you want some breakfast?"

Micki was shaking her head before he finished speaking. Not even trying to mask her feelings, she gazed up at him, her eyes honest and direct.

"I want to go back to bed."

"Good Lord," he breathed huskily, his arms drawing her closer. "What did I ever do to earn you as a reward?"

Pleasure radiated through her entire body at the warmth of his tone, the emotion-darkened gray of his eyes. Her arms, made clumsy by the too-large raincoat, encircled his neck to draw his head closer to hers. A shiver of anticipation skipped down her spine as his hands slid slowly over the smooth, stiff material of the garment.

"Are you wearing anything at all under that slicker?" His face was so near, his cool breath fanned her lips.

Mesmerized by the shiny, tautened skin of his mist-dampened cheeks and the motion of his mouth, Micki whispered a bemused, "No."

His parted lips touched hers in a brief kiss before she felt her lower lip caught inside his mouth, felt his teeth nibble gently on the tender, sensitive skin. Moaning softly, she flicked his teeth with her tongue. Instantly his arms tightened, crushing her against his hard body, and his lips pushed hers apart to receive his hungry, demanding mouth.

Awareness of him sang through every particle of her being. Squirming inside the stiff, confining coat, she strained her body to his, thrilled to the feeling of his body straining to hers.

"Wolf, Wolf." The words filled her mind, whispered past her lips to fill his mouth.

Lifting his head, he stared deeply into her eyes, his own eyes now nearly black with desire. His gaze dropped to her mouth.

"Why are we standing here?" His murmured groan held near pain. One arm clasped firmly around her waist, he led her along the slippery deck, down the steps, and into his cabin. Releasing her, his hands moved to the buckles on the coat.

"I swear, if I don't soon feel the silkiness of you against my skin, I think I'll burst into flames."

And in a sense he did, engulfing her in the conflagration.

They didn't leave the boat all that day or night. In fact they hardly set foot out of his cabin, except when hunger drove them to the tiny galley for sustenance.

At those times they worked together, mostly getting in each other's way. Micki, clad in her mid-thigh-length beach coat, juggled a frying pan around Wolf's large frame as she endeavored to prepare a cheese omelet on the small two-burner cooking unit. Wolf, wearing a belted, knee-length velour robe, stretched long arms around and in front of her in his effort to make a pot of coffee and open a jar of olives.

When Micki opined that had they followed the simple method of flipping a coin to determine who would get the meal the job would have been completed a lot faster, Wolf retorted that it would also have been one hell of a lot less fun.

They went through the same bumping into and laughing procedure while preparing a canned soup and canned corned beef sandwich supper, washed down with canned beer.

And both times, after appeasing the hunger of their stomachs, they went back to the appeasement of their seemingly insatiable hunger for each other.

They slept for short periods when exhaustion could no longer be held at bay, waking every time to come eagerly together, resentful of the hours of separation the need for sleep had imposed.

At one of those times, late in the night, Micki woke first and lay quietly, unmoving beside Wolf's sleeping form. Touching him with her eyes only, she studied him minutely, imprinting his likeness on her mind, in her soul.

Although by now she knew him fully in a physical sense, he was still a stranger. A stranger she was deeply, unconditionally in love with. It was a sobering thought. Sobering and somewhat frightening, for although he had murmured countless, impassioned, exciting love words to her, none had been words of love for her. But then, she had not spoken of her love for him either. Maybe it was all too new, too sudden for both of them. And maybe, she thought with a sageness beyond her years, the avowals of love now would ring false, take on the shadings of an excuse for their wild coming together. Micki shrugged mentally. It didn't matter. She'd face the reality of it all tomorrow. For right now, she knew she loved him, would probably always love him.

Micki's eyes misted over as she stared at his face. He had made her so unbelievably, joyously happy. She loved her father dearly, yet she knew that should Wolf ask her, she would go with him anywhere in the world with never a backward glance. She had had no promises of undying love, had had no solemn words spoken over her, still she felt like a bride on her honeymoon. And no girl's honeymoon, she was certain, had ever been more idyllic, more perfect than this one.

"Why are you crying?" Wolf's tone, though soft, held hard concern.

Blinking against the moisture, Micki snuggled close to him.

"Because I'm happy," she whispered, her lips brushing his taut jaw. "Haven't you ever heard that females cry when they're happy?"

"Yes, I had heard that." The movement of his lips at her temple sent tiny shivers down the back of her neck. "In fact there have been several occasions when I have been the recipient of those happy tears." The admission was made tonelessly, without conceit. "But never for so little."

"Little?" Tilting her head back, Micki looked up at him, her eyes reflecting her confusion. "I don't understand. What do you mean—for so little?"

Lifting his head, he studied her expression, as if trying to determine if her confusion was authentic. Obviously deciding it was, he shook his head in wonder. "Always before, the tears were in response to a gift from me." Wolf's eyes held hers steadily, gauging her reaction. "Jewelry, flowers, things like that," he shrugged, "but always a tangible, usually expensive, object."

Micki gazed back at him, trying, but failing, to keep the hurt from her eyes.

"And you think," she asked softly, "your gift of this weekend, being an intangible gift, has no value?"

"Honey, I didn't—" Wolf began.

"You're right." His eyes widened slightly at the firm words that cut across his protest. Blinking against the hot moisture that clouded her eyes, Micki placed the tip of her finger over his mouth, silencing whatever he was about to say. "There can be no price tag attached to the gift you've given me, simply because, to me, this weekend has been priceless." Despite her efforts, two tears escaped, rolled slowly down her face. "I never dreamed this kind of happiness, this perfect contentment, was possible to achieve."

Her voice faltered and she lowered her eyes. Hesitant but determined, she went on softly. "This is the gift you've given me, Wolf, and that's why I was crying."

A stunned silence followed her small speech and Micki began to tremble, certain she'd shattered the harmony they'd shared till now.

"Good God, can this woman be real?" Wolf's hushed tone held a hint of genuine awe. Glancing up at him, Micki saw he was no longer looking at her, but was staring at the night-blackened porthole. As if unaware of her, he went on, in the same hushed tone. "She offers me her innocence, her youth, her trust, then absolves me with her tears for my greedy use of them."

In the shadowy light Micki thought she saw his eyelashes flutter suspiciously, then all thought stopped as she was hauled, almost roughly, into his arms.

"You can have no idea what your words mean to me," Wolf whispered raggedly, "because I have no idea where to begin to express my feelings. But what I said was true. I am greedy and I don't want to waste one minute of our time together."

They left the boat in a once-again mist-shrouded pre-dawn. Like the morning before, Micki woke to find Wolf getting dressed.

"Wolf?" The one softly murmured word held both a question and a plea for him to come back to bed.

"I was just going to wake you." Wolf's eyes devoured her. "It's time to go, baby."

"But, I don't—" Micki's protest died as his features settled into lines of hard determination. Trying a different tactic, she asked innocently, "Aren't you going to kiss me good morning?"

Although a smile curved his lips, he shook his head emphatically. "No way, honey. If I come over there, it'll be noon before we get off this tub. I want to get you home while there's at least a chance no one will see you, for if

72

anyone even suspects we've spent the weekend together, your reputation will be shot to hell."

"I don't care about that—" Micki began earnestly.

"I care." Wolf's tone was suddenly harsh. "And you should too." The fingers of his right hand raked through his hair and rubbed absently at the back of his neck. Wolf sighed and went on less harshly. "God, honey, I'm eleven years older than you. Can you imagine your father's reaction if he found out about this?"

Micki could, only too well. The thought alone sent a shudder rippling through her slender frame. She groaned softly.

"Exactly," Wolf said flatly. "At any other time I wouldn't give one goddamn what your father, or anyone else for that matter, thought about me. But right now I can't afford that unconcern. So don't argue, babe. I'm going to go make some coffee. By the time it's ready I want to see you in the galley fully"—his eyes shifted to her discarded bikini and beach coat and his tone went dry— "dressed."

They stepped off the boat into a pearl-white cloud. Halfway along the narrow pier Micki paused to look back at the apparitionlike outline of the craft, bobbing gently in the ruffling bay waters. When she turned back to Wolf, her face was wistful, her eyes sad. One strong arm encircled her waist, drew her close. Bending over her, he murmured, "We'll come back, honey."

Micki's eyes lit up. "When? Can we come back tonight?" The light dimmed as he slowly shook his head. Meekly, she walked beside him to the car park.

"Although I'm crazy about the way you look in a bikini, I want you to get all dressed up to go out for dinner tonight."

"Can't we have dinner on the boat?" The light was back and for a moment he didn't answer, seemingly bemused by the sparkling blue of her eyes.

"You'd rather have dinner on the boat than go out somewhere?" Wolf laughed.

"Yes," Micki answered gently. "Can we? Please?"

"You're absolutely something else, youngster." Wolf's tone shivered over her skin like a caress. He stopped walking and turned to her, his arm tautening as he crushed her to him. In complete opposition to his crushing hold, his kiss was a tender blessing that robbed her lungs of air, her legs of strength.

"All right, we'll have dinner on the boat." He started moving again, his arm possessive around her waist. "But I still want you to get dressed up. I'll come for you about eight. I have an appointment in Cape May this afternoon." He stopped beside a late-model Ford, unlocked the door, and held it open for her. Seated in the car, Micki watched him, loving the long, lean look of him, as he strode around the front of the car and slid into the seat beside her. Frowning, he turned to her. "If I can shorten the meeting, which I doubt, I'll call you. But I can't make any promises."

His tone held such finality Micki didn't have the courage to argue.

"All right, Wolf, you're the boss."

Her tone of meek acceptance amused him and a devilish grin flashed, revealing strong white teeth. "And don't you forget it," he drawled softly.

When he pulled up in front of her home, Wolf reached across her body to open her door, gave her a quick, hard kiss, and growled, "Get out of here, babe. I've got to get home and grab some rest or I'll be useless at the meeting this afternoon." The soulful eyes Micki lifted to his turned the growl into a groan. "Oh, God, baby, will you get out of the car?" His hands came up to cradle her face, his mouth was a hungrily searing brand. Then he moved back behind the wheel with an ordered, "Go."

Micki went, on the run, not stopping until she was inside her own bedroom. After stripping off the very wilted beachwear, she dove, stark naked, between the sheets. Laughing and crying at the same time, she hugged herself fiercely. Oh, Lord, she was so crazily, wildly in love with that man, it was almost scary.

She woke late in the afternoon, automatically reaching for the solid bulk of Wolf's body. When her hand found nothing but emptiness, she opened her eyes and sighed on finding herself in her own bed. Stifling a yawn, she stretched contentedly. The sensuous movement of her body between the smooth sheets evoked the sensuous thoughts of Wolf's expertly arousing hands and she gasped softly at the sudden, sharp ache that invaded the lower part of her body, the small hard points that thrust against the sheet covering her breasts. God, she was well and truly caught, she thought fearfully, if the mere thought of him could have this kind of effect.

Rolling her head on the pillow, she stared at the fake-gem-encrusted tiny alarm clock on her small nightstand. Two fifty-eight. Micki groaned aloud. Five hours until she'd see him. Kicking off the sheet, she jumped out of bed. She had to do something to fill those hours. Pulling on a light cotton duster, she left the room and went to the kitchen.

Forty-five minutes later, Micki stood at the sink, a small smile curving her lips, washing the dishes. She hadn't realized she was so hungry! It had required a large glass of orange juice, two poached eggs, three slices of toast, and three cups of coffee to appease her suddenly ravenous appetite.

Leaving the kitchen spotless, she went back to her room, made her bed, then headed for the bathroom for a shampoo and a shower. Humming softly as she stood under the warm shower spray, Micki didn't hear her father and Regina enter the house. She was standing before the medicine cabinet mirror, blow drying her hair, when her father tapped on the door and called, "Hi, honey, will you be very long? I feel the need of a shower."

75

Shutting the dryer off, Micki disconnected the plug and opened the door. "Hi, Dad," she said as she leaned toward him and kissed his whisker-rough cheek. "Welcome home, have a good trip?"

"Gruesome," Bruce grimaced. "You know what New York is like in August. Why the hell these realtors had to have their conference there is beyond me." He sighed wearily. "I was tied up in meetings most of the time, which didn't do a thing for Regina's patience. She should have listened to me and stayed at home."

Fleetingly, and for the first time since her father's marriage, Micki thanked the powers-that-be for Regina's stubbornness. "Well, you're home now and the bathroom's all yours. You can have your shower. And, Dad"—one slim hand caressed his cheek—"have a shave too."

"Brat." A larger hand made contact with her bottom.

Smiling happily, Micki went to her room. She was plugging the blow dryer into the wall socket by her dressing table when the phone rang. Wolf! The dryer dropped onto the table's mirror-bright surface with a clatter as Micki ran across the room. Flinging the door wide, she dashed along the hall and started down the stairs.

"Hello."

Micki was halfway down the stairs when she heard Regina answer the phone. She took one more step down then froze, her hand gripping the railing at Regina's velvety, incredibly sexy-sounding words.

"Wolf, darling, couldn't you wait? We haven't been in the house a half hour. I know how impatient you are and I was about to call you."

Eyes widening in disbelief, Micki waited breathlessly through the small silence while Regina listened to whatever Wolf was saying. When she spoke again, her words sent a shaft of pure hatred through Micki.

"The trip was exactly as you warned me it would be— dreadful. I could have kicked myself for not staying here to go with you as you wanted me to." There was another short pause, then, "Bruce? No, he's having a shower, how could he know? I told you we just got in. Yes, of course, darling, I want that as badly as you do."

Feeling she couldn't bear to hear any more, Micki, moving like a zombie, started back up the stairs. The sound of her name stopped her.

"Micki? No, she's not here. But then, she rarely ever is." Regina paused to listen again, then replied with a sigh, "I don't know, possibly with Tony Menella, she's been seeing a lot of him lately. She does not confide in me, but I'm sure she doesn't know."

Ordering her numbed body to move, Micki retraced her steps to her bedroom. Standing in the middle of the room, she stared sightlessly at the wall. Wolf and Regina? The words became a tortured scream in her mind.

Wolf and Regina? Oh, dear God, could Regina be one of the women who had cried on receiving a gift, usually expensive, from Wolf? Shaking all over, Micki blinked her eyes and when she did, her gaze touched the bed. Hot color flared into her cheeks on the thought that Wolf had robbed her father like an outlaw. First his wife, now his daughter.

Choking back the bitter gall that rose in her throat, Micki silently berated herself. *You fool, you young, stupid, virginal fool. Correction,* she thought, fighting against a growing hysteria, *ex-virginal fool.*

"Micki?"

The sound of Regina's soft voice, followed by a gentle tap on her door, turned the budding hysteria into cold fury. Before she could answer, the door was opened and Regina entered the room, closing the door behind her.

"I thought you were out. Have you been in your room all this—"

"What do you want?" The voice that slashed across Regina's words held cold contempt and a new maturity.

"Micki." Regina hesitated, then asked bluntly, "Were

77

you out with Wolf Renninger while your father and I were away?"

"That's none of your business." Striding across the room, Micki brushed by Regina on her way to the door. At the contact, her duster parted at her throat, revealing the abrasions David's plundering mouth had left on her skin.

"Did Wolf do that?" Regina gasped, pointing at the dull red mark.

"That's also none of your business," Micki snapped, one hand covering the spot. "I want you to leave my room." Her other hand grasped the doorknob to yank the door open but released it again at Regina's sharp words.

"You are a fool."

Spinning to face her, Micki looked her straight in the eye and spat, "Aren't we all?"

"Micki, you don't know this man." Regina's tone held an oddly pleading note. "Believe me, he lives up to his name. The women buzz around him like fleas at a honey pot. I must make this my business if you're to be kept from being hurt."

"I can take care of myself." Micki actually had to fight the urge to laugh in Regina's face. Hurt? Regina didn't know the meaning of the word.

"With a man like Wolf?" Regina asked, then answered her own question. "I hardly think so. He told me he was picking you up at eight." At Micki's nod a strange, almost crafty look entered her eyes. Very softly she said, "Don't be surprised if he's—well—somewhat tired. Or were you aware of the fact that he's spent the afternoon with a woman in Cape May? He was calling from her home actually."

Micki didn't want to believe her, but how could Regina know he was in Cape May unless he'd told her? Sickness churning in her stomach, Micki fought to maintain a cool facade. Wanting to get Regina out of the room before she humiliated herself by throwing up in front of her, Micki waved her hand airily, forced herself to laugh lightly.

"I had no intention of going out with him," she lied. "I told him I would to get rid of him." Drawing a deep breath, she rushed on. "Do me a favor, Regina. When Wolf comes, tell him I'm out," she paused, then added, "with Tony."

CHAPTER 5

A chill rippled through Micki's body, partly from the dampness, partly from her thoughts. Tugging the edges of the sweater together, she stood up and went into the house. After locking the doors and hanging the sweater in the closet, she went up the stairs slowly, her face blank of expression, her eyes dull.

Six years! For six long years she'd suppressed all thoughts of him. And now, after being home only one day, he filled her mind to the exclusion of everything else. Why? Why had he been on the street at the exact time she stopped for that car? If she hadn't seen him, spoken to him. But she had seen him, had spoken to him. More stupid still, she had snapped at his tauntingly tossed bait.

Closing her bedroom door quietly, she walked across the darkened room, sank wearily into the fanned-back peacock chair, clasped her hands tightly in her lap. She was trembling all over and she felt sick to her stomach, as sick as she'd felt that night.

She had not gone with him that night, had not seen him. But she had heard him. From her bedroom doorway, she'd heard her father, innocently, for he really thought what he said was the truth. *Tell Wolf that she'd gone out with Tony Menella.* And she'd heard Wolf reply, "But we had a date for dinner," his voice rough with anger and confusion.

A shudder shook Micki's slender body. Closing her eyes, she rested her head back against the smooth wicker. He had called every day during that following week, and each time either Regina or her father told him the same thing. She was with Tony. She hadn't been, of course. She'd been hiding in her bedroom like a fugitive. And like a fugitive on the run, she stole away the next week without seeing him or talking to him again. Her father never knew the real reason she insisted on going back to school early.

But running away had not ended it. Oh, he had not tried to see her at school or contact her in any way, but he was with her in more ways than one. Although remembering the hurt caused actual pain, she had been unable to stop thinking about him. The feel of him, the scent of him, the taste of him, was in her blood and no amount of self-determination had succeeded in repelling him. And then, four weeks after she'd returned to school, she knew the life of him was inside her too.

Strangely, the realization that his child was growing inside her body banished the pain, replaced the hurt with deep contentment. She'd decided that even if she could not have the man, she could, and would, cherish his seed. There would be problems, not the least of which was her father, but thoughts of the baby had eased the ache in her heart and she grew daily more determined to have it.

Her euphoria had lasted two weeks. A euphoria only slightly dampened by her sudden aversion to eggs in the morning. Then horrible cramping pain in the middle of one night and a sticky, wet, red-stained sheet had burst her bubble of happiness. When she wakened in a hospital near the campus, one look at the faces of the doctor and nurse who were beside her bed told the story. She was one again, her body had repelled Wolf's issue. It was while she lay in that sterile room alone, once again hurting unbearably, that her mind repelled Wolf's image.

No one except the hospital personnel knew of the abortion and three weeks after her twentieth birthday she left school. Luckily she had found a job and a room within a week of her arrival in Wilmington. She had not gone back until her father's illness two years ago. At that time she had not seen Wolf, nor had his name been mentioned. She had assumed he was no longer there, had moved on to greener pastures.

Over the years she had dated at least a dozen different men. And, in fact, was seeing one man exclusively before she came home. His name was Darrel and he'd asked her to marry him. She had been completely honest with him, without mentioning a name or circumstances. He knew he would not be the first, yet he'd asked her to marry him. Darrel was handsome, and Darrel was rich, and Darrel was successful. The perfect answer to any young woman's romantic dreams. But Micki was not any young woman. She had left him in Wilmington, two nights before, with her promise to think about his proposal.

Micki moved her head restlessly back and forth against the wicker, not even attempting to wipe away the tears that ran freely down her face. She knew what her answer to Darrel would be. She liked him, she respected him, but she did not love him. She loved Wolf. It was crazy. It was stupid. It was also an irrevocable fact. Nothing that had happened over the last six years had changed that. Within two nights and one day he had wrapped himself immovably around her heart. She had suspected even then that she would always love him. Now there was no doubt in her mind at all, and she could not go to Darrel loving Wolf.

Sighing softly, Micki stood up and began to undress. She would have to contact Darrel soon, give him her answer, and that answer would have to be no.

In sudden anger Micki tossed her clothes into the hamper, tugged a silky nightie over her head, and flung herself across her bed. Burying her face in her pillow, she wept quietly, damning the night she'd laid eyes on Wolf Renninger, damning the love for him that consumed her, and damning her own stupidity in accepting his challenge. She had been all right as long as she could not see him, be near him. But she knew that if she went with him Friday night it would just be a matter of time before she found herself in his arms, and in his bed, again. The urge to surrender that had swept through her that fateful afternoon had been all the proof she needed. She loved him and in loving him she wanted him desperately.

Rolling onto her back, Micki brushed impatiently at the tears on her cheeks. For six years she had repressed all her normal physical wants and needs. She had been called frigid. Some had even suggested therapy was called for. Micki had laughed at some and ignored them all. She knew exactly how normal her response could be. She had felt the hunger fire her blood. That hunger was for one man only. She had found the kisses, the light caresses, of several men pleasing. But only one man's mouth and hands could set her whole being alight. And now that one man, that Wolf, was stalking her again.

"No!"

The firm exclamation sounded loud in the dark room. Sitting up in the middle of the bed, Micki clenched her hands into fists. She could not go through that pain again. She would not expose herself to it. This time when Wolf came to pick her up she really would not be home. The decision made, Micki lay down again and went to sleep.

On Thursday Micki called the shop in Atlantic City to ask if it would be convenient for her to stop in sometime Friday afternoon. The enthusiastic reception her request was met with left her with a feeling of deep satisfaction.

Friday afternoon she bathed and dressed with extra care, then went looking for Regina to tell her she would not be home for dinner.

"If Cindy or anyone calls," she tossed casually over her shoulder, as she headed for the door, "tell them I expect to be late getting home and I'll return their call tomorrow."

Not wanting to field any questions Regina might throw, she hurried out the door and into her car. During the drive up the coast she determinedly pushed all thoughts of Wolf and his possible reaction to her action out of her mind.

It was a beautiful, hot day, the sun a bold yellow disc in a cloudless, blatantly blue sky. A day, Micki thought reminiscently, for healthy young things to laugh and romp on the scorching hot sand.

After parking the car near the hotel in which the shop was located, Micki walked along slowly, craning her neck like a tourist at the many changes that had taken place in the years since she'd last been in the city. So many of the old familiar buildings along the long boardwalk were gone, replaced by the large, elaborate hotels. The air literally reverberated with the sounds of construction.

Inside the hotel the air hummed a different tune. The place was crowded with people, all, it seemed, with one objective in mind—to get into the casino as quickly as possible.

Weaving in and out of the throng, Micki made her way to the reception desk. The cool, unruffled young man behind the desk gave her directions to the boutique politely, while running a practiced eye over her face and figure. When she thanked him, equally politely, he gave her an engaging grin and asked if she was free that evening.

"No, sorry," Micki grinned back. "I have an appointment."

"Why is it always some other guy that has all the luck?" He smiled sadly, then turned to the very impatient lady standing next to Micki.

The short exchange amused her, and with a jaunty step Micki walked through the lobby to the escalator the young man had indicated. As the steps moved up, her eyes roamed over the interior of the casino. The room was huge yet, incredibly, every square inch appeared to be occupied by humanity.

At the top of the escalator Micki paused to get her bearings. Directly across from her was the small cocktail lounge the desk clerk had mentioned, so the boutique should be a little farther down this wide expanse of hall. She found the shop exactly where he'd said she would.

With a knowledgeable eye Micki studied the displays inside the small windows on either side of the entrance to the shop. The one window proclaimed sun and fun with slightly reduced summer togs. The other window was a forecast of coming fall with soft plaid skirts and cashmere blazers. Very nice, Micki mused, very, very nice.

The manager of the shop turned out to be the woman Micki had spoken to the day before, and she was turned out very well indeed. A few years older than Micki, the woman, though not really beautiful, gave a good impression of being so. Her hair was a natural flaming red. Her skin a sun-kissed ivory. She was taller than Micki and her very slender body was beautifully clothed in an exquisite raw silk sheath that had Micki murmuring a silent prayer of thanks for the urge that had made her dress with such care.

While Micki had been studying the woman, the redhead had been making her own evaluation and they seemed to reach the same conclusions at exactly the same time. For just as Micki was giving thanks, the redhead smiled and extended a slim, long-nailed hand.

"Jennell Clark," she offered in a soft drawl. "And you must be Micki Durrant."

"I am." The hand Micki stretched out was just as slim, the rounded nails every bit as long. "How do you do?"

"Very well, actually." Jennell's soft laugh was a delight to the ears. "Glad to have you with us." Her eyes ran over Micki again. "If you buy for the shop as well as you buy for yourself I have a feeling I'll be doing even better."

"Thank you," Micki laughed with her. "I'll do my best." Then unable to exactly place the soft drawl in Jennell's tone, she asked, "Are you from the South?"

"Yes," Jennell again favored her with a laugh. "But not too far south, Richmond, Virginia. Where are you from?"

"Only a little south of here," Micki grinned. "Ocean City, New Jersey."

Jennell introduced her to the shop's other two employees, a petite, pretty young woman named Lucy and a strikingly beautiful black woman named Georgine. The three of them filled Micki in on the running of the store in no time.

The rest of the afternoon flew by so quickly, Micki was surprised when Jennell said it was time to close the shop. She was on the point of saying good-bye when Jennell asked, "Do you have plans for dinner? I mean do you have a date or are you expected home or anything?"

Micki thought fleetingly of Wolf, then shook her head. "No, no date or plans or anyone expecting me."

"Then come have dinner with us," Jennell coaxed. "Lucy's guy is out of town. Georgine's between guys and I"—an impish smile curved her red lips—"I'm punishing my man at the moment."

"Punishing?" Micki laughed.

"Well, just a little," the redhead drawled. "He was getting much too possessive and I'm letting him know I won't be owned. Will you come?"

As both Lucy and Georgine added their pleas to Jennell's, Micki agreed and the four of them left the shop, all talking at the same time.

They had dinner in a small restaurant where the decor was unexceptional and the food out of this world. While they ate, Micki learned that all three women came from other shops in the chain. Jennell from one in Washington, D.C., Lucy from one in Baltimore, and Georgine from one in New York City.

"I've been here for over a year," Jennell volunteered.

"Georgine came a few months after I did and Lucy joined us three months ago. Your predecessor came from Philadelphia at the same time as I did." She fluttered her lashes dramatically, drawled oversweetly. "She's been transferred to Miami." Jennell smiled derisively. "She went too far with the boss."

"You didn't like her?" Micki's question was greeted by rolled eyes and snorts of laughter.

"Honey," Jennell drawled softly, "I could sooner like a rattlesnake."

"She really wasn't very pleasant to work with." This from the small, somewhat shy, Lucy.

"She was a first-rate bitch," Georgine, every inch as worldly as she was beautiful, stated flatly.

"Yes," Jennell concurred. "Our buyer decided to play footsie with the owner. He shipped her out when she became demanding. I mean"—the drawl was laid on thick —"one just does not fool around with that man. Let alone demand marriage."

Micki frowned. When Jennell had said the boss, Micki assumed she'd been referring to their regional manager, Hank Carlton. But she'd just now said the owner and Micki had never met the owner, had not, in fact, ever heard his name mentioned. She was about to ask Jennell who the owner was when Lucy said something about finding a new man for Georgine and the thought went out of her head.

Their suggestions to Georgine ran from the ridiculous from Lucy.

"You could take an ad in the personal column like: Wanted: good-looking man between the ages of twenty-five and forty, must be fantastic dancer." To Micki she confided, "Georgine would rather dance than eat."

To the outrageous from Jennell.

"You could always station yourself on the boardwalk and smile sweetly at all the better-looking men. Of course," she drawled heavily, "you'd have no idea which ones could dance. But then, look at all the fun you could have teaching them."

"The way my luck's been running," Georgine grinned, "if I took a newspaper ad I'd only get replies from the uglies and the crazies." The grin grew wider and her eyes sparkled impishly. "And if I stationed myself on the boardwalk, I'd probably wind up with my fanny in the canny."

A smile teased Micki's lips as she drove home that evening. She had enjoyed the dinner and the company very much. They had lingered, laughing, over their coffee until the arched look of the proprietor sent them, still laughing, out of the restaurant.

The three women had insisted on escorting Micki to her car, where they stood talking for an additional twenty minutes. By the time Micki drove her car off the parking lot she felt as if she'd known them all her life.

She'd had a good time, she told herself as she drove the car up the driveway of her father's house, a very good time. She had hardly thought about Wolf all evening, she realized as her fingers turned the key, shutting off the engine. Well, she mentally qualified, she hadn't thought about him too often, she admitted as she pulled on the hand brake. So, okay, he'd been in her thoughts constantly, she finally confessed disgustedly as she swung out of the car and headed for the kitchen door. But she had enjoyed her day and her evening.

"That you, princess?" her father called as she closed the door.

"No," Micki called back. "I'm a burglar, I've come for the silver."

"Good luck," he laughed. "We are strictly a stainless-steel family."

"Well, in that case, I guess I'll go back to being the princess." Micki smiled, entering the living room. "At least I'll have a title, even if there is no silver to inherit."

"Hi, honey." Although her father smiled, one brow

went up in question. "Did you forget you had a date this evening?"

"A date?"

Even with the sudden acceleration of her pulse, Micki had somehow managed to keep her tone innocent.

"With Wolf Renninger," Bruce prompted gently, then he winced. "I wouldn't say he was exactly happy when I told him you weren't here." He paused, his eyes narrowing in thought. "I had the oddest feeling that I'd gone through the same thing before." A frown leveled his brows. "What are you up to, young lady?"

"I—I'm not up to anything," Micki murmured nervously. She hated deceiving her father, yet she couldn't bring herself to confide in him. "I got caught up in the business of the shop and when the shop manager asked me to join her and the two women who work in the store, I accepted. I simply forgot I'd made the date with Wolf."

Micki wet her dry lips, trying not to see the sharp-eyed glance Regina gave her. Her father's memory might be a little cloudy, but Regina's certainly wasn't.

"Wolf has called twice in the last hour," Regina supplied quietly. "He seemed to be becoming angrier every time I had to tell him you hadn't come home yet."

"I think if the phone rings you had better answer it," Bruce advised. "You forgot the date and you can apologize your way out of it."

The words were no sooner out of his mouth when the doorbell rang. Micki's body jerked as though someone had touched a live wire to her.

"Go to it, girl." Her father flipped his hand in the direction of the front door. "I think there's little doubt who that is." He stood up, his hand reaching for Regina's. "We'll be discreet and give you some privacy."

The bell sounded again and Micki started for the door, her steps betraying her trepidation. Her father's soft laugh sounded from the stairs.

"You're not going to the gallows, honey," he chided.

"Just give him your sweetest smile and he'll forget why he's angry."

I'll bet, Micki thought grimly, her hand shaking as she reached for the doorknob. She swung the door open bravely, then bit her lip fearfully. Wolf, looking hard-jawed and cold-eyed and madder than hell, stood, hands thrust into his pants pockets, staring balefully at her. Stepping out onto the porch, Micki closed the door softly behind her, her mind searching for something to say. Wolf brought her search to an end.

"I don't believe it." His cool tone, so opposed to the hot anger in his eyes, sent a tremor bouncing down her spine. "I really don't believe it."

"What?" Micki was almost afraid to ask.

"You did it again." A touch of wonder colored the cool tone. "Do you get your kinky little kicks out of standing up many of your dates, or do I alone hold that honor?"

"Wolf." Micki had to fight to keep her voice even. "I'm sorry."

"Yeah." Wolf smiled crookedly. "I'll bet you are."

"All right, I'm not," Micki snapped. "If you'll recall, I didn't want to go out with you in the first place."

Angry herself now, she moved away from him, down the porch steps, and along the front walk to the pavement without the slightest idea of where she was going.

"But you did agree to have dinner with me." His long strides brought him alongside her before she'd taken six steps on the pavement. "Didn't you?"

"Yes," she admitted, turning south when she reached the corner.

Matching his stride to hers, Wolf walked beside her silently. *At least he didn't ask me where I'm going,* she thought wryly.

"Where the hell are you going?"

His impatient words followed on the heels of her thought and Micki couldn't repress the smile that tugged at her lips.

"I said something funny?" His tone was not amused.

"No," Micki sighed. "It's just that I don't know where I'm going."

"That's pretty damned obvious," Wolf drawled sardonically, leaving little doubt in her mind he meant the direction of her life, not her impromptu walk.

"I just felt like walking," Micki shrugged in annoyance.

"I see," Wolf drawled softly.

"You didn't have to come along," she snapped irritably.

"True," he agreed, with a maddening calmness.

Their quick stride ate up the blocks during their exchange and when they had to stop at a corner to wait for traffic Micki realized with surprise that they were near the city's shopping district. Grasping her arm, Wolf began walking east.

"Where the hell are *you* going?" Micki flung his words back at him.

"To the boardwalk," he answered imperturbably.

"Whatever for?" she demanded.

"Why does anyone stroll the boards?" She shrugged, elegantly. "To gaze at the ocean, to feel the sea breeze against the skin, to wander in and out of the shops." He slanted a barbed look at her. "To have something to eat. At least those who have been stood up and didn't eat any dinner do."

His hand placed firmly at the back of her waist propelled her up the ramp and onto the boardwalk still crowded with people at ten o'clock at night.

"Come on, babe, I'll buy you a slice of pizza at Mack and Manco's." His eyes raked her face. "Not exactly what I'd planned but," he shrugged, "I like the pie and it will fill up the hole in my stomach."

Unsure if he was telling the truth or not about not having eaten, Micki allowed him to lead her to the pizza stand. The stand's outside counter was three deep with people and, grasping her hand, Wolf edged around the bodies and drew her inside the shop. While they waited for

92

two seats to become vacant Micki watched, as fascinated as she'd been as a young girl, the swift, dexterous movements of the young men behind the counter as they assembled the pizzas and slid them into and out of the ovens. And the aroma! Even though she'd had dinner, Micki ran her tongue over her lips in anticipation.

Once seated, they were served quickly and Micki was soon convinced Wolf had not been lying about not eating. He consumed four slices of pizza to her one and as soon as they were out of the shop said, "Let's walk awhile, then we'll hunt up some dessert."

"On top of all that pizza!" Micki exclaimed.

"Look at me, Micki," Wolf urged chidingly. "Tom Thumb I'm not. I've got a big body and it's got to be filled occasionally. It is now"—he glanced at his watch—"ten thirty-five. That pizza was the first solid food I've had since somewhere around noon." His tone went bland. "Yes, I am going to sink some dessert on top of all that pizza."

"Solid food?" Micki jabbed at him, as if that's all she'd heard of his statement.

"Did I ask you if you'd been drinking?" Wolf jabbed back harder.

Fuming, Micki walked beside him, uncomfortably aware he was laughing, if silently, at her. After several quiet minutes, curiosity and a concern she didn't want to feel got the better of her.

"Were you drinking, Wolf," she asked softly, "on an empty stomach?"

"I had a couple of beers in a bar over at the Point," Wolf replied equally softly. "To pass the time while I waited for my date to put in an appearance."

Feeling her face flush, Micki looked away from him and glanced into the faces of the people moving around them. Up until that point her mind had been so full of Wolf she'd been only surfacely aware of the hum of voices, the sound of laughter around her. Tugging her hand free of his grasp, she walked to the rail and stared out at the dark, white-capped water.

"Why didn't you keep our date?"

Wolf bent his long frame beside her, rested his forearms on the top rail, propped one foot on the bottom rail. He had removed his suit jacket and it dangled in the air over the beach, held in the fingers of one hand.

Micki's eyes clung to the gentle movement of the jacket, held so carelessly in those strong fingers. Not unlike the way he handles women, Micki thought suddenly, a shiver feathering her back. The idea of being held in those strong hands, even carelessly, made her feel sick with longing.

"I asked you a question." Wolf's edged tone jolted her back to reality.

"I went up to Atlantic City this afternoon to introduce myself to the manager of the shop I've been transferred to," Micki explained nervously. "We got talking shop talk and the time slipped away. By the time the shop closed, I'd forgotten about our date and when she asked me if I'd like to have dinner with her and the other two women who work there, I said yes."

"You are a very bad liar, babe," Wolf grated, not looking at her. "Now would you like to tell me the real reason?"

"Honestly, Wolf, you are—" Micki began angrily.

"Honestly?" He cut her off. "I don't think so, sweetie. I honestly think you've been lying through your teeth. Why the hell won't you level with me? Did you go out with another guy?" He was on the attack now and Micki felt cornered by his stinging tone. "Someone you ran into after you agreed to go with me? If so, why the hell didn't you call me and break the date?"

Micki turned to face him, her eyes bright with anger. "Would you have let me break the date?"

Wolf's silvery eyes turned the color of cold steel as he stared into hers. "Probably not," he finally snapped, after a few long, nerve-racking seconds.

"That's what I thought." Micki wrenched her eyes from his, stared sightlessly out over the ocean. "So I simply decided not to keep it."

"*Were* you with another man?" Wolf's tone held a strange, breathless quality Micki couldn't define. For a brief moment she considered telling him she had been out with another man, then she sighed and murmured, "No."

She heard her sigh echo beside her before his voice, close to her ear, sent tiny little chills skimming over her body.

"What are you afraid of, honey?"

"Wh-what do you mean?" she stammered. "Afraid of?"

"Are you afraid, if you go with me, I'll get you alone and want to touch you?" His breath fluttered the hair near her ear; his words started a fluttering in her mid-section. "Afraid I'll want to hold you in my arms and kiss you?" His voice went low. "Afraid I'll want to make love to you?"

Micki's hands gripped the rail. She couldn't answer, she couldn't move. In fact, she could hardly breathe.

"You'd be right." Wolf's voice was very low now, low and urgent. "I do want to do all those things."

Motionless, unseeing, Micki stood as if fused to the boards beneath her feet, the need to have him do all those things draining all the color from her face. Oh, God, how she ached to be in his arms, and yes, in his bed. Her own thoughts frightened her into action. Pushing herself away from the rail, she dashed across the boardwalk, dodging in and out, around the startled faces of people. Wolf caught up to her as she came off the ramp.

"Running away again?" His tone was now sharp with exasperation.

"I simply want to go home." Micki shrugged his hand from her arm. He slid it around her waist, held on tightly.

"What are you running from, do you know?" Wolf asked tiredly. "Did you know six years ago?"

"Shut up," Micki cried, then lowered her voice at the

95

sharp glance a man passing them threw at her. "I don't want to talk about six years ago. I don't even want to think about it."

"Why?" Wolf rapped softly. "Why don't you want to talk about it?" Micki was almost running in her urgent need to get home. Wolf tightened his hand at her waist even more, forcing her to slow down. "Why don't you want to think about it?"

"I told you why in your apartment the other day." Micki lied frantically. "It's dead and there's nothing as dead as a dead love affair."

Wolf came to an abrupt halt and grasped her shoulder to turn her toward him.

"So that's what it was," he rasped, "a love affair." His soft laughter had the sound of rusty metal being scraped. Micki felt fear clog her throat. "I'll give you a hundred dollars against a Mexican peso I can breathe life into it again." His fingers dug into her soft flesh to draw her closer. "What kind of gambler are you?"

His mouth touched hers and at that moment a car full of teenage boys drove by. Laughing and hooting, the boys called encouraging suggestions to Wolf and though he released her, he threw them a wicked grin.

Micki used his momentary inattention to move away from him. Wolf was right behind her.

"For God's sake, kid, slow down." His big hand swallowed hers, held fast. "I wasn't going to hurt you."

The mere thought of you hurts me, Micki's mind cried silently. Shaking her head to dislodge the thought, she said bitingly, "I know that, but I hate being put into a position to receive that kind of taunting catcall." She tried to tug her hand free, shot him a sour look when his fingers tightened. "And I'm not a kid."

"Then stop acting like one," he bit back. "Those boys didn't mean any harm." Micki withdrew into a stony silence. Walking steadily, her eyes straight ahead, she sighed with relief when they turned the corner onto her street. She couldn't wait to get into the house for the simple reason she wanted to be with him so badly.

Wolf stopped, pulling her up short, several yards from the house. With a casual wave of his hand he indicated a flame-red Ferrari parked at the curb.

"Come have a drink with me," he coaxed. "I haven't had my dessert yet."

"I don't want a drink," Micki said flatly, swinging away from him again. "I'm not thirsty, I'm tired."

Hurrying up the front walk, she prayed her father had not come back downstairs and locked the door. She had to get away from Wolf. She knew it. She had been tempted to go with him, had wanted to go with him. And she knew that given even the few minutes it would take her father to come down and open the door for her, Wolf would be able to persuade her into going with him.

"Why are you so tired?" Wolf's hand on her arm made her pause in front of the door. "It's only eleven fifteen."

"I'm not physically tired, Wolf." Micki had not turned her head, and her words seemed to bounce off the door, back into her face.

Wolf's hand left her arm to circle her waist and she felt her throat go dry when he stepped closer to her. With trembling fingers she clutched the doorknob as if grasping for a lifeline.

"Micki, baby." Wolf's soft voice, only inches from her ear, was a nerve-shattering temptation. "If you're not really tired, come with me."

"But I am really tired," Micki insisted in a dry, crackling voice. Her hand turned the knob and pushed, relief washing over her when the door gave under pressure. "I'm tired of this conversation. I'm tired of defending myself." Turning her head, she forced herself to meet his gaze levelly. "I'm tired of your company, Wolf."

Wolf stepped back as if she'd actually struck him. His face drained of all expression and quite a bit of color. His lips thinned. His eyes narrowed.

"Okay, baby." His lips barely seemed to move around the muttered words. "I guess you can't make it any clearer than that." He turned away, started down the porch steps, then turned back swiftly. "But if you change your mind, you'll have to call me. I won't be calling you." His lips twisted, almost as if he were in pain. His voice rasped against her ears. "I've had about all I can take of your brand of rejection."

Micki gasped audibly. Stung by what she considered was the unfairness of his taunting words, she retaliated without thinking.

"Don't hold your breath."

"Very classy," Wolf drawled stingingly. "And you say you're not a kid. You've said very little to prove otherwise tonight."

His silvery eyes, sharp with scorn, moved dismissively over her body, then, with a shrug, he turned away again. Hurt unbearably by his sarcastic words and the scorn in his eyes, Micki was goaded into trying to hurt back.

"If you hurry, Wolf," she called softly, as he started down the walk, "you can drink a gallon of dessert before the bar closes."

"Grow up, kid," Wolf tossed back disparagingly, not even bothering to look back.

CHAPTER 6

Wolf's parting shot nagged at Micki's mind for most of the following week. She just could not decide what exactly he'd meant by it. Not "Grow up, kid." She understood that well enough. But the prior one, the one about his having had enough of her brand of rejection, that bothered her. She was sure the gibe could not be taken at face value, for that would indicate his being hurt, and that concept she could not accept.

During that week, the last of her vacation, Micki kept very busy and away from Regina's questioning eyes. She spent hours on the beach, soaking up sun, acquiring a deep tan that made her eyes look an even brighter blue. She saw, or spoke on the phone to every one of her friends still at home, including Tony, who called and asked her to have dinner with him on Saturday night. She accepted eagerly for two reasons. One, she would be truly delighted to see Tony again and two, she was ready to jump at any excuse to get out of the house.

Determined to keep her mind occupied every waking minute, she lived that week on the run. From house to beach, back to the house to shower, then out again to have lunch or shop with Cindy, or visit her old haunts. For several hours on Tuesday afternoon she lost herself in the nineteenth century by way of the Historical Museum. All other thoughts were sent packing as her imagination was caught, then consumed, by the lifelike reality of the priceless antique furniture and household articles used in the display areas set up as living room, dining room, bedroom, kitchen, and nursery.

A small smile tugged at her bemused expression as she imagined herself and her friends dressed in the apparel worn at the turn of the century, carefully preserved and kept in glass cases, in the Fashion Room.

As she moved slowly through the Sindia Room, she could almost feel the anxiety of the crew of the four-masted bark when it was driven onto the beach in a gale on December 15, 1901.

The contemplative state induced by her visit into yester-year stayed with her through the remainder of the day and evening and left her with the surety that an individual life was indeed too short to be wasted.

On Thursday evening she agreed to go with her father and Regina to the Music Pier for the concert given nightly by the Ocean City Pops. Her father and Regina went inside the large building on the pier while Micki sat on a bench outside as she had years before, watching the ocean's constant movement while she listened to the music.

The strains of Rodgers and Hammerstein music, blending with the muted roar of the sea, evoked memories of her girlhood. In the years she'd been away, she hadn't consciously realized how much she'd missed it all. And now, the atmosphere, the ambience, seemed to seep through her skin into her heart. Irrevocably her wandering thoughts led to Wolf.

Moving restlessly on the slatted wood bench, she fought in vain against the image that would no longer be pushed away. Silvery eyes mocked her struggle. Sighing softly, Micki closed her eyes while the essence of him took control of her senses, her emotions. Where was he tonight? What was he doing? Most importantly, who was he doing it with? Her own thoughts bedeviled and hurt her, yet she could no longer keep them at bay. She was resentful, hurt, jealous of his activities, his companions, even though she knew she had no right to be. She loved him distractedly, passionately, and that love had the effect of slashing her to ribbons inside.

She needed him in every way, and the growing intensity of that need sparked near panic. With a sickening feeling of humiliation clogging her throat, Micki faced the realization that unless she found a way to dislodge his occupation of her mind she would be reduced to calling him, as he had suggested she should.

With determination spawned by desperation, she made plans for the rest of the summer, pushing aside the nagging reminder that the best laid plans . . . She had to overcome her emotional obsession with him. She had to—somehow. For one tiny moment she allowed herself the remembered breathlessness aroused by his arms, his mouth, then, with a quick, sad shake of her head she wished him to Siberia, or some other, much hotter, place.

The sound of the sea and the music lulling her into a somewhat dreamlike state of wishful thinking, Micki convinced herself of her eventual success. She would throw herself vigorously into her new job and fill her non-working hours by finding and settling into a new apartment. Even though she had made arrangements to have her things packed and trucked to her father's house when her lease ran out at the end of August, she could take a run up to Wilmington to oversee the removal. Born of desperation, ideas popped into her mind. There were any number of things she could do to stay busy and, she vowed fervently, she would do them, all of them, to escape the hold Wolf had on her.

Riding the crest of optimism as bravely as a surfer skimming a wave, Micki walked home from the concert with a jaunty stride, humming snatches of the music she'd heard.

"I get the distinct impression you enjoyed the concert," her father teased.

"Very much," Micki affirmed, flashing him a smile. "I always have. The tenor soloist was pretty good, at least what I could hear out at the rail sounded good."

"I liked the aria the soprano sang," Regina inserted quietly. "Even though I can't remember the name of it and your father knows absolutely nothing about opera. Do you know it, Micki?"

Know it? Micki hadn't even heard it. Shaking her head, she frowned.

"No, I'm sorry, Regina, I'm afraid I don't know any more about opera than Dad does."

"It doesn't matter really," Regina smiled. "It's just been tantalizing the edge of my memory, if you know what I mean?"

Did she ever, Micki groaned silently. When it came to a subject tantalizing the memory, she was an expert. Veering sharply from the thought, she launched into another song, singing where she knew the words, humming where she didn't.

"Do you have plans for the weekend, honey?" Bruce's soft voice cut into her slightly off-key version of "A Cock-eyed Optimist."

"Yes," Micki nodded. "I've been invited to Cindy and Benny's for dinner tomorrow and I have a date with Tony Saturday."

Micki didn't miss the sharp-eyed glance Regina shot her at the mention of Tony's name. In an effort to block any questions from her stepmother, she rushed on. "Why? Was there something you wanted me to do?"

"No, no," Bruce assured her. "We were invited to a cookout Saturday evening and you were included, if you were free."

"A cookout? Where?" Micki asked curiously.

"At Betty and Jim Grant's," Regina answered for her husband. "Betty wanted to meet you and thought this might be a good time and way."

"And I would like to finally meet her," Micki assured her. For Micki, Regina's friend Betty had been a warm voice on the phone. They had become friends while Micki was away. Although she had not intruded at the time of Bruce's illness, her voice had been a bracing encouragement at the other end of the line during those nerve-racking days. "Ask her if I may have a raincheck."

"Not necessary," Bruce put in smoothly. "I would like you to keep two weeks from Saturday open, honey. There's a celebration party being planned for that night and, as the Grants will be there, you will meet Betty then."

"A celebration party?" Micki's brows went up. "For what?"

"A big-time developer and several realtors, myself included, are on the verge of closing a very big deal. It's been in the works for some time, and we decided a celebration was in order. We'd like you with us for two reasons. First, simply to have you join us in celebrating the successful conclusion to some very long, hard negotiations. And secondly, because it will be the last evening we'll spend together for a while as"—he paused to glance at his wife—"Regina and I will be flying to the West Coast the following afternoon."

"You're actually going?" Micki cried happily. "Terrific. How long will you be gone? Where are you going? I mean, are you going to stay in Frisco the whole time or are you planning to take in other places—Vegas, Mexico?"

"I believe you are nearly as excited as we are," Bruce laughed when Micki finally ran down. They were almost home and as they turned onto the front walk he dropped an arm around her shoulders. "The minute we get into the house we'll show you our itinerary."

He removed his arm to unlock the door. "We plan to be gone the last two weeks of August." With a wide courtly sweep of his arm he ushered them inside. "So will you go to the party with us?"

"Yes, of course, if you want me to go," Micki answered quickly. "Now, lead me to your itinerary."

They sat around the kitchen table, tall, moisture-beaded glasses of iced tea in front of them, until after midnight, Regina and Bruce talking at the same time, cutting in on each other as they outlined their plans for Micki.

For Micki, Friday evening was an unqualified success. Cindy had gone all out in her preparations for dinner and the dining-room table gleamed with her best china and crystal (Micki's wedding gift to them). The menu complemented the entrée of fried chicken. The consommé was delicious, the small parslied potatoes cooked to just the right peak, and the tiny creamed peas and pearl onions tender. For dessert Cindy served a rich homemade cheesecake Micki was sure she could not possibly manage, but she did.

"Is this the same girl who could not boil an egg seven years ago?" Micki asked Benny with not altogether mock surprise.

"Can you believe it?" Benny laughed. "You should see the pile of cookbooks this woman has collected." His eyes caressed Cindy's face. "She has been a very busy lady since you left, Micki. She's learned to sew so well she now makes most of her own clothes and now she is knitting." His tone was so full of pride, his eyes so full of tenderness as he gazed at his wife, Micki felt the hot sting of tears behind her lids. "I swear," he murmured, "she began knitting tiny things the day after she conceived."

"You big oaf, will you stop?" Cindy's glowing face proclaimed her love as she chided Benny. "You're embarrassing me."

"Why?" Benny's hand caught and held Cindy's tightly. "Because I love you and I don't care who knows it?" He lifted her hand to his lips, bestowed a light kiss before adding, "Besides which, Micki's our friend, our best friend, why would you be embarrassed before her?"

"Oh, Benny."

Cindy's half sigh, half whisper brought a lump to Micki's throat and in an attempt to dislodge it she drawled dryly, "I can do a fantastic disappearing act if you two want to be alone."

"Would you?" Benny teased.

"Don't you dare," Cindy gasped.

The banter flew back and forth all evening. The closest they came to a serious subject was while they considered the best location for Micki to begin her apartment hunting.

Micki was in a mellow mood when she left and as she drove along the almost deserted streets a gentle smile curved her lips. Cindy and Benny were so perfectly suited and so obviously in love it was a joy just being in their company. Who would have believed it, back when Cindy was tossing insults at Benny every five minutes? Had, Micki wondered, Cindy been attracted to him even then? Very likely, Micki decided. The insults and taunts were probably the adolescent Cindy's way of venting that attraction. And Benny? Micki's smile grew tender remembering how good-naturedly he had taken Cindy's constant ribbing. What a delight they were to be with, Micki mused. If only Wolf were . . . Micki put a brake on her thoughts abruptly. Scathingly she told herself *if only* must surely be the most overworked words in the English language. You can *if only* from now until the first day of forever, she scolded herself mentally, and it will change nothing. So forget it. Forget him.

Her date with Tony the following evening was a mixture of fun and sadness. The fun began the minute she opened the door to him, for she was caught in his arms and twirled around in the air.

"Micki." Tony laughed down at her when she stood once more firmly on the floor. "You look as gorgeous as ever, only more so. God, what a sight you are for these weary old eyes."

"Weary old eyes, my Aunt Sara," Micki laughed back. "It's good to see you too, Tony. What are you up to these days?"

"Oh, about five-eleven," Tony drawled. "Maybe six feet."

"I'd have been disappointed if you hadn't said that."

Although Micki's tone was teasing, there was an underlying note of seriousness to it. It was silly, she knew, yet she would have been disappointed. His predictable rejoinder had reaffirmed their friendship, their closeness.

She had been around twelve the first time he'd quipped the reply to her. It had been summer then, too, and on that afternoon Micki had felt deserted and alone as all her girl friends were otherwise occupied. Without much hope of finding a companion, she had scuffed her way forlornly to the playground. She had found the fourteen-year-old Tony, looking every bit as dejected and forlorn, leaning against the playground fence. He had been watching, with lofty teenage amusement, the antics of a group of toddlers and had not seen Micki approach.

"None of the kids are around today," Micki had grumbled as she leaned against the fence beside him. "What are you up to, Tony?"

Maybe it was the sound of abject self-pity in her voice. Micki never knew, but when Tony turned to look at her, all signs of his own dejection had vanished. His expression was one of consideration and when he answered his tone was serious.

"Oh, about five-three, maybe four."

"Huh?"

She was wrapped up in her own misery, so his quip had gone completely over her head. She had gazed up at him blankly for several seconds before the dancing gleam in his sky-blue eyes and the betraying shake of his skinny shoulders turned the light on in her head. Her reaction was way out of proportion to the humor in his remark. The young, very naive Micki became convulsed with laughter.

"You goof!" she had gasped when her giggles had subsided somewhat. Balling her hand into a small, tight fist, she swung it at his arm. Tony caught her by the wrist before her fist made contact and shook it gently.

"Come on, you silly ass." Tony's grin had held amusement, and a dash of superiority. "Since we're both alone, we may as well be alone together."

They had kept each other company for the rest of the day and until nine thirty that night. After they had plumbed all the diversions offered by the playground, they moved onto the beach and from there to the bay to watch the fishing boats return. From the bay they went to Tony's home where Micki had promptly been invited to supper. After a quick phone call to her father obtaining permission for her to stay, Micki and Tony earned their supper by pulling weeds out of his mother's flower bed. And from the time they left the supper table until Tony's dad ran her home at nine thirty, they had engaged in a hotly contested game of Monopoly—which Tony won.

From that day until Micki left to go back to college six years ago, their greeting to each other had been the nonsensical, "What are you up to?" the only variance being the inches in Tony's reply.

Now, they stood, one twenty-five, the other twenty-seven, laughing into each other's face exactly as they had all those years ago.

"Tony, you are still a goof." Micki shook her head sharply, fighting the tears of affection that suddenly threatened. Sliding her arms around his waist, she gave him a quick, hard hug. "Do you think we'll ever grow up?"

"God, I hope not," Tony murmured fervently into her hair, returning her hug fiercely. When he released her, he glanced around curiously. "Where's your dad and Regina?"

"At a cookout." Micki's laughter, finally under control, threatened to break out again at the crafty expression that stole over Tony's face.

"We're all alone here?" he whispered slyly.

"Yes," Micki whispered back. "Why?"

"You want to stay here?" he leered exaggeratedly. "Fool around a little." His voice went very low. "We could play doctor."

"No!" Micki exploded into gales of laughter all over again. Grasping his arm, she urged him toward the front door. "Come on, you nut, you asked me out to dinner, so let's go dine. I hope you brought an enormous amount of money with you because I'm starving."

"How much do you consider enormous?" Tony eyed her warily.

"Oh, at least twenty-five or thirty dollars," Micki said airily.

Tony exhaled a long, exaggerated sigh of relief as he stepped out onto the front porch. "You lucked out," he replied jauntily. "I think I have around thirty-two."

"Are you serious?" Micki turned to look at him, all traces of merriment erased from her face.

"Of course not," he chided gently. "When were we ever serious?"

They drove to an Italian restaurant in Wildwood, where Micki declared the food almost as good as Tony's mother's. Tony did most of the talking while they ate, telling about his job in Trenton, why he had decided to make the move home, and all about his present job and apartment.

A soft light in her eyes, Micki watched him while he talked, noting the changes in his face. He was, she decided, one fine-looking young man. His swarthy skin tone and wavy dark hair were set off, given an appealing look by his light-blue eyes and perfect white teeth. A small pale scar, earned in a high school football game, which broke the line of his left eyebrow, added a rakish touch to his visage. Yes, indeed, a very fine-looking young man.

After dinner Tony took Micki to a bar that catered to the dance crowd. The minute the waitress had taken their order and turned away from their minuscule table, Tony stood up and tugged at her arm.

"Come on, Micki, let's show them how it's done."

Tony had always been a good dancer and Micki quickly discovered he'd improved with age. Lithe, agile, he moved around the floor, and her, in a sensuously serpentine way.

From that afternoon in the playground Micki had never felt awkward with Tony, and after only a momentary hesitation, she gave herself fully to the music and the beat.

"Yeah, do it, girl," Tony encouraged, undulating smoothly in front of her. "Crank it up."

By the time they left the bar some four hours later, Micki's head was slightly fuzzy from a combination of the loud music and the drinks she'd consumed. Her body was damp with perspiration and she felt as if her legs might fall off at any moment.

As they drove back to Ocean City, Micki leaned her head back against the seat with a contented sigh. The breeze rushing in through the car's windows cooled her overheated skin and Micki inhaled deeply, savoring the scent of the sea.

"Do you want to come to my place and see my etchings?" Tony's quiet voice nudged her out of a half doze.

"Do you have some?" Micki asked innocently with deliberately widened eyes.

"No," he admitted ruefully, then added brightly, "but I make pretty good coffee. Would that do instead?"

"That would do perfectly," Micki laughed, unsuccessfully trying to smother a yawn.

Tony's apartment was on the third floor of a large, old building, kept in excellent repair. Mumbling, "Why didn't you warn me about the stairs?" Micki groaned as they trudged upward. The apartment comprised the whole of the third floor and consisted of a fair-sized bedroom, a large kitchen-living room combination, and a small bathroom. The furniture was sparse, but what there was was comfortable and well chosen.

"Make yourself at home," Tony tossed casually, walking to the kitchen area. "Coffee will be ready in a few minutes, I have one of those almost instant things."

Micki sank onto the overstuffed sofa and sighed sleepily as the soft cushions seemed to envelop and cradle her tired body. Half asleep, the sound of Tony's quiet movement touched the fringes of her mind. There was the rattle of a tray being placed on the coffee table and a record dropping onto a turntable, then, as the cushion beside her depressed from Tony's weight, the voice of Bruce Springsteen came to her softly from the stereo.

"Are you asleep?" Tony's voice was low and soft and very, very close.

"Almost."

Lifting her heavy lids, Micki smiled into the light-blue eyes only inches away from her face. One arm resting on the back of the sofa, he leaned over her, his expression serious, somewhat sad.

"I'm going to kiss you, Micki," he murmured. The scent of alcohol came to her as his warm breath whispered over her face. Micki knew her own breath held the same tinge.

"I know."

His lips touched hers gently and then, with a low groan, his arm slid around her waist, his chest crushed hers, pushing her body deeper into the cushions, and his mouth became a driving force that searched hers with an urgency that held near desperation. At first, startled into stillness by the very intensity of his action, Micki lay unresponsive in his embrace. Then, her own feelings of desperation swamping her, she curled her arms around his neck, returned his kiss with equal fervor. Stretching his frame beside her, his hand moved down her back to the base of her spine, urging her body to meet his. Hope flaring that maybe this time she'd feel something, if only a tiny quickening of desire, Micki arched her body to his, her arms tightening around his neck.

Other than the mild, pleasant sensation she usually felt when being kissed, there was nothing. No spark of excitement danced along her limbs, no fire rushed inside her veins, no longing to give herself up to sensual pleasure clouded her senses. She yearned for those sensations, longed to feel them, yet, even when Tony's hand moved over her rib cage to stroke her breasts, there was nothing. She could have wept in frustration and disappointment. Attuned as she was to those emotions, she felt them reciprocated from Tony when, with a strangled moan, he released her and flopped back against the sofa.

"It's no good, is it, darlin'?" It was posed as a question, yet it wasn't one. She answered anyway.

"No, it's no good, I'm sorry."

"It's not your fault." The sigh he emitted seemed to come from the depths of his being. "It's mine."

Leaning forward, he poured coffee into the two cups on the tray, lifted one, tasted it, then stood up abruptly.

"Better drink your coffee while it's still hot," he advised softly, walking to the window on the other side of the room.

Shifting to the edge of the sofa, Micki added milk to her coffee and sat staring at it, her eyes sad and misty.

"Goddamn!"

Tony's sharply expelled curse startled her upright, her eyelashes fluttering in bewilderment.

"Tony?"

Her soft entreaty brought his body around to face her, a small, apologetic smile on his lips.

"I'm sorry, Micki." Tony's lips twisted. "But I was hoping, no praying, that something would ignite between us. It would have been perfect, we're so compatible. We can laugh and talk so easily together without strain that I thought—maybe—we could make love together as easily."

Micki frowned, and knowing she misinterpreted his words, he added hastily, "Not just sex, but love—you know." His lips twisted more harshly. "The real thing, stars and music, the whole shootin' match."

"Yes, I do know." Micki's frown deepened. "It would seem that we're suffering from the same malady. You've been hurt badly, haven't you?"

"God, yes!" Tony's softly groaned exclamation tugged at her heart. Then, as the full content of her words sank in, his eyes sharpened on her face. "You too?" At her nod he probed. "Do I know him?"

Unblinking, Micki stared at him steadily until, turning palms out, he lifted his shoulders and pleaded, "Forget I said that. Bad, was it?"

"Yes."

"I know the feeling." He laughed humorlessly. "I've been there. Hell, I'm still there."

"She didn't"—Micki paused to choose her words carefully—"care for you?"

"That's the stinger." Tony's smile hurt her. "She loved me."

"But then, why?" Micki's face wore a puzzled expression. "Tony, I don't understand."

"Neither did I." He laughed harshly, puzzling her even more. Reading her expression, he lifted his shoulders again in a weary, defeated way. "I threw it away, honey," he stated flatly. "I had it all in my hands and I threw it away."

"Tony!" Micki cried in exasperation. "You are not making any sense."

"Nothing new about that," Tony sighed. "I haven't made much sense for some time now." Tilting his head, he asked quizzically, "Was I always stupid, Micki?"

"Tony!" Micki begged. "Will you stop wallowing in self-pity and explain?"

"Am I doing that?" he asked, startled, then he smiled.

"Yes, I guess I am. Sorry, hon. Are you sure you want to hear it?"

Micki nodded emphatically. "Of course. We're friends, aren't we?"

"Yes, friends." Tony's smile softened. "Okay, friend, you asked for it." Drawing a deep breath, he began. "I met her in Atlantic City. She's a supper-club singer." At the slight rise of Micki's eyebrows, his hand sliced through the air dismissively. "Oh, she had no great ambitions, no burning drive to be a star or anything. But she has an appealingly soft voice, perfect for the supper clubs, and it was a way for her to earn a good living. She comes from upstate New York and she arrived in Atlantic City via New York City." He paused and his smile turned whimsical. "We met—introduced ourselves—at a blackjack table."

"She's a gambler?" Micki exclaimed.

"Lord, no!" Tony laughed, then sobered. "Even though she gambled, and lost, on me."

"But how?" Micki cried. "Tony, *will* you explain?"

"All she wanted was marriage, children, and believe it or not, she wanted me for their father."

"You didn't want to get married?" The idea didn't surprise Micki. Many young men shied away from that total commitment.

"Hell, yes," he disabused her at once. "I wanted that more than anything in the world. But, Micki, she was so lovely and I had so damned little to offer her."

"Ah, Tony—" Micki began, but Tony's self-derisive chuckle cut her off.

"That's exactly what she said. In exactly that tone of voice. But, you see, I wanted to have everything perfect for her. I wanted to wait until I could give her a home and all the nice things that go in it." He smiled ruefully. "She didn't want to wait, told me she'd enjoy working with me to get the things we'd need." He drew a deep breath, went on slowly, painfully. "I wouldn't listen, wouldn't even consider it."

"But, Tony, most young couples work together to set themselves up." Micki's face revealed her astonished reaction to his words.

"I know, I know, but—" He paused to wet his lips. "Micki, you know me, I'm great in the light moments, like earlier this evening, but when it comes to the heavy stuff, well, I freeze up. And with her it was even worse. I wanted her so much, yet I was almost afraid to touch her. I didn't merely love her, I put her on a pedestal, literally adored her. I—"

He turned away from her, his shoulders slumping, and Micki's heart ached for him all over again. When he turned back to her, his face was pale.

"She wrote me a letter." His soft tone betrayed the strain he was feeling. "Told me a friend she used to date had come down to A.C. to see the casinos and had looked her up. He asked her to marry him." Tony grimaced, but continued. "She said she couldn't wait anymore, so she was going back home with him, was going to accept his proposal." Suddenly his eyes shot blue sparks and his fingers raked his hair roughly. "I should have dragged her off the pedestal and into my bed. That's what I meant when I said I threw it away."

Micki sat staring at him long moments before, rising quickly, she walked around the sofa, her mind working at what it was about his narration that bothered her.

"Did she love you, Tony?" she finally asked.

"Yes," he answered at once. "I'd bet everything I own on that, Micki."

"Oh, Tony!" she exclaimed impatiently. "Did she take your brain with her when she left?"

"What do you mean?" he bristled.

She ignored his question to ask one of her own. "How long ago did she leave?"

"Two months, one week, and four days ago. Why?"

"Oh, for heaven's sake," she groaned. "Tony, you don't need a friend, you need a keeper. Didn't it ever occur to you she might be trying to get you off dead center?"

"In what way?" he snapped.

"Probably the second oldest way there is," she snapped back. "You made sure she couldn't use the first. She took a powder, took off, leaving a letter designed to make you jealous. You, dumbhead, were supposed to go after her."

"Do you really think so?" he asked hopefully.

"Is she married?" Again Micki brushed off his question to pose one of her own.

"I don't know."

"Why don't you?"

"For God's sake, Micki, you sound like a trial lawyer," Tony growled. "How would I know?"

"Men!" Micki's eyes lifted as if beseeching help from above. "Do you know what town she comes from? Her parents' name?"

"Well, of course." He sounded almost angry. "But what has th—"

"Call them, ask them," Micki cut in sarcastically. "They very likely know if their daughter has gotten married."

"Just like that?" Tony snapped his fingers. "Just call and ask? Come on, honey, I can't do that."

"Why not?" Micki nearly shouted in her exasperation with him. "What's so unusual about a friend calling to find out if a proposed marriage came off? A friend might want to be sure before sending a wedding gift."

Tony's eyes grew bright, then dimmed again. "What do I do if she answers the phone?"

"Ask her, you leadbrain," Micki chided. "And if the answer is no, then coax, plead, beg her to come back to you. Promise her anything, but—" she paused, her eyes twinkling. "Give her yourself, your love."

In a few long strides, Tony crossed the room, caught her

to him and hugged her fiercely before releasing her to gaze fondly into her eyes.

"You're wonderful," he said clearly. "I'll do it. Oh, baby, the guy that let you get away had to be completely crazy."

Micki winced, as much from the name *baby* as the rest of his words. Tony was instantly contrite.

"Oh, Micki, I'm sorry. What happened? Don't tell me he acted as stupid as I did?"

"No," Micki shook her head, her gentle tone robbing the denial of its sting. "He didn't put me on a pedestal." Her tone went rough. "In fact he treated me like a silly fool, called me a youngster, a juvenile." Feeling her cheeks flush, she dropped her eyes. "And he didn't have to drag me into his bed, I practically jumped into it."

"I know what it cost you to say that, honey." Tony's hand caressed her hot face. "But what happened? What went wrong?"

"I found out, after it was too late, that he was using me." Biting her lip, she lifted overbright eyes to his. "I was a very willing, convenient plaything for a weekend."

"He told you that?" Tony demanded, outraged.

"No, of course not," Micki sighed. "But the way I found out, well, it left no doubt at all as to his intentions. Oh, I'm sure he would have been willing to fit me into his schedule every now and then, as long as I didn't become difficult—or boring."

"Micki, stop." Tony's eyes were anxious, his tone concerned.

"Don't worry, Tony," Micki shook her head at him. "It all happened a long time ago. I'm fine now, really."

"Oh, sure." His tone called her a liar. "That's why you tried so hard to work up a response to me a while ago. The experience shattered you so badly you're still trying to put the pieces together." His eyes grew soft. "I can see why it would. If you know me, I know you as well. I was around, I saw how fiercely you guarded your innocence.

116

For you to give it up so willingly, you would have to be very much in love. And it still hurts, doesn't it?"

"Yes," Micki whispered.

He gazed at her silently several seconds, then his eyes narrowed in thought.

"You said it all happened a long time ago." He hesitated before probing. "Was it that time six years ago, right before you went back to college, when you called me and begged me to say yes if anyone asked if we were seeing each other regularly?"

"Yes," Micki admitted with an apologetic smile. "I'm sorry, Tony, but I'm afraid I used your name a lot at that time. I literally hid behind it."

"Sorry? Now who's being a leadbrain?" he scolded. "You may hide behind my name, or me, anytime the need arises. Now come on, it's late, I'd better get you home."

When he stopped the car in front of her house, he kissed her gently on the mouth and whispered, "If things go right, I'll send you an invitation. Okay?"

"You'd better," Micki warned.

"A promise," he vowed. "And, Micki, toss off that load of guilt and shame you've been toting."

"Yes, Tony," Micki promised meekly.

CHAPTER 7

As she slipped into bed, Micki prayed her hunch about Tony's girl had been right. She was almost sure it was, as it was exactly the sort of thing she might do in the same situation. Anxious for him, wanting to see him happy, she hoped it would not be long before, keeping his promise, he sent her an invitation to his wedding.

As to her promise to him, there was no need to worry about that, simply because she never had felt guilty or ashamed. At first, sure she should have them, she'd wondered about her lack of those feelings. The searing pain, the disappointment, the anger she'd had, hadn't had the power to change what had been a joyous experience into anything else. She'd discovered sheer delight, an exquisite Eden in Wolf's arms, and nothing that happened after that had been able to erase it from her mind.

What disturbed her was her inability to find that Eden in any other man's embrace. It was not a man's mouth that ignited the spark, but Wolf's mouth. It was not a man's hands that fanned the flame, but Wolf's hands. And it was not a man's body that could consume her in the blaze, but Wolf's body. With sad defeat, Micki faced the possibility that no other man but Wolf held the key that could unlock her emotions.

What do I do in that case? Micki wondered sleepily. Marry another man, any other man—Darrel—and act out a part the rest of my life? The thought sent a shudder down her spine and her last coherent thought was *I must call Darrel.*

It was mid-morning before Micki woke. Fuzzy minded, heavy lidded, she stumbled down the stairs and into the kitchen. Her father paused in the act of pouring a cup of coffee to give her a grin devoid of any sign of sympathy.

"Hangover?" he chirped brightly.

"No," Micki denied honestly. "But I do feel like a washout. I think I'll just loaf around the house today if I want to be in decent shape to start my job tomorrow."

"Sound thinking," Bruce intoned. "By the way, you had two phone calls last night, Wolf Renninger and a Darrel Baxter."

"Wolf?" Micki pounced on the name. "What did he want?"

Bruce shot her a sharp glance before lifting his shoulders in an I-don't-know shrug. "You'll have to ask Regina, she took the calls." Heading for the doorway Micki had just come through, he added, "If anyone wants me, I'll be on the front porch reading the paper."

Micki itched with the desire to go in search of Regina but deciding to be prudent, she poured herself a small glass of juice and a cup of coffee, dropped a slice of bread into the toaster, and sat down to wait for Regina to find her. She didn't have long to wait. Regina came into the kitchen as Micki was finishing her toast and starting on her second cup of coffee.

"Good morning, Micki," Regina greeted quietly. "Did you have a good time last night?"

"Yes, thank you," Micki answered warily, studying her stepmother's face for maliciousness. Finding none, she blurted, "I hear I had some calls last night."

"Yes," Regina nodded. "A young man named Darrel Baxter called soon after you left, and a short time later Wolf called."

"What did they want?" Micki asked quickly.

"To speak to you, of course," Regina replied smoothly.

"What did you, tell them?" Micki demanded sharply.

"Really, Micki." Regina's eyes flew wide at Micki's tone. "What could I tell them? I informed them both that you were out for the evening with Tony Menella. You were, weren't you?"

"Yes, yes, of course," Micki sighed contritely. "I'm sorry, Regina. I got in very late and I'm irritable this morning."

"I've experienced the feeling," Regina smiled. "Oh, yes, Mr. Baxter said he'd call sometime today."

"And Wolf?" Micki was almost afraid to ask. What, she wondered, was he up to? Why had he called when he had assured her he would not?

"Wolf said thank you very coldly and hung up," Regina replied from the counter, where she was getting herself a cup of coffee. Turning to Micki with the pot held aloft, she asked, "Can I heat yours up?"

"Yes, please."

Micki brought the cup to her lips, gulped most of the lukewarm brew down her suddenly parched throat, then handed the cup to Regina. After refilling the cup, she carried both cups to the table and sat down on the chair opposite Micki.

"Micki." Regina's tone held confusion. "What's going on?"

"Nothing's going on," Micki returned quickly. "I don't know what you mean by going on."

"You know perfectly well what I mean," Regina sighed. "The day you came home you absolutely refused to discuss Wolf Renninger. In fact you would not allow me to speak that person's name. Since then he has called here several times and you have seen him at least once that I

121

know of. Last night Wolf's tone was not only cold, it was"—Regina hesitated, as if searching for the exact word —"proprietorial." Having found the word, she placed hard emphasis on it before going on. "I don't like feeling in the middle, while still in the dark."

When she paused for breath, Micki seized the opportunity to declare flatly, "He has no right to sound proprietorial."

"Right or not, he did," Regina retorted. "Which leads me to suspect he will be calling again. Now don't you think it's time we talked frankly about what happened six years ago and clear up that mess once and for all?"

"No!"

The chair scraped the floor and nearly toppled over as Micki jumped up. She was at the doorway when Regina's voice, sounding both tired and impatient, stopped her.

"Micki, you don't understand," Regina argued. "There are things you must know. Things about Wolf and—"

"I don't want to hear it," Micki cried, rushing through the doorway. "And I won't listen."

"For heaven's sake, Micki," Regina called after her. "This is ridiculous."

"So, okay," Micki shot back as she swung around the banister and started up the stairs, unaware of her father standing in the front doorway holding the screen door open. "I'm ridiculous."

"What in the— Micki?" Bruce's voice was sharp with concern. "What's all the shouting about? I doubt any of the neighbors missed a word."

"I'm sorry, Dad, but I can't—I won't—" Micki paused at the growing look of confusion and alarm on his face. "Oh, hell," she sighed, running up the stairs.

"Micki!" Bruce called after her, then called sharply, "Regina!"

Micki didn't wait to hear any more. She ran inside her room, slammed the door, and leaned against it, breathing heavily and fighting tears. Oh, why did Regina persist in tormenting her? If she really wanted a smoother relationship between them, why didn't she let the subject drop?

Still tired from her physical and emotional exertions of the night before, Micki's thoughts tumbled, none too rationally. Were Regina and Wolf still seeing each other behind her father's back? But if they were, why had Wolf insisted she go out with him? Wasn't one woman at a time enough for him? *Damn Regina,* Micki silently cursed her, *if she hurts Dad again I'll* . . . Not knowing exactly what she'd do, Micki's fury turned to Wolf. Why was he doing this? And why, after stating so flatly that he would not call her again, had he called last night? Were Regina and Wolf working together to drive her away? That thought brought her up short.

"Please, no."

Moving her head back and forth against the smoothly finished door, Micki wasn't even aware that she'd whispered the words aloud. The very possibility of her reasoning being correct tightened a band of pain around her head. If it was true, if their affair was still going on, she, simply by being her father's daughter, and being in the house, was a definite threat to them.

Her breathing suddenly constricted, Micki stumbled across the room and dropped onto the bed. Six years ago she had thought the intensity of the pain she suffered at the image of Wolf and Regina entwined together, exactly as she and Wolf had been, could not possibly be deepened. She had been wrong. The anguish she felt now far superceded what had been before.

"Goddamn you, Wolf Renninger."

The muted curse held more the sound of an animal's snarl than the lucid words from a reasoning mind. And like an animal's claws, her elegantly long, painted nails dug viciously into the rumpled bedcovers on the unmade bed.

Harsh, rasping breaths were drawn in roughly around the unreleased sobs gripping her throat. And eyelids were anchored firmly against hot tears she refused to let run free. Curled up tightly into the fetal position, Micki's slim ball of a body caused the mattress to tremble with the force of the shudders that shook through her.

Dear God, the silent plea was wrenched from the depths of her being, *I take it back, don't damn him. Just, please, please, make him go away and leave me alone before I give in to my need for him and damn my own soul in the giving. You see, God,* the chaotic thoughts run on, *I love him so terribly, and if he manages to get me alone, I don't know how long I can hold out against the urge to lose myself, my very identity, inside his arms. If you have any mercy, help me. And, if you have any justice,* she added irreverently, bitterly, *you'll give a small slap to Regina's conscience.*

By the time she finished her somewhat unorthodox prayer, Micki's sobs filled the room and her tears soaked a patch of the sheet under her face. The sound of her sobs blocked out the quiet tap on her door and a second later the click the latch made as the door was opened. Nor did she see the alarm that filled her father's eyes as they encountered her shaking form. The anxious sound of his voice told her she was no longer alone.

"Princess, what is wrong?" Bruce probed gently, bending over the bed to stretch his hand out and smooth her hair from her damp face. "What has happened to make you cry like this? Was it something Regina said or did?"

Yes, it was both those things. Micki had to bite back the words as, rolling onto her back, she shook her head and lied. "No, of course not." Swallowing down her sobs with the air she drew into her lungs, she hiccupped, then rushed on. "I'm tired. Tony and I danced for hours last night and despite what I said, I'm afraid I drank too much. After that I went to Tony's apartment with him and—"

"You did what?" Bruce's voice, sharp with sudden anger, cut across her babbling explanation. "That's why you're crying, isn't it? What did he do to you?"

"Do?" Micki asked blankly. "What do you me—?" She

stopped, stunned, as her mind caught up with his train of thought. Before she could deny his impression, he was speaking again.

"Answer me!"

Never before had Micki heard quite that harsh a tone from her father, seen such fury in his eyes. Struck momentarily speechless, Micki stared at him in wonder.

"Well, if you won't answer me"—he swung away from the bed—"maybe he will."

"What do you mean?" Micki squeaked. "What are you going to do?"

"I'm going to call him," Bruce snapped, moving toward the door. "Better still, I think I'll go see him."

"Dad, stop!" The sobs, the tears, were forgotten as Micki scrambled off the bed to run after him, clutch at his arm. "It's not what you're thinking. I swear nothing happened."

"He didn't try to make love to you?" Bruce rapped.

"Well, not really—he—" Micki floundered.

"That's what I thought." Bruce shook her arm off, continued toward the door.

"Dad, please, nothing happened."

At the frantic, pleading note in her voice, Bruce turned to look at her, his angry eyes raking her face.

"Suppose you tell me exactly what did happen."

"Tony did kiss me," Micki admitted. "But he didn't really want me." His body stiffened and again she caught his arm, explained. "Dad, Tony is crazily in love with a girl he met in Atlantic City. What he really wanted was someone to pour his heart out to."

"And that's all?"

Watching the anger drain out of his face, Micki expelled a long sigh of relief. Her father's fury was an altogether new experience for her, never having been exposed to it before. If she hadn't seen it with her own eyes, she would not have believed it. For a few seconds there, that furious man had been a stranger, not the gentle father she thought she knew. Subdued by this new facet of her father's personality, she avowed, softly, "That is absolutely all."

"All right." Although the anger had left his expression, it still edged his tone. "But what the hell possessed you to go to his apartment in the first place?"

"But why shouldn't I have gone with him?" Micki asked, genuinely puzzled.

"Why?" Bruce exclaimed. "You know full well why. You're not that naive."

"No, I'm not," Micki returned with force. "And I'm no longer a little girl. And Tony's is not the first bachelor apartment I've been in. Good grief, Dad, I'm twenty-five years old, not sixteen."

"And everyone knows twenty-five-year-old women never get attacked." Bruce's voice dripped sarcasm. "Or hurt. That only happens to sixteen-year-old girls."

"Oh, Dad," Micki sighed. "I'm fully aware of what goes on out there in the big bad world, but I can't hide myself behind locked doors, or wrap myself in cotton."

"No, you can't," he agreed, then qualified, "but you don't have to invite trouble or go looking for it either."

Knowing there was no way she could win, but unwilling to give in, Micki insisted, "I don't go looking—"

"Micki," Regina's call ended the argument. "You're wanted on the phone."

Casting a rueful glance at her father, Micki left the room. Who, she wondered in amazement, would have believed he'd react like that. And what in the world would he have done had he ever found out about the weekend she'd spent with Wolf? A shudder rippling through her, she started down the stairs only to stop suddenly, her breath catching in her throat. Could that be Wolf on the phone now? Slowly, her steps lagging, Micki descended the stairs, went into the living room, and picked up the receiver.

"Hello?"

"Micki?"

The well-modulated sound of Darrel's voice left Micki weak with relief and, contrarily, a bit disappointed.

"Yes, Darrel. How are you? I was planning to call you this afternoon."

"Where?"

His query stopped her for a moment. What did he mean, where?

"At your apartment, of course," she finally answered. "Where else would I call?"

"Since yesterday afternoon"—Darrel's voice held a smile—"my mother's summer place in Cape May."

"You're calling from Cape May now?"

"Isn't that what I just said?" He laughed indulgently. "I'm glad I finally found you at home." No laughter or even a tinge of a smile now. "Did you have a good time last night?"

Something—was it censure—about his tone annoyed her, so she answered oversweetly. "Yes, I had a wonderful time." Well, she had, for the most part anyway. Her answer met a short silence. When he spoke again, his tone conveyed a worried mixture of anger and hesitation.

"How—nice." Again there was a tiny silence. "Micki, mother's having a small dinner party this evening and she expressly asked me to bring you. Will you come?"

Expressly? I'll bet. Micki's mouth curved wryly. She was very well aware that his mother did not consider her nearly good enough for her precious son. Should she go? Why not? she asked herself. Mrs. Baxter would know before too long that Micki posed no threat to her plans for Darrel's future.

"I'd love to," she lied blandly. "What time should I come?"

"I was hoping you'd agree to my coming up there now," he said quickly. "Then we could have some time alone together before returning here for dinner. Also it would afford me the opportunity to meet your father and stepmother."

Don't bother, buster, you're on your way out. The outrageous thought skittered into Micki's mind, only to be swept quickly out again. Whatever was the matter with her? Why was she feeling so bitchy? It's all Wolf's fault, him and his damn phone call after telling her he wouldn't call. The fact that there was no sense at all to her reasoning didn't bother her in the least.

"Micki? Are you there?"

"Yes, yes, Darrel," Micki assured him. "I was just trying to remember if I'd made any commitments for the day." *Liar*. "As I can't remember any, yes, you can come up. Say, in an hour?"

"Good, I'll be there."

"How should I dress?"

"Oh, casually I'd say. See you in an hour."

After she had replaced the receiver, Micki stood staring at the instrument, the wry smile back on her lips. Oh, casually, the man said. Oh, sure. As casually as labels that read Dior or Halston and that ilk. In other words, girl, she told herself as she left the room, you had better dress casually—to the teeth.

Micki spent the entire hour on her appearance, choosing carefully everything she put on down to the shade of varnish she brushed on her nails. On opening the door for Darrel, she counted the time well spent by the expression on his face.

"You're so lovely," he said softly. He took one step, his arms reaching for her, then, realizing where he was, he stopped, placed his hands lightly on her waist and bent to kiss her cheek. "I've missed you, darling."

"And I've missed you," Micki replied, trying in vain to infuse conviction into her tone.

After making the introductions, Micki stood aside watching Darrel charm her father and Regina. No one she had ever met could be quite as charming as Darrel. Intelligent, handsome, urbane, his athletically slim body encased in perfectly tailored clothes, he was every parent's dream of a husband. By both her father's and Regina's reaction, they were not any exception.

After a two-week separation, her own reaction to him surprised her. Watching him, listening to him, she heaved a silent sigh of relief that she had decided not to marry him. He was almost too perfect. Too good-looking, too well turned out, too charming. How, she wondered, could she have ever lived up to that, or with it, twenty-four hours a day? A picture of her own jean-clad, barefoot, tousle-headed form, as she usually was when around the house, rose in her mind, and she had to fight the grin that tugged at her lips. While working, Micki always looked like she'd stepped off the cover of a high-fashion magazine. But when she was at home, well, that was a different story. To her own way of thinking she was more real when she was at home.

After they had left the house and were in his car—a custom-made black Cadillac—driving south, Micki continued with her train of thought. Studying him and the situation objectively, she was convinced that had she married him she would have lost her real self, the essence that was Micki Durrant.

With a small jolt of surprise Micki suddenly realized that Darrel had seen her only in her workday facade. What, she mused, would he think of the tomboyish Micki who could still scamper up a tree with the best of them? Or, the curves revealed by a bikini not withstanding, become joyfully covered with gritty particles as she erected a sand castle of enormous proportions? She did not have to witness his reaction to know it. Again an impish grin tugged at her lips, more successfully this time.

"What amuses you?" Darrel's tone held just a touch of the petulant child left out of a secret. Yes, indeed, she decided, Darrel would be very hard, if not impossible, for her to live with.

"Life," Micki answered, her bright-blue eyes dancing. "And its funny little twists and turns."

"I find very little amusement in twists and turns," Darrel intoned. "I like my life well planned and ordered. After we're married"—he seemed unaware of Micki's small gasp—"you'll have no more twists and turns, and I'm sure you will find life less unnerving."

Not to mention a lot less exciting, Micki thought scathingly. How was it possible, she asked herself, for a man to be so charming one minute and so pompously dull the next? She didn't even try to work out the answer to that one, as having already rejected him in her mind, she proceeded to do so in fact.

"But we're not going to be married." Although her tone was gentle, it was also flat with finality.

"Not going to be—!" The big car swerved slightly before Darrel's white-knuckled hands gripped the wheel and straightened it. "But I thought it was settled."

"I don't know why you should have thought that," Micki said quietly. "The only promise I made to you before I left Wilmington was to think about your proposal. I have, and I've reached the conclusion that it simply would not work."

"But of course it would work," he insisted. "Why wouldn't it?"

"In the first place," Micki replied calmly, "your mother does not approve of me. And—"

"You're wrong," Darrel interrupted sharply. "At least she no longer objects to the union. She has reconciled herself to the—"

"And in the second place," she cut him off forcefully, "I'm not in love with you."

"But you would learn to love me." He was actually pleading! "I could make you love me."

"No, Darrel, you could not," she assured him gently, but firmly. "Of that I am very sure."

"There is someone else?" His eyes had left the road for a moment as he asked the question. Micki's momentarily unguarded expression was all the answer he needed.

"Yes," he sighed, glancing back at the road. "I can see there is."

"I'm sorry." The words sounded inadequate, even to her own ears, yet they were all she had to offer.

"Sorry? Sorry?" His tone held an anger she'd never heard from him before. "What good is sorry? Why didn't you tell me at once? When I first asked you to marry me?" His voice died away, then came back more strongly. "Why the hell did you let me hang like that when you knew the answer was no all along?"

"But I didn't—" Micki began, then stopped, aghast at what she was admitting to him.

"You didn't know?" he finished for her. "You mean it's some man you've met within the last two weeks?"

"Yes—no!" Micki cried.

"What do you mean, yes—no?" Darrel demanded. "For God's sake, Micki, make up your mind. It's either one or the other."

Having arrived at their destination, Cape May's charmingly quaint shopping mall, Micki was allowed a few minutes to form her answer while Darrel searched out a parking space.

The second the car was motionless, he turned to face her, his expression grim.

"Well?"

"Well," Micki began slowly, "both yes and no are correct." At his look of disbelief, she hurried on. "Yes, really, Darrel." Micki hesitated, wet her lips, then admitted, "I met, and fell in love with, him some years ago. I was very young." Again she moistened her dry lips, looked in every direction but his. "I had hoped, was sure, that it was all over." She paused to draw breath and he took the opportunity to question her.

"That's why you really came home, wasn't it?" His voice was heavy with accusation. "To see him."

"No, it was not," Micki denied. "I never expected to see

him again. When I ran into him, purely by accident, I—I realized nothing had changed for me."

"For you?" Listening carefully, Darrel had caught the inflection in her last two words. "He doesn't love you anymore?"

"He never did." It wasn't easy but she managed to lift her head and meet his penetrating glance. "All he ever wanted was an affair. He still does."

"And you've agreed to this?" he exclaimed, astonished. No man knew better than Darrel exactly how cool and unresponsive Micki could be.

"Of course not," Micki snapped icily.

"Well then," he argued, "if there is no future for you with him, why not—" That was as far as he got before Micki trod on his words.

"I'll tell you why not. Very simply, I can't marry or sleep with one man while loving another." She smiled sadly. "I'm sorry, Darrel, but that's not my style."

"Yes, I know." Darrel's smile matched hers for sadness for several minutes before he shrugged. "I suppose, under the circumstances, dinner at mother's would not be a good idea. She was halfway expecting an announcement of our engagement." His shoulders moved again. "I'll call her and tell her we can't make it, and face the questions tomorrow." The sadness left his smile, replaced by all the charm he was capable of. "You will have dinner with me, won't you?"

"No pressure?" Micki asked warily.

"No pressure," he vowed. "I may not know you all that long, but I know you well enough to be sure no amount of pressure would change your mind."

Micki had a sudden urge to cry. The words *no amount of pressure* brought home to her more than anything else how very vulnerable she was. It would, she knew, take very little pressure from Wolf to turn her into a pliant, shivering love slave. *How very little we know each other,* she thought sadly. She was considered very strong-willed and near frigid by most, if not all, of her friends. What would Darrel's reaction be, she wondered, if he were exposed to a tenth of the passion that had consumed her while on Wolf's boat? A conjured picture of Darrel's shocked visage exchanged the hovering tears for a fleeting smile.

"What are you thinking?" he probed. "You're so quiet, and for a second there I wasn't sure if you were going to laugh or cry."

"For a second there, I wasn't sure either," Micki laughed softly. "I wanted to cry for what might have been. Darrel, would you do something for me?"

"Of course," he answered at once. "Anything. What is it?"

"Would you buy me a sandwich?" Her eyes bright with the recent moisture teased impishly. "I just realized I haven't eaten for hours and I'm starving."

Up until then the car's engine, which he'd left on to run the air-conditioner, had purred softly. As he turned to shut off the engine, he shook his head ruefully.

"You're unbelievable, Micki." As if against his will, he smiled. "To use a very trite phrase, how can you think of food at a time like this?" His smile deepened and grew into a grin. "But now that you mention it, I could eat a sandwich myself."

They left the cool confines of the car to brave the fierce assault from the sun and the waves of heat rising from the sidewalk. Strolling along the perimeter of the shopping mall, they came upon a restaurant with a low-walled patio. On the patio were a half dozen umbrella-shaded tables surrounded by wooden deck chairs. Only two of the tables were occupied, and the waitress, looking somewhat forlorn, cast them a hopeful look.

"What do you think?" Darrel laughed softly. "The patio? Or would you prefer the air-conditioned dining room?"

"Oh, the patio," Micki grinned. "I don't think I have the courage to bypass that waitress."

Chatting pleasantly, the waitress took their orders of grilled cheese and bacon sandwiches and iced tea before reluctantly disappearing through a door at the far end of the patio.

"Well," Darrel sighed, pushing back his chair. "I may as well find a phone, face the music, and get it over with. I'll be back in a minute, if I'm lucky."

"Take your time, I'll be fine." Micki waved him away. "Please convey my regrets to your mother." A low grunt was the only reply she received.

A mild breeze ruffling her hair, Micki leaned back in the chair and let her gaze roam over the surrounding area. Moving lazily, her eyes passed a glare of red, then, a soft gasp escaping her parted lips, her eyes honed in on the flame-colored car.

With something akin to panic, Micki watched as the sports car was maneuvered into a small parking space. Even without a good view of the man behind the wheel, Micki knew who was driving that brazenly painted, rich man's toy. She very seriously doubted there were two cars like that on the whole of the south Jersey coast.

A growing ache gripping her throat, Micki watched as Wolf stepped out of the car, walked around to the other side to assist his passenger in alighting. Hating herself, yet unable to tear her eyes away, Micki studied the woman as she stepped onto the street and straightened up. At that distance Micki could only get an impression of the woman. That impression was tall, willowy, her platinum hair gleaming in the sunlight, her face partially concealed by overlarge sunglasses, her teeth flashing whitely in a crimson mouth.

"Here's your tea, miss." The waitress's lilting voice drew Micki's attention. "Your sandwiches will be along in a moment."

"Thank you, I need that," Micki croaked. "I'm parched."

Sipping gratefully at the cold drink, Micki kept her eyes firmly on the glass, determined not to look at him again. An instant later, unable to stop herself, she lifted her head and froze, the ache in her throat culling forth a corresponding one in her chest. Fighting a desire to jump up and run, she watched as the couple walked in a direct line toward her. Aware that as yet, due to the obviously deep conversation they were engaged in, Wolf had not spotted her, Micki had to force herself to stay in her chair.

Let him pass by without seeing me, please, Micki begged silently. Apparently it was not her day with the deity, for at that moment Wolf turned from the woman and saw Micki. His step quickened and his eyes widened, then, looking beyond her, narrowed.

"God!" Darrel's harassed voice reached her an instant before he slipped into the chair beside her. "My mother should have gone into law, she would have made a fantastic D.A."

Tearing her gaze from the silvery eyes fastened on her, Micki stammered, "Bad, was it?"

"Rock bottom," he groaned. "She had more questions than an end-of-term exam." Raising his glass, Darrel took a long swallow. "Oh, that's good, even though I'm sorry now I didn't order something stronger."

Micki barely heard him. An odd, eerie feeling cloaking her, she knew without looking that Wolf and the tall woman had entered the patio. She didn't even blink when his low voice drew her head around.

"Hello, Micki."

Blue eyes locked with silver and for one mad second Micki was tempted to ignore him. The sure knowledge that in no way would Wolf allow her to get away with it chased temptation out of her mind.

"Hello, Wolf," Micki replied with amazing coolness. "Cape May seems to be a very popular place today."

135

"Yes, doesn't it." Until that minute his eyes had refused to release hers, now they swung pointedly to Darrel, who had risen at Wolf's greeting.

"Darrel Baxter," Micki smiled painfully. "Wolf Renninger and—" The breath died in her throat as, shifting her gaze, Micki got a good look at the woman by Wolf's side. Her hair was not platinum, but a beautiful true silver and, although she was still strikingly lovely, she appeared to be somewhere in her middle sixties.

"Mrs. Bianca Perriot," Wolf finished for her. "Bianca —Miss Micki Durrant and Mr. Darrel Baxter."

Returning the woman's enchanting smile, Micki extended her hand, felt her fingers grasped in a firm handshake at the same time the two men performed the same act.

"Micki." Bianca's voice was every bit as enchanting as her smile. "What a delightful name. Is it a given name or a nickname?"

"Given," Micki answered softly. "In honor of my Irish grandfather, who by all accounts, was a real Mick."

Bianca's laughter tinkled on the air like the sound of tiny bells before, turning to Darrel, she placed her hand in his and queried, "Baxter? Are you by any chance related to Martha Baxter?"

"My mother." Darrel's tone betrayed his surprise. "You're acquainted with her?"

"I know her very well. I knew your father also." Once again that enchanting smile came to her lips. "My late husband was as avid a golfer as your father was. They played together quite often, leaving your mother and me to amuse ourselves at the clubhouse."

During this exchange, though Micki determinedly kept her attention centered on Bianca Perriot's animated face, she was uncomfortably aware of Wolf's eyes devouring her. When Darrel spoke again, his words went through her like a blast of arctic air.

"Were you and Mr. Renninger planning to have some-

136

thing to eat here?" At her assenting nod, Darrel asked, "Then won't you join us? We'd love the company, wouldn't we, Micki?"

What could she possibly say? Her eyes wide with shock, she swung her gaze to Wolf. The glittery spark that blended with the silver told her she'd get no assistance from him. He was enjoying her discomfort. Biting back a moan, she curved her lips in a parody of a smile and lied.

"Yes, of course, we'd love to have you join us."

CHAPTER 8

Uncomfortable and uneasy, Micki stole another glance at Wolf as he seated Bianca. At the same moment his glance shifted to her, his eyes glittering wickedly.

"All set to start the new job tomorrow, Micki?"

The lazily drawled question turned her unease into dismay. With those few words Wolf had managed to convey a familiarity between them to Darrel and Bianca. Pretending she didn't notice Darrel's startled reaction, Micki glared daggers at Wolf, her lips straining to keep her smile in place.

"Yes," she answered softly. "I've enjoyed my vacation, but I'm ready to go back to work."

"Micki is a buyer for Something Different boutiques," Wolf informed Bianca, adding to the familiarity. "She has just been transferred to the Atlantic City store."

"Oh! But—" Bianca began, her face mirroring confusion.

"Promoted."

The sharp word Darrel flung at Wolf cut across Bianca's quiet voice. For several seconds his eyes blazed a challenge at Wolf, then, as if suddenly realizing his rudeness, he smiled at Bianca and murmured, "I'm sorry I

139

interrupted. Micki was promoted." His eyes flashed to Wolf. "Not transferred."

"Yes, of course." Wolf's cold as steel eyes contradicted his smooth tone. "I knew that."

Feeling caught in their crossfire and growing angry at the childish way they were squaring off at each other, Micki snapped, "Transferred, promoted, what difference does it make?"

Without waiting for a reply from either of them, Micki continued, "Either way, I begin tomorrow and I'm eager to start. Now," she finished strongly, "can we drop the subject?"

Bianca's puzzled expression slowly changed to one of amusement as her eyes shifted from one to the other of them. Her lips twitching, she soothed, "Micki's right, it is unimportant and—oh, good, here's our waitress."

The tension around the table eased with the arrival of the waitress, even though Micki felt the angry stiffness in Darrel when his arm brushed hers as he drew his chair closer to the table.

The waitress placed the delicious-looking, open-face sandwiches in front of Micki and Darrel, whipped two menus out from under her arm, and offering them to Bianca and Wolf, chirped, "Can I get you folks something to drink?"

"I don't need that." Wolf waved the menu away. "I'll have a Reuben and a beer."

"And," Bianca smiled, "as those sandwiches look good enough to eat, I'll have one of those and a glass of Chablis."

"You can bring me a beer too," Darrel inserted as the waitress moved to turn away. "Micki?"

"Another iced tea." Micki smiled faintly at the woman before, in a chiding way that left little doubt she was reminding Darrel of his manners, she emphasized, "Please."

At any other time Micki would have enjoyed being in

Bianca's company, even though the exact relationship between the attractive woman and Wolf tormented her more than she cared to admit to herself. Being a permanent year-round resident of Cape May, Bianca was a fund of information on the town's history. Had it not been for her enlightening conversation, the atmosphere around the table would have been much more uncomfortable.

Even so Micki could hardly wait until the food had been consumed and the check was presented. Sighing with relief, Micki smiled brightly at the waitress when she placed the check on the table. The smile turned to a silent groan as hostilities were resumed between Wolf and Darrel.

"I'll take care of that."

Moving swiftly, Wolf's hand grabbed the check out from under Darrel's.

"But I invited you to join us." Darrel's angry glance clashed with glinting silver.

"But we intruded on your, er, privacy." Hard finality laced Wolf's tone as, turning away check in hand, he strode toward the building's entrance.

Finally they were back in the car heading for Ocean City.

"He's the man, isn't he?" Darrel shot the question at her savagely after some fifteen minutes of total silence. The suddenness of his attack startled Micki out of the blue funk she'd drifted into.

"W-what man?" she hedged.

"You know damned well what man," he growled frustratedly. "The bastard who's willing to fit you into his schedule now and then."

"Darrel, please."

"Please, hell," he snorted. "Do you have any idea how it makes me feel, knowing you turned me down for a man like that? Oh, I grant you," he sneered, "he's got the kind of looks that attract the females. Of all ages apparently. As lovely and charming as Bianca Perriot is, the fact remains she is old enough to be his mother."

141

"Darrel." Micki's tone was sharp with admonishment. "Don't jump to conclusions. You don't know—"

"Don't kid yourself," Darrel interrupted jeeringly. "A man like Wolf—how apt, that name—doesn't waste his time on any woman unless she's coming across."

"Darrel!" Micki's shocked exclamation revealed the depth of pain his words had inflicted.

"Darrel what?" Unrepentant, he continued to fling words at her like blows. "Face the facts, Micki, he's a user and age means nothing. What does he do to earn a living?"

"I . . ." Micki paused, wet her lips, then admitted, "I don't know."

"I thought not." He shot a pitying glance at her and went on mercilessly. "I'll tell you what I think he does. I think the polite term is paid escort but, to call a spade a spade, I think he's a stud for hire."

"Be quiet!" Micki shouted angrily. "Don't you dare say another word. Even if what you say is true, it is none of your business." Her voice dwindling to a soft sigh, she added, "Or mine either."

They covered the remaining miles to her home in uneasy silence. The minute he stopped the car in front of the house, Micki flung the door open and ran out.

"Micki, wait," Darrel pleaded. "I'm sorry, I—"

"I don't want to talk about it," Micki snapped coldly.

"May I call you later in the week?" he called after her.

"No," Micki flung over her shoulder. "Or ever again."

"Micki!"

Walking quickly, she went into the house and closed the door on the sound of his voice. Her breath coming in gasps, Micki ran up the stairs and into her room. Taking short, agitated steps, she paced her room, around the bed to the window, then, turning sharply, back to the door again.

It wasn't true, she assured herself. What Darrel said wasn't true, it couldn't be, could it? No, of course it couldn't be. But what did he do for a living? What kind of job was it that paid enough to afford him the expensive clothes he wore, that boat and—she winced—that fantastic car. How much did a car like that cost anyway? More bucks than an ordinary job paid, of that she was sure. And the slacks and shirt he was wearing today! Micki's trained eyes had told her they were hand tailored and had very probably cost him more than she earned in a month. And Bianca Perriot's simple little summer frock had practically screamed the words *created in Paris*. Was she very wealthy? Very, very likely, Micki decided. And the suspicious little thought crept into her mind: Had Bianca's still-smooth, diamond-bedecked slim hand written the check that had paid for Wolf's clothes?

Aghast at herself, Micki tore out of her room and along the hall to the stairs, running from her thoughts. It didn't work; her thoughts followed her. A note on the kitchen table informed her that her father and Regina had gone out for dinner. Alone, the quiet of the house pressing in on her, she curled up in a corner of the sofa, paperback in hand, in a vain attempt to lose herself.

She was reading a paragraph for the third time when the phone rang. Silently apologizing to the author, she put the book down and lifted the receiver.

"Hello?"

"Micki?" Tony's exuberant voice attacked her eardrum. "I couldn't wait to send you an invitation, I had to call you."

"You called her?" Micki exclaimed. "You talked to her?"

"I'm with her now," Tony laughed. "I didn't sleep at all last night. I kept thinking about what you said, asking myself should I, shouldn't I? Anyway, I called her first thing this morning and damned if you weren't right. Not only is she not married, or getting married—except to me—there was no ex-boyfriend at all." His laughter this time held a rueful note, and Micki could imagine him shaking his head. "I'll tell you, friend, it's a good thing I spilled my guts out to you last night; she was about ready to give up on me."

"After waiting this long?" Micki chided. "I somehow doubt that."

"Yes, well, she's not waiting any longer," Tony said determinedly. "And neither am I. We're getting married next Saturday and we want you to come. Can you make it, Micki?"

The anxious note that had crept into Tony's voice brought a rush of tears to Micki's eyes. "Can birds fly?" she shot back at him with a shaky laugh. "Just tell me what time, where, and give me directions and I'll be there with wedding bells on."

"If you'd want to, you could fly into Albany and I could meet the plane," he suggested. "Save you all that driving."

"You're on," Micki agreed. "I'll check into flight schedules tomorrow. Suppose you call me sometime midweek and I'll let you know what time."

"Will do. And Micki?" Tony's voice went rough with emotion. "We both thank you."

"You're both welcome," she whispered. Then she added, "Tony, does she have a name?"

"Shirley," Tony laughed. "Don't you love it?"

After she'd replaced the receiver, Micki went back to the sofa, a small smile curving her lips. Tony Menella getting married! Unbelievable. Memories rushed over her, and caught up in the flow, the tormenting suspicions about Wolf were pushed to the back of her mind.

The first thing that greeted Micki when she walked into the shop Monday morning was an announcement. Georgine, her large, dark eyes bright with excitement, was fairly twitching with news.

"I've been transferred."

"Transferred?" Micki cried. "Where? When?"

"The boss was in the day after you were here," Georgine laughed. "Told me they were opening a new store, asked me if I'd like to manage it."

"Manage? Georgine that's wonderful," Micki enthused.

"That's what I thought," she drawled. "Then, when he told me where the store is he asked if I still wanted it." Her dark eyes rolled expressively. "I asked him if he'd like my eye teeth." Her beautiful face was drawn into a sober cast and her voice rasped deeply. " 'No, thank you,' the man said, 'I've got a good set of fangs of my own.' "

The word *fangs* sent a picture of Wolf flashing into Micki's mind, and shaking her head impatiently, she pleaded, "Georgine, will you tell me where the store is?"

Georgine mentioned a large hotel chain, then said casually, "The one in Honolulu."

"Honolulu?" Micki repeated in an awed tone, then, much louder, "Honolulu?"

Jennell's soft laughter drifted to her from across the width of the shop, where both she and Lucy had stood watching Micki's reaction to the news. Then she drawled huskily, "Isn't it a shame? I mean, some poor girls have no luck at all. First Georgine can't find a man, now she gets shipped almost to the end of the earth—poor thing."

Georgine's excitement infected them all and Micki's first week at the store flew by without a hitch. Even her plans for attending Tony and Shirley's wedding went smoothly. Plans were also made by Micki, Jennell, and Lucy to take Georgine for dinner on Friday night, as she was leaving for Honolulu on Monday.

When she learned Micki was flying to Albany Saturday morning, Jennell suggested she pack a valise, bring it with her to the shop Friday, and spend the weekend at her apartment.

"I'll drive you to the airport Saturday morning and pick you up again Saturday night," Jennell said. "That way you won't have to leave your car at the airport."

All Micki's arguments about not wanting to put Jennell

145

out ended up against a stone wall. Jennell was determined and Micki finally, laughingly, gave in.

Friday night was pure fun. After a wildly expensive dinner they went bar hopping, having decided there was safety in numbers, flirting madly and dancing until Micki thought she'd drop.

Saturday morning, still half asleep, Micki waved goodbye to an equally sleepy Jennell, boarded the plane, and promptly fell asleep, dead to the world until the plane touched down in Albany. A grinning Tony woke her completely with a bear hug and resounding kiss on the mouth.

"What are you up to?" Micki grinned back at him when he released her.

"Oh, five-eleven, et cetera," Tony chirped. "I wanted to bring Shirl with me to meet you, but I'm not allowed to see the bride before the ceremony." His grin flashed again. "So come on, friend. You and I are going to have some lunch and you can hold my hand between now and then. Maybe you can even prevent the nervous fit I feel coming on."

Micki's first glimpse of Shirley was just before the ceremony and with that quick look she knew why Tony had put the young woman on a pedestal and had hesitated about making love to her. Small, fragile Shirley had the face of a modern-day Madonna. Her own breath catching in her throat, Micki could well imagine the impact Shirley had on a supper-club crowd.

Although the ceremony was brief, it was beautiful and moving, and as Micki left the small church, she had to dab quickly at her eyes to blot the tears.

At the champagne supper given by the bride's parents, Micki discovered the girl behind the breathtaking face was not only very nice, but intelligent and quick-witted as well. When they saw her off at the airport, Micki kissed Shirl on the cheek and whispered, "I know you'll be very happy." Then loud enough for Tony to hear, "Keep this clown in line, won't you?"

"This clown wants a kiss too," Tony retorted, repeating his bear hug performance of that morning.

Tears in her eyes, Micki kissed him, warned him he'd better take damned good care of her new friend, then walked away from them with the advice they get on with the honeymoon and let her sniffle in peace.

Jennell was waiting as promised and had to hear all the wedding details on the way back to her apartment. Micki had all day Sunday to rest in the apartment by herself, as Jennell decided to do her boyfriend a favor and spend the day—and night—with him.

The nighttime part Micki found out about when Jennell telephoned the apartment around nine.

"Would you be all right on your own tonight, honey?" Jennell drawled the question hesitantly.

"Of course," Micki said at once. "Why?"

"Well, this deliciously bad man wants me to stay with him tonight, but I told him I'd have to confer with you first."

"Would you like to stay?" Micki asked devilishly.

"Is the ocean salty?" Jennell laid the drawl on thickly.

"Then stay," Micki laughed. "And Jennell."

"Yes, sugar?"

"Be good."

"Are you crazy?" Jennell purred. "I'll be terrific."

Laughing softly, Micki replaced the receiver, then went still as a strange thought struck her. Why was it, she wondered, that she was so liberal-minded about her friends' sleeping arrangements and so rigid about her own? She knew, because Jennell had been open and frank, that this "deliciously bad" man was not the first Jennell had slept with, yet she in no way thought of Jennell as promiscuous.

In fact, now that she gave it some thought, Micki could not come up with one name out of all her female friends who had not unashamedly admitted to sleeping with their current man. Why did she have to be odd woman out? Were her moral guidelines too narrow? Micki had never thought so, but, damn, she was the one alone tonight, every night.

The questions, all with the same theme, chased each other around in her mind as she prepared for bed. As she slid between the sheets the answer, which had been demanding exposure, finally broke through her self-imposed mental barrier. Very simply, she had felt no desire or even the slightest urge to be with any man other than one Wolf Renninger. And that one man scared the hell out of her. What had Darrel called him? A user of women? From her own experience Micki was very much afraid Darrel's judgment was correct. And what scared her was the almost certain feeling that should he get his hands on her again she would revel in his using, lose herself completely, and when his use of her was over, be lost forever.

Micki's second week in the shop sped by as quickly as the first. Georgine's absence was felt in more ways than one. Not only did they miss her droll sense of humor but her help in the shop as well. A sudden spurt of business kept them all on the run, and by the end of the week had nearly wiped out their stock of marked-down merchandise.

Saturday morning, half asleep and yawning, Micki walked into the kitchen to find her father and Regina talking over their after-breakfast coffee.

"Good morning, princess," Bruce smiled gently, studying her sleepy-eyed face. "You look tired, rough week?"

Returning the greeting, Micki nodded in answer. She had seen little of them all week, as staying late after the store closed to help Jennell straighten and restock the shop, she had shared a quick meal with her before driving home. She had found the house empty every night but Monday and had been asleep before they had returned.

Now Micki smiled her thanks as Regina placed a glass

of juice and a cup of coffee on the table in front of her and murmured, "How was your week?"

"Oh, not bad," Bruce replied casually, too casually. That and the bright sheen of excitement in his eyes alerted her. "As a matter of fact we concluded that deal I was telling you about a couple of weeks ago. Do you remember?"

"Yes, I remember," Micki emphasized with a nod. "It's a very big deal?"

"Involving millions eventually," Bruce grinned. "And it's all signed and sealed and tonight we celebrate."

"I remember that also," Micki laughed before jumping up. Then she went over to her father and hugged him. "Congratulations. You've been working on this some time, haven't you?"

"A good long time," Bruce sighed, shaking his head. "With all the maneuvering and negotiating and people involved—several years." He exhaled harshly. "For a while there, when I was hospitalized, I was afraid I was out of it. But this one," he nodded at Regina, "was fantastic. She became my legs, did all the running around for me, eased the pressure. And she shares equally in the rewards. So you may extend your congratulations in her direction as well."

Stunned, Micki stared at Regina for a moment. Regina's expression, a mixture of hesitancy and hope, loosened her tongue.

"Congratulations, fantastic lady." Micki's tone, though light, held real sincerity.

"Thank you."

The two simply spoken words conveyed an equally simple message to Micki. The hostilities between them were over. Micki nodded her head sharply once, sniffed, cleared her throat, then asked overbrightly, "What time does the celebration begin and where?"

"It began right here a moment ago," Bruce answered huskily. "It will continue at another realtor's place with a cold buffet lunch between one and two thirty and a clambake supper at seven. We'd like to leave here around twelve thirty, as the place is some miles inland. Can you be ready by then?"

"Yes, of course." Micki smiled, swallowing around the tightness in her throat caused by the suspicious brightness in his eyes. "How many people will be there?"

"Thirty or forty I expect." He grinned at the look of dismay that crossed her face. "Don't worry, honey, you'll know quite a few of them."

On arrival at the large country house Micki judged her father's estimate to be short by at least ten. But he had been right about one thing, she did know quite a few of the people.

Micki stayed with her father and Regina until after they had finished lunch, then she wandered off on her own to explore the extensive and beautiful grounds.

The place looked like a picture out of a magazine, and content with her own company, Micki strolled across the putting green, around the tennis courts, and onto the fringes of the pool area. Shading her eyes against the fierce glare of the sun's rays striking off the water, Micki watched a group of teenagers playing Follow the Leader off the diving board.

Continuing on, she completed her wide circling of the grounds, ending up on the other side of the house. It was another hot, humid day in a long summer that had grown monotonous with hot, humid days. As she threaded her way through the cars parked in front of the three-car garage, Micki brushed her hand over her perspiration-slick face, shivering as sweat trickled between her breasts and down her back.

Walking around the front of the house, she headed for the patio from where she'd begun her exploration. There were few people there, as most of the younger ones were either in the pool or engaged in other outdoor games and the older ones had retreated into the air-conditioned house

150

where several bridge games were in session. After unwisely gulping down two gin and tonics at the small bar that had been set up at the end of the patio, she found a lounge chair in the shade, sank onto it, and was asleep within ten minutes.

As the sun trekked its way west, it inched up Micki's body, waking her when it touched her face. Bathed in sweat, her clothes plastered to her, feeling headachy and half sick, she went to the ground floor powder room. The cool interior of the house was a shock to her overheated body, and after rinsing her face and neck, she stood long minutes resting her forehead on the cool tiles. The rattle of the doorknob jerked her upright, and leaving the room she smiled wanly at the woman waiting to enter.

"They're about ready to serve the clambake," the woman informed her as she stepped into the powder room.

The thought of food made Micki's stomach lurch. She made her way slowly back to the patio and was about to step outside when she stopped cold, her breath suddenly constricted in her chest.

Wolf, looking cool and relaxed in lightweight tan slacks and a pale blue shirt, stood at the bar talking to two men. About to retreat and find another way to the area where the tables had been set up for supper, Micki heard the one man say, "Since you're alone today, Wolf, what do you say we do a disappearing act after supper and hunt up some action?"

"No, thanks." Wolf's soft laughter sent a shiver through Micki. "When this Wolf goes on the prowl, he prowls alone."

The sickness increasing inside, Micki turned away sharply. His own words seemed to confirm Darrel's opinion of him. How could she be in love with a man like that? And what was he doing here anyway?

She was halfway across the room when her steps faltered, then stopped, her hand reaching out for something to hang on to. The room seemed to be moving around her

151

and she felt funny, almost floaty. Then her fingers were caught by a hard male hand and a sharp voice demanded, "Micki, what's wrong? Are you sick?"

"I—I feel funny." Was that watery voice hers?

"Sit down." As he spoke, Wolf guided her into a chair, lowered her head gently to her knees, muttering, "Damn, no one's around, they're all at supper."

The light-headedness passed and Micki urged, "I'm all right now. Please go back to your friends."

"Don't talk so damned dumb," Wolf snapped. "I'm taking you home."

"But—"

That's as far as she got, for scooping her into his arms, Wolf ordered, "Be quiet," and carried her out of the house. He deposited her in his car and had turned to walk around to the driver's side when she exclaimed, "Dad and Regina! They'll wonder what happened to me."

"Relax," Wolf soothed. "I'll tell them."

Within minutes he was back sliding behind the wheel. Her head resting against the seat, eyes closed, Micki heard the engine roar to life, felt the car move slowly as he drove onto the road, then with a sudden surge, the Ferrari seemed to literally fly along the highway. Afraid to open her eyes, Micki listened for the siren's wail from a patrol car all the way home.

When Wolf brought the car to a stop in front of her home, Micki stirred lethargically and murmured, "Thank you."

He didn't bother answering. He picked up her handbag and dug through it until he found her keys. Holding them up, he asked, "Which one?"

Ignoring her protests that it wasn't necessary, he helped her from the car and into the house. Once again the air-conditioned coolness went through her like a shock, and dropping into the first chair she came to, Micki closed her eyes against the renewed dizziness. She heard Wolf moving away and had to bite back a plea for him to stay.

Tears were slipping out from under her tightly closed eyes when she felt something cool and wet touch her face. Wiping gently, Wolf bathed her face and neck.

"That's good," Micki sighed. Nearly unconscious, unaware that she spoke aloud, she murmured, "I haven't felt this bad since the abortion."

The damp cloth stopped moving and stirring restlessly she pleaded, "Don't stop."

"What abortion?" There was an odd, breathless quality to Wolf's husky tone that confused her already fuzzy mind. "When?"

She'd forgotten the question, and moving her head from side to side, she frowned and murmured, "What?"

"Your abortion, Micki," Wolf urged, his voice sounding strange. "When did you have it?"

The mistiness was clearing now, and opening her eyes, Micki stared in confusion into Wolf's pale face. He looked strained with white shadowy lines around his mouth.

"When, Micki?" The tone of his voice flicked at her like a lash.

"While I was still in college," she answered honestly, actually afraid to lie to him. "Six years ago."

CHAPTER 9

"Six years ago?"

The question emerged softly through lips that barely moved. Wolf was absolutely still for long, frightening moments then, his hands grasping her arms painfully, he pulled her to her feet to face him.

"You got rid of my baby?" he whispered hoarsely. When she didn't answer at once, he began to shake her hard. Fear closed her throat, making it almost impossible for her to answer. Feeling the faintness closing in on her again, she forced two words past the fear.

"Wolf, please."

He didn't even hear her. His face a terrifying mask of rage, he shook her harder and shouted, "You killed my baby?"

With a low moan Micki welcomed the blackness that covered her mind, blanking out the harsh sound of Wolf's voice.

When she opened her eyes again, she was lying on her bed. Wolf was sitting on its edge bending over her, his silvery eyes cold and blank. The expression of contempt on his face sent a shudder rippling through her and she began to shake. When he moved, her heart thumped wildly, and when his hands again grasped her arms, she brought her palms up against his chest, pleaded, "Wolf, please."

Before he could speak or even move, there was a loud exclamation from the doorway.

"Micki, Wolf!" Bruce said sharply. "What in the hell's going on here?"

Micki froze, her mind, her whole body seemingly turned to stone. His face becoming amazingly calm, Wolf released her and stood up with an easiness that was contradicted by the tenseness she could feel in him.

"Not what you apparently think," he replied smoothly. "Micki fainted."

Bruce obviously didn't believe Wolf, for he snapped, "You have no right in Micki's room."

"Not yet," Wolf returned. "But I will have very soon. Micki and I are going to be married."

"No!"

"Married!"

Micki's choked whisper went unheard, covered as it was by her father's loud exclamation.

"Yes." Wolf's flat tone held a ring of finality and the icy silver glance he threw at her told her he'd listen to nothing from her.

Panicstricken, Micki moved to get up to run to her father for protection, but the look of delight on his face stopped her.

"Wolf, that's great news." Smiling broadly, hand extended, Bruce walked to Wolf and clasped his hand warmly. "I couldn't be more pleased." Losing its brightness, his smile turned rueful. "I must admit that, for a minute there, I thought you—"

"We *have* been lovers, Bruce." Wolf's cool tone sliced across Bruce's words.

In shocked disbelief Micki's eyes darted from Wolf to her father, who looked, for a moment, like a time bomb ready to go off. His eyes had a murderous gleam and a

156

muscle in his jaw twitched from the pressure of his clenched teeth. Was Wolf trying to get himself killed? What had possessed him to say such a thing? Trying to ward off the fight she felt sure was coming, Micki rushed into speech.

"Dad, let me explain." Micki scrambled off the bed and ran to her father, placing a detaining hand on the bunched-up muscle in his arm. "It happened—" That was as far as she got.

"It happened," Wolf repeated her words with cold finality, "because we both wanted it to happen." Ignoring her gasp, he stared coolly into Bruce's furious eyes. "Cool off, Bruce. So, okay, we didn't wait for the words, the ring, the document." He paused, then underlined, "Did you?"

The question caught Micki by surprise and in unwilling curiosity she glanced at her father's face.

"No."

Even though the light of battle had gone out of Bruce's eyes and Micki could feel the tension easing in his arm, Bruce had not given the answer. The softly spoken word had come from Regina who stood, until now unnoticed, in the doorway. Bruce turned his head to gaze for several seconds into his wife's composed face then, turning back to Wolf, Bruce echoed honestly, "No, we didn't wait."

"I *am* going to marry her, Bruce."

Wolf's statement, delivered with what Micki thought was overbearing confidence, vanquished what was left of her father's anger while at the same time igniting her own. Before she could voice her protest however, her father again clasped Wolf's hand.

"You've made your point, Wolf. I'm sorry if I came on a little heavily as the outraged father, but Micki's my only child and very important to me."

"I understand." Wolf accepted his surrender gracefully. "I'll take very good care of her, Bruce."

Feeling invisible, anger seethed inside Micki. Wasn't she going to be allowed to speak at all? Apparently not, for before she could open her mouth, Regina suggested from the doorway, "We still have that bottle of champagne we were saving for a special occasion, Bruce. Don't you think this is the time to open it?"

"The perfect time," Bruce agreed, grinning broadly. "What are we standing here for? Let's go crack it open." He turned, began walking to the doorway, then, as if in afterthought, glanced back at Micki. "You feel all right now, honey?"

She wasn't even allowed to hand out her own health reports, for Wolf answered for her.

"She's fine now. I think the excitement got to her."

Excitement! You fatuous jerk, Micki thought furiously, *I'll excitement you!* Frustrated anger searing her throat, Micki watched her father drape his arm around Regina's shoulders as he left the room. The moment they were out of hearing she turned on Wolf.

"Have you gone mad?" Incensed, she spat the words at him. "I wouldn't marry you if I was ugly as sin and desperate. And, as you got yourself into this, you can damned well get yourself out of it. I'm going down there and stop them before they open that stupid bottle."

She spun away from him only to be spun right back again forcefully. Wolf's hand grasping her upper arm held her still. His voice, cold as ice, sent a chill skipping down her spine.

"No, you're not." His eyes bored into hers like steel drill bits. "You are going down there with me and accept their toast, and, as soon as they are back from the coast, you are going to marry me. You owe me."

"I owe you!" In her astonishment at his charge Micki missed the menace in his tone. "I owe you nothing."

"You owe me," he repeated coldly. "One child. When you produce that child, you may have your freedom."

Eyes widening in disbelief, Micki stared at him. *He isn't mad*, she thought wildly, *he's a raving maniac*. Fighting to control the renewed panic in her voice, she sneered,

"You have got to be kidding. There is no way I'd share a child with you."

"I didn't say share it," Wolf sneered back. "I said produce it. You chased my baby," he added crudely, "and you're going to damn well replace it."

"But that was six years ago!" Micki cried, not even attempting to correct him about how the child was lost.

"I don't give a damn if it was a hundred and six years ago. You're going to give me my child, my legitimate child. So stop arguing and let's go down and join the celebration." He started toward the door, dragging her with him. Before stepping through the doorway he paused, cocking one eyebrow at her. "Unless, of course, you want me to give your father—in minute detail—a blow-by-blow description of the weekend we spent together?" Again he paused before adding silkily, "And exactly how old you were at the time? You have"—he glanced at his watch unconcernedly—"fifteen seconds to decide."

A picture of her father's outraged expression of a few minutes ago followed by the fury he'd displayed about her being in Tony's apartment flashed through Micki's mind. Decide? What was to decide? She knew positively that should Wolf tell her father about that weekend their relationship would be irreparably damaged. Oh, he would not stop loving her, but he would never trust her again. The taste of defeat burning bitterly in her throat, she lashed out at him unthinkingly, "You rotten son-of-a—"

"Watch it." Wolf's warning, though soft, silenced her. Releasing her, he strode out of the room and along the hall. For one rebellious second Micki hesitated, then, hating herself, she hurried after him.

Wolf stayed long after the last drops of wine had been drained from the bottle. Stretched out lazily on a chair in the living room as if he belonged there, he smilingly lied through his teeth to her father and Regina.

Yes, he had been seeing Micki for some time, he assured them. And yes, they were both sure they did not want a large wedding. And no, unfortunately, they would not be able to get away on a honeymoon trip at this time, as, he was sure, Bruce and Regina could fully understand.

That part puzzled her. Why could her father and Regina fully understand that of all things? That question was answered for her after Wolf finally left, making a big production of drawing her out onto the porch with him, ostensibly to bestow a good-night kiss, in reality to warn: "Don't say anything stupid."

Flaming mad, Micki went back into the house prepared to take her chances and tell her father the truth. Her father's first words to her rang the death knell on that idea.

"You've made me very proud and happy, honey," he praised her seriously. "With the permissive attitude that seems to be the standard with young people today, well, I must admit I've had some very uneasy moments the last few years worrying about your future." Pausing to heave a sigh of relief, he grinned. "Like most fathers I hoped you'd marry well, but I've never dared to hope you'd do this well."

Her guns effectively spiked, Micki pondered his words in confusion. Somewhere along the road she had definitely missed something. Her father spoke as if he not only knew Wolf, but knew him well. And it was more than apparent that his opinion of Wolf differed vastly from Darrel's. Choosing her words carefully, Micki tried to close her intelligence gap.

"I'm relieved that you're pleased," she said slowly. "I was a little apprehensive about your reaction."

"Apprehensive?" Bruce's eyebrows shot up. "But why?"

"Well." Micki stole a glance at Regina. "He does have something of a reputation with women, doesn't he?"

"Micki," Regina inserted urgently before her father could answer. "Please let me explain."

"What's to explain?" Bruce waved his hand expressively. "So over the years he's been seen with a lot of different

160

women. He chose you. Good Lord, did you think I wouldn't realize what a compliment that is? The man is a millionaire several times over and a damned attractive one in the bargain. I'd have to be out of my mind to object to him as a son-in-law."

Micki's attention to her father's small speech ended with the words *millionaire several times over*. Wolf, a millionaire? Micki shuddered. Forcing herself to concentrate, she caught her father's last words.

"—and I have enormous respect for him. You just put your mind at rest about the other women, honey. At thirty-six he's obviously been waiting for the right woman. I'm delighted that woman is you."

What could she possibly say? There was no way she could look into his happy face and say, *Look, Dad, I hate to burst your bubble, but the threat of a firing squad wouldn't make me marry Wolf Renninger. Why? Because you see, Dad, he only wants me for the length of time it will take to produce one child. A child he mistakenly thinks I owe him. He may be wealthy and he may be attractive, but he is also vindictive and he wants what he believes is his due. And, Dad, I'm afraid that in the process he is going to tear me into tiny little pieces.* No, she very definitely could not say that.

What to do then? Micki shuddered. There was nothing she could say to him. Fatalistically Micki determined to give Wolf his due then run for what was left of her life. Hell, she shrugged mentally, everyone got divorced today anyway. Her mind made up, Micki pushed aside the small voice that cried, *That attitude may work for other people but not for you, it will destroy you.*

Presently the conversation switched from that of Micki's future wedding to the more immediate topic of Bruce and Regina's vacation trip. After receiving her father's repeated instructions on what to do if . . . with a gentle smile, Micki excused herself and went to her room. Convinced she wouldn't sleep, yet deciding she may as well be comfortable while awake, she had a tepid shower, slipped a nightie over her head, and slid between the sheets, where the exhausting events of the day caught up with her and she fell promptly asleep.

The morning was half gone before Micki woke. Feeling dull and still tired, she lay staring at the ceiling trying to come to grips with the unbelievable happenings of the night before. That Wolf was a millionaire was in itself plenty to think about, especially as she had begun to suspect Darrel was right in his assessment of him. But that her father obviously knew him much better than she did herself, and liked him as well, was almost too much to assimilate. How had they originally met? And not only how, but why had they become so well acquainted? Wolf had called her father Bruce. Not sir, or even Mr. Durrant, but Bruce, and to Micki that indicated a friendship, at least of sorts. Frowning, Micki got out of bed. She would simply have to ask someone.

She found that someone sitting at the kitchen table drinking coffee.

"Good morning, Micki." Pushing his chair back, Wolf rose to his feet, his eyes cautioning her to watch her reaction to his presence.

"Good morning," she managed huskily. "What are—I didn't expect to see you this morning."

"Wolf's going to drive us to the airport," Bruce said placidly. "He's got the motel station wagon."

"How nice," Micki cooed, looking away from the silvery eyes that sparked with fire at her tone. "And at exactly what time does the exodus begin?"

Unaccustomed to sarcasm from her, Bruce and Regina turned surprised eyes to her.

"Are you all right, princess?" Bruce asked, a frown creasing his forehead.

"Yes, of course, I'm sorry." Micki was instantly contrite. For heaven's sake, she chided herself, a sarcastic mouth won't solve anything. Lowering her eyes, she murmured, "I think I'm missing you already, and you haven't even left yet."

"I knew it," Regina wailed in dismay. "I knew it was too soon after her homecoming to go away."

"No, Regina, really," Micki rushed to assure her. "I don't mind. I guess I'm still a little washed out from yesterday."

Bruce's eyes flicked from his wife to his daughter, an indecisive expression on his face. While Wolf sat silently, his eyes narrowing on Micki.

"Bruce," Regina said softly, "maybe with the wedding coming up this isn't the best time—"

"This is the perfect time," Wolf interrupted quietly. "If anyone has earned a vacation, you two have." His glance, cold and hard, sliced back to Micki. "You leave the 'princess' to me."

"We-ell, if you're positive," Bruce asked hopefully.

"I'm positive," Wolf replied in a hard tone. Then, his tone lighter, he grinned. "By the time you get back, all the arrangements will have been made and you can sit back and enjoy watching me hang myself."

Bruce and Regina returned his grin and the bad moment was past, except for Micki, who wanted very badly to slap Wolf's grinning face.

The jet made its charge down the runway and then it was airborne, its nose lifting regally toward the sky. Biting her lip, Micki watched the plane until it was swallowed up into the sun-splashed expanse of blue.

"Come on, Micki," Wolf chided dryly. "I'll take you home and let you cry on my shoulder."

Micki flinched away from his voice and the hand he placed at the back of her waist. Ignoring the hard thump her heart gave at the forbidding lines his face set into, Micki moved away from him quickly. At the car she again shook off his helping hand and slid onto the seat without looking at him. The way he palmed the gear lever as he shot out of the parking area told her clearly how angry she'd made him.

The silence was broken only one time on the drive back to her home. That was when he asked, "Would you like to stop for dinner?" And she answered, "No, thank you."

When he stopped the car in front of the house and reached for his door release, she said sharply, "Please, don't bother to get out. I'm tired, I have to work tomorrow and I'm going to bed."

His detaining hand prevented her from leaving the car. His voice low, almost pleasant, advised, "I think you should give a week's notice tomorrow."

"Give notice?" she repeated incredulously. "I'll do nothing of the kind. I have no intention of quitting my job."

"I won't have you working after we're married, Micki," he stated flatly.

"We're not married yet," she snapped. "Now let go of my arm, I want to go in."

Surprisingly he did, but she could feel his icy eyes boring into her back until she closed the front door and heard the car roar away from the curb.

The week that followed was nerve-racking for Micki. Business was slow at a time she very badly needed to keep busy. Wolf did not come to the house or call all week, and by Sunday night she had to mentally chide herself to stop pacing.

What was he trying to do? She had heard him tell her father that all the arrangements would be made when he and Regina got back and they would be home in one more week. Was he trying to upset her? Make her nervous? The questions tormented her as she paced from room to room, tired but too uptight to sit still.

Monday afternoon, busy at last checking over the arrival of a shipment of clothes purchased for the holiday season, Micki went into the shop to question Jennell on an item, not bothering to look up when the door opened.

"On your toes," Jennell drawled softly. "The boss just walked in with a very enticing piece on his arm."

Glancing up, Micki felt her stomach flip and heard her breath hiss through her dry lips. Cool, relaxed Wolf walked toward her, his head bent slightly to one side as he listened to what the woman beside him said. A small smile playing at his lips, he nodded, then lifted his head to stare coolly into Micki's eyes.

"Hello, Jennell." Wolf's smile deepened. "This is Brenda Rider, Micki's replacement."

During the short, shocked silence that followed Wolf's announcement, Micki felt her hands go cold while her temper flared red hot.

"Micki's re—?" Jennell stopped short, her eyes flying to Micki's. "You're leaving?"

"Yes," Wolf answered for her. "To get married." A wicked light sprang into his eyes as he tacked on casually. "To me."

"Married!"

"Married!"

Jennell's outcry was echoed by Lucy, who at that moment came out of the stockroom to see what was keeping Micki.

"But she never said a word," Jennell moaned. Turning reproachful eyes on Micki, she asked. "Honey, why didn't you tell us?"

"I think I can answer that." Wolf again answered for her. "Micki wanted an easy, comfortable working relationship with you girls and she was afraid if she told you that would not be possible."

"Yes, I see," Jennell murmured, then, her eyes widening in alarm, she gasped. "Oh, Micki, that first day, I told you about—"

"It doesn't matter," Micki, fully aware that Jennell was referring to the previous buyer, cut in hastily. "It's of no

165

importance really." Ignoring the questioning look Wolf leveled at her, she turned to the woman with him. "How do you do, Brenda. I'm, as you heard, Micki and this is Jennell and Lucy." A small devil taking sudden possession of her, Micki lifted her hand, waved it in a shooing motion at Wolf and ordered, "Go away, Wolf, we'll take care of Brenda."

Another small silence followed Jennell's and Lucy's barely concealed gasps. Smiling sardonically, Wolf walked up to Micki, bent his head, and kissed her soundly on the mouth. When he lifted his head he grinned wickedly before, strolling to the door, he drawled, "You're the boss, baby—for now."

When she left the shop he was waiting for her, as she knew he would be. Falling into step beside her, he said, "We're having dinner together. I think it's time we talked."

He took her to a small, elegant, dimly lit dining room in another casino hotel. As it was still fairly early, only two of the room's tables were occupied, and given their choice of empty tables, Wolf indicated his preference for a secluded corner on the far side of the room. As they waited for their pre-dinner drinks, Micki's eyes scanned the room, the other diners, the black-jacketed waiter, everywhere but Wolf's face. When the drinks were served, Micki smiled vaguely at the waiter and studied his slender, retreating form, wondering irrelevantly if he had to lay flat on his back to close his skintight slacks.

"Now that you've done a complete inventory of the place and its occupants," Wolf inquired dryly, "do you think you could force your attention in this direction?"

Micki turned her head slowly, a disdainful expression on her face. Her icy glance didn't quite come off, however, as the flush that tinged her cheeks robbed it of its effect. Wolf, sipping at his Rob Roy, watched Micki intently, which deepened the heat in her face even more. Unable to maintain his narrow-eyed survey, Micki lowered her eyes to the frothy piña colada in front of her. His soft, weary-sounding sigh drew her eyes back to his.

"How did it go with Brenda this afternoon?" His even tone warned her he was just about at the end of his patience.

"Very well," she answered tightly, not even trying to hide her resentment. "As I'm very well aware you knew it would."

"Cool off, Micki," he advised softly. "We're not going to get anywhere if you blow your cork."

"What gives you the idea I want to get anywhere?" she asked coldly.

"Step down, honey," Wolf cautioned. "Okay, you're steamed, but damn it, Micki, I asked you to give notice. Why the hell didn't you?"

"I told you I didn't want to give up my job." Micki spat the words at him. "And I will not be ordered—" She broke off as the waiter approached their table to take their dinner orders. The minute he'd walked away again, Micki snapped angrily, "I will not be ordered around."

"And I told you I don't want my wife working," Wolf snapped back.

"I'm not your wife yet." Micki had to speak very softly to keep from shouting. "And I don't want—"

"I don't particularly care what you want," Wolf cut across her soft voice coldly. "It's done, you've been replaced, face it. Face this as well, there is no way you're getting out of this marriage, I want what's mine, and I usually get what I want."

"Spoken like a dyed-in-the-wool spoiled brat," Micki sneered. "It must be wonderful to be rich."

"It sure as hell beats being poor," Wolf taunted, his lips twitching with amusement. "I'll give you six months, then ask you if you agree." Then his face sobered and the near-smile disappeared. "You may have anything your tiny little heart desires as my wife, Micki."

For some reason the hard emphasis he'd placed on the

word *tiny* caused a sharp pain in the area mentioned. Hating the idea that he could hurt her so effortlessly, Micki taunted nastily, "In exchange for one child?"

"Precisely," Wolf answered coldly.

Once again they fell silent as the waiter served their meal. Staring at the food disinterestedly, Micki felt her eyes burning suddenly with a rush of memories. How totally different this was compared to the makeshift meals they had laughingly prepared and shared that long-ago weekend.

Automatically Micki put food in her mouth, chewed without tasting, desperately loving the Wolf she'd known then, desperately trying to hate the Wolf who sat opposite her now. When he spoke, his tone had thawed, but the taunting note remained.

"Would you care to hear my family's history?"

"If I must." Glancing up sharply, Micki leveled an accusing look at him. "I've been working for you right along, haven't I?"

"I honestly didn't know it, Micki." Wolf's tone held the clear tone of truth. "I seldom bother with the shops in any way. Not, that is, until the last few months."

"The previous buyer?" Micki asked oversweetly.

"The previous buyer," he agreed calmly. "She was no babe-in-the-woods; she knew the score. I suspect her vision was clouded by dollar signs. When she became possessive, I shipped her out." He paused, one brow raised as if asking if there were any questions. When there were none, he continued. "As I had done the shipping, I was given the job of replacing. I asked for a list of qualified possibles; your name was on it."

"You chose me deliberately?" she asked tightly, hating the thought of the previous buyer, yet refusing to let him know.

"Yes," Wolf answered bluntly.

"As a replacement in the store?" Micki asked smoothly. "Or—other places?"

"Don't push it, Micki," he warned softly.

"Okay." Micki backed off hastily. "Commence with the history."

"It's a long story," Wolf began. "But I'll cut it to the bone. It started with my great-grandfather who, as a young man, bought an inn with rooms for overnight guests along the Lancaster Pike near Lancaster, Pennsylvania. He prospered and as he did, he bought more inns and several small hotels in the southeastern part of the state. He was a rich man by the time he declared he was ready to retire. Leaving the running of his business in the capable hands of his only child, my grandfather, he grabbed his long-patient wife and took off for Florida."

Here his story was interrupted as the waiter came to clear the table and take their order for coffee and liqueurs. When that service had been completed, Wolf continued his narrative.

"Like most men who survive on work, he couldn't rest until he'd explored the possibilities in Florida. Before he died he'd acquired six hotels along the southeast coast. When he died he was a millionaire. My grandfather followed bravely in his footsteps. Deciding to take a chance, he invested heavily in a new type of travelers' accommodations: the motels. Payday, bonanza, and the whole bit. It was a smashingly successful venture."

Now he paused to light the darkest, slimmest cigar Micki had ever seen. After puffing contentedly several times, he resumed his tale.

"My grandfather's marriage had produced two sons. My father," he grinned, "Wolfgang the third, and my uncle Eric, who was ten years his junior. Eric was killed in the last days of Korea. His death triggered a heart attack that killed my grandfather a few months later. As Eric was childless, the growing monster, as we called the family business, went to my father. Here's where my mother enters the picture. Working beside him, she learned the business inside out. My father had one passion

169

besides my mother. He loved to sail. He was drowned, blown overboard, during a yacht race off the coast of South America. That left my mother and the rest of us to manage the business."

"The rest of you?" Micki probed.

"My father had better luck than his father and grandfather," Wolf supplied. "I have two brothers and a sister. My sister's the baby." Taking a test sip of his coffee, he glanced around the now-crowded room. "Family history to be continued," he said quietly. "Drink your coffee, Micki, and let's get out of here."

CHAPTER 10

They were quiet as they left the hotel, the quiet broken only when Wolf asked if Micki would like to gamble awhile before going home. Her only answer was a sharp shake of her head, which he accepted without comment.

"Go on with your story," Micki urged as soon as they'd left the heaviest traffic behind. "Or should I say your saga?"

"Got you interested against your will," Wolf taunted gently. "Didn't I?"

His soft, teasing tone did strange things to her breathing and for a flashing instant she ached all over for the feel of his arms around her. The mere thought of his mouth against hers drew a low moan from her throat that she somehow managed to turn into a whispered, "Yes."

"Where was I?" he asked himself. "Oh, yes, my brothers and sister. Eric is thirty-four, dark, unbelievably handsome and married to a rather plain, incredibly lovely young woman we all adore. They have two fair-haired, beautiful little girls. Eric takes care of the southeast, and now Honolulu, operations."

"Where does he live?" Micki asked when he stopped to draw a deep breath.

"Near Miami," Wolf replied. "Brett is thirty-one, taller than I, very slim, fair like our mother, not quite as handsome as Eric, and married one year to a vivacious redheaded ex-airline stewardess. They have no children—too busy having fun. They live in Atlanta. Brett handles things in the mid-Atlantic coastal area. While I, as you've probably figured out by now, take care of the northeast coastal area business."

Wolf grew quiet as he lit another cigar. Deciding she liked the strong, aromatic odor of the tobacco, Micki inhaled slowly before enquiring. "Is your mother retired?"

"My mother?" Wolf laughed. "Hardly. At sixty-one, she is still beautiful, energetic, and she holds the reins on the rest of us with iron control. She saw the potential in condominiums a long time ago. It was through her that the company branched out to include them. Now"—he shot her a smile that made her heart skip—"I've covered everyone but Diane. As I stated, Di is the baby of the outfit. She just turned thirty. She's blond, a beautiful reflection of our mother, and every bit as headstrong. When she finished college, she told mother she wanted to work but she wanted to do something different." He threw her a what-can-I-tell-you look. "Mother listened to her ideas, thought about it all of ten minutes, then, presto, we're in the boutique business. Di worked like hell in the shops until going into semi-retirement when her first child was born five years ago, she has two boys. Di and her husband also live near Miami, as does our mother. Her husband took on the mantle of manager."

"Hank Carlton," Micki inserted his name.

"Yes." They had been parked in front of her home for several minutes. Now, stepping out of the car, Wolf finished. "And there you have it. Any questions?"

"Yes," Micki answered, sliding off the seat. "Several."

"How about posing them over a cold drink?" he chided softly when she'd stopped short at the door. "All that talking has dried me out."

Micki stared at him for some moments before, giving in with a short nod, she unlocked the door and went in. Heading for the kitchen, she waved at the living room and murmured, "Make yourself comfortable. I can't offer you a Rob Roy, will scotch and soda do?"

"Plain water," he called after her. "Two ice cubes."

When she went into the living room, his drink in one hand, a glass of iced tea for herself in the other, he was sitting on the sofa, long legs stretched out in front of him, his head back, eyes closed. He had removed his jacket and tie and had opened the first three buttons of his shirt and the sheer, masculine sight of him sent a shaft of longing through her that was so intense her hands trembled. His eyes opened at the tinkling sound made by the ice tapping the insides of the glasses. Straightening, he took the glass she extended, patted the cushion beside him, and said, "Light and fire away."

Micki sat in the very center of the cushion, then stared into her glass to avoid looking into Wolf's amusement-filled eyes.

"How and when did you meet my father?" she blurted suddenly.

"I met him a few months before I met you." Although Wolf's tone was serious, it held a fine thread of laughter. "He handled the real estate transaction on the property where the motel now stands. He has been involved in every one of our property transactions in this area since then."

Micki turned wide, astonished eyes to him. "The big deal they were celebrating Saturday a week ago, that was yours?"

"The company's," he corrected gently. "Yes. And the big deal concerned not only another motel in the area, but a condominium in Cape May as well. Your father, several other realtors, and I had our work cut out for us talking Bianca Perriot out of the land the condo's going up on. Over six years of work as a matter of fact."

"Bianca Perriot?" Micki repeated faintly, a sick feeling invading her stomach.

"You remember, you met her a few weeks ago," Wolf prompted.

"Yes, of course, a lovely woman." Micki hesitated, but she had to ask, had to know. "You said over six years ago?"

Nodding, Wolf smiled ruefully. "The property had been in her husband's family for years. She wasn't sure if she should let it go." His tone took on a bitter edge. "She's the person I had an appointment with the day I brought you home from the boat. She batted all of us back and forth like tennis balls until a few weeks ago. It was motels and condos that brought me into this area in the first place."

Feeling foolish and stupid for the suspicions she'd harbored about Bianca, Micki was only too glad to change the subject.

"Brought you from where?"

"I was fairly well established in a New York office when I received orders from H.Q. to scout out the possibilities along the south Jersey coast," Wolf enlightened her. "At first I sent my assistant, whose reports were not very promising. I relayed the reports to H.Q. and received in reply just eight words. They were *If you want a job done right, move.* I moved."

Unable to believe anyone would dare issue an order like that to him, let alone that he'd meekly obey it, Micki stared at him in wide-eyed wonder.

At the look of shocked incredulity on her face, Wolf threw his head back and roared.

"Oh, honey," he finally managed between gasps for breath. "I assure you I did—post-haste. When that chairlady of the board gives an order, people better jump, most especially her sons. Since she took over, she has nearly tripled the company's combined income. No one argues with her."

174

"I see," Micki said softly, then a trifle fearfully, "and will I be expected to meet this business wizard?"

"Most certainly," he grinned. "She's looking forward to it breathlessly. But don't let the thought throw you, it's only her sons she cracks the whip at. Away from the office she's the most charming woman you could meet and a very understanding mother-in-law to my brothers' wives."

"You said," Micki rushed in as soon as he'd finished, "she's looking forward to meeting me. She knows about me?"

"Of course," Wolf answered easily. "I told her I was getting married when I flew to Miami to fill her in on the latest developments here." He paused before adding sardonically, "I was gone all last week—in case you hadn't noticed."

Micki felt her cheeks grow warm at the piercing look he gave her, and trying to hide her nervousness, she jumped up and asked, "Can I get you another drink?"

"No, thank you." Wolf's tone had changed. All business now, he went on briskly. "Sit down, Micki, we have plans to make."

"What plans?" Micki asked sharply, sitting down on the exact same spot she'd just vacated.

"You know damned well what plans," Wolf sighed tiredly. "I told your father that everything would be taken care of by the time he and Regina got home and I intend to see that everything is." His tone went brisk again. "Now we can do this the easy way, or we can do it the hard way, but, either way, it will be done. So, if you have any preferences, let's hear them."

"Like what, for instance?"

"Damn it, Micki." Wolf stood up abruptly, as if having to get away from her, and strode across the room. Turning suddenly, he raked his long-fingered hand through his hair and barked, "You know like what. Like do you want a church wedding with all the attendant hoopla, or would you prefer something more simple? If you want a big

175

splash, we have got to get it together. As I understand it, a large wedding takes several months to arrange. Personally I'd just as soon get it over with. The sooner the better."

Subdued by his outburst, Micki sat silent so long Wolf growled, "For chrissake, Micki, talk to me or I'll go ahead on my own and make all the arrangements."

"You seem to forget," Micki shouted at him. "I don't want to get married at all."

Striding back across the room, Wolf bent over her and said harshly, "I haven't forgotten a thing. Not one single thing. Do you understand?"

Cringing back into the sofa, Micki whispered, "Yes, damn you." Closing her eyes against the hard glitter in his, she added, "Make any plans you like. It means nothing to me."

She felt him move closer to her, felt his warm breath whisper over her skin an instant before his mouth covered hers. Steeling herself against an onslaught, she was completely undone by the gentleness of his kiss. His lips explored hers tenderly, coaxing them apart as he sat down beside her and drew her gently into his arms. Determined to remain cold in his arms, Micki groaned with dismay when her mouth, then her body, responded hungrily to his. Bringing her hands up to his chest to push him away, her fingers, as if with a mind of their own, sought his warm skin at the opening of his shirt. She was trembling on the brink of surrender when he lifted his head and whispered, "I think I'll very much enjoy making you eat your words. But don't worry about it, I'll sweeten them for you."

Shocked into cold reality by his taunt, Micki pushed at his chest. Breathing harshly, she growled, "Get out of here. I don't want you to touch me or even look at me. You sicken me."

Anger flared in his eyes before his narrowed lids concealed it. Rising to his feet in a quick, fluid movement, he picked up his jacket and headed for the door tossing over his shoulder, "I'll call you when the arrangements are completed."

"Drop dead," Micki called after him, feeling very childish when she heard his mocking laughter.

Micki heard nothing from him until Friday morning. During the interval she received three post cards from her father and Regina, alternately extolling the beauties of the West Coast and their growing excitement about her marriage. Moodily, she'd considered jumping off the Ninth Street Bridge.

Wolf's first words to Micki when she answered the phone Friday morning were "I'll pick you up in half an hour. We're going for the license."

Three hours later they were back at the house, everything taken care of. They would be married, Wolf had informed her coldly, late Tuesday afternoon. It would be a civil ceremony, no fuss, no bother. Even the witnesses would be impersonal county employees.

Wanting to weep and forcing herself not to, Micki held her head high and snapped, "That's fine with me," and walked into the house, forcing herself not to run.

Panic built steadily during the rest of that day and all day Saturday. Sunday brought relief in the form of her father and Regina's return, and chagrin in the form of Wolf's arrival at the house soon afterward.

For several hours Micki managed to avoid speaking directly to Wolf. Intent on keeping her father and Regina talking, she coaxed an almost hour-by-hour description of their activities from them. Finally, unable to pull one more question from her mind, Micki grew silent and tense.

"Now that my inquisitive offspring has apparently run down," Bruce laughed teasingly, "perhaps one of you will answer a few questions for me."

Leaving Wolf to the answering, Micki went to the sink to make a pot of fresh coffee, and as it was already past dinnertime, to prepare a light supper of salad and sandwiches.

Both Bruce and Regina voiced protest at the meager wedding plans. Wolf listened to all their arguments patiently but remained adamant in his resolve to go through with them as stated. The shuffling around as Micki served the hastily put together meal ended the argument. By the time Wolf left, Bruce and Regina had resigned themselves to the inevitable.

Monday morning, Labor Day, Micki stared out her bedroom window at the bright, hot day, and wished she'd accepted Cindy's invitation to join them for a barbecue. Sighing at the memory of Cindy's excitement on hearing that Micki was getting married, she turned listlessly when Regina entered the room.

"We have really got to talk now, Micki," Regina said nervously, "about Wolf, and what happened six years ago."

"I don't see what good—"

"Maybe none," Regina interrupted, closing the door. "I'm afraid I made a bad error in judgment that day."

"Error in judgment?" Micki repeated blankly. "In what way?"

"In the depth of your feelings for Wolf. I thought you an immature teenager infatuated with an older, exciting man. And it wasn't like that, was it? You were very much in love." Without waiting for Micki to comment she went on. "You still are."

"Am I?" Micki asked carelessly.

"Your cool facade doesn't fool me, Micki," Regina chided. "I've watched you ever since you came home. As much as you try to hide it, you light up at the mere mention of his name."

"Why are you doing this, Regina?" Micki whispered.

"Because I must," she answered tightly. "Because I can't let you marry him thinking there had been something between us. There wasn't."

Micki went cold. Then she got hot, blazingly hot.

"Then why did you infer that there was?" Micki asked bitingly. "What was the purpose?"

"I thought I was protecting you," Regina explained. At the look of disgusted disbelief that crossed Micki's face, Regina insisted. "I truly was, Micki. Wolf had been involved with several women that I knew of. But they were mature women able to take care of themselves. You were only nineteen, and when I saw that mark on your neck—" Regina shrugged. "I just felt I had to do something to keep you from getting hurt."

"But I heard you talking to him on the phone," Micki argued.

"On the phone?" Regina looked blank, then confused. "But as far as I can remember, all we talked about was real estate. I had gone to New York with your father against Wolf's advice, and he as much as said I told you so. He had stayed to talk to Bi—"

"I know," Micki cut in weakly.

Later, after Regina left, Micki paced her room like a caged tiger. Six years! The words hammered in her brain. She had run away for nothing! What a fool she'd been! What a child! All this time she could have been with him. That thought brought her to a standstill. But could she? Wolf had had, did have, a reputation with women. How long would she have lasted before he shipped her out of his life? But she had been carrying his child. That he would have wanted. That he still wanted. And that, she thought sadly, was all he wanted.

Even so, she faced Tuesday morning with hope. Wolf had said she could have her freedom after she'd produced a child, but maybe, just maybe, she could make him change his mind. She loved him. She had to try and make him love her too.

Palefaced and trembling in her off-white shantung sheath, Micki stood beside a pearl-gray-suited Wolf and repeated the traditional vows.

The one concession her father had won from Wolf was

that he and Regina would take Micki and Wolf for dinner after the ceremony. He chose a well-known restaurant in Wildwood where, over bright red lobsters, he solemnly lifted his glass of champagne and wished them happiness. Wolf was pleasant and amusing and Micki was trembling with nervousness.

The dinner seemed unending but finally it was over. Her stomach churning, Micki added very little to the banter that flew back and forth between Wolf and her father and Regina as they drove back up the coast.

They were met at the motel by the manager, who wished them smiling congratulations, and a grinning good night. Wolf was quiet as they walked up the stairs and along the hall, so quiet Micki felt all her nerves tighten. The minute he closed the door, she made for the window like a homing pigeon.

"Would you like something to drink?" Wolf's voice came to her from the direction of the kitchen.

She had eaten very little all day, had barely touched her dinner, and had had three glasses of champagne but she said, "Whatever you're having," hoping it would calm her nervousness. She turned as he strolled into the room, a glass in each hand.

"That's a fantastic view," she murmured breathlessly, taking the glass he extended.

"There's one exactly like it in the bedroom," Wolf drawled softly, his eyes lingering on her lips.

Suddenly parched, Micki lifted her glass and drank thirstily, then, her throat on fire, her eyes smarting, she gasped, "What is that?"

"Scotch and water," Wolf laughed softly. "You did say whatever I was drinking."

"Yes," she exhaled deeply. "But if you don't mind, I don't think I can finish this." She handed the now-half-empty glass back to him and turning, added jerkily, "I—I think I'll have a shower."

Forty-five minutes later, clothed only in the filmy nightgown and matching peignoir that had been a bridal gift from her father and Regina, Micki stood in her bare feet, staring out the huge square bedroom window that looked out over the beach and ocean. The bedroom was decorated in the same earth tones as the living room, the furniture modern with straight, clean lines.

Hearing the shower shut off, she shivered and curled her toes into the soft fiber of the carpet. Wolf had come into the room while she was brushing her hair and, with hardly a glance at her, had gone directly into the bathroom. When the bathroom door opened, she closed her eyes. The thick carpet muffled Wolf's light tread and when his finger touched her shoulders she jumped, startled.

"Relax, honey." Wolf's warm breath ruffled the hair at her temple. "This isn't going to hurt a bit."

His hands moving slowly, he slid the peignoir over her shoulders and down her arms to her hands, where the garment dropped soundlessly to the floor. She shivered as his fingers trailed back up her arms to the ribbon bows on her shoulders that kept the gown in place. His lips teasing the sensitive skin behind her ear, his fingers tugged open the bows and the sheer gown slithered sensuously down her body.

For tormenting moments his hands caressed her shoulders, her throat, before he turned her slowly to face him. Raw desire shimmered darkly in his silvery eyes. As he bent his head to hers, Micki, torn between apprehension and anticipation, breathed.

"Oh, Wolf."

Expecting the searing brand of his mouth, Micki closed her eyes. His lips barely touched hers. Light as down he brushed her mouth with his, again and again, slowly building in her a need for his kiss. Adding to the tantalizing touch of his lips, his fingertips drew maddeningly fine lines down the side of her neck. When the tip of his tongue danced along her lower lip, she moaned with the urgency only this man could arouse in her.

181

With a small sob she coiled her arms around his neck and at that moment his mouth crushed hers, while his arms, encircling her body, drew her close to him. His kiss was hard, demanding and giving at the same time, and Micki gave herself up to the sheer joy of it.

Without breaking the kiss, Wolf straightened. His arms, holding her tightly, drew her up with him, then, her toes dangling inches above the floor, he carried her to the side of the bed. Sliding her body against his, he set her back on her feet. Wordlessly he lowered her to the bed and stretched his long length beside her.

All thought ceased for Micki. All she wanted was the feel of his mouth, his hands, his body. It had been so very, very long, and she loved him so very, very much.

Wolf's mouth played with hers, teasing her, delighting her. His tongue pierced and explored while his hands caressed and grew bold, exciting her to the edge of endurance. When his lips left hers she threw back her head to give him access to her throat. Making a moist path, his lips moved down the arched column to the hollow at its base where he paused to explore with his tongue, then, moving on, his lips climbed the soft mound of her breast to its summit, closed around its hard peak.

Micki was unaware of the soft moaning sounds she was making deep in her throat until Wolf, returning to kiss and tongue-tease her neck near her ear, whispered, "That's right, honey, purr for me. Purr like the amoral little cat you are."

It took ten full seconds for his words to sink in and when they did Micki froze.

"What did you say?" Her voice sounded loud after the murmurings of lovemaking.

"I think you heard me." Lifting his head, Wolf looked at her coolly.

"You think I'm immoral?"

"Not immoral, honey, amoral," he corrected. "Like a cat that doesn't know any better."

"Let me go," Micki whispered around the pain in her throat. "I said let me go," she snapped when he made no move to obey. "I don't want you."

"Oh, but you do, and I know it," Wolf whispered. "I'm a male and that's all that's required, isn't it?"

Micki didn't think; she reacted. Curling her hand into a small fist she lifted her arm and punched him right in the mouth. Wolf's head jerked back and then he laughed.

"I really am going to enjoy making you eat your words and anything else that comes to mind."

Moving swiftly he caught her mouth with his, kissing her sensually, erotically until she was breathless and had stopped struggling against him. Then with slow deliberation, using all the expertise he possessed—and that was considerable—he set a blaze burning inside her that only one thing would quench. His own breathing ragged, he growled, "I'll make you forget Tony, and Baxter and God knows how many others. By the time I'm through with you, no other man will ever satisfy you. You may hate me everywhere else, but you'll beg for me in bed."

"No." Micki's head moved from side to side. What did he mean Tony and Baxter and the many others? Surely he didn't think . . .

"Wolf, no, I—"

"Yes," Wolf rasped against her mouth, silencing her.

It was past noon when Micki woke up. She was alone in the bed, and, if the still quiet was any indication, in the apartment. Turning her head wearily on the pillow, she gazed out the huge window at yet another blatantly blue sky. Now, in early September, after a long summer filled with blatantly blue skies, Micki wished for chill, cloudy days to match her mood.

Stirring restlessly, she closed her eyes. Where the hell were all the cold, rainy days people were always singing about? Spreading her fingers, she smoothed her palm over the sheet where Wolf had lain, humiliating heat warming her body. He had made good his threat—several times

183

over. She had not only welcomed him she had urged him to join with her; she had literally begged.

With a groan she rolled over, her body replacing her hand on the now-cool sheet, her face burrowing into the indentation Wolf's head had made in the pillow.

Curling into a tight ball, she wept the tears of the damned. He had stripped her of all pride, all pretense. Inside her head she could hear the echo of her own damnation.

"Wolf, please—please," she had pleaded.

"You'll have to do better than that," Wolf had taunted.

"What do you want of me?" she'd wept.

"Everything," he'd growled harshly. "Your body, your soul, your mind. I'd ask for your heart, but I know you don't possess one."

That, more than anything that followed, had hurt her the most. He thought her amoral. A hedonistic little alley cat incapable of deep affection or love. A hard shudder shook her body. She had made one attempt to tell him how she felt. Nearly incoherent, sobbing into his shoulder, she'd pleaded, "Wolf, please, don't do this to me. I love you."

Wolf had become still for a moment, and then his harsh laughter struck her with more force than if he'd used his fist on her.

"Oh, sure," he'd taunted coldly. "Me and Tony and Baxter and probably every other male you've ever met in between. Save your love song for the naive ones. I don't need or want it. But I do want everything else. So coax me, honey. Change your love song to a lust song and I just might hear you."

And all the time he'd been inflicting those hurtful words on her he'd also been inflicting an exquisite brand of torture. With his hands, with his mouth, with his entire body, he had pushed her up one side of the mountain called desire and chased her down the other side.

Mindless, lost, and groping in the world of the senses

he'd created around her, she had clutched at him, pleading, sobbing, begging him to find her, save her.

And when, finally, he had, not once, but over and over again, she had completed her own damnation by humbly thanking him.

Now, alone, eaten alive by a love that no amount of humiliation could change into anything else, Micki wept into the pillow that still held his spicy, masculine scent.

By the time Wolf returned to the apartment, most of the day was gone—as were all traces of the tears she'd shed.

Barefoot, dressed in jeans and a cotton pullover, Micki sat curled up in a chair, an unlooked-at magazine on her lap.

Coming to a stop three feet in front of her chair, Wolf, looking drawn and bone tired in an obviously hand-tailored business suit, studied her makeup-free face broodingly.

"How young you look," he said softly. "Young and innocent and untouched."

"Wolf."

Her anguished cry seemed to snap something inside of him. Flinging himself into the chair opposite hers, he closed his eyes and massaged his forehead with his fingertips. As his hand moved, he raked his fingers through his hair and looked up at her.

"I'm sorry, baby." His voice was raw and soft. "I've had one hell of a day reliving all I said to you, did to you last night. And the damning thing is I meant to do it. Planned to do it."

"Why, Wolf?" Micki whispered brokenly.

"Because I couldn't stand the thought of all those other men," he replied harshly. "Or that you had rejected my child." His eyes, glinting with resentment and anger, pierced hers. "You didn't have to get rid of it, Micki. All you had to do was call me." His voice went raw with emotion. "I'd have taken care of you. I wanted to take care of you."

"But, Wolf, I—"

"You had no right, damn you." Wolf's stinging words cut across hers as if he hadn't heard her. "You had no right to have it scraped from your body like a detested growth."

"Wolf, stop," Micki commanded in sudden anger. "I—oh!" With a gasp she cringed back against the chair, for Wolf had jumped to his feet, crossed the space between them, and stood looming over her.

"Stop, hell," he snarled. "Let's have it out in the open. It's been festering in my guts long enough. I'd have kept it, Micki. I thought that weekend was beautiful and to have a child from it would have made it perfect."

Really afraid of him now, yet unwilling to admit it even to herself, Micki glared up at Wolf and challenged him. "Are you going to beat me, Wolf?"

"Beat you?" Wolf frowned, then followed her eyes as they dropped to his tightly clenched fists. Sighing deeply, he backed up, his fingers slowly uncurling. "No, Micki." He smiled ruefully as he lowered his body wearily into the chair. "I did enough damage to you last night without taking my fists to you." His eyes flashed briefly. "But I felt I had to obliterate in my mind as well as yours the memory of all those other men."

Hot, swift anger seared through Micki's mind. He had said those words one too many times.

"Goddamn you, Wolf, there were no other men!" Micki cried. "There has never been any other man." With a sudden violence that startled him, she flung the magazine across the room and said bitterly, "And I didn't kill or get rid of or chase your baby." The spurt of fire died as quickly as it had flared, leaving her pale face with a haunted look. "I wanted your baby, Wolf." Her voice was husky with remembered pain. "I wanted it desperately. I lost it."

"But you said abortion." Wolf's tone revealed his mental torment. "Your exact words were, 'I haven't felt this bad since the abortion,' don't lie to me, Micki, not now."

"Yes, I said abortion, because that is the correct term." Wolf winced and she added strongly. "That is the correct medical term, Wolf. I did not reject your baby, my body did."

The eyes that stared into hers lost their silver clarity and grew uncertain with doubt. Her eyes filled with tears.

"I don't have to lie to you, Wolf. Go to the hospital. Check the records," she urged. "If the doctor that took care of me is still there, talk to him." Her voice caught on a sob, and brushing the tears from her cheek, she whispered, "I held the thought of your baby very closely, Wolf. Losing it was like losing part of myself."

Wolf was quiet a long time and Micki watched, her bottom lip caught between her teeth, as the clouds of doubt left his eyes.

"Good God!"

The whispered words were more a plea than a curse. Dropping his head back onto the chair, he stared through the window at the sky. When his eyes came back to hers, the silver had changed to a bleak gray.

"Why did you run away from me six years ago, Micki?" he asked wearily. "Was I too old for you? Had I frightened you?"

"No!" Micki exclaimed.

"Then why?" he demanded. "For six years I've asked myself that question. Why, after that fantastic weekend, had you run? When I came for you that night I wanted to give you"—his hand waved in an encompassing circle—"everything. Damn it, Micki, I was prepared to do anything to keep you with me. I wanted to marry you so badly my teeth hurt with the wanting." His tone went ragged. "Why did you run?"

Tears stinging her eyes, Micki swallowed against the tightness in her throat and whispered, "I thought you were having an affair with Regina."

"WHAT!"

The word seemed to bounce off the walls.

187

"I know, now, that it wasn't true," Micki said quickly. "But for six years I thought it was. And I couldn't stay with you thinking you and she had—" Micki shuddered.

"God," Wolf groaned, then, "Tony?" Before she could reply he added harshly, "How I hated that name. It seemed every time I called you all I heard was that name. Tony. Tony. Tony. Even when I mentioned your name in the shop I heard, 'She's in Albany with Tony.' Were you?"

"I went to Albany to attend Tony's wedding," Micki said quietly. "He's a friend. A very good friend. Nothing more."

"And Baxter?"

"Darrel asked me to marry him," she explained. "I said no. And as for any others over the years, casual dates, all of them."

"Come here to me, babe," Wolf coaxed, holding out his arms to her. "You can do whatever you like when you get here. Kiss me, punch me in the mouth again, anything. But come let me hold you."

Jumping out of her chair, Micki ran to him, snuggled into his arms.

"We make a pair," he murmured into her hair. "Me, going out of my mind thinking you're jumping in and out of bed with every guy you meet. And you, eating your heart out because you believed I was sleeping with your stepmother, and God knows how many others. Oh, yes, we make a fine pair. We deserve each other."

"Don't we though?" She laughed up at him.

There is something incongruous about grocery bags sticking out of an open Ferrari, thought Micki suddenly while she lifted the bags off the seat. A small smile curving her lips, she closed the car door with a quick sideways thrust of her hip.

Wolf, waiting at the open kitchen door of the large beachfront rancher, relieved her of her burden with a terse, "Where the hell have you been all this time? Your father and Regina and my mother and the rest of the clan will be here in less than two hours."

"I know, I'm sorry," Micki apologized, dropping her glasses, keys, and handbag onto a chair. "The store was packed," she explained, beginning to empty the bags he'd placed on the table. "And the checkout lines didn't seem to move." She sighed. "And then I ran into Mrs. Jenkins and she talked and talked and—"

"Somewhat like you're doing right now?" Wolf asked dryly.

"Oh, Wolf—" Micki began, then broke off, alarm-filled eyes flying to his at a loud wail from the interior of the house. "Is something wrong with Cub?" she asked anxiously.

"No, of cour—" Another wail reached them.

Dropping the box of snack crackers she was holding, Micki started for the doorway, only to be brought up short by Wolf's hand grasping her wrist.

"Cub is fine," he said firmly. "The nurse is giving him his bath." He grinned. "And you know how much he loves that."

Micki sighed with relief, then gave a gasped "oh" when Wolf, with a quick tug at her wrist, pulled her against him. Holding her loosely in his arms, he complained, "Cub is fine, but I'm feeling neglected." Bending his head, he caught her lips in a light kiss that very quickly turned into a hungry demand.

Bemused, lost in the scorching wonder of Wolf's mouth, Micki was raising her arms to circle his neck when another irritated wail brought her to her senses. Sliding her mouth from his, she scolded, "Wolf, stop it. What if your mother should walk in right now?"

"She'd understand perfectly," Wolf replied blandly. "And say I was a true Renninger," he teased. "Mother's been over that mountain."

Feeling her cheeks go pink, Micki made a move to break

free of his arms. All she accomplished was to find herself held more tightly against him.

"You look tired," he murmured. "I think you should go lie down for a half hour or so. If you like, I'll come with you, rub your back." His eyes gleamed wickedly. "And your front."

While he was speaking, his right hand was moving. Under her sweater, up her side and, on his last word, over her breasts. Even through the lacy material of her bra the hardening tip his fingers found, caressed, proclaimed the effect he was having on her.

Stepping away from her suddenly, he clasped her hand and strode through the room, taking her with him.

"Wolf, the groceries!" Micki yelped, practically running to keep up with him.

Without breaking stride, he growled softly, "That's what I pay a housekeeper for."

When he reached the master bedroom with its wide, sliding glass doors facing the ocean, he swung her inside, slammed the door, and said softly, "We have two hours before the horde descends on us for the birthday party for the Wolf's cub." His eyes caressed her, inflaming her senses. Without conscious thought her fingers went to the zipper on her skirt. Silvery eyes followed her hands and his voice went husky. "I've been waiting for you all afternoon, planning a party of our own."

Watching him yank his gray-and-white velour shirt over his head, desire flared inside Micki, sweeping all thoughts from her mind but one.

Within seconds the floor was littered with their clothing and they were on the large bed, mouth to mouth, flesh to flesh, together.

Her soft throaty moans inflaming him, Wolf husked, "Oh, God, I love you, baby. I love you."

Later, wrapped in Wolf's arms and the afterglow of their lovemaking, Micki sighed in contentment.

"After the way you celebrated your cub's birthday," she

teased softly, her hand stroking over his hip. "I can hardly wait to see what you have planned for our anniversary."

Fleetingly the memory of their wedding night invaded her mind and her hand paused in its caressing movement.

Wolf's soft laughter dissolved the memory. His hand covered hers, urging it onward on its journey down his long, taut thigh.

"Maybe I should put you in charge of planning that party," he murmured against her hair.

Tilting her head back, she looked up into his wickedly gleaming eyes.

"You're getting pretty inventive in that department." Dipping his head, he covered her invitingly parted lips with his own, his hand leaving hers to spread possessively, protectively over her still flat belly. When he lifted his head, his eyes traveled down her body to his hand.

"When are you going to make your announcement?"

"Oh, not until after Wolfgang has been duly honored," she grinned. "Do you think I should tell them I'm already positive this one's a girl? Wolf, what?"

Sitting up suddenly, Wolf had replaced his hand with his lips.

"I love you, my daughter," his warm breath fluttered across her skin, exciting her, warming her. "And I love your mama."

Micki felt tears sting her eyes even as her body moved sensuously under his mouth as he trailed his lips up to her throat.

"And I love her daddy," she whispered huskily, some long moments later.

MORGAN WADE'S WOMAN

CHAPTER 1

Sam pushed through the doors of the tall building that housed the offices of Baker, Baker, and Simmes, Attorneys-at-law, and stood tapping her foot impatiently on the sidewalk. Where was her driver? She was only vaguely aware of the admiring glances turned her way by men passing, both on foot and motorized. She had only to step onto a public street at any time to receive these glances and, quite often, to her disgust, remarks as well.

That Samantha Denning was a strikingly beautiful woman there was no doubt. She stood five feet eight inches in her slim, stockinged feet. She was very slender, with long perfectly shaped legs and softly rounded curves exactly where they belonged. Her face was a perfect oval, the skin fair, with creamy pink cheeks, and a short, straight nose above full red lips that covered perfectly shaped white teeth. Dark brows arched gracefully over large, deep-green eyes, the lids heavily fringed with long, dark lashes. But what one saw first was her hair. Thick, long, wavy, not quite red, but more the color of highly polished, expensive mahogany. It seemed, when it hung loose, to have a will of its own. Subdued now in a coil around her head, it offset perfectly the severely but expensively cut hunter green suit she wore. With a large leather shoulder bag, snug leather gloves, and high-heeled boots, all black, her somewhat somber look was the only concession she would give to mourning clothes. They were none too effective, however, as a few curly tendrils at her temple and in front of her ears had escaped their pins and danced merrily on her face in the soft spring breeze, defying the impression of the dark suit and black accessories.

Samantha tapped her foot even more impatiently as, glancing at the narrow platinum watch on her slim wrist, she thought, *Damn, where is that man?* Looking up, she saw the long, midnight-blue Cadillac glide to a stop opposite her at the curb. Before she took the few steps required to reach the car, the driver had jumped out of the front seat and was holding the door to the back open for her. As he touched her elbow lightly to help her enter, she said crossly, "Where have you been?"

"Sorry, Miss Sam, but the traffic's pretty heavy," he murmured. She glanced out the window to note the truth of his excuse, realizing she had been so deep in thought while she waited she hadn't even noticed.

"Yes, I see, I'm sorry I snapped, Dave. I'm going home now."

Dave smiled to himself as he pulled the big car into the stream of traffic. It was like her to apologize for snapping at him. She was self-willed, haughty, and imperious most of the time with her family and friends, but rarely ever did she speak sharply with the employees.

Dave had been with the Dennings fifteen years now, he as chauffeur and his wife, Beth, as a cook. They respected Mr. Denning, liked his petite, delicate, second wife, and were fond of her young half-sister Deborah. But they both adored Sam, this rebellious, redheaded firebrand, from the day she had come to the big house on Long Island to stay. Dave smiled again as he drove the car expertly through midtown Manhattan toward home, remembering that day seven years before.

What an uproar the house had been in, Mrs. Denning wanting everything perfect for the first meeting with her stepdaughter. Even Mr. Denning's normal reserve seemed about to crack as he and Dave waited for her plane to land. They had expected a shy seventeen-year-old and what they saw walking toward them was a queen.

She had said lightly and unselfconciously, kissing his cheek, "Hello, father," and then had turned as Mr. Denning said in introduction, "This is our driver, Dave Zimmer."

He had been wearing the usual gray uniform and he chuckled to himself now as he remembered the way her eyes had looked him up and down.

"Not mine, not dressed like that at any rate. I'd as soon drop dead as be seen being driven by a liveried chauffeur."

That said, she'd given him the most beautiful smile he'd ever seen and added, "Please, Mr. Dave, could you not wear your everyday clothes if you have ever to drive me?"

He had been lost from that moment. It had been about the same when they had reached the house. Within ten minutes she had overawed her tiny stepmother and equally small halfsister and enslaved the rest of the employees. She had ruled the roost ever since.

He had heard the story years ago, how the quiet, reserved Charles Denning had gone to England on a business trip and returned four months later with a ravishingly beautiful wife from a wealthy British family. Being a wealthy man himself, he had bought the huge house on Long Island for her. But nothing seemed to content her, not her husband or the house or even the daughter she bore eighteen months after their marriage. She missed her friends at home and refused to make new ones in her husband's homeland, referring to them all as gauche. When Samantha was two, she fled to her family, taking the girl with her. Though Charles Denning had fought for custody of his child, his ex-wife's family was powerful and he had to be satisfied with a few visits during those years.

Immediately on Samantha's mother's death, he had instructed his lawyers to notify the family that Samantha was to come to him. She had been back at school in Switzerland when she received the news and requested he allow her to finish her schooling and go ahead with plans made to do her tour of Europe with an American girl she'd been friends with in school for years. Her father had acquiesced to her request but had sworn that when he finally had her home he would keep her there.

Taking a cigarette from her bag and lighting it, Sam leaned back against the pale-blue plush upholstery, looking completely calm and relaxed. Inside she was fuming. How could he do this? Why? She went over it again in her mind, the meeting she had just come from and what had precipitated it.

They had gathered in the library the afternoon before. Her stepmother, Mary, calm now from the tranquilizer her doctor had given her, her half sister, Deb, still looking pale and a little lost, Deb's fiancé, Bryan Tyson, and Sam. Mr. Baker had asked them to assemble at three for the reading of the will. The reading had gone along smoothly without interruption with Mr. Baker's voice droning on about bequests for the employees; then he went on to the family. He went into great detail about what was to be left to Deb and Bryan after their marriage. Sam was very surprised as she learned of the enormity of her father's estate and was deep in thought when Mr. Baker said her name and proceeded with her father's wishes concerning her.

At first Sam stared at him, stunned, then almost sprang from her chair.

"I will not do it. I'll contest the will."

Mr. Baker coughed slightly. "My father thought you would react this way," he replied, "so he instructed me to ask you if you could see him in his office to discuss this tomorrow morning at ten?"

"I'll be there," she said grimly and left the room, not waiting to hear the rest of the will. She had gone to her bedroom to pace the white fur rug, unseeingly touching furniture and the lovely things she had collected over the years. The beautiful room, all white and gold, failed to give her the soothing feeling it usually did. She had been thoroughly agitated and wondered how she could stand it till the morning.

As Sam snubbed out her cigarette, she went over that meeting of an hour ago. Both young Mr. Baker and old Mr. Baker (he had to be in his eighties, although he looked twenty years younger) had been there. Mr. Baker the elder had come directly to the point.

"Miss Denning, I see no way you can possibly break your father's will."

She had been in the process of lighting a cigarette, and he was watching her hands, beautiful hands with long, slender fingers, the nails gracefully oval-shaped, covered with pink polish. The lighter closed loudly in the quiet room. Sam inhaled deeply before replying.

"I don't see why. The terms are ridiculous."

"Not at all, Miss Denning, and not at all unusual."

Well, they certainly seemed so to her. She heard again in her mind Mr. Baker's voice yesterday as he read the stipulations to her inheritance.

11

1. If she married an American citizen by the day she was twenty-five (just five months away) she would receive the sum of five million dollars, to be controlled by the husband and Mr. Baker, with a generous monthly allowance for her own personal use.
2. If in five years time the marriage was still intact; the control of the money would revert to herself and her husband jointly.
3. If the marriage was dissolved within said five-year period, the money would revert back to her father's estate, leaving her with a much smaller monthly allowance.
4. If she chose not to marry within the stipulated time, she was to have a small monthly allowance and a home with her stepmother until such time as she did marry or died.

"I'll forfeit," Sam had declared. "I still have my inheritance from my mother." She knew that amounted to approximately two hundred thousand American dollars.

"I'm afraid not, Miss Denning," Mr. Baker murmured. "You see, before your mother died, she changed her will, leaving your father in complete control of your inheritance, and that money is included with your father's."

Sam sat staring at him, speechless. He then went on to explain why he thought she would be unable to break the will, as her father had certainly been in a sound mind when it was drawn up, also his reasons for so stipulating. Oh, Sam knew his reasons. First, he had thought her too headstrong and concluded she needed the firm hand of a husband to control her. Second, he wanted her to make her home permanently in the States, thus the stipulation she must marry an American citizen. The fact that he had set her twenty-fifth birthday as a time limit probably meant he thought the sooner she was safely married the better.

Mr. Baker told Sam that her father had changed the age limit three times in as many years and had given instructions to have it changed again one month before Sam's birthday. His death negated those instructions.

Sam had left the lawyers' office with her mind in turmoil. Now she was almost home and still had not sorted out her thoughts very well. The amount of the inheritance alone staggered her. Five million dollars! Notwithstanding the strings attached, it was an enormous amount of money. Perhaps she should have expected it, for Deb's share was an equal amount. Yet she would not have been hurt or felt left out if she'd have received much less. She had spent a total of nine of her twenty-four years with her father, Deb had been his from birth.

The Cadillac turned in and along the curved driveway slowly, and Sam looked up at the house. It was a beautiful house, an anachronism really, and the cost of maintaining it was staggering. Yet her father would not give it up. He had loved it, and had considered the money well spent.

Sam entered the house and went directly to the small sitting room in search of her stepmother, thinking how unusually quiet the house had seemed since her father's death. She found both Mary and Deb there, sitting close together, talking quietly. Sam sat down in a chair near them, lit a cigarette, dropped her bag and gloves onto the floor beside her, and said, "It seems it would be useless for me to contest the will." Her voice was low and her eyes had an almost lost look.

"Oh, my dear," her stepmother murmured, reaching her small hand out to her. "Please believe I knew nothing of these conditions in your father's will. If I had, I would have tried to dissuade him. They are quite impossible."

"I know, but I don't think it would have helped anyway. He was determined, in his own mind, to tie me down and keep me here." Then, in a stronger voice laced through with anguish, she added, "Didn't he know how much I'd come to love him and this country?" Her voice dropped to a whisper. "Didn't he know?"

Mary and Deb looked at each other helplessly a moment. They had never seen Sam like this. They had seen her angry often, she and her father had gone into battle regularly and they suspected both thoroughly enjoyed it. They had seen her cool and disdainful. But never had they seen this hurt, vulnerable look.

"Samantha," Mary said softly, "you needn't feel you must fulfill these conditions. I'd be happy to supplement your allowance with some of my own."

Sam's voice caught slightly as she replied, "Thank you," and picking up her bag and gloves stood up and said as she walked quickly to the door, "I'll be in my room if you want me, Mother."

Mary called, "Sam," but Sam was already across the hall and on the stairs. Mary turned to Deb with tears in her eyes. "Go to her."

Deb followed Sam up the stairs and into the bedroom. Standing uncertainly inside the door she asked, "Would you like some company?"

Sam smiled at her gently. "Of course, Poppet, sit down, we can talk while I change." Deb sat on the bed and watched as Sam pulled her boots off, slipped off her skirt and jacket, walked across the room to the closet that completely filled one wall, and hung her clothes away neatly.

Deb's eyes went over her half-sister admiringly as she

stood there in nothing but panty hose and bra. *What a beautiful thing she is,* Deb thought, and wished again, as she had many times before, that she had met Sam's mother. Deb did not envy Sam anything, except, perhaps at times, her height. Like most petite people she sometimes longed to be tall. But as far as looks went, Deb was honest enough with herself to admit she was not lacking in that department. With her dark hair and very fair skin, she was a lovely woman. Deb also realized that the love she had for this tall sister who had come into her life when she was just thirteen bordered on hero worship.

Pulling the pins out of her hair, Sam walked to the white and gold dressing table, sat down, and picking up her hair brush, began brushing her hair in long slow strokes. Set free, her rich auburn hair hung in deep waves halfway down her back. Deb watched her for a short time, her eyes dark with compassion. "What are you going to do, Sam? Do you know?"

Sam's eyes lifted and met Deb's in the mirror. "I really haven't a clue, Poppet. It's quite a bind."

Deb knew how deeply upset Sam was, for the British accent was heavy. Generally there was just a tinge of it in Sam's speech, becoming thick only when she was very angry or upset.

Pensively Sam added, "My first thought was to find a job, but then, what sort of work could I do?" She paused before adding, "You realize, love, I've been extensively and expensively educated, all of which prepared me to do nothing of use. I can ride, swim, play tennis, and golf with the best, I'm also a fair decoration in any room or gathering. None of these things will earn me a dime." She sighed. "Oh, I suppose I could apply for a post as a salesclerk, but who is going to hire the daughter of Charles Denning once they know?"

Deb didn't answer, understanding Sam was sorting it out for herself as well as explaining her options.

"That leaves marriage within five months," Sam went on, "or depending on your mother. The allowance father stipulated in the case I fail to marry in five months' time is less than I've been receiving since the day I first came to this house to live."

"And your mother's inheritance—" Deb began.

"Is tied up with Father's," Sam finished.

"Is there no one you could marry?"

"Oh, there are quite a few I could marry." Sam waved her arms airily. "I must have had at least five proposals of marriage within the last two years, but you see, Poppet, I have no wish to marry any of those men. The idea of spending five days, let alone five years, with any one of them gives me the horrors."

Sam laughed lightly as she walked to the closet and withdrew a white terry robe. "I'm going to take a long hot bath before lunch, maybe that will relax me some. Will you ask Mother to hold lunch a few minutes?"

"Of course," Deb smiled to herself as she left the room. Sam had stopped calling her stepmother Mary and began calling her Mother after their father's death of a heart attack just a week before. The suddenness of his death had shattered his wife and Sam had seemed to take a very protective attitude to both Mary and Deb.

Sam slid her body down into the warm bubbly water and sighed deeply. She wondered now, as she did so often of late, whether she could be an emotional cripple of some sort. She knew she had normal physical urges because she had felt, at times, an almost hurtful, aching need. Yet whenever any of the young men she knew, and there were many, tried to make love to her, she froze. She could respond only lightly to a good-night kiss, and it worried

16

her a little. What she had told Deb was true—the idea of marriage to any of them horrified her. She really didn't know what to do.

Sam woke the next morning to spring sunshine streaming in her windows and a letter postmarked Nevada on her bedside table. "Babs," she said softly, pushing herself into a sitting position as she slit the envelope open. She hadn't heard from her best friend for two months, when Babs had called to tell her her second son had arrived. Sam scanned the pages quickly. Babs began with sincere condolences for all of them, then went on to rhapsodize on the virtues of her youngest. She then came to the most important part of her letter:

> We are having the christening next week and, darling, both Ben and I so want you to be Mark's godmother. You could, of course, stand by proxy, but it would probably do you good to get away for a while at this time, and I do long to see you. Please say you will come. Give my love to the family.

Babs

Sam let the hand holding the letter drop into her lap and mused on it. Should she go? The urge to run had been on her since she'd left the Messrs. Bakers' office. Here was a place to run to. Here was someone to run to. She'd not fallen asleep till very late the night before worrying over what she should do and had reached no decisions. Perhaps talking it over with Babs would help. She had a way of putting things into their proper order of importance. Laughing all the while, Sam thought now, shaking her head and smiling. Sam then sat up straight, swung her long legs off the side of the bed, and picked up the receiver of the white phone that sat on the gilded white and gold table next to her bed. She called her travel agent and made plane reservations for the following Wednesday, then sent a wire to Babs informing her of her arrival day and time.

The big jet was airborne and the seat belt sign blinked out. Sam unfastened her seat belt, moved her seat back, closed her eyes, and relaxed. She felt good and looked it. She hadn't missed the admiring glances sent her way, both in the waiting room, and as she boarded the plane. She was wearing a white crepe long-sleeved blouse with a matching tie at her throat and a soft wool pants suit in a deep shade of pink that set off her almost red hair to perfection. She carried no purse but instead had slung over one shoulder a rather large flight bag in a creamy beige color and wore soft leather high-heeled boots to match.

When she had packed her suitcases she hadn't been quite sure what to take with her. The weather in the East had been unseasonably mild for early March, so she had laid out lightweight clothes. Then on reflection she had put some back into her closet and added a few heavier things. She did not know what the weather was like in the part of Nevada where Babs lived.

Sam smiled slightly to herself with the thought of Babs. Babs of the laughing eyes. Oh, the scrapes Sam had had to extricate her from while they were in school. Babs had an impish streak and had been forever in hot water. Nothing serious, but zany things, usually involving their teachers or later, when they were older, young men. She was bubbly and full of fun and mischief, and to Sam, always cool and composed, fell the task of smoothing the rippled waters. They had become fast friends when they were both twelve years old. The friendship had deepened and

18

matured as the girls grew. They had made the grand tour after leaving school and when Sam had gone to her father in Long Island, Babs had returned to her family in Nevada.

They had been to Europe and Asia together since, and Babs made several shopping trips a year to New York. Then three years ago on one of her trips East, Babs had told Sam she was getting married, almost immediately, to Benjamin Carter, a name Sam had heard often over the years. Babs had assured Sam that she was very much in love, but as she was also very pregnant, couldn't Sam go back to Nevada with her right away and be her maid of honor? Sam went.

Sam had liked Ben Carter on sight. He was a tall, quiet, good-looking young man, and he blatantly adored Babs. The wedding had been a hasty and, as everything involving Babs, hilarious affair, the only off-note being the man whom Ben had wanted as his best man was out of the country and unable to make it back in time for the wedding, much to Ben's disappointment.

Sam had spent just four days in Nevada, and had not seen Babs again until she had made a five-day shopping trip to New York in last August. She had told Sam she was buying a new maternity wardrobe, as she was three months pregnant. They had had a wonderful five days together, making their home base the apartment on the East Side that Sam's father kept for the convenience of the family whenever they had extended stays in the city. She and Babs had torn around shopping all day and had seen a few shows in the evening. Yes, it would be good to see Babs again.

The sign flashed on, Sam fastened her seat belt, then the wheels touched down, and the big plane rolled to a stop. The Las Vegas terminal was, as usual, very busy and Sam stood hesitant a moment. On hearing Babs call her name, she turned to see her and Ben hurrying forward. She smiled as Babs gasped breathlessly, "Oh! We were afraid we were late, we just this minute landed." Ben and Babs lived in the copper regions of the state and kept their own plane for easier mobility.

Babs would always be Babs, and she almost flung herself into Sam's arms, giving her a warm hug. When she stepped back she exclaimed. "It's positively demoralizing for anyone to look as ravishing as you do, Sam . . . how are you?"

"I'm perfectly well, thank you," Sam said, smiling. "You look lovely yourself," she added, her cool eyes going over her friend's slightly full figure. "The extra weight looks good on you."

"Oh, I gained too much carrying Mark." Babs smiled ruefully. "I've still got some to take off."

"You've been saying that for two months," Ben chimed in, but his voice was gentle, and the look he gave his wife caused a odd twist inside Sam.

"Welcome, Sam," he added, putting one arm around her shoulders giving her a light squeeze. "Babs is right, you look terrific."

"Hi, Ben, and thank you, sir," she answered, slipping her arm around his waist to return his hug. "You both look wonderful to me."

Ben laughed. "Now if we can adjourn this meeting of the mutual admiration society, suppose we stop blocking traffic and get out of here."

The women laughed and started moving, Sam asking Babs about the children. That set Babs off, and she went into a discourse about her offspring, talking nonstop, with Sam barely able to get a word in edgewise, while Ben took up Sam's case and led them outside to find a taxi. Finally

Babs came back to earth to say, "We're going to spend the night in Vegas, and fly out to the house in the morning. Okay?" Sam barely had time to smile and nod as Babs rushed on. "I haven't really had a night out since Mark was born and this darling man here has said he is going to buy us a lavish dinner and let me gamble all night if I wish."

"Up to a financial point," Ben said softly, lovingly, as his wife snuggled even closer to him in the back of the cab.

They're so completely, unselfconsciously in love, Sam thought and again felt that twist inside, hating to admit to herself that it was envy. She had always wished only the best for Babs but she could not help thinking if there had been a Ben somewhere for her she would not have this stupid mess she found herself with now. Then she gave a mental shrug, deciding firmly to enjoy her visit with the Carters.

The taxi deposited them at the M.G.M. Grand and Sam looked around curiously as Ben registered for them. It was almost too much to take in at once. The hotel was fantastic, but what caught Sam's attention was the number of people about. It was the middle of the afternoon and everything was crowded.

Babs, watching Sam's face as she looked around, laughed. "You think this is something, wait until tonight." Sam just smiled and still glancing around followed Ben and Babs as they were shown to their rooms. The room was beautifully impersonal, in the manner of good hotels everywhere. Used to staying in the best, Sam nodded her head, glancing around in satisfaction.

They had decided, while still in the cab, to let Sam rest after her flight, and meet for dinner at seven. Babs stated firmly that she intended to nap, as she fully planned to make a night of it.

Sam opened her suitcase, removed the things she'd need for the evening and gave her apple-green lace gown a shake before hanging it up. She then sank into a warm, scented tub. She felt sleepy, she didn't know why, but every plane flight lasting over an hour always left her feeling this way. She was glad Ben and Babs had wanted to stay over. She had never been in Vegas. When she'd come before, she hadn't left the airport, but had gone from one plane to a much smaller one, and flown straight to Babs's parents' home. Sam was curious, as nearly every one of her friends had been to Vegas at least once and had been astonished at finding Sam had not.

Her bath finished, Sam slipped a nightie over her head, called the desk to request a wake-up call at six, and slid between the sheets. She felt deliciously relaxed and wondered idly whom Babs had asked to stand as godfather as she drifted into sleep.

Sam left her room a few minutes before seven, to find Babs and Ben right outside her door. Her eyes went over the two of them appreciatively. Babs was still something to see, even with the added pounds. Small and very fair, with almost white-blond hair and dark-brown brows and lashes on a lovely face with flawless skin, she had a small, pert nose and big brown eyes that forever danced merrily. She was dressed in a burnt-orange chiffon pants suit and looked decidedly delectable. Standing next to her, Ben looked even taller than his six feet and very handsome in the pale blue suit that matched his eyes. A wildly patterned silk shirt in varying shades of blue set off his ruddy good looks and shock of sandy-colored hair.

Babs's eyes went over Sam slowly, taking in the combination of green gown, red hair, and flawless skin. Brown eyes laughing, she gave a small pout.

"Oh, Sam! Any woman that looks as gorgeous as you should be outlawed."

CHAPTER 2

What a night! They had dinner and Babs did some gambling at the M.G.M. but she would not stay in one place. They hit the Sands, Caesars, and other casinos, and while Babs and Ben stood at the tables or played blackjack Sam wandered through the rooms. Sam didn't gamble, but she assured her friends she was completely happy just watching. And watch she did. She was fascinated. She had been to all the posh casinos in Europe but never had she seen anything like this. The magnificence of the decor in the different hotels was worth seeing, but what absorbed Sam were the people. All kinds of people, from all over the world, from the very elegantly dressed to the almost (but not quite) down at heel. Many looked to Sam as if they hadn't slept for days, and the very air seemed to be charged with the excitement of a living thing.

Except for a light tinge of color in her cheeks and an added sparkle in her green eyes, Sam looked as always as she drifted in and out of the rooms—cool, composed, her bearing almost regal. And in a town full of almost unbelievably beautiful women, eyes followed Sam wherever she went. Male eyes avidly; female, enviously.

She had a wonderful time and when Ben announced that they must leave, she was surprised to see it was light outside. They dashed into the M.G.M. to get their valises, change and then taxied to the airport. Within an hour Ben was circling Vegas and heading the Piper toward home, and Babs was strapped into her seat fast asleep. It was a short flight and soon they were at the house.

Sam exclaimed her delight over the large, rambling ranch house set in beautifully landscaped grounds, as Ben grinned at her. "Our mine might not be as grand as the Ruth, but it keeps the wolf from the door." Sam grinned back. She knew that copper was not the only thing Ben's family had, but timber and cattle, and different industries as well.

The house was designed in a U-shape with hallways leading off the large foyer. Babs linked arms with Sam, leading her down the hall to their left to a large airy room, one wall of which was practically all glass. Sam looked around at the light Danish furniture, the deep rose carpet, pale pink walls, and scarlet draperies drawn open at the wall. "What a lovely room, Babs," she murmured, walking to the glass wall to gaze out at what was obviously the back of the house. A beautiful lawn dotted with shrubbery and trees in early soft green bud, due to the unseasonally warm weather, greeted her eyes. At the base of the lawn to her left was a kidney-shaped pool with a patio surrounding it and across from it to Sam's right was a tennis court. Also to Sam's right but closer to the house sat several umbrellaed tables with lawn chairs placed around them. Altogether it was a lovely view. Sam turned back to Babs with a soft smile. "You have a beautiful home, Babs."

Babs nodded in agreement, obviously pleased. "Now come see the most beautiful of all." She led Sam back along the hall near the end where Sam surmised the family bedrooms were and into the nursery. A young girl approximately seventeen sat in a rocking chair, reading to a chubby, towheaded toddler and Sam could see an infant asleep in a crib against the wall. On seeing Babs, the boy cried "Mommy," slid off the girl's lap, and ran into Babs's arms. She swung him up to her, turning to Sam, "Benjie, this is your Aunt Sam," and to Sam proudly, "Ben, Jr." Sam took a chubby little hand into her own, smiled, and said quietly. "Hello, Ben, Jr. I hope you and I will be great friends."

Benjie stared at her with huge brown eyes a moment, then a beautiful smile breaking his face, he stretched out his arms to her, gurgling, "An Sam."

Laughing, Sam took him into her arms, enjoying his sweet, clean smell, while Babs looked on proud and delighted at her son's easy conquest.

"A charmer, just like his father." A voice came from the doorway, and Sam glanced up to see Ben, his face reflecting his wife's pride.

"He certainly is," Sam laughed. Her eyes went back to Benjie. "Would you like to show me your new brother?" He nodded, his face becoming eager as he turned in Sam's arms and pointed a small finger at the crib. Sam walked to the crib and looked down at the small duplicate of the child in her arms. Before she could say anything, Benjie's small finger moved to his lips and he whispered, "Baby seep." Laughing softly, Sam turned to a beaming Babs, "I envy you." It was not a casual compliment, it was true. Sam had felt a shaft of pure envy go through her as she gazed at the sleeping child, and had felt surprised and slightly shocked. Never being around small children much, she had never experienced their enslaving charm. She was completely captured.

Babs smiled at the young girl who was now standing by the rocking chair. "And this is Judy Demillo, my housekeeper's daughter and the baby's nursemaid, among other things. Please be very nice to her, for we must keep her happy." She grinned teasingly. "I could not possibly cope without her."

While Babs was speaking, Sam studied the girl. She was a beauty, very slender, with dark hair and brows and big dark eyes set in a thin, heartshaped face. Her skin had a creamy magnolia texture that was probably the envy of all her friends.

"Hello, Judy," Sam extended her hand, smiling gently, thinking the girl had the look of a timid doe.

"How do you do, Miss Denning." Judy returned Sam's smile shyly. Her small hand was as soft as a baby's, her voice was light, sweet. "Shall I take Benjie now?" Sam gave the boy a quick hug before handing him to Judy.

"I want a shower before lunch," Babs declared, turning toward the door. "And I imagine you do too, Sam." As they left the room Sam smiled at Judy and blew a kiss to Benjie from her fingertips.

Back in the hall Babs went to a door directly across from the nursery. "Lunch in two hours, Sam, and don't fuss. Wear jeans or whatever you're comfortable in. I'll come for you a few minutes early and show you around the house."

Babs knocked on Sam's door an hour and a half later. Sam had unpacked her suitcases, had a quick shower and a short nap, which had taken the edge off her tiredness. Now, dressed in pale-green denim slacks and a hunter-green ribbed pullover, her face devoid of makeup, she looked lovely, if a little pale. Babs had a slightly drawn look herself. She was in blue jeans and a white knit top, which stole all color from her face. She had a fuzzy look around her eyes, which told Sam she had also had a nap. "I'm not used to the night life anymore." Babs laughed tiredly. "I think I'd better have another nap before dinner, if I don't want to fall asleep at the table." As they strolled down the hall, Sam yawned, then grinned apologetically. "I think I'd better do the same."

Sam loved the rambling house. As they went from room to room she noted that the keynote here was comfort. The furnishings were expensive, but casual, and some pieces, Sam's practiced eye told her, were priceless. Yet everything blended perfectly, giving the house a warm, relaxed atmosphere. The contrast between it and the elegant house in Long Island was astonishing. Again Sam felt that odd twinge in her chest, thinking, this is a home for a family, a house for raising children and sharing love, a reflection of the contentment Babs and Ben shared.

Babs saved the kitchen for last. Although Sam's love of cooking would greatly surprise anyone who knew her, other than her own family, Babs knew of it better than any other person. She had followed in Sam's wake into the kitchens of private homes and restaurants for years, standing back, watching Sam beguile and coax recipes from master cooks and chefs. Babs knew of the notebooks full of recipes Sam had collected from all over Europe. Now she watched, a smile on her lips, as Sam stood entranced in the middle of the large, spotlessly clean, fully equipped room. She led her to the small, slim, dark-haired woman preparing lunch at the stove.

"Sam, this is my housekeeper Marie Demillo."

"How do you do," Sam smiled, looking closely at Marie. "I see where Judy's beauty came from."

"Thank you, Miss Denning," Marie beamed. They chatted a few moments, Sam voicing appreciation of the well-kept kitchen, Marie appreciating Sam's appreciation. Lunch was a slow, relaxed affair, Sam and Ben bantering back and forth like longtime friends. Babs smiled contentedly. The man she loved and the friend she had always adored were fast friends. She was completely happy.

They had their coffee in the living room sitting comfortably in the big roomy chairs. Babs, glancing at her husband, murmured lazily. "When can we expect Morgan, darling?"

"I talked to him while you had your nap, and he said to tell you he promised to be here for dinner."

"I don't believe it!" she exclaimed. "Then he'll be here a few days with us. That man could certainly do with a rest." As Ben nodded, Babs caught the look of mild inquiry on Sam's face. "Ben's best friend, Morgan Wade," She explained. "He'll be godfather to your godmother for Mark. As a matter of fact, he's Benjie's godfather too." She paused a moment before chiding, "Come to think of it, you'd be Benjie's godmother, too, if you hadn't been traipsing around Vancouver or wherever at the time."

"I'm sorry now that I was away." Sam grinned at Babs. "I would have loved to have been Benjie's godmother." Searching her memory, she frowned. "Morgan Wade, the name sounds familiar, have I met him?"

"No, I don't think so," Babs mused. "Of course not, he was to be Ben's best man but he couldn't get here in time for the wedding, remember?"

Sam smiled and nodded but thought grimly, *Some wretched friend if he couldn't have made a better effort at the time, considering the swiftness of air travel.* She had thought the same at the time of the wedding, but then, as now, said nothing.

Ben leaned forward offering cigarettes to the women and after he lit them, he said, "I hope you'll like Morg, Sam."

"Morg's like an older brother," Babs chimed in, then

lifted her eyebrows at Ben. "How old is he? Thirty-two, thirty-three?"

"Three," Ben replied, and went on, laughter in his voice, "I dogged his feet like a puppy while I was growing up."

Sam's eyebrows went up in question. Babs supplied the answer. "Morg's a cattleman, has an immense spread upstate. His ancestors were headed for California, got as far as Nevada, and liked what they saw. They settled and the Wade spread has been here ever since. All of them cattlemen, till Morg's father, George. He was a maverick. A friend got him interested in photography while he was still a teen-ager and he was lost to ranching forever."

Ben took up the narrative. "The ranch came to him when Morg was about fourteen, and he installed a manager, allowing himself freedom to accept assignments all over the world, mostly wildlife. As he and my father were close friends, Morg came to us whenever George took on a new assignment. He was with us through most of his teens, seeing his father only at holidays and summer vacation."

"And he's a throwback." Babs laughed. "A cattleman to the core. He loves that spread with a passion. Hates to leave it, that's why I was surprised when Ben said he'll be here today, three days before time. I wouldn't have been at all surprised if he'd have arrived Sunday morning, just in time to go to the church."

Ben lay back in his chair, his legs stretched out, his eyes looking back on memories.

"Old Morg even tried to opt out of college," he reminisced, "but his father finally convinced him that a well-rounded education was necessary, even to a rancher. He worked like hell during his college years, went every summer, did the work of four years in three and still graduated near the top of his class. His father died in Africa of one of those rare things we'd never even heard of while Morgan was in his senior year. Then it was my father who had to talk to him like a Dutch uncle to keep him in school."

Babs again took up the story. "As it turned out, the manager George had hired had not been a good one. When Morgan came home from school at age twenty-one, he found the ranch run down and finances fairly well depleted. And he's been working like a fiend the last twelve years to build it up again. Practically lives on the land, being in the house just about long enough to eat and sleep, if that. Even though he has the best housekeeper this side of St. Louis."

"I don't believe that." They were the first words Sam had uttered in the last half hour.

"Oh, but it's true," Babs laughed, "and Marie would be the first one to tell you that Sara Weaver is a gold mine. She came out here from the Pennsylvania Dutch country with Morgan's mother, Betty, when she married George. And as Betty died in a car accident when Morgan was two, Sara is the closest thing to a mother Morg has ever known." She glanced at Ben. "Except maybe your mother."

Ben nodded. "Yes, Morg's fond of Mother but he was in his teens when he came to us and by then he was Sara's."

"She must have missed him during those years," Sam put in, and again Ben nodded. "And I know he missed her. When he finally came home to stay, even with the money so tight, he re-did the ranch house for her."

Babs piped in, "You should see his kitchen, Sam, it'd blow your mind."

Sam stared at her in disbelief, this from a woman whose

kitchen would blow any cook's mind. Babs laughed gaily and held up one hand.

"Honest injun, it's something else. Marie turns green at the mention of it."

"Then I shan't mention it," Sam promised softly. Babs stood up, stretching and yawning. "I'm going to spend some time with the kids before I go for another nap. Want to join me, Sam?"

"I certainly do," came the reply from an equally drowsy Sam. As they left the room they both smiled fondly at Ben, already half asleep in his chair.

They spent the next hour in the nursery and Sam was given the honor of feeding Mark his bottle. As she held the tiny baby in her arms, Sam again experienced that small shaft of envy. He was so small, so very beautiful, and for the first time in her life Sam wondered what it would be like to have a child of her own. When the boys were put down for their naps, Sam and Babs made for their own beds.

In her room Sam drew the scarlet draperies over the glass wall, pulled her top over her head, then slid out of her sandals and slacks. Stretching out on the bed in her bikini panties and bra, she was instantly asleep. The late afternoon sunrays, the glare muted by the draperies, crawled up the bed, waking Sam when they touched her face. She glanced at the clock by the bed quickly, remembering Babs's parting words: "Dinner at eight, cocktails in the living room at seven thirty."

It was not quite six, so Sam lazed another half hour, not quite asleep yet not fully awake, before she rose to get ready for dinner. She had a long, warm bath, the water scented with salts, and as she soaked she wondered idly what Ben's friend would be like. Shrugging her shoulders carelessly, she stepped out of the tub, patted herself dry, slipped into a lacy bra and briefs and made her face up lightly. After dropping a hot-pink, raw silk caftan over her head, she slid her feet into soft leather sandals while she pulled the pins from her hair, thinking she should have removed them before lying down as her scalp was smarting at spots from their digging in. As she brushed her hair, she decided to wear it loose this evening to let her scalp heal. Giving one last flick with the brush, she looked into the mirror, decided she'd do, and left the room.

Although it was past seven thirty when she entered the living room, she found it empty, and hesitating only a moment, she made for the kitchen, pausing in the doorway to ask, "May I come in, Marie?"

"Of course, Miss Denning," came the reply from Marie, standing at the sink washing vegetables.

"Sam."

"Miss Sam," Marie emphasized.

"Done." Sam walked across the room to stand looking down over Marie's shoulder and added, her voice eager as a child's, "What's for dinner?"

Marie turned a smiling face up to Sam, "Mr. Morgan's a steak man, so I'm broiling Delmonicos on the charcoal grill outside. The foil-wrapped potatoes have been in the coals for an hour already. With that you'll have broccoli hollandaise and a tossed salad."

"Dressing?"

"My own."

"Hmmm, I can't wait," Sam laughed. "And dessert?"

"We'll let that be a surprise."

"Sounds super." Sam smiled, retracing her steps out of the kitchen. She heard voices as she neared the doorway to the living room. On entering, she paused and three heads were turned toward her. For a few moments she had the unreal feeling of a stop-motion effect and was unaware

33

of the picture she made, framed in the doorway. The moment was broken as she stepped out of the frame into the room, and at the same time the three people came to their feet out of their chairs.

Babs walked over to Sam, a vision in teal-blue chiffon, her voice teasing, "We had just decided you were still asleep, and I was delegated to go tip the bed." Sam shook her head lightly and replied softly, "I was in the kitchen with Marie."

"I should have known," Babs laughed.

In the few seconds that this exchange lasted, Sam was sizing up the man standing beside Ben. He was, she judged, at least six feet two inches, perhaps six feet three inches tall. Broad-shouldered, narrow-hipped, long-legged, and slim almost to the point of gauntness. Feeling the short hairs on her nape bristle, Sam thought, *That's the most dangerous-looking male animal I've ever seen.* On the heels of that thought she felt a tiny curl in her stomach which she recognized, in some shock, as fear. Fear? Then she was standing in front of him, hearing Babs say simply, "Samantha Denning—Morgan Wade."

Lifting her eyes, Sam was struck, as if from an actual blow, by the direct, riveting stare from the coldest black eyes she had ever seen.

It seemed the curl grew inside her as she automatically answered "Mr. Wade" to his "Miss Denning," spoken in a disturbingly soft voice. She was fighting an alien sense of panic, his eyes still on her, as she nodded yes to Ben's "Martini, Sam?" The eye contact was broken when Morgan turned to Ben's query to refill his glass, and Sam sank thankfully into a chair.

Sam sat very straight, almost rigid, on the edge of her chair, her face composed, if somewhat pale, showing nothing of the turmoil in her mind. With growing amazement, she wondered at her reaction to this man. Instant dislike she'd have understood. She had experienced that at times. But fear? Yes, a very real, if small, jolt of fear. That she had never experienced before. It was almost as if, in some way, he was a threat to her. She heard Babs's chatting and smiled in her direction. What was she talking about? Sam hadn't the vaguest idea. When Morgan turned back to her to hand her her drink, Sam saw his eyes glitter briefly at her barely whispered "thank you." Hearing the slight tremor in her own voice, she mentally pulled herself up short thinking, enough of this nonsense. Feeling a slow anger beginning to burn inside, she lifted her chin. As she did, black eyes again struck hers, but this time the glance bounced off eyes as cold, as hard as the emerald they matched in color. And as the sun strikes sparks from the stone, her glance struck sparks of challenge. She saw his own glint in acceptance. She had thrown the glove. He had picked it up.

Warfare silently declared, voices slowly penetrated. Something was being said on their roles at the christening, and she made herself relax against the back of the chair, hearing Babs say, "Okay with you, Sam?" Again she smiled and nodded. She would have to question Babs later on this point. Was what okay with her? Sam hadn't the least clue.

Ben asked Morgan Wade something about the ranch, and the conversation switched to ranching in general. Putting a look of interest on her face, Sam sipped at her drink and studied him over the rim of her glass.

He sat lazily in his chair, his long legs stretched out, crossed at the ankles. His arms formed a triangle, elbows on the chair arms, holding his drink with both hands in front of him. His hands were big, the fingers long and slender, and Sam felt a small shiver skip down her spine on seeing his right index finger rub and caress the rim of his glass. She shifted her gaze to his clothes—a lightweight suit, expensive, in a rich brown that almost matched his skin color, with a pale yellow shirt open at the throat, the sight of which also disturbed her vaguely.

Again her gaze shifted, upward, to his face, not quite in profile as he looked at Ben, who was speaking. Decidedly good-looking, almost devastatingly so, saved from being handsome by the almost harsh bone structure. The jaw firm, hard, the nose longish, but straight, well-defined, hard lips, the cheeks high, and overall the brown skin stretched tight, smooth, with shallow hollows under the cheekbones adding to the look of gauntness. Hair as black as his eyes, thick and wiry, growing a little long to curl at the collar and behind the ears. Full black eyebrows, with a slight arch, and the longest, thickest black eyelashes Sam had ever seen on a man.

Babs interrupted the men's talk with "Dinner, bring your drinks" and they drifted into the dining room. It was a disaster. Sam found herself sitting directly across the table from Morgan and every time he spoke, whether to her or to the others, she felt her anger and resentment grow. It wasn't what he said, but the tone in which he said it. In fact, she was hard put to remember what was said all evening. She only knew that by the end of it, she had labeled Morgan Wade as that blasted arrogant cowboy.

She tried to do justice to Marie's dinner, but only pushed it around on her plate with her fork. The surprise dessert, which turned out to be an exceptional mousse, she barely touched. When Babs questioned her on it, she pleaded fatigue for the loss of her appetite. Having done so, she used fatigue again to excuse herself shortly after they had finished their coffee in the living room. There was no demur, but she caught the arched brow and mocking look Morgan gave her as he wished her a quiet good night. In her room she thought in agitation she would be unable to sleep, but she fell asleep at once.

Sam wakened to bright, spring sunshine and a feeling of well being. Stretching in contentment, she laughed and chided herself on her feelings of the night before, telling herself, he's a man like every other, a little full of his own importance, but certainly no threat to her. She would make an effort to be pleasant in the face of his arrogance and in four days time they would both be gone. He to his ranch, and she to Long Island.

That settled, she had a shower, dressed quickly in flat sandals, jeans, and a pullover. She brushed her hair, pulled it back, twisted it, and pinned it to her head with a long barrette. Feeling famished, she left her room in search of breakfast. She found Babs alone at the breakfast table, and was informed that Ben and Morgan had left an hour ago on business of their own. The knowledge dismayed her not at all. The morning passed swiftly. Sam made periodic trips to the nursery, falling more in love with the two boys every time.

The men were back for lunch, and Sam felt relief as Babs again ran over the procedure to be followed at the church two days hence. Sam, changing the conversation, determined to stick to her earlier resolve, told Ben and Morgan what she and Babs had done all morning, and in turn, asked what they had been up to.

Morgan cast her a quick, surprised look, a question in his eyes then, as if he understood her purpose and agreed with it, he answered her, his voice deep and pleasant. Sam almost sighed audibly in relief. Maybe, just maybe, they would get through the next few days without coming to blows.

They again took their coffee into the living room, the

men following slowly behind the women. Sam was already seated when they strolled into the room and as she glanced up, her breath caught at the appearance Morgan made. His slim length alone was arresting. He was wearing a white cotton shirt that was a glare against his dark skin as he walked through a ray of sunlight shining into the room from the french doors. The shirt was tucked into skin-tight jeans that rode low on his hips and across his stomach, which was not just flat but almost concave, causing his belt buckle to tilt forward slightly at the top. Both men were in stocking feet, as they had been riding and had removed their boots before entering the house.

After their second cup of coffee the men excused themselves, claiming work and Babs, drawing her mouth into a mock pout, complained of being neglected. The pout changed to delighted laughter as Morgan, passing her chair, reached down and ruffled her hair. "There isn't a man alive who could neglect you, gorgeous," he drawled as he sauntered from the room, his entire form a picture of unconscious grace. Sam moved uneasily in her chair.

Babs turned to her, laughter still in her voice. "What a charming liar that man is." The tone of her voice told Sam the deep affection she had for him. Sam resolved again to keep it light, she would in no way have Babs hurt.

Babs poured herself more coffee and settling back, cradled her cup in her palms with a sigh. "Well, finally, now we can have a long talk." She proceeded to inquire after Mary and Deb, asking if the wedding was still on for October and then, gently, of Sam's father's death. Sam answered her questions, then told her the details of her father's will.

Babs sat staring at her a moment, the look on her face one of sheer disbelief. After long seconds she exclaimed, "My God, Sam! That's pure Victorian."

"I know," Sam smiled. "I had exactly the same reaction."

"What are you going to do?" Babs asked as everyone else had who heard the conditions of the will.

"I haven't the foggiest, love," Sam said wryly. "I simply do not know."

"Unreal," Babs murmured, "positively unreal."

"Quite."

The subject was dropped as they decided to visit the boys. As they left the room, Babs's head still shook in wonder.

They had been with the boys perhaps an hour when Ben and Morgan came in. Sam had been sitting with Benjie, who, on seeing Morgan, slid off her lap to run toward him, little arms outstretched, shouting, "Unca Mog, Unca Mog." Bending down, Morgan caught the child under the arms, swung him off his feet, and tossed him into the air over his head, teasing. "What's up, hotshot?"

Sam caught her breath at the rough handling of the child, releasing it slowly when Benjie squealed, "Ben is," just as big hands seemed to pluck him out of the air. Benjie piped excitedly, "Again, again," but Morgan shook his head. "Not today, chum, let's have a look at your brother." Walking to the crib, Benjie repeated the words he'd said to Sam the day before, "Baby seep."

"Then we'll be very quiet," Morgan whispered as he reached the crib and stood looking down. Then, his voice tone normal, "Playing possum, he's wide awake."

Sam drew her breath in sharply and held it as suddenly she saw his arm tighten around Benjie's small bottom and bending, slide the other arm under Mark. Straightening slowly he turned, the baby securely caught against him. Sam expelled her breath on a rush, hearing Babs laugh.

"It shook me the first time I saw him do it, too, Sam."

Morgan gave her a wicked grin, delighted in knowing he'd frightened her—twice. Still grinning, which made a lie of his words, he drawled mockingly, "I'm sorry if I shook you, Miss Denning."

Before Sam could retort, he turned to Judy, "Did I frighten you too, beautiful?"

Sam watched color stain Judy's cheeks thinking, *Babs is "Gorgeous," Judy's "Beautiful," and I'm Miss Denning, I guess that'll keep me in my place.*

"You couldn't frighten me, Morgan," Judy laughed, the color deepening in her face.

She's got a crush on him, Sam decided, watching the color mount in Judy's cheeks. Shifting her gaze, she studied Morgan's smiling face, his teasing eyes. This one, she thought, is used to female adoration—very used to it. For some strange reason the thought was unsettling.

A short time later Babs announced, "Nap time." To Benjie's cried "not yet" Morgan replied in mock sternness, "Sack out, wrangler," and handed him to Judy and Mark to Babs. Kisses were given and received, and Sam, Ben, and Morgan left the room, Babs calling, "I'll be out in a minute."

Sam headed for her room but was stopped by Ben's invitation. "Come have a drink, Sam." She hesitated, but then followed them into the living room.

Ben started for the liquor cabinet but was stopped by Morgan's hand on his arm. "Sit, I'll get it." Without asking, he mixed two Martinis, turning to hand one to Sam and place the other at Babs's usual chair. Then taking two more glasses he put an ice cube into each, filled the glasses halfway with Jack Daniel's, and handed one to Ben. Moving to stand in front of the fireplace, he took a long, appreciative swallow of his whiskey.

Babs came into the room, dropped into her chair,

picked up her drink, sipped, and murmured, "Hmm good. Benjie's a love, isn't he?" She asked the room in general, which brought a laugh from them all. The talk was light and easy for a time. Then, refilling his glass, Morgan moved to the doorway with a casual "I'm for a bath." Ben soon followed, claiming a nap wouldn't hurt either.

Sam and Babs sat quietly for a time, sipping their drinks. Suddenly Babs sat up, looked at Sam with an odd expression on her face and exclaimed. "Of course! That's the answer, Sam, Morgan."

"Whatever are you talking about?" Sam asked lazily.

"You can marry Morgan," came the jolting reply. Sam's eyes flew wide, and her voice rose slightly.

"Have you gone mad?"

"Not yet," Babs answered serenely. "It's the perfect solution to the will, Sam."

"Really Babs?" Sam began. "But I don't see . . ."

"Of course it is, Sam," Babs interrupted. "You need a husband within five months, right?" Sam nodded. "Yet you have no wish to marry any of the men who have already offered." The nod was more emphatic. "You think they'd want a regular marriage? A normal male–female relationship?"

"I know they would."

"Okay," Babs went on. "You get a husband. No demands. Morgan gets a wife with money, which he needs."

"It couldn't work," Sam stately firmly. "In the first place I hardly know the man." She held up her hand as Babs started to interrupt. "And in the second place, although he may need money, he doesn't strike me as needing a wife overmuch."

"That's where you're wrong," Babs denied. "He can hardly step off the place but that the females are falling all over him, trying to drag him down the aisle. And he is

41

simply not interested. Oh, he's had his flings, as a matter of fact quite a few, but he is too wrapped up in that ranch to be bothered with a wife."

"But then why do you think . . ."

"That's the beauty of it, Sam. This way, with a wife, he gets a modicum of immunity from the felines, without the demands of a more, er, normal marriage. And what does your barely knowing him have to do with it? Will you think, Sam? You could use the house, a place he spends very little time in, as a home base and travel around to wherever you please. As long as you touch home for a short stay occasionally, in this day and age, who could call that a separation?"

She paused to draw breath, but before Sam could say anything Babs went on. "At the end of five years, you get a quiet divorce and go your separate ways. Morgan financially in the black at last and you with, I'm sure, the bulk of your inheritance intact."

"Oh, Babs, I don't know, you make it sound as if it almost might do."

"What else is there?" Babs insisted. "It would be lovely if you could fall in love, but really, Sam, if in all these years you haven't met Prince Charming, I somehow can't see him tooling down the pike in his Maserati within the next few months." Babs grinned impishly at her.

Sam grinned back. "I can't either, but, good God, how would one go about it? I mean really, one can't just walk up to a comparative stranger and declare, 'I say, would you care to marry me for my money?' "

Babs giggled and Sam had to smile, but added, "I mean it, Babs, I couldn't do it."

"You don't have to," Babs told her, "I'll explain to Ben and he'll talk to Morgan."

"Do you really think?"

42

"I do."

Sam hesitated long moments, then sighed. "All right, I don't like it, but I don't see any other way short of sponging off Mary."

Babs knew that was the deciding factor.

CHAPTER 3

As she dressed for dinner, Sam felt nervous to the point of being sick. She should not have told Babs to go ahead. If that arrogant cowboy mocked her offer, she'd leave at once for Long Island, christening or no christening. No, she'd hit him first, then she'd leave.

She had made up her face carefully and now, standing in front of the closet, she decided, since the evening was cool, to wear a longsleeved hostess gown in apple green. Cut like a shirtwaist, it clung snugly at the top, tapering to the small, belted waist, the skirt hanging in full soft folds to the floor. Giving herself a last glance in her full-length mirror, she lifted her shoulders in resignation, then left the room.

Dinner went smoothly, Ben and Morgan carrying most of the conversation, discussing the merits of different breeds of cattle, much to the disdain of Babs. For her part, Sam was happy to remain quiet and concentrate on forcing her food down. Back in the living room, with coffee cups in hand, the talk centered on various activities of their mutual friends. As soon as Morgan had set his cup down, Ben excused the both of them, to a surprised look from Morgan, and they again left the room.

Sam got up and circled the room, only to sit down again with a sigh, upon which Babs shot her a look and stated firmly, "We need a drink." Babs then proceeded to make a pitcherful of Martinis. She poured out two and handed one to Sam, who downed it in four fast swallows.

"Good grief, Sam, relax. You do much more of that and you'll be flat on the floor."

Sam shrugged and refilled her glass, but she sat back into her chair, drawing her feet under her, and sipped at the drink. Babs launched into a discussion of clothes and from there to her children. The time seemed to drag and Sam, pouring her third drink, was beginning to fidget when they heard the men returning.

Morgan went directly to the Jack Daniel's, but Ben stopped inside the doorway saying softly, "I think Benjie is calling for us, Babs." Babs literally jumped out of her chair, glanced at Sam, and left, Ben right behind her.

Sam sipped her drink watching Morgan warily. He dropped the cube into the glass, then splashed the whiskey over it and turned. As he walked slowly to Sam, she had the urge to run, and kept her seat out of sheer will power. Morgan was wearing a white denim suit with a patterned shirt in shades of blue, and he looked completely at ease. He stopped a few feet from her, still silent. His eyes on her, he lifted his glass and took a long swallow. She could tell nothing from his face or eyes and was having trouble keeping her fingers from trembling, when he lowered the glass. His soft tone sent a shiver down her arms. "I hear you want to make a trade."

"A trade?" she whispered, thinking she sounded rather stupid.

He gave a short nod and stated bluntly, "My name for your money." She bristled, but forced herself to answer, "Yes."

"When?"

"Why, I don't know, there's my family and . . ." she faltered.

"No, as soon as legally possible," he cut in adamantly.

"But, really—" she began, but he cut her off again.

"I want to get back to the ranch, and do you really want your family here? How long do you think it would take them to get wise? Better to let them think you've had a whirlwind affair that ended at the altar. Right?"

"I suppose so."

"Good. Bargain?"

"Bargain," Sam answered weakly.

"Okay," he said briskly. "Tomorrow we'll go into town and apply for a license and do whatever else has to be done. Then as soon as we can, we'll get married and go home."

"Whatever you say," Sam murmured faintly, wondering if she was going to be sick as she gulped at her drink.

At that moment Babs stuck her head around the doorway. "All right if we come in?"

Morgan laughed, white teeth flashing in his dark face. "Of course, it's your house."

They talked for over an hour, Ben and Babs advising them on what must be done. Then Sam rose, stating, "If we're having an early start, I think I'll turn in," and left the room quickly. Babs caught up to her in the hallway outside her room and putting her hand on Sam's arm whispered, "Are you all right, Sam?"

"Of course," Sam assured her. "It's just . . . everything's happening so fast."

"I know, but I think it'll work, really," Babs urged.

"I hope so." But Sam's voice didn't sound very hopeful.

The next three days blurred together for Sam. She woke Saturday morning tense and headachy, telling herself she couldn't go through with it, she'd have to beg off somehow. The headache and most of the tension drained away under a shower. Calmer now as she dressed, she thought hopefully, *Perhaps Morgan is having second thoughts.* It may be quite easy to call it off. They might even joke about it.

She stepped out of her room to see Morgan closing the door of his own directly across the hall, next to the nursery. Before she could open her mouth and without even a good morning he said almost curtly, "I was just going to knock on your door, breakfast is ready. Ben and Babs just sat down." Glancing at his watch impatiently he went on, "We better get moving."

"Mr. Wade," Sam started, but he broke in dryly.

"Don't you think you'd better call me Morgan, Samantha? The days of a wife calling her husband mister are long gone." Taking her arm he propelled her down the hall to the dining room, she practically running to keep up with his long-legged stride. She was breathing quickly when she reached the table and not only from the trip down the hall. She was emotionally shaken as well. Her only clear thought being, *I'm not going to be able to stop this.* With a rising sense of unease she turned to Babs, who had just wished her good morning, ready to plead, you've got to get me out of this. Babs, not waiting for Sam's return greeting, went on. "We're going into Ely with you. Ben has some things to look to, and unless you have a white dress with you, you and I have some shopping to do."

"A white dress! What for?" Sam repeated in surprise, catching the quick, sharp-eyed look Morgan threw at her.

"What for?" Now it was Babs's turn to repeat. "Why, to get married in, silly. Do you have one with you?"

Before Sam could answer, Ben, laughing softly, said, "I don't think our bride is altogether awake yet." Thinking *I don't think your bride's all together, period,* Sam answered Babs, "No, I don't have one, but I don't think it necessary to wear white." Morgan and Babs spoke simultaneously.

"I don't see why not."

"Of course it is."

"But . . ." Sam started.

"Samantha," Morgan interrupted sharply, "I know I said I'd like to do this as fast as possible, but I didn't mean we shouldn't do it right."

"Exactly," Babs stated firmly.

Sam's hands fluttered, turning palms out, and she gave in with a barely audible, "All right, we'll shop." Taking a roll from the bun warmer in the middle of the table, she sat crumbling it onto her plate. Feeling Morgan's eyes watching her, she glanced up.

"You'd better have some breakfast."

"I'm n-not really h-hungry," she stammered. Blast it, she'd never stammered in her life. "Coffee and juice will do."

"Then drink your juice," he ordered. Picking up the coffee carafe, he filled her cup and then the mug in front of him.

Anger burned through her at the tone of his voice. As if he were speaking to a child! She emptied the juice glass and placed it carefully on the table, observing coldly, "You're not eating."

At her words he cocked an eyebrow and smiled mockingly. "I ate over an hour ago. Unused to the good life, I get up early."

Babs chuckled. The burn deepening inside her, Sam turned and watched, in some disgust, as Babs polished off her bacon and eggs with sickening gusto.

Ben had already cleaned his plate and had just lit a cigarette. Turning to him, Sam asked, "May I have one, please?" Before Ben could reach for one, Morgan was holding his pack across the table. She took one, watched as he placed one between his teeth. His lighter flared, was touched to first hers then his cigarette. Teeth still clamped to the filtered end, he drawled, "Now drink your coffee so we can get moving."

Sam's green eyes flashed, but she emptied her cup. Crushing out the half-smoked cigarette, she left the table, hurried to her room, brushed her teeth, applied a light coat of lipstick to her mouth, grabbed her handbag, and joined the others, who were waiting for her beside a very dusty Buick station wagon parked in the driveway. Settling herself onto the back seat beside Babs, Sam could barely keep her nose from wrinkling. The inside of the car was every bit as dusty as the outside. At that moment Morgan slid behind the wheel and caught her reflection in the rearview mirror. As if he read her mind he drawled, "May as well have the heap washed while we're in Ely."

The heap being all of six months old, Sam had to assume he referred to all vehicles as heaps. Pulling her eyes from his mocking black ones, she stared sightlessly out of the window. The drive into Ely didn't take long enough for Sam. In fact none of the things they had to do seemed to take long. From filling out the marriage license form to speaking with Babs's pastor and arranging to have him marry them in his study on Wednesday morning at ten. Babs had insisted on the last, stating emphatically that a dusty civil office just would not do. With a mounting feeling of having won the battle but lost the war, Sam went along with everything decided, voicing no preference.

They separated, agreeing to meet again in two hours time for a late lunch; the women to shop, the men to follow their own pursuits, the nature of which Sam hadn't the vaguest idea. Except of course, the cleaning of the Buick.

Sam did not buy a dress. She found nothing she liked, admitting to Babs the fault was not in the shops or the merchandise. They had seen some lovely things. She was, as she told Babs, simply not with it. She shopped for the boys instead, to voiced disapproval from Babs.

Joining up with the men again, they entered a small coffeeshop. Morgan and Ben chose a booth and sat across the table from Sam and Babs. After giving their order of four cheeseburgers and coffees to the waitress, Babs told the men of the failure of the shopping trip.

Ben laughed, giving his wife a fond, teasing look. "Somehow that doesn't surprise me. I don't know a woman who can suit herself shopping inside two hours." Babs made a face at him but didn't answer. Sam, glancing up at Morgan, gave a small sigh. He wasn't laughing. Quite the opposite, his face had gone still, his mouth a hard, straight line. He sat silent while the waitress served their meal but as soon as she had walked away, he spoke to Ben, his eyes steady on Sam's face.

"May I use your plane Monday?"

"Certainly," came the prompt reply from Ben around a mouthful of burger, "Where are you headed?"

"Vegas. I'll fly the girls in early in the morning and Sam may take the day to shop. Hopefully she can suit herself there." This last on a decidedly mocking note.

Sam nearly choked on her burger and was about to protest, but catching the danger signals flashing from Morgan's eyes, changed her mind, thinking she could veto the plan later. Babs disabused her of that thought almost at once. "Oh, Sam, what luck, two trips to Vegas in the same week." Sam managed to give Babs a weak smile, then turned to frown at Morgan thinking, *All right, your*

point again, cowboy, but I swear I'll buy the first damned
white dress my eyes land on, even if the wretched thing's a
rag.

They left the coffeeshop and made their way to the car
which, Sam discovered, minus its coat of dust, was a lovely
deep green. On the way back to the house Sam and Babs
managed a half-hearted conversation, and once there, they
went directly into the boys' room. Benjie squealed with
delight at Sam's presents.

Sunday flew by for Sam. She was up early, helping
Marie with the last-minute preparations for the buffet
lunch to be served to the relatives and friends Babs had
invited to the christening celebration. Then it was time to
leave for the church. Sam held Mark throughout the service, he sleeping contently through it all. They drove directly back to the house, a long line of cars behind them.

Confusion reigned. The guests overflowed the house.
Sam, silently giving thanks for the fair, mild weather, kept
on the move. Steering clear of Morgan, she circulated,
being greeted like a long-lost daughter by Babs's parents
and younger sister, getting reacquainted with Ben's parents, and stopping to talk and laugh with people she had
met at Babs and Ben's wedding. If she came upon a group
that included Morgan at the time, she went right on by,
but she was not unaware of the number of young, pretty
females who seemed to hang on him, or of his deep, somewhat disturbing laughter that rang out frequently.

Sam had been on her feet, except for the time spent in
church, for over sixteen hours and she had had too much
champagne, she admitted to herself ruefully, when she
sank gratefully onto her bed sometime after eleven. Pushing everything out of her mind she was asleep at once.

She woke slowly to a light tapping on the door. Before
she could talk herself into moving, Babs poked her head

inside, calling, "Wake up, sleepyhead, Morgan said to tell you to hit the deck, he wants to leave in an hour." On the verge of saying "Tell Morgan Wade to go to hell," the sight of Babs's happy, laughing face stopped her and she murmured, "Be with you in thirty minutes."

Grumbling to herself that he was some kind of flaming idiot, she showered and dressed in the pink pants suit she had flown west in. As she slid onto her chair at the table, she raised her eyebrows in question at the two empty places where Morgan and Ben usually sat.

Babs, sipping her coffee, her breakfast finished, stated, "They ate earlier. Ben's gone, had some people to see. Morg's changing his clothes, be with us in a minute."

"Aren't we the favored ones?" Sam purred acidly, attacking the dish of grapefruit in front of her, unaware of the quick, concerned look Babs gave her.

She was still jabbing listlessly at the fruit when Morgan strode into the room looking vital and alert in the white denim suit of a few nights ago, with a dark copper-colored shirt that, Sam grudgingly admitted to herself, looked terrific.

Without sitting, he poured himself coffee and stood drinking it, watching Sam quietly a few minutes before chiding softly, "No breakfast again." It was a statement, not a question. Sam, not bothering to answer or even look up, lay down her spoon, pushed her plate away, and lifted her cup to stare moodily at her coffee before sipping it.

Babs laughed a little nervously, knowing Sam's temper when aroused, and implored Morgan, "Have a care, Morg, Sam's still tired and a bit testy this morning."

Black eyes glinted with devilment and his tone was sardonic as he cooed, "Poor baby."

Sam jerked to her feet, her face a mask of cold hauteur.

"If we must have this shopping trip, then let's do so and have done with it."

The flight was too short for Sam's taste. She sat enjoying the panorama below her, occasionally asking questions of Babs, ignoring Morgan, which didn't seem to bother him in the least.

In Vegas they parted company, agreeing to meet for lunch. Sam did buy the first white dress she saw, simply because it was perfect—a sheath with long sheer sleeves and a cowl collar that stretched from one shoulder tip across her throat to the other, draping down the back revealing the upper half of her lovely shoulders and back. She chose soft white leather pumps and a large white leather bag against Babs's advice, who chided softly, "Don't you ever buy a handbag other than those huge ones?" Sam answered "never" shortly and declared herself outfitted, much to the delight of Babs, who decided to shop for herself as they still had an hour before meeting Morgan.

They left Vegas right after lunch, returning in time to play with Benjie before his nap. They idled the rest of the day away and Sam excused herself early to go to bed.

Sam's tension grew steadily Tuesday until, late in the afternoon, she had to force herself to laugh and reply lightly to Babs's concerned questioning.

"One doesn't get married every day, pet."

"I know," Babs replied, "But do you realize, Sam, you've barely spoken to Morgan for two days. I know this isn't a love match or anything, but you could try to be civil."

Chastising herself for her boorish behavior in her friends' home, Sam made an effort to hold her end of the conversation at dinner. Later in the evening, as she poured her fourth Martini, she decided she was running out of

53

banalities when Morgan, stretched out lazily, rose to his feet in a fluid move, strolled across the room to her, and plucked her drink out of her hand.

"Walk outside with me for a while, there's something we have to discuss." Giving Babs and Ben a brief "excuse us," he led her from the room. He waited at the dining room for her to get a coat, then they went through the sliding glass doors in the dining room and onto the soft grass. He strolled toward the tennis courts and when he paused to light a cigarette for her and himself he said suddenly, his voice harsh, "What the hell are you trying to say with the booze?"

Caught off guard Sam stammered, "W-what?"

"Babs told me you're a very light drinker," he rasped. "Yet that drink I took from you was your fourth. Yesterday it was wine. As a matter of fact you've been belting it away since Friday. If you're having second thoughts, you don't have to drink yourself insensible, just say it and we'll drop the whole thing."

"I don't understand."

"I think you do. Do you want to call it off?"

"No, of course not," she answered quickly, too quickly.

"There's no *of course* about it," Morgan grated. "You better be sure, Samantha, very sure, before it becomes a fact. An irrevocable fact."

She thought his phrasing a bit odd, but again answered quickly, "I am."

He said nothing for some time, then, "All right, but let me suggest you lay off the booze and get some rest. We've got a long day tomorrow, starting early and ending late." Grasping her forearm in his big hand, he started back to the house.

Sam was speechless. Who did this man think he was? No one had ever presumed to tell her she had had too much to drink or when to go to bed. Angry now, she snapped, "What do you think you're doing?" For, going through the dining room, he bypassed the living room, and was practically dragging her down the hall to her room. His fingers tightened painfully as she tried to stop and pull her arm free. She was shaking in fury when he stopped at the door to her room. Grasping her other arm he held her still and bending over her, said softly, "Calm down and stop acting like a spoiled child. You're so uptight you're about ready to go off like a firecracker." His voice held laughter as he ended, "Get some sleep. You want to be a beautiful bride, don't you?"

"Oh, you—" Sam began, only to gasp as, dipping his head swiftly he brushed his lips across hers and whispered, "Good night, Samantha." Pushing open the door he gave her a gentle shove into the room and pulled the door closed firmly behind her.

Sam stood inside the door, still, rigid, her hands tightly fisted at her side. *I must be mad,* she thought wildly. *Why didn't I stop this when I had the chance? It can't possibly work, he has nothing but contempt for me and I hate him.* She was uncomfortably aware that her mouth tingled from that brief brush of his and her arms felt hot where his hands had held her. She felt a very real fear. *I must stop this,* she thought desperately.

But she didn't. It was over quickly. She stayed in her room until it was time to leave. Babs brought her coffee, which she drank, and toast, which she ignored. She dressed and paced the room until Morgan knocked on the door with a quiet, "It's time to go, Samantha." Sam hesitated, stepped back, then lifting her chin, walked to the door and opened it to stand straight and still as his eyes went over her body, then back to hers.

"You look lovely."

"Thank you." Her face was perfectly composed, her voice icy. She walked past him and down the hall to Babs, waiting at the door. The drive into town was uncomfortable, Morgan and Babs eyeing Sam warily. If someone had asked Sam to describe the pastor's study five minutes after leaving it, she would have been unable to do so. Yet the brief service was vividly imprinted on her mind. Morgan's voice, deep, firm, repeating, "With this ring I thee wed, with my body I thee worship, with all my worldly goods I thee endow," as he slid a narrow platinum band on her finger. Her own voice low but clear, repeating the same vows and placing a ring, the larger twin to her own, on his finger. The ring, hastily handed to her by Babs, was a complete surprise to Sam. Even as she slid it into place she could not believe he'd leave it there. He simply did not come across as the type of man who would advertise his marital status. But then, Sam still had a lot to learn about Morgan Wade.

When the pastor said, "You may kiss the bride," Morgan brushed her lips as he had the night before and then Babs and Ben kissed her. Minutes later they were back in the car. They went directly back to the house as Marie was preparing what she called a wedding luncheon for them. Ben drove and, as they had entered the back seat, Sam sat as close to the door panel as she could, giving a short nod, but not even looking up as Morgan said, "Excuse me," when he stretched his long legs across to her side of the floor, bumping her foot with his.

Without speaking, Sam sat staring out the window, seeing nothing, unaware that her fingers twisted at her ring, or of black eyes watching her, anger building in them. What she was aware of was the same tingling feeling on her mouth that she had felt the night before.

Marie and Judy were waiting to toast the newlyweds

with champagne when they returned to the house. Sam didn't know whether to laugh or cry, and she felt sorry for Judy, whose eyes, whenever they touched Morgan, grew sad and forlorn. Drawing Babs aside Sam asked, "Will there be time for me to call home before lunch?"

"Of course," Babs answered with a small laugh, as Benjie had joined the group and was jumping up and down in noisy excitement. "Use the phone in Ben's study, it'll be quiet there."

Sam entered the study, then turned in surprise as Morgan followed her into the room, closed the door and leaned back lazily against it. "I'd like some privacy, if you don't mind," she snapped.

"I do mind," he replied flatly. "I'm staying."

She glared at him, but he returned the look coolly, not moving. Turning her back to him sharply, she perched on the edge of Ben's desk, reached for the receiver, and dialed the Long Island number. Beth answered.

"This is Sam, Beth, is Mary about?" Then to Beth's inquiry of herself, "I'm fine. How are you?" Beth told Sam she was also fine, then asked her to hold on as she went in search of Mary. A few minutes later Sam heard Mary's gentle voice. "Hello, Samantha? Is something wrong, dear?"

Forcing her voice to lightness, Sam answered, "Not at all, just the opposite." Breathing deeply, she closed her eyes. "I was married this morning." Silence.

"Sam, are you joking?"

Sam, hearing the note of concern in Mary's voice, plunged on. "No, darling, I'm not joking, we just returned from the church a few minutes ago."

"But, my dear, who? Do I know him?"

"No, you don't know him, Mother. I just met him myself." She managed a light laugh. "Swept me off my

57

feet. His name's Morgan Wade, a friend of Ben's, little Mark's godfather. He's a rancher here in Nevada," she added quickly before Mary could ask what he did.

"Sam, is this wise?" Mary's soft voice was tinged with suspicion.

"I don't know," Sam said gaily. "Is it ever? I don't much care, I'm in love." She was amazed she didn't choke.

"Are you truly?" Mary asked hopefully.

"Yes, Mother, truly," she affirmed, uncomfortably aware of Morgan leaning against the door.

She was not prepared for Mary's next question. "May I speak to him, Sam?" Without thinking, she turned a frantic face to him. As if he'd heard Mary's voice, Morgan walked across the room, and took the receiver from her hand. Sam was amazed at the gentleness of his tone.

"Hello, Mrs. Denning, this is Morgan."

Sam watched him as he listened and when he spoke again his voice was warm, seemingly sincere. "Yes, I know it was very fast. But I assure you it will be all right."

Again he listened then answered, "No, we can't come east just now. This is a very busy time for me at the ranch." There was a pause. "I appreciate that fact, and I promise you I'll bring Sam east as soon as I can. Yes, of course." Another pause, then, "Hello, yourself, how are you?" His tone was lighter and Sam knew he was now talking to Deb. She knew Deb's question had been, "How is Sam?" by his answer: "Sam's fine." His tone grew teasing, "In fact she's beautiful, isn't she?"

Oh, brother, Sam thought, his tongue should fall out of his head. She heard him say, "Of course you may," then he handed the receiver to her and walked back to the door.

Sam thought to forestall Deb's questions by saying, "Hello, Poppet, will you do a favor for me?"

"Of course, what is it?" Deb answered.

"Well, call the Messrs. Baker and inform them of the situation. Tell them I'll send copies of the marriage certificate right away." Before Deb could answer, she added, "And would you pack a few of my things and send them to me?"

"Yes, what do you want me to send?"

"I'll make a list and drop it in the mail. Now, I really must go, love, as Babs is holding lunch for us, and this phone call is going to cost the earth."

"But, Sam," Deb protested.

"I'll call you from the ranch in a few days and answer all your questions, but right now I must run, as Morgan is starting to glower at me. Kiss Bryan for me. Bye for now." Sam hung up quickly.

"Neatly done." Morgan's voice came softly. "Was I glowering?"

Sam chose to ignore him as she walked to the door. He didn't move. "Let me pass," she snapped.

"Not just yet, I have something to say."

Sam felt a shiver run down her spine. Gone was all warmth from his voice. It was cold, hard, and it matched his face.

"I've had enough of your sulkiness, Samantha. Now you'll either shake yourself out of it, or I'll do it for you."

"How dare you—" she began, but he cut in roughly, "I dare one hell of a lot and if you want to find out how much, keep pushing. You had your chance to back out and didn't. So put a smile on that beautiful face, for we are leaving this room now and joining our friends for lunch and you'd better behave like the lady you're supposed to be, or believe me ycu'll wish to heaven you had."

Sam stood stiff with anger a few seconds, but his reference to Babs and Ben had hit home. She was being unfair to them. She thought, with shame, of the uneasy glances

59

both had given her all morning. Turning to him with a half smile she murmured, "You're quite right, shall we declare a temporary truce?"

"No, Samantha," he shook his head firmly. "Not temporary, it will have to be a permanent one. This bargain of ours can't work if we don't."

Lunch went well, Sam not missing the look of relief on Babs's face at her thawed attitude. As Sam kissed and hugged Babs, Ben, and Benjie and said good-bye to Marie and Judy, Morgan stashed their suitcases in the car, promising Babs he'd bring Sam to visit soon. They drove the first twenty miles in silence and Sam jumped when Morgan asked suddenly, "Who's Bryan?"

"What?" Then, remembering her phone call, "Deb's fiancé. Why?"

He shrugged in answer, changing the subject. "Sara will have supper ready for us when we get home."

Home? She was going to a house she'd never seen, with a man she didn't know. Home? Her home was in Long Island. She said none of this out loud. Instead she raised delicate brows. "Sara?"

"Sara Weaver, my housekeeper."

"Oh, yes, Babs mentioned her," Sam murmured. "She knows about us?" He glanced at her quickly and nodded, then turned his eyes back to the road. A good driver herself, Sam had been watching him and decided he drove expertly, his big hands easy on the wheel. But as he also drove very fast, except for a few quick glances shot at her, he kept his eyes on the road.

Suddenly he slowed the car, pulled it off to the side of the road, and brought it to a stop. Sam looked at him, startled. "Something wrong?"

"No." Reaching around to the back seat he produced a Thermos bottle. "Marie supplied us with coffee, we may as well stretch our legs and drink it." Pushing his door open he got out and walked around to her as she slid out her side.

Standing together, he leaning against the car, they drank coffee from plastic cups and he said casually, "You seemed surprised that I'd called Sara." Sam nodded. "I had to give her some warning." At her questioning look he added, "She's house proud, probably been cleaning the place ever since I called her." He laughed ruefully. "If I'd have sprung you on her without giving her time to do her thing, she'd have had my hide nailed to the kitchen door."

"I see," Sam said, then asked hesitantly, "Does she know the circumstances?"

He grinned, his eyes laughing at her. "As to sleeping arrangements?" Sam felt her face grow hot and she looked away from him nodding. The beast was laughing at her, she could hear it in his voice.

"No, I simply told her what room to get ready for you. She didn't like the idea very much." His voice went dry. "I explained that within the social stratum in which you were raised, it is not at all unusual for a husband and wife to have separate rooms. She accepted that grudgingly."

Sam looked up at him in amazement. Accepted grudgingly? An employee?

He read her face and the easy, relaxed look on his own became hard, his voice cold. "Understand this, Samantha, Sara is not the hired help. She's family."

Sam, who had started to relax as they talked, stiffened, not from his words, but his tone.

Misunderstanding her withdrawal, he went on. "If Sara dislikes you, she'll still tolerate you because you're my wife. But if she likes you, she'll probably adopt you and be ordering you around and fussing over you before the weekend's out. Either way you will treat her with respect." Turning, he jerked the door open. "Let's get moving."

She got into the car without looking at him and sat rigid, staring straight ahead. She wanted to explain that she did understand his feelings in regard to Sara, had understood since Babs had told her of it. But his cold face stopped her.

He slid under the wheel, tossed the Thermos onto the backseat and put his hand on the key, but didn't turn it. Swearing softly, he turned angrily and grabbing her shoulders forced her to face him. The hardness vanished from his face when he saw hers. Her eyes held a hurt look and her lips trembled slightly. His eyes hung on her mouth a long moment before glancing up to her own. "I didn't mean to sound harsh, but I had to make it clear that I will not have Sara hurt." His tone had softened. "Do you understand?"

"You love her very much, don't you?" Sam whispered, wondering at the small twinge of pain she felt inside when he answered simply, "Very much." He let go of her suddenly, as if just realizing he was still holding her. "Jacob too." Taking two cigarettes from the pack on the dash he lit one, handed it to her, then lit his own.

"Who's Jacob?"

"Sara's husband." Dragging deeply, he narrowed his eyes against the smoke. "Didn't Babs mention Jake?" At the brief shake of her head, he explained. "When my father and mother got married, Sara stated firmly her Miss Betty was not going to Nevada without her." Sam nodded, indicating she knew this. "At the same time, Jake stated equally firmly that Sara wasn't going without him. They were married three days after my parents."

"What does Jake do?"

"Name it. The place would fall apart without him." He

grinned at her easily, relaxed again. "In fact, if my father had left him in charge when he went traipsing the world, instead of hiring that damned manager, I'd have come home to a much different situation."

His eyes looked back through the years a few seconds, then he gave a short laugh. "Mainly Jake keeps the place in order and takes care of anything that grows." At her raised eyebrows he added, "He was a farmer in the Pennsylvania Dutch country, and I wouldn't be surprised if he could make a fence post grow."

She laughed, the tension gone again. Smiling, he started the engine and pulled the car onto the road. The big car ate up the miles with Morgan's foot on the gas pedal. Sam, growing tired, rested her head back and fell asleep. She woke when the car stopped. Opening her eyes slowly, she asked, "Why are we stopping?"

"We're home."

Sitting up quickly, she looked up to see Morgan watching her, his body slightly turned toward her, his left forearm resting on the steering wheel. She looked around in confusion, not fully awake, and saw they were parked on a drive in front of a garage. The house was to the left of it, a breezeway connecting the two. She opened her door and stepped out awkwardly. Massaging the back of her neck, she looked the place over as Morgan took their valises from the back.

The house was a rancher, built in the shape of an L with a smooth lawn surrounding it. In the distance off to the left, Sam could see the ranch outbuildings and a white-railed corral. A flagstone walk ran from the driveway to the front of the house. Morgan led Sam along it to the front. As they neared the door, it was flung open to reveal a full-bodied woman of medium height with a smile on her plain, unlined face.

"Welcome home, and congratulations, Mr. Morgan."
She fairly beamed at him, then turned expectantly to Sam.
"Thank you, Sara," Morgan said, turning to Sam.
"Samantha this is Sara Weaver—Sara, my wife, Saman-
tha."

Sam put out her hand. "How do you do, Sara?" Sara
grasped Sam's fingers in her broad, work-roughened hand.
"I'm fine and I hope you'll be happy here, Mrs. Wade."

"Sam," Sam replied automatically. Sara said almost the
same as Marie had done just one week ago. "Mrs. Sam."

"All right, Sara," Sam laughed, looking around as they
moved into the room.

They were in the living room, and the door they had
come through was in the corner of it. The front wall had
a large bow window with a deep window seat onto which
big, plump gold velvet cushions were tossed. Two com-
fortable-looking chairs with a low table between them
were placed in front of the windows. On the far left wall
was an archway leading into a hall and in the far left
corner were a long, curved sofa with a long oval coffee
table in front of it and a wooden rack holding papers and
magazines at each end. On the right wall, Sam had noticed
as she entered an archway through which she'd glimpsed
the dining area. And in that wall between the archway and
the back wall was a large, stone fireplace in front of which
was another coffee table and two huge chairs with matching hassocks. The floor was hardwood with furry rugs
scattered about, and the walls paneled in dark walnut. The
ceiling was opened beamed, the beams darkly gleaming
against the flat white plaster between. The room was all
in white and gold and shades of brown, none of the pieces
matching, all blending, and it was as inviting as a pair of
warm arms. But what drew Sam was the back wall, like
the one in her room at Babs's—it was entirely glass, with

64

sliding doors which led, as Sam saw as she walked up to them, onto a broad porch with outdoor furniture casually placed. Three steps led off the porch to a flagstone walk set in the lawn which sloped gently fifty feet to a shallow bank with a rock garden. Three stone steps down the bank the lawn leveled off, smooth and flat as a putting green and at the base of it a flagstone patio encircled a kidney-shaped swimming pool, its water now reflecting the last long rays of the late afternoon sun. This was Sam's favorite time of day, when those last golden rays bathed everything in a deep, warm glow, softening even the most harsh of outlines. *How perfect to have my first look at this time,* Sam thought fleetingly, and turned back to the two people who had watched her silently the last few minutes. Her eyes alive with pleasure, she turned to Morgan. "It's beautiful, Morgan."

"Yes," his voice echoed her softness. No stiltedly polite "thank you" or overly casual "glad you like it." Just simply, "yes."

Turning to Sara, her eyes still glowing, Sam sighed, "How I envy you this house."

Sara understood. Sam had acknowledged her place in the house. Sara granted Sam's own with, "I happily give it to you." As had happened so many times before, Sam had entered and conquered. Sara was hers. Morgan stood, a small smile tugging the corner of his mouth, as the bond was forged between the two, so different, women.

"Now come with me, Mrs. Sam," Sara said briskly, moving to the suitcases inside the door. "I'll show you your room. You'll want to wash up, and supper's ready to be served."

Morgan also reached for the suitcases. Sara, snatching Sam's up, scolded, "I'll take that, Mr. Morgan, you get cleaned up yourself, if you want to eat." Sam laughed, as

Sara added, as if to a grubby little boy, "Don't you dare come to the table in those jeans."

The idea of anyone speaking like that to that big, arrogant, black-eyed devil amused Sam greatly and she had trouble controlling her face as Morgan replied dryly, "Samantha's wearing jeans."

"Well, they're different somehow on a lady. Don't you dare, Morgan," Sara tacked on warningly, forgetting the Mister.

Morgan laughed out loud, shaking his head as he watched Sara lead Sam across the room to the arched hallway.

It was a short one, some twelve or fourteen feet, Sam thought, leading into another at a right angle. There was a door on each wall and Sara nodded to the one on their left. "Mr. Morgan's office." Eyeing Sam, she indicated the one on the right. "*His* bedroom."

They turned to the right at the joining and Sam saw a much longer hall, realized this part of the house was the downward stroke of the L. A few steps along the hall and Sara stopped, opened a door on the left, and waited for Sam to enter. Sam's breath caught and she stood quietly a few seconds glancing around. The room was done completely in white and shades of green: the deep-piled carpet in forest, so deep it looked almost black, the walls and ceiling in pale apple, and the draperies at two large windows on the far wall and bedspread in a deep summer leaf green. The woodwork and furniture were in sparkling spotless white. Sam loved it.

"I hope you'll be comfortable here." Sara looked around doubtfully. The idea of a husband and wife not sharing the same room obviously did not sit well with her.

Sam, smiling slightly, murmured, "I don't see how I could help but be, it's a lovely room."

"And here's your bathroom," Sara added, walking across the room to the left. She opened the door to reveal a large bath in deep pink and gold. *It's as if someone knew my colors,* Sam thought.

"Now don't bother unpacking," Sara said, going to the door. "I'll do that later. You wash up and come right in for supper."

Sam smiled as the door closed with a snap, remembering Morgan's warning that if Sara liked her she'd be fussing and ordering her about. Laughing softly, she went into the bathroom. Apparently Sara liked her.

CHAPTER 4

Sam stood staring out through the glass wall, idly smoking a cigarette. The late afternoon sunrays again bouncing and dancing off the pool's water. She didn't really see it, as she was deep in thought. She had been here ten days now, and so far things had gone much more smoothly than she had anticipated. She saw very little of Morgan, as he was gone by the time she got up in the morning and seldom returned to the house before seven. Then he'd come striding through the house to his room to have a quick shower and change in time to sit down to dinner at seven thirty. After dinner he'd sit with Sam in the living room long enough to drink his coffee then, going to the liquor cabinet built into the wall between the dining room archway and the fireplace, he'd drop the inevitable one ice cube in a short, fat glass, splash Jack Daniel's over it, murmur "excuse me" and go into his office. Sam would not see him again except for a quick glance into the office when she said good night on her way to her own room a few hours later.

He had told her the first evening after her arrival that he'd leave the office door open a bit in case she had any questions as to where anything was. Sam had replied lightly, not looking up from her book, "That's quite all right, don't bother, I'll ask Sara if I need anything." She'd looked up in shock when he said quietly, "Sara does not sleep in the house, Samantha. She and Jake have their own small place on the other side of the garage."

"But, I thought—" she began. He cut in, his eyes wicked, the corner of his mouth twitching in amusement. "There's nothing to be afraid of, I'll be here." Laughing softly under his breath, he'd gone to his office.

Sam had not slept well those first few nights, but on finding that once in her room she heard nothing, not even Morgan going to his own room, whatever time that might be, she had shaken off the uneasy feeling and had slept well since.

On her first day at the ranch Morgan had not worked, at least not on the property. He had wakened her early, tapping on her bedroom door insistently until she'd groaned, "Yes, what is it?"

"Roll out, Red," he'd ordered. "My men will be expecting to meet you this morning. You have twenty-five minutes, so you'd better get moving."

Still groaning, Sam had bitten back some very nasty words as she dragged herself off the bed. Twenty minutes later she'd strolled into the kitchen, still half asleep but looking perky in jeans, a heavy knit pullover, and a soft suede jacket.

Morgan's eyes had skimmed over her coolly before shifting to the wall clock. Handing her a cup of coffee, he'd said, "That'll have to do for now. We'll eat later."

Sam had gulped down the hot brew, then followed him through the still, pink dawn to the outbuildings she'd spotted briefly the day before. A small group of men stood, hats in hands, waiting for them. With surprising abruptness Morgan made the introductions, then turned away from her to give the men work instructions.

Feeling dismissed, wondering at the hot shaft of pain the feeling caused, Sam walked to the corral fence, breath catching at the sight that met her eyes. Standing inside the corral, elegant head arched high, bathed in the first sharp rays of morning sun, was the most beautiful golden palomino Sam had ever seen. As if recognizing she had a captive audience, the mare tossed her head and danced delicately to the corral fence, allowing Sam to stroke her long nose.

"She's a beauty, isn't she?"

Not having heard Morgan walk up to her, Sam jumped at his softly drawled voice.

"Yes, she is," Sam sighed, hand dropping to her side.

"She's yours."

With a small gasp, Sam spun around to stare into his strangely watchful face. "But—"

"To ride," Morgan inserted softly. "When I have the time to take you out." Before she could ask him when that would be, he added, as if he had read her thoughts, "After you've become accustomed to the house—and me."

How many times since then had she gone over his words trying to determine exactly what he'd meant? Sam asked herself now. He had not mentioned taking her out again and pride demanded Sam not ask him.

Sam blinked her eyes and saw that the daylight was just about gone. She knew she should go bathe and dress for dinner, but she lit another cigarette and stood still, wondering how Morgan would react to Sara's dinner surprise.

She and Sara had become quick friends, chatting easily and comfortably on any subject that came to hand. Though shocked at the idea when Sam first mentioned it, Sara had given in to Sam's pleading to help with the housework as she found time hanging on her hands. Sara had assigned Sam light duty, as Sam called it, admonishing her sternly not to let Morgan find out about it. Sara considered Sam, to Sam's deep amusement, too much a lady for heavy housework. But two days ago Sam had managed to invade Sara's kitchen.

On Thursday, Jake had carried the large cardboard carton containing the things Sam had asked Deb to pack and send her into Sam's room. Sam had liked Jake at first meeting. Not much taller then his wife, he was broad in the shoulders, strong as an ox and gentle as a kitten. His wife bossed him around outrageously and he loved it, as did his boss.

"Here are your things, Mrs. Sam," he'd called to her through her bedroom door. Sam had flung open the door with an "Oh, thank you, Jake, I imagine you were all getting a trifle tired of seeing me in the same clothes all the time."

"Oh, I don't know about that." He gave her a shy grin. "I think you always look pretty, no matter what you wear," he complimented as he left the room. His tone was that of an affectionate parent. Jake had adopted Sam too.

Sara had come into the room to help Sam unpack the bulging carton. Touching things lovingly, exclaiming in delight, she had put the beautiful clothes, shoes, and handbags in the closet, placed books in the case by the bed and records next to Morgan's in the rack in the TV-stereo unit built into the wall on the other side of the fireplace. Then her eyes lit up when she realized what was in the notebooks at the very bottom of the carton. Sam's recipes were her passport to Sara's kitchen.

They had sat, drinking coffee, at the kitchen table every moment Sara could spare since. Sara studied the recipes, Sam translating the ones in French, and just yesterday had declared she would try one on Morgan, with Sam's help of course. "Do we dare?" Sam had asked impishly.

The meals Sam had eaten since arriving had all been delicious and perfectly prepared, most with a decidedly

German flavor, some strictly American. But due to the wide variety of foods Sam was used to, quite a few of which she had cooked herself in the big kitchen in the house in Long Island, she was well ready for a change.

"Oh, Mr. Morgan's been around," Sara had returned airily. "I wouldn't be surprised to find he'd tasted most of these at one time or other." Sam, considering Morgan's unconcerned attitude to whatever was placed before him at the dinner table, forbore to comment.

They had studied and discussed the different recipes when Sara finally chose a Viennese cream torte. Sam, thinking, they wouldn't have to face the music till the end of the meal.

Now she turned sharply as Morgan strode into the living room. His brows shot up as he glanced at his watch before his eyes skimmed over Sam's jeans and ribbed top. "Aren't you changing for dinner?"

"What time is it?" she asked, her own eyes taking in his stockinged feet, dusty jeans and shirt, and the broad-brimmed Andalusian hat he had brought home from a trip to Spain that he wore low on his forehead. "Seven thirty," he supplied and laughed softly as she cried, "It can't be," making a dash for the hall, his long stride right behind her.

She had a swift shower, hurried into her bikini panties and bra, applied makeup lightly, pulled the pins from her hair, and shook her head to loosen its long coil. She brushed her hair quickly and glancing at the clock, decided there was no time to recoil it. It would have to hang loose. Sliding her feet into gold sandals, she pulled a silky gold and brown caftan from her closet and over her head. She gave her hair a last smoothing with the brush, then, tossing the long, heavy hair back off her shoulders, left the room.

Morgan turned from the liquor cabinet, a drink in each

hand, as Sam entered the living room. He watched her as she walked across the floor to him and she felt her chin lift and her back stiffen as he studied her. His eyes were insolent as they went over her face and hair, his brow inching at the mass of it freed from its usual coil. Slowly his hooded eyes moved down her body and back up again, to linger long seconds on the neckline of her gown where it plunged deeply between her breasts. She felt her face grow warm at his appraisal and in retaliation coolly raked her own eyes down the length of his body. That he looked unnervingly attractive she had to admit to herself. His black hair curled at the nape of his neck, shiny and still damp from the shower. His lean brown face, the cheeks smooth, gleamed with a freshly shaven look. His black brows rose over eyes amused at her survey. His silk shirt was startlingly white against the dark skin of his throat and chocolate brown slacks that fit snugly on his slim hips and down the long legs to flare gently at the bottom. When her eyes lifted to his, his voice held mocking laughter. "Enjoy the view?"

Anger flashed from cold green eyes and she replied icily, "Just another man."

His laughter was derisive, his voice low. "And for five million dollars you expected more, is that it?"

Sam went rigid with fury. Barely able to control her voice, she seethed, "How dare you!"

He answered softly. "I think you'll find out before too long, Samantha, that I dare anything." The amusement had left his voice and his face was deadly serious. Sam felt a small twinge of fear. Before she could answer he put in smoothly, "Shall we have our dinner?" He strolled into the dining room, leaving her to follow him.

She seated herself across from him, refusing to look at him, and forced herself to smile at Sara as she served dinner. The dessert took on more significance as they ate silently, and Sam was sorry she'd ever asked Deb to send her the notebooks. Finally Sara sat the torte in front of him and stepped back, an anxious look on her face, waiting for him to taste it. *Good Lord,* Sam thought, *one would think she was afraid he'd beat her if he didn't like it.*

One eyebrow raised, he looked first at Sara, then at Sam before tasting it. "An excellent torte, Sara," he complimented quietly. "I don't recall you serving this before."

"Thank you, Mr. Morgan." Sara's voice was tinged with pride. "You're right, I haven't made this before. It's one of Mrs. Sam's recipes and she helped me make it."

"No kidding," Morgan answered sardonically. "I hadn't realized Mrs. Sam was so domesticated." He smiled gently at Sara's confused look, which turned to relief at his smile. Smiling happily, she left the room.

Sam glared at him across the table as he calmly ate his dessert. When he had finished, his eyes again slowly raked over her. "My heavens," he mocked, "all this and she cooks too."

They drank their coffee in silence, Sam's eyes smoldering, Morgan's amused. As soon as he put his cup down, he stood up, poured his whiskey, and went to his office. Tonight he did not excuse himself.

Sam carried the coffee tray to the kitchen and complimented a beaming Sara. At her suggestion they try another recipe soon, Sam voiced a vague, "Yes, well, we'll see," and hastily left the room. She went straight to her bedroom, not bothering to say good night to Morgan as she passed the office door. Once inside her room she kicked off her sandals and sat down at her small desk to write to Deb.

She had written four lines in twenty-five minutes when she threw the pen down and stood up. Pacing back and forth in agitation, she thought, *Damn that cowboy for annoying me like this, what is the purpose of it?* She couldn't think of any reason and, giving up, decided to read, hoping that would calm her, and glanced about for her book. Not seeing it, she went back into the living room in search of it and was drawn to the wall of glass by the shimmering glow of moonlight. Standing still, transfixed by the dance the moonlight was doing on the pool's water, she didn't hear Morgan come up behind her. She jumped, then spun around sharply at his softly whispered words. "Still mad, Redhead?"

Her voice was a hiss through her teeth. "I detest being called Red."

He laughed, low in his throat, and caught her off guard saying, "That's a beautiful dress." She was groping for a retort when he bent his head, brushed her lips with his own, as he had done twice before, and whispered. "And you're a beautiful woman." His mouth brushed hers again and, one big hand going around her neck under her hair, the other around her waist, he pulled her to him. His mouth pressed down on hers, his lips forcing her own open. Sam went still in his arms a moment in shock, but his hard, demanding mouth seemed to be robbing her of strength. She couldn't think, felt oddly lightheaded, and without her willing it, her arms slid up around his neck, her body went soft against him. His arms became hard, coiled bands that pulled her tightly against the hard length of him, robbing her of breath.

His mouth left hers, went to the curve of her neck, sending tiny shivers down her spine. The hand at the back of her neck slid to her arm and grasping her firmly drew her back away from him as his lips trailed along the neckline of her gown to stop and caress the soft skin at the V between her breasts. His other hand slid sensuously over her hip.

Sam felt like her body had been set on fire. Desperately trying to fight a confusing urge to surrunder, she gasped, "Morgan, you must stop."

Lifting his head, he bent low over her. His lips almost touching hers, he said fiercely, "I must not stop. I want you, Samantha, and I'm going to have you. Now." With those words he clamped his mouth on hers passionately, his lips bruising hers. All resistance went out of her and she clung to him feeling she could no longer stand up. Feeling her go limp against him, Morgan bent and scooped her up. Holding her tightly in his arms he carried her into his bedroom.

Sam lay tightly against Morgan's body, her head resting on his chest. She couldn't move, for although he was asleep, his arm still held her. She had made one tentative attempt to move away once and the arm had tightened. Now she pressed against him almost afraid to breathe. She didn't want to wake him. She wept silently.

He had been an expert lover, if a little rough at first. When she had cried out in pain, he had become very still. His voice an incredulous whisper, he exclaimed. "My God, Samantha, I had no idea!" Her outcry had not stopped him, but he had become gentle, almost tender, his hands, his mouth, caressing, building in her a hunger almost as great as his own. Her cheeks burned now, remembering how she had surrendered, willingly, eagerly, to his possession of her, making her his. But she had been his, she admitted to herself now, the damp, matted hair on his chest soft against her cheek, from the beginning. From the minute she had walked into Babs's living room and had felt the impact of his black eyes on her, she had been his.

She shivered and his arms tightened. She didn't want to

love him. She thought of Ben, tender, affectionate, his eyes warm with love when he looked at Babs. That was the kind of man she had wanted to love. Not this hard, unfeeling, cold-eyed cowboy who laughed at her mockingly. That he wanted her physically, he had just proven. Seemingly tireless, he'd drawn her to him again and again, murmuring softly of a hunger that gnawed, a thirst that raged. In a mindless vortex of pleasure created by his caressing hands, his exciting mouth, Sam had floated in an unbelievably beautiful state of sensual sensation, until sheer exhaustion caught him, sent him into a deep sleep. No, she didn't want to love him, yet she faced the fact she was his. She did love him. She wept silently.

Sam woke slowly and stretched languidly, feeling completely relaxed and free of tension for the first time in weeks. Opening her eyes fully, she stiffened, shame flooding through her as she remembered the night before. She was alone, the house was very quiet, and she knew by the bright sunlight shining through the window that faced the porch, the only window in the room, that it was late in the day. Good Lord! Had she slept most of the day away? She had been exhausted till she had finally slept. The blackness of the room had changed to a pale gray. Now, the room in bright light, she looked around, she had not been in Morgan's bedroom before, not even when Sara had shown her the house. The bed she was lying in was huge, the biggest bed Sam had ever seen in her life, and at this moment was quite rumpled, a fact which made Sam's face warm. The walls and ceiling between the open beams were white, the furniture dark walnut. The carpet and matching draperies Mediterranean blue. Through the open bathroom door she could see that room was in black and white tile, even the towels were black and white. No frills, almost Spartan, definitely a man's room.

She jumped out of bed suddenly, thinking, I've got to get out of here, and her cheeks flamed again. She had not a stitch on. Her caftan and undies lay draped on the white chair in the corner, and she knew Morgan had picked them up, for when he had removed them the night before, they had been dropped carelessly in a heap on the floor.

Snatching them up and holding the gown against herself she opened the bedroom door cautiously, peeking out. Seeing the hall empty she dashed for her own room, sighing with relief as she closed the door behind her.

The salty drops mingled with the water as Sam stood numbly under the jet spray of the shower. She had to go, she decided, and it tore at her heart. Not to be near him, not to see him—the thought was almost unbearable. But she knew she had no choice, for how long would it be, if she stayed, before those mocking black eyes, filled with contempt, told her he knew how she felt?

Sam moved back and forth in the room packing her suitcase. She'd take only what she needed, Sara could send the rest of her things East later. She knew Sara was not in the house now, as she always had Sunday free after preparing the noon meal. And it was now after five. Sam had no idea if Morgan was in the house or not, as she had not left her room after fleeing his.

She went into the bathroom to collect her toiletries and stopped in her tracks as she came back into the bedroom. Morgan was leaning lazily against the bedroom doorframe, his thumbs hooked through two of the belt loops on his close-fitting jeans. The breath caught in Sam's throat. *What a magnificent male animal he is,* she thought. *Like a huge cat, at ease, relaxed, yet giving the impression of being ready to spring in an instant.* She felt a slight shiver as she watched him. His eyes went over her clothes and valise on the bed, the open closet door and bureau drawer. Then his cool glance came to rest on her. His voice was unconcerned.

"Running away, Redhead?"

Sam had control of herself now. She had had her cry, and in a cool, composed voice she answered, "I'm going home."

One black eyebrow arched and he drawled, "Really, I thought you were home." Before she could say anything he went on, "How are you going to explain your sudden appearance alone? Don't you think it will sound a little strange if, after assuring them you were in love, you tell them that after two weeks of marriage your husband raped you?"

Without stopping to think Sam gasped, "But you didn't," then stopped, shocked at her own denial.

Morgan laughed softly. "I know, I just wanted to make sure you did."

"I won't stay here," Sam snapped angrily.

"Why not?" Black eyes went over her slowly and Sam felt herself grow warm. She had not dressed after showering, but had slipped on a terry robe, belting it tightly. She moved away from his look, her bare feet silent on the carpet as she went to place her makeup bag in the suitcase. "You know why," she flung over her shoulder.

"Yes," he answered dryly. "Because you thought you'd bought yourself a man's name, and now you find the man came with it."

"How dare you," she breathed indignantly. "We made an agreement, a marriage in name only."

"I warned you last night, Redhead, I dare almost anything."

"I told you not to call me that," Sam said hotly, but he went on as if he hadn't heard her. "And I made no such agreement, not when Ben first talked to me about it or

79

when you and I discussed it later. If there were terms and conditions, it seems you forgot to tell me at the time, and it's a little late now." He paused, then added gently, "I'm sorry if I hurt you last night, but I had no way of knowing of your—er—virginal state."

"What kind of girl did you think I was?" Sam cried.

"I thought you were a woman," he snapped sharply. "My God, Samantha, you're going to be twenty-five soon. I didn't think any young woman reached that age and remained innocent today and I'll call you Redhead or anything else I damn well please."

Sam's cheeks were hot, and she opened her mouth to protest, but he hadn't finished. "I said I'm sorry I hurt you and I mean that, but I'm glad I was the first." Sam lowered her eyes so he could not read them as she thought, *I'm glad too.* Turning from him, she walked to the closet and reached blindly toward her clothes. Her hand stopped, became still, as his voice, hard now, lashed at her. "So you're going to run, throw it all away, because you haven't the guts to grow up."

Sam spun around, glaring at him. "What do you mean, throw it all away?"

Morgan's eyes were as cold as his voice. "I mean there'll be no polite little visits every now and then, so you don't lose the money. I'll divorce you, Samantha, and you can live off your stepmother until you find a man who'll marry you under your conditions. Or you might fall in love, if you're capable, and the physical side of it won't be so abhorrent to you."

"You really are a beast," she whispered.

"Maybe so," he said, his voice flat. "But that's beside the point. It's up to you. You can go or stay. But make no mistake, if you stay, what happened last night will happen again regularly." His voice hardened. "You can hate my guts for the next five years, but you'll stay put, I'll see to that. There will be no little side trips alone. If you want to go anywhere, it will be with me. And don't think I can't keep you here—I can." At the look which had come into her face as he spoke, he sighed in exasperation, rasped, "What the hell did you expect, Samantha? Did you really think we could live in the same house for five years without sex? Or did you suppose I'd keep a girl friend somewhere and drive back and forth after working fourteen hours a day?" She opened her mouth to answer him, but he went on harshly. "If you go now, it will be final. So make up your mind. What's it going to be, go or stay?"

Sam's eyes were wide, unbelieving. "You want an answer now? This minute? You won't give me time to think about it?"

He had moved into the room as he talked and now he stood, not more then two feet in front of her. His face was expressionless, his voice rough. "I've given you two weeks to think. As a matter of fact you should have thought it out before you married me. If you'll remember, I asked you if you had second thoughts the night before we got married. You assured me then that you didn't. You've had more than enough time, Samantha. What's it going to be?"

Sam turned away so he couldn't see her face. *He means it,* she thought wildly, *he'll divorce me. I won't see him again.* He had said, not knowing how she felt, she might fall in love. But she knew, somehow, deep inside, there would never be another man for her. It would be hell, she knew, if she stayed. Not being able to show her love, having him use her body to relieve his physical needs. But it would be worse not to be near him, not to see him at all. In a small, tired whisper she said, "I'll stay." Without a word, he turned her around and pulled her into his arms.

CHAPTER 5

Spring fever, lovesickness, Sam had both, and though she readily gave in to one, she silently riled at the other. What had she ever done to deserve Morgan Wade? The mere thought of his name set off a tingling reaction throughout her system that left her weak, longing for the sight of him.

From the time she was fourteen, Sam had been besieged by admirers. Some coaxed, some pleaded, a few even begged for a chance to make her care for them, but Sam had blithely gone her way, untouched, unmarked by any of them. The idea that, of all the men she'd known, this lean, long-legged cowboy could ignite her senses to the point of near madness, was a very bitter pill to swallow. For Morgan didn't coax, and Morgan didn't plead, and most emphatically, Morgan didn't beg. Morgan demanded. The fact that she gave in without demurs to his demands was the confidence-shattering self-knowledge that Sam riled against.

Sam slowed the mare to a walk and drank in the sweetness of spring on the land. *Being the complete idiot I am,* she thought wryly, a small smile of self-mockery twisting her lips, *I not only allow myself to become enslaved to the man, I go off the deep end for his land as well.* Bringing the horse to a complete stop, Sam idly stroked the mare's beautifully arched, golden neck, her eyes pinpointing the ranch buildings. When he had had the palomino cut out of the corral for her, Morgan had warned her not to lose sight of the buildings when she rode alone. Green eyes flashing rebelliously, Sam had turned on him angrily, but he cut off her hot protest before she could voice it.

"I mean it, Samantha. I don't want you riding out alone. I don't have the time, nor can I spare the men, to launch a search for you if you get lost. Which you probably would." Morgan paused, black eyes hard with determination. Then, seeing the disappointment she couldn't hide on her face, his voice gentled. "I'll take you out when I get the time." A teasing light entered his eyes. "If you're a good girl, Redhead, maybe we'll ride out on Sunday."

They had, and from that first ride across his property, Sam was a goner. Morgan's manner, though teasing, was easy, relaxed, as he showed her the land he so obviously loved. The mountains, with their color shadings at different times of the day, the Indian paintbrush, larkspur, and other spring flowers all had their effect on her. Whether it was the countryside or her guide, Sam wasn't quite sure, but for the first time in her life she felt as if she were home.

As spring faded into summer, and that too wore on, Morgan seemed to work even harder. He looked tired. The smooth skin over his cheeks and jaw grew tight and drawn and his hard slim body became even harder. When he held her at night the muscles in his arms, shoulders, and thighs felt like corded steel. He was drawn to a fine, tough edge and he frightened her a little at times.

Over coffee one evening in late spring Morgan casually told Sam he was thinking of buying a plane, a Lear jet, and just as casually asked her what she thought of the idea. Surprised, and flustered that he'd even bother to ask her, Sam had told him stiffly to do what he thought best, then watched in dismay as his eyes went flat and expressionless.

With a sharp nod of his head he'd left the room, murmuring cryptically, "I always do."

He'd bought the Lear and Sam hoped the plane, enabling him to get around faster, would give him more time. It hadn't. If anything, he seemed to have less.

Unsure of her position in their strange relationship, Sam asked few questions and Morgan volunteered little information. But she did learn, from the few things he did say, and the off-chance remarks made by Sara and Jake, that his interests did not lay wholly in the ranch as she had thought. He was in partnership in ranches in South America and Australia, owned interests in mines in Nevada and Africa, and was involved in other ventures in the States and Europe. She saw little more of him now than she had in the first two weeks of their marriage. He spent most of his time, the evenings he was at home, in his office, usually on the phone. If she had thought at first he had married her with the idea of her money making his life easier, she knew now how wrong she'd been. She had never known a man who worked harder. She felt a deepening respect for him, and she loved him to the point of distraction.

Most nights, when he was home, they slept together. He coming to her room when he'd finished in his office, usually very late. Other than the first time, she had spent only one night in the huge bed in his room.

It had been a particularly lovely night in late spring and Sam, curled into one of the big chairs in the living room, was reading. Morgan had been in his office not much more than an hour when he sauntered into the room and up to her chair. Bending over, he plucked the book from her fingers and as he dropped it to the floor, his voice was low, almost raw.

"It's too nice a night to waste, Redhead."

Scooping her into his arms, he'd carried her to his bedroom. Sam liked it there in that big bed. For some strange reason she felt more his wife in his bed. He had not taken her there again.

Her tears still wet his chest before she slept, but no longer from a feeling of shame. She honestly admitted to herself that her own physical need of him matched his for her. She wept now from frustration and fear. Frustration at having to wear a mask, hiding her true feelings from him. Fear that his own seemingly insatiable appetite for her would slacken and she'd find herself alone at night as well as in the daylight.

She was alone too much and now, in early August, it was beginning to show. She was losing weight. She ate very little when Morgan was home and hardly anything when he wasn't. Sara fussed over her to no avail. She simply was not hungry. Not for food.

Time was heavy, the days too long. The small jobs Sam found to do, the light housework, a small amount of cooking, puttering in the small garden Jake had helped her lay out, did not take nearly enough time. She went riding, but though she had always before enjoyed riding alone, it had somehow lost all appeal. She swam and sunbathed, her normal light tan turning to a deep golden color. She read. She paced. She wanted to scream. She grew tense and strained and was consumed with jealousy. Morgan was away often. He'd tell her casually the night before he left that he'd be away a few days. A few days often stretched into a week. She was positive there was another woman, possibly more than one. She knew that with a man like Morgan, handsome, charming when he chose to be, with a look of complete sensual masculinity, the women would gravitate to him, unable to keep their eyes or hands off him. When he was away, she hated him fiercely.

Sam had been away from the ranch only twice in the almost four and a half months she'd lived there. And for a young woman who was used to tearing around the world at the merest suggestion, the confinement was not easy to live with.

On a Friday evening not long after he had bought the jet, Morgan told Sam he had to fly to San Francisco in the morning. That statement alone surprised her as he never bothered to tell her where he was going, just that he was. After a small pause her surprise changed to an almost childlike excitement when he asked her if she'd care to go with him, adding that she could do some shopping while he took care of his business and then they could have dinner, perhaps see a show, and fly home Sunday morning. Sam forced her voice to sound calm, not wanting to appear overeager, and said she'd enjoy that, as she did have some shopping she could do. At the odd look that flashed quickly across his face, she had wondered miserably if he'd hoped she'd refuse. Nevertheless she had enjoyed the trip. Morgan was relaxed, charmingly attentive, which Sam attributed to their being in public, and seemingly quite willing to take Sam anywhere she wished to go.

Sam had shopped for hours but bought only a few things. A pair of riding gloves, two silk shirts, and a pair of terribly expensive white jeans that she couldn't resist, even though, when she'd pulled them on in the fitting room, they fit as though they'd been painted on her. She'd been completely happy with her day and was amused, on entering the hotel room to find Morgan already there, one brow raised at her few packages.

"It took you this long to buy that?"

She hadn't offered to show him what she'd bought, sure he wasn't in the least interested, and after a few long seconds he'd shrugged, dropped onto the bed, said he was going to grab a nap before dinner, and fell promptly asleep.

Their dinner on the Wharf had been superb, the show excellent, and on returning to their hotel room, Morgan's lovemaking ardent. Sam had returned to the ranch content. Her contentment didn't last long, however, as Morgan was away most of the time the next few weeks.

At the beginning of June, when Morgan was again away, and Sam was in what she'd always thought of as her bad time of the month, she thought that although she loved it, if she didn't get away from the house she'd go mad. On the spur of the moment she decided to visit Babs for a few days. Although they talked often on the phone, Sam had not seen Babs since her wedding day. She knew the silver gray Jaguar that Morgan had bought, again consulting her first, was in the garage. She had heard Morgan ask Jake the night before if he'd drive him to the small airfield where he kept the plane, as he wanted to go over some papers on the way, and she'd heard Jake put the car in the garage when he'd returned.

Hurrying into the kitchen, she told a startled Sara to go home and take care of Jake as she was going away for a few days, then had left the room on the fly before Sara could question her. She had thrown some clothes into her suitcase and left before she could change her mind. She was not concerned about driving the Jaguar—she had driven powerful cars ever since she became old enough to drive. What did nag at her was Morgan's words the day he'd given her the choice of go or stay. "If you go anywhere it will be with me." With a snort of impatience at herself, she shook off the feeling of unease and decided firmly she would enjoy herself. She had, although the warm, family atmosphere in Babs's home left her with a lonely, hurt, ache inside.

Morgan came home the day after Sam did. Waiting, like a coward she thought, for the right time to tell him where she'd been, he caught her off guard, as glancing up at her across the dinner table he said softly, "Have a nice vacation, Samantha?" Unable to believe that either Sara or Jake had said anything to him, Sam stammered, surprised, "H-how did you—?"

"You really should have filled the tank, you know," he cut in, his voice like silk. "That Jag eats up the gas." His voice rapped, "Where did you go?"

"To see Babs," she'd snapped, resenting his tone. "We all missed you," she added sweetly, then wished she hadn't, as she saw his eyes narrow.

He stared at her silently a few moments, his eyes glinting warningly. When he spoke, his voice was a threat.

"Next time you want to see Babs, tell me, and if I can take time off we'll go together, or invite them here. Don't go off by yourself again." At the flash of defiance in Sam's eyes he added, much too softly, "I mean it, Samantha."

The spark of fight went out of Sam, and she looked away from him. Why? Oh, why, she thought in self-disgust, did she allow this man to intimidate her like this? She had never in her life retreated from a man before. She didn't like the feeling.

That had been over two months ago, and although Morgan had not gone away as often in the last few weeks, Sam saw very little of him. They ate dinner later, as he stayed out as long as the light held, coming in dusty, his shirt sticking to him in dark wet patches. He slid into Sam's bed earlier than before too, sometimes, but not often, not even making love to her, just taking her into his arms and falling into a deep sleep within minutes.

Sam worked in the morning sun, fitfully pulling weeds in the herb garden behind the kitchen. Morgan had gone away two days before, the first time in weeks, and Sam was feeling moody and as surly as the weather. It had become mucky and close the day before, storms threatening which so far had not materialized, and Sam was hot and sticky and lonely.

She jumped up, pulling the gloves from her hands, on hearing the roar of the Jag as Morgan pulled into the drive. She was around the house and halfway to the car before he cut the engine.

She made herself slow down as she walked to the car, watching him hungrily as he unfolded himself from the driver's seat, then reach back inside for his suitcase. As he turned to her, she felt a stab of pure jealousy, positive he had been with another woman. The lines of strain were gone from his face and he looked rested for the first time in weeks.

He grinned at her, and she almost believed he was glad to see her. "This weather's a bitch isn't it?" Arching a brow at her sweat-soaked shirt and grubby knees below her shorts he added, "What in hell are you doing working in this heat, you crazy redhead? Why aren't you in the pool?"

Sam frowned at the word *redhead,* though she felt an icicle thrill go down her spine. She would never admit it, but she loved the sound of it on his lips. It had become, for her, a substitute for the endearments she never heard.

"You work in the heat." She kept her voice as light as his, not wanting to sour his good mood.

He laughed softly and dropped an arm over her shoulder as they walked toward the kitchen door.

"I wouldn't if I didn't have to," he lied.

The look Sam shot at him called him a liar and he laughed again softly, easily, and the stab of jealousy tore deeply into her. What was she like? Sam tormented herself with the thought. This woman who could make Morgan look and act like this.

He lifted his arm from her shoulder and opened the kitchen door for her to proceed him into the house. Inside he stood still for a second, looking around the empty, silent room. Then he turned sharply to Sam and her heart sank. His face had gone stiff, his eyes hard, and his soft, laughing voice of a moment ago now had a raw edge.

"Where's Sara?"

"She went into town with Jake to do some shopping," Sam answered as lightly as she could.

"You're alone here?" The edge was sharper.

Sam turned away biting her lip. *You don't have to worry, I won't run away,* she wanted to snap, but what she said was, "I don't mind, I like being alone."

"I know." His voice had an odd inflection that Sam couldn't understand. "And what about lunch?"

"Morgan, I am completely capable of preparing my own lunch, for heaven's sake." Sam felt let down and exasperated and now her own voice had an edge.

"I'm aware of that fact."

For some reason Sam didn't understand, his manner had changed again, he was relaxed, his voice light and teasing. "What I'm wondering is, are you prepared to make mine as well?"

"Well, of course!" The face she turned to him wore a surprised look at the abrupt change in him. Would she ever understand this man? Glancing at the clock and noting it was only ten thirty she asked, "Are you hungry? Do you want lunch now?"

"No, I'm not hungry—for lunch." Then he surprised Sam even more by adding, "Suppose you give me a half hour or so to check any messages Sara left on my desk

91

while I've been away, and then we'll have a swim together before we have lunch."

Sam's face looked even more surprised. He'd said it casually, as if they swam together regularly, when in fact they had never shared the pool. She answered quickly, forcing her voice to stay light, "All right, I'll have a shower while you're in your office." And she walked ahead of him out of the kitchen.

Standing under the shower, Sam felt the curl of excitement that had started with Morgan's words building inside. *Don't be a silly child,* she told herself softly, but she couldn't stop the feeling of happiness that washed over her. She felt almost grateful to that unknown woman who had sent Morgan home in such a relaxed mood. She had stepped out of the shower and was wrapping a towel around herself as she thought this and she became perfectly still. *I must surely be going mad,* she thought now, the feeling of happiness dying. The idea that she was thankful to another woman for any small crumb of pleasure Morgan might offhandedly offer her made Sam feel sick. A picture of herself six months ago flashed through her mind. Samantha Denning, laughingly turning her lips away from the mouths of the men she'd gone out with, coolly turning down their offers of marriage, frigidly telling them to keep their hands to themselves when they had reached out to touch her. And now, Samantha Wade, who trembled in the arms of this tall hard-eyed man, whose own arms slid around his neck eagerly as her mouth hungrily accepted his. *Oh, God!* she thought now. *Why should love be like this?* And she felt, for the first time, a measure of compassion for the men who had pleaded with her to marry them.

She stood there quite still, dripping on the bathmat for

a long time, and was jerked into movement by a short rap on her bedroom door as Morgan called.

"Hurry up, Redhead, I'll see you in the pool."

Sam quickly blotted herself off and twisted her hair back as she walked into the bedroom. Taking a long barrette from her dresser, she fastened the silky red mass to the back of her head, then stepped into the bottom of her bikini and gave a sign of dismay, for it hung on her hips. Shaking her head slightly, she reknotted the material, taking in the slack and put on the skimpy top, noting she had to tie that more tightly than before also. She turned to the full-length mirror on the closet door and gave herself a long, critical look. She was not happy with what she saw. She was much thinner, her collarbone and pelvic bones sticking out prominently. She had a dark, bruised look under her eyes and her face had a drawn, strained look. She grimaced in distaste, then turned sharply away, not wanting to look on the pitiful woman reflected there.

Sam stood at the side of the pool, watching Morgan's sinewy, powerful arms slice through the water. As he reached the far end and turned, he saw her and shot back across the pool. Placing his hand on the edge he lifted himself smoothly from the water. He stood in front of her, legs slightly apart, and brushed the shining black hair from his face. Standing still, his eyes raked over her. His voice soft, almost silky, chided, "You look like hell, Redhead, how much weight have you lost?" Reaching out his hand, he trailed his forefinger along her collarbone. "Haven't you been feeling well?" His voice sharpened as his hand moved to grasp her shoulder. "You're not pregnant, are you?"

Sam winced as his fingers dug into her soft flesh. "Of course not," she gasped, wondering at the strange look that sped across his face. "And I'm perfectly well, I've just

93

been minding the heat, I guess." Wanting to change the subject she added quickly, "Doesn't it ever rain here?" It worked, for he laughed, then drawled, "Not much." Looking up at the black clouds moving in the distance he added, "Even though it looks like it might before too long. So let's get our swim while we can." With those words he grabbed her hand and grinned at her squeal as he leaped into the water pulling her with him.

They swam side by side for some time, he matching his strokes to her shorter ones. When she stopped to catch her breath, he slid his big hand around her neck and drew her to him. His mouth close to hers, he whispered, "Let's get out of here, Redhead, I'm hungry." He laughed softly as she gasped and pulled away from him muttering, "Oh! Men!"

Sam stood in her room patting herself dry with the huge towel draped around her and turned swiftly on hearing her door open. Morgan sauntered into the room and Sam turned her back to him feeling her face flush as she clutched the towel firmly to herself. He was wearing nothing but a towel draped loosely about his lean hips and she went tense and rigid as he came up behind her, his arm coiling around her waist. Sliding under the edge of the towel and moving it aside, his hand caressed the smooth, still damp skin underneath. As she felt him lower his head, slide his lips along the sensitive skin on the side of her neck, Sam said breathlessly, "I thought you were hungry?"

His mouth close to her ear, he murmured in amusement, "Yes, but I didn't say what I was hungry for, Redhead." Giving her towel a quick hard tug he dropped it onto the floor as he turned her around into his arms.

"There are those who eat," he purred, "and those who eat."

Her body stiff, Sam decided firmly that this time she would not respond, but her decision wavered when his mouth found hers, his lips hard, demanding, urgent. In the next instant, as she felt his tongue search for and find her own, she sighed and went soft against him, her arms going around his neck, her fingers digging into his hair. He drank even more deeply of her mouth and his arms tightened, the one dropping to her hips, flattening her body against the length of his, letting her know his need of her.

Later, much later, Sam stood at the stove in her robe, watching the eggs she had just poured into the pan. Morgan sat stretched out on a kitchen chair, looking relaxed and somewhat smug. She could feel his eyes on her back, and she jumped at the sound of his voice, low and deep.

"One of the messages on my desk was to call the lawyers Baker."

Sam spun around, her brows raised in question.

"Don't scorch our lunch, kid."

"But what did—?"

"It will wait until we eat," he interrupted.

Sam turned the omelet onto a plate and sat it on the table next to the molded salad she had made early that morning. Seating herself, she turned to Morgan questioning, "What did the Bakers want?"

"Mmm, you really are a terrific cook, Redhead." He put another forkful of eggs into his mouth.

"Morgan." Her voice was low, tinged with warning.

His eyes stared blandly into hers as he slowly chewed and swallowed, the corner of his mouth twitching in amusement as he watched the green eyes start to spark with anger. Just as she was about to explode, he said calmly, "It seems there's a question concerning our

95

finances and they'd appreciate my going to New York to straighten out the problems."

"Are you going?" she asked softly, hesitatingly.

"I suppose I might as well, as Mr. Baker strikes me as the type who would just keep calling until I did," he answered offhandedly.

Sam nodded slowly, pushing the food around on her plate disinterestedly. *He'd said I, not we, but I.* She looked down at her plate and asked softly, a little fearfully, "May I go East with you, Morgan?"

He looked at her silently a few minutes, then his voice mocked. "Have you been a good girl, Samantha?" His eyes gleamed with deviltry as he watched her jerk upright in her chair.

Green eyes blazing, she sputtered, "Really Morgan, I'm not a child, I'll be twenty-five in a few days and you have no right to speak like—"

He cut in sharply, "Calm down, Redhead, and eat your lunch, you're thin enough." He paused, then went on, "That's right, you'll be celebrating a quarter century in a few days." He laughed at the look she threw him. "Now be nice, kid, and I'll think about it while you get my dessert. You do have dessert for me?"

Sam nodded, afraid if she opened her mouth she'd scream at him. She went to the refrigerator and removed the rich creamy rice pudding Sara had made the day before. She served him, then sat stiffly in her chair, poking at the jelled salad in front of her.

"Eat your salad," he ordered, then continued, "The pudding's very good. Aren't you having any?"

She shook her head, her lips tightly compressed. He was deliberately tormenting her, she knew, but she refused to give him the satisfaction of answering him back. Morgan finished his pudding and wiped his mouth with his napkin.

96

As he tossed it onto the table he said seriously, his face expressionless, "I'll make a bargain with you, Samantha."

Sam looked at him, not answering at once. What was he up to now? she wondered. "What sort of bargain?" she asked finally.

"I'll take you East with me, even stay a week or so in Long Island for you to spend your birthday with your family." Sam caught her breath, but he was going on. "On two conditions."

"What conditions?" Sam breathed, almost afraid to ask.

His eyes held hers, his voice was completely without emotion. "One, tomorrow morning you move your things into my room and, as of tonight, you sleep in my bed. I'm pretty damned tired of crawling out of your bed and trotting to my room to dress every morning." Sam felt her face flame, but his eyes held hers, which widened as he added. "Two, there'll be no more tears, late in the night, every time I make love to you."

So he hadn't been asleep as she'd thought. She hesitated a second and he said impatiently, "Well, will you bargain?" She managed to break the hold of his eyes and lowering hers, she whispered, "Yes."

He pushed his chair back, stood up, and walked around the table to her. Taking her by the shoulders, he lifted her from her chair. He bent his head, kissed her hard, then, lifting his mouth from hers, said softly, "It's a bargain sealed. Can you be ready to go by the end of the week?" Again she whispered, "Yes." Nodding almost curtly he removed his hands and left the room.

CHAPTER 6

Sam rested her head against the seat of the rented Ford and sighed in relief. She had forgotten what New York in August was like.

"Tired?" Morgan glanced at her, then returned his eyes to the highway.

"Not really," Sam settled more comfortably on the seat. "The air-conditioning feels lovely after the heat outside the airport."

He nodded, not looking at her, his eyes steady on the highway, a driver's nightmare with its usual Monday morning traffic heading into New York. Sam lowered her eyelids and looked at him through her lashes, studying him a moment. With his weight loss over the summer the sharply defined lines of his profile were intensified. The skin stretched firm and smooth over the high cheekbones and strong, hard jaw. The color of his skin exposed on his face, throat, and hands had deepened to a rich copper. Sam felt her face grow warm, remembering that except for a lighter swath around his hips, the rest of his body was the same dark color. And she wondered, a little uneasily, when and where he had acquired that color on his long straight legs. The more pronounced leanness had not detracted from his looks. If anything, he was more handsome than when she had first met him.

Morgan felt her eyes and, as one brow inched slowly upward, he drawled, "Something?"

Sam cast about in her mind in confusion and grabbed at the first thing that entered her head. "I—I was just wondering what everyone will think of you." She called herself all kinds of an idiot as she watched the corner of his finely defined lips twitch in amusement.

"I've been meaning to talk to you about that, Redhead." The soft drawl heavier, he added, "I suppose, when we get to Long Island, like it or not, we'll have to play the role of newlyweds."

"Yes, I know." Sam wondered how she had managed to keep her voice so cool. His choice of words had hurt, even though she felt relief wash over her at them. She had become more tense and nervous about this every day since she had agreed to his bargain six days ago. The added days had not helped. Morgan had not been able to get away at the end of the week as he'd planned and had told Sam the trip East would have to wait.

Sam turned her head away from him and closed her eyes, letting her mind drift back over the last six days. She had kept her part of the bargain, and as the threatened storm had finally broken that night, was glad to huddle close to Morgan in the big bed. She had never been afraid of storms, but somehow out there in the space between the mountains, it had seemed so much more threatening. The thunder had rumbled angrily, the lightning cracked long and sharp, brightening the bedroom with its fierce but cold light. Sam had clung to Morgan, feeling safe in his strong, hard arms and ignored the silent laughter that shook his broad chest.

The first few days had not been too bad. She and Sara had been busy, first with transferring Sam's things into Morgan's room, Sara's face telling Sam plainly she

99

thought the move right and proper, then straightening the now empty room. After Thursday night, when Morgan informed her they could not leave until Monday, the tension started to build inside her. She had called Mary and Deb to tell them they were coming, then had had to call them back telling them of the change in plans. She had become steadily more tense, afraid that for some reason or other they would not be able to leave, and if they did, what would be the reaction of her friends and family to Morgan. Then this morning, before daylight, she had awakened to Morgan calling her name softly and had opened her eyes to find his face close to hers as he whispered, "If you're going with me, Redhead, you'd better get moving. I'm leaving in one hour." She'd jumped from the bed and ran to the bathroom, his laughter following her. The flight East had been smooth and uneventful. Morgan flew the jet exactly as he drove the car, expertly.

Sam, bringing her thoughts to the present, opened her eyes and felt a thrill of excitement seeing they were close to the city. Morgan had an appointment with the Messrs. Baker which, Sam noted glancing at her watch, he would make just in time. She planned to do some shopping, her weight loss being such that few of her clothes fit properly. Sam decided she'd look for a special dress, as Mary was planning a belated wedding party and birthday celebration for Friday evening. The thought caused her pain. This was her twenty-fifth birthday. Morgan had forgotten. She gave herself a mental shake, whyever did she think he'd remember.

They reached their hotel and dispensed with the rented car. In the large room Morgan asked if she needed money, which she didn't, told her he had to go or he'd be late, said he'd see her whenever, and left.

Sam went into the bathroom to freshen up and looked

100

at herself in the mirror. She didn't like what she saw. Her hair pulled back into the usual coil around her head made her face look even thinner than it was. Something had to be done, she decided. She walked quickly to the phone and called her hairdresser. She knew the shop was always closed on Mondays. She also knew he was usually in the shop on Mondays, and was not surprised when she heard his smooth, clear voice answer, something he never did when the shop was open, as he paid a receptionist a very high salary to do it for him.

"Charles?" Sam said, not waiting for a reply as she knew it was him, "Samantha Wa—Denning."

"Samantha," Charles purred. "Wherever have you been, darling? I haven't seen you in ages."

"I've been away, getting married." She answered evenly, and smiled at his reaction.

"What in the world did you want to do that for? Oh, well, no matter, what can I do for you, sweetheart?"

Sam smiled again at the way the endearments rolled off his glib tongue. She knew that many people had doubts about Charles's masculinity, but she had none. If she had ever had any, they had been dispelled the day she found herself alone, not by accident she was now sure, with him in the shop and he'd tried to seduce her in the beautician's chair. She'd had a fight on her hands that day, but she'd won it. He had accepted his defeat graciously, and they were good friends.

"My hair's a sight," she laughed, "and there's a big to-do the end of the week." Sam inserted a pleading note, "Charles, you must help me."

She heard him chuckle softly. "You know I'm closed Monday, you beautiful baggage, but come around and I'll see what I can do with that red mop."

"Thank you, Charles, you're a love." Sam heard him

chuckle again as she replaced the receiver. Six hours later Sam stepped into the hotel elevator and pushed the button for their floor. She felt tired but good, and although she carried only one package, she had spent a lot of money, having all but one outfit sent to the address on Long Island. She smiled to herself as her hand went up to her hair, the long slim fingers sliding into the loose curls. She loved the cut Charles had given her. He had called it a savage cut, short and loosely curled at the top and temples, the crown and sides tapered in length to blend into the long deep waves that fell halfway down her back, which he hadn't touched. She laughed aloud, softly remembering his words as he'd stood back to look at her and admire his own work. "Lord, Sam, you're a beautiful creature. That cut gives you a wild, free look. Why did you do an idiotic thing like get married?"

Her face sobered, *Wild and free.* Well, she certainly hadn't been too wild lately, and she'd never be free again.

She walked into the room and stopped, closing the door softly behind her. Morgan sat sprawled lazily in the chair by the window, reading the *Times,* his long legs stretched out in front of him. He looked up as she entered and went dead still, the paper held motionless. She endured his scrutiny as long as she could. Somehow she managed to keep her voice cool. "Do you like it?"

He folded the paper and dropped it on the floor, his eyes on her, before answering, his voice deep. "You look like a redheaded witch. Are you?" Before she could say anything, he added, "You must be. Cast a spell too. I can feel it doing strange things to me already." His voice went lower. "Come here, Samantha."

"Morgan, I'm hot and tired, I—"

Even lower. "Come here."

"I'm starving, I want my din—"

Almost a whisper now, and a definite warning. "Samantha."

Sam walked across the room slowly, dropping the package and her handbag on the bed as she passed. She stopped in front of him and as his hand went to her waist she saw something flash in the late afternoon sunlight coming through the window. His hand drew her down to her knees on the floor between his legs then, taking her left hand, he removed a ring from the end of his finger and slid it along hers till it touched the narrow band of platinum already there. Her eyes widening as she stared at it, she exclaimed. "That's the most beautiful thing I've ever seen!"

The large emerald-cut emerald, set in platinum with two diamond baguettes on either side looked almost too heavy for her slim hand. The deep, clear color of the stone matched the eyes she lifted to his. "Morgan, what—?"

"Happy Birthday, redheaded witch," he murmured.

"I—I don't know what to say," Sam stammered.

He leaned back in the chair, his hands, clasped on her waist, drew her up to him, against him. His mouth an inch from hers, he whispered, "We'll think of some way for you to thank me."

"Are you hungry?" The words were spoken softly when Sam opened her eyes. She turned her head to see Morgan, fully dressed, sitting in the chair by the window.

"Famished," she murmured, her voice blurred with sleepiness. She closed her eyes again. She felt absolutely hollow. She had been looking forward to dinner with longing as she returned from shopping yesterday, and she hadn't had any. Morgan had said he'd think of some way for her to thank him, then had proceeded to show her exactly where his thinking led. As on the first night, he'd been tireless, and she had wondered at the almost desperate urgency of his lovemaking. When, finally, he'd stretched out on his back and drew her into his arms, pulling the covers over them both, she was exhausted, all thoughts of food gone.

"What time is it?" She yawned. Her eyes flew open as he drawled, a hint of laughter in his voice, "Nine thirty."

"Nine thirty! Why didn't you wake me? Dave will be here with the car at eleven." She sat bolt upright, then blushing, clutched the sheet around her nakedness. Morgan laughed out loud and she sat glaring at him. He returned her stare, the corners of his mouth twitching. Sam could see he had no intention of either turning around or leaving the room and her voice became a plea, "Morgan, please."

He shook his head and grinned at her. "You have one hour and thirty minutes to get yourself dressed, fed, and ready to leave this hotel by the time the car gets here. But first, you must get from that bed to that bathroom and I'm quite comfortable where I am, thank you." His grin widened as eyes flashing, she snapped, "Damn you," lifted her chin, threw back the sheet, jumped from the bed and ran for the bathroom.

They walked through the hotel doors just as the midnight-blue Cadillac slid alongside the curb. Dave jumped out to open the door to the back seat, his eyes going over Sam anxiously before, growing guarded, he turned to Morgan.

Sam hurried across the pavement, looking cool and lovely in the pale pink shift and matching sandals she had brought the day before. Stretching out her hand to him she said softly, "Hello, Dave, how are you?"

"I'm fine." He clasped her slim hand firmly a moment, his eyes warm. "Welcome home, Miss Sam."

Morgan stood tall and quiet behind her and, a little breathless, she introduced them. "Dave, this is my husband, Morgan Wade." Turning her head slightly to Morgan, she smiled coolly, and added without a catch, "Darling, our driver and friend, Dave Zimmer."

Morgan was silent, his face expressionless. In confusion Sam turned back to see Dave's eyes study Morgan briefly before extending his hand, Morgan's arm shot past her and as his hand clasped Dave's he said, a small smile twitching his lips, "I assure you, Dave, I'm taking very good care of her."

"Yes, sir, Mr. Wade."

They settled themselves on the back seat and Dave's face, as he slid behind the wheel, told Sam he was satisfied. With a few quiet words, Morgan had acquired a follower.

Sam was tense, and although Morgan had not even blinked when she had called him darling, she was worrying over what attitude he'd assume when meeting Mary and Deb. She glanced at him quickly. He looked healthy and full of vitality and altogether too handsome in a tan suit with a white and brown striped silk shirt, the white contrasting sharply with the dark brown of his face and throat. *The wretched man hasn't even the grace to look tired,* she thought peevishly, and felt her cheeks grow warm remembering the night before. Catching her look, Morgan arched a brow and grinned wickedly at her as if he'd read her thoughts.

Her tension mounting, Sam gave a sigh of relief, wanting to have it over with, when the big car turned into the drive and slowed to a stop in front of the big house.

"Very elegant," Morgan said softly, stepping out of the car and turning to help Sam before Dave had cut the engine.

As Sam stepped from the car, the front door opened and

a small, dark-haired figure ran lightly down the steps and in a soft, lilting voice cried, "Sam," as she hurtled herself into Sam's arms.

Sam hugged her half sister, then held her away from her, laughing softly. "Poppet, you're looking positively radiant."

"Oh, Sam, I've missed you so much. It's seemed like ages," Deb said softly and Sam felt the breath catch in her throat, for Deb had tears in her eyes. Then Deb turned, an unsure look on her face, and tilted her head way back to look at Morgan, who had stood quietly watching. She put her hand out slowly. "Morgan?"

Morgan took her hand into his, and Sam was astonished at the look of tenderness on his face as he said gently, "I've never had a sister, Deb, but if I had, I'd want her to be just like you, small and dark and captivating." He paused, then added, "Will you be my sister, Deb?"

Sam watched, some of the tension inside her lessening, as the unsure look on Deb's face changed to one of enchantment. "I'd love to be your sister, Morgan," Deb answered, a radiant smile curving her lips.

Stepping forward, Morgan let go of Deb's hand to scoop her off her feet and into his arms, kissing her soundly on the mouth.

"Don't enjoy that too much, Deb." The pleasant warning came from Bryan as he came slowly down the steps.

Morgan sat a laughing Deb back on her feet and she turned to Bryan, who came to a stop next to her. "Darling, this is Morgan and as he is my new brother, you must be nice to him."

"As long as he doesn't make a habit of kissing you," he answered dryly, looking up at Morgan, who stood a good four inches taller than he did. The two men eyed each other silently a few seconds, each taking the other's measure, then seemed to reach a decision simultaniously as both grinned and put forth a hand.

"Bryan."

"Morgan."

Bryan turned to Sam and Morgan saw the same warm look in his eyes that he'd seen in Dave's as he murmured almost the exact same words. "Welcome home, Sam."

"Hello, Pet." Smiling, Sam walked into his outstretched arms.

Morgan's voice was as dry as Bryan's had been a few moments ago. "As long as you don't make a habit of that, Bryan."

Laughing easily together, the four mounted the steps and entered the house. The feeling of ease left Sam abruptly when, once inside the large hall, Deb said, "Mother's waiting in the small sitting room, Sam." Arm in arm, she and Bryan walked in the direction of that room.

Sam's steps faltered and without saying anything or even looking at her, Morgan took her hand, entwined his fingers in hers and drew her along behind the other couple.

"Settle down, Red," he drawled softly. "I promise I won't let you down. Be a good girl and your family will be as ignorant of our deception when we leave as they are right now."

Sam shot a startled, uneasy glance at him, but they were at the sitting room doorway before she could form a reply.

As they entered the room, Mary stood, hands outstretched, saying in her sweet, cultured voice, "Samantha, darling, I can't tell you how good it is to see you and have you home again."

Morgan loosened his hold. Steps hurrying now, Sam went to Mary, put her hands in hers and, bending, kissed her soft cheek. "And it's wonderful to be here with you, Mother." Then, turning, "Here's Morgan."

107

Her stepmother was delicate and sometimes seemed a trifle vague, but everyone in the house knew that very little escaped her attention. So Sam held her breath as Morgan, bending over the petite woman, enclosed her tiny hand in his large one. "I'm happy to meet you, finally, Mrs. Denning. May I call you Mary?" On her nod, he continued. "Though I could hardly believe her, you are every bit as lovely as Sam said you were."

Mary's cheeks pinked becomingly. "How charming you are." Her eyes dancing, she added, "And I'm afraid a bit of a rogue."

Morgan grinned, his black eyes laughing. "You won't tell anyone, will you?"

Mary's soft, sweet laughter floated through the air. "I hardly think that will be necessary, my dear. Now, I'm sure you both want to freshen up. Samantha, dear, you're in your own room, of course. Take Morgan up and join us for lunch whenever you're ready."

Sam closed the door gently behind her, watching Morgan as he sauntered into her room, his eyes missing nothing. "Thank you," she whispered.

He turned slowly, his eyes pinning her to the door. "What for?"

"For being so nice to them. They're very important to me."

His voice was very low. "I know that. It was easy to be nice to them, they're very nice people." His voice took on an edge. "For God's sake, Sam, what did you expect me to do?"

She shrugged helplessly, despite his words earlier, she had been worried. "I don't know, but, I was afraid." Her breath caught; she could say no more.

His eyes mocked her, his voice was impatient. "I know

that too. Five months and you don't know me at all, do you, Redhead?"

She straightened, moving away from the door. She was home, in her own room and she was determined, no matter how much she loved him, he would not intimidate her here. "I know you as well as I care to," she said coolly, walking to the bathroom. Her hand on the doorknob, his laughing voice stopped her.

"It won't work, Samantha."

Sam felt a small shiver trickle down her stiff spine. Forcing her voice to remain cool, she snapped. "I don't know what you mean."

His laughter deepened, as did his voice. "No? I think you do. Planning to put me in my place while we're here, aren't you? You won't, but have fun trying, Redhead, because I'm going to enjoy watching you."

She spun around, her eyes blazing and without taking time to think, bit out, "You really are an arrogant bastard, aren't you?" She stopped, appalled at herself.

He was across the room in a few strides, gripping her shoulders painfully, his eyes and voice hard with anger.

"Is that how you think of me?"

"Morgan, I'm sorry."

"Don't ever be sorry for saying what you think to me. I'm your husband and regardless of what you think of me, we have a bargain and you'll stick to it." The anger seemed to drain out of him and dropping his hands to his sides he said calmly, "We don't want to keep your family waiting too long for their lunch." Pulling the bathroom door open for her he added, "Don't be too long—darling."

Sam's hands shook as she washed her face and applied fresh makeup lightly. She was more frightened of him when he was cool and calm than when he was angry.

Sam's nerves grew taut over the next few days. She felt like she was living with two different people. When they were alone in the bedroom, Morgan was reserved, withdrawn. He barely spoke to her and for the first time since he'd carried her to his bed and made her his, he didn't touch her at night. When they were with other people he was charming and attentive, the endearments coming smoothly and easily from his mouth.

Mary and Deb had told no one they were coming, wanting to have Sam to themselves for the few days before the party. Sam and Morgan spent those days horseback riding with Deb and Bryan or lazing by the pool, for all the world like a happy family group.

By Friday morning Sam felt slightly sick with apprehension. Morgan would be meeting her friends for the first time at the party and she wondered nervously what they would think of him and, more importantly, what he would think of them.

Sam found herself alone soon after breakfast, Mary and Deb having gone shopping for some last-minute items for the party. Morgan was gone when she woke and hadn't returned for breakfast. Restlessly she paced her room, then, grabbing up her purse, she left the room and ran down the steps. She'd go for a drive. Always before, whenever she was upset, she drove alone, and it had always soothed her, calmed her down. She hadn't driven her car since coming home, hadn't even looked at it, and now as she left the house by a side door and hurried along the graveled walk to the row of garages in back, she was eager to get behind the wheel again. Although she knew that Dave would have kept her car in perfect running condition, it would probably do it good if she gave it a good run.

Hurrying along, head bent, Sam was deep in thought, remembering the last time she'd had to let off tension by driving alone. She'd quarreled bitterly with her father. Over what? She couldn't remember, but she remembered leaving the house in anger and driving, much too fast, for over an hour. When she'd returned, the anger was gone and she'd calmly gone to her father and smoothed over their argument. Two weeks later he was dead and she was thankful now that she'd—

"Going somewhere, Redhead?" Morgan's voice cut across her thoughts, and she stopped, startled, looking up quickly. He stood leaning against the Cadillac parked in front of the garage.

"I didn't hear the car," Sam said in confusion. He'd been riding and Sam's eyes ran the length of him. He wore flat-heeled boots and his long legs and slim hips were encased in tight black jeans. A white shirt open at the throat, sleeves rolled to the elbow, was an assault on the eyes in the bright morning sunlight. Within seconds every detail about him registered in her mind. The gold watch gleaming against the dark skin on his wrist, the narrow platinum band on his finger, the crisp black hair, the ends given a silvery look by the sunlight. His eyes were hidden from her by large wire-framed sunglasses, and his mouth, sensuous, the lips perfectly outlined, which could become suddenly straight and hard, now curved in mild amusement.

Sam took him all in and was shattered emotionally. As she moved, began walking toward him, she admitted to herself that the only thing on this earth she wanted was to walk up to him, slide her arms around that slim waist, fasten her mouth to his and feel the long, lean hardness of his body against hers. Her thoughts brought her up short, and she eyed him in resentment. Why, why, of all the men she'd met, did it have to be this one? This cowboy who looked at her in contemptuous amusement.

"I've been here awhile." His voice was pure silk. "And I asked you a question."

Anger burned through her. Who the hell did he think he was? Her voice frosty, she said, "I'm going for a drive."

"Dave driving?"

"Of course not! I'm taking my car." Sam ground her teeth as she watched one black brow arch above the rim of his sunglasses.

"I'll go with you," he said softly.

"No," she almost shouted the word at him.

The tone lowered, became a soft purr. "I said I'll go with you."

Sam glared at him, then stormed into the garage, slid behind the wheel and backed the red Stingray out of its stall.

Now both brows peeked over the glass rims and as Morgan folded himself into the seat next to her, he murmured, "Nice little toy you have here."

She smiled sweetly at him. "I hope you're comfortable —darling."

Morgan grinned at her and in fury she tore along the drive and onto the road and for the next thirty minutes drove like the demons of hell were tailgating her. He sat silent until she had ripped back up the driveway and into the stall, stopping the car a bare half inch from the back wall. Watching her, his attitude one of complete boredom, he removed his sunglasses, held them by one earpiece between thumb and forefinger and gently swung them back and forth. "Feel better now, Redhead?" he drawled. Bending and leaning to her, he kissed her lightly on the lips.

His utter indifference exploded the already seething anger inside her. Sam didn't think, she reacted. Her hand flew up and across his face, then back to her mouth. In horror at what she'd done, she watched his eyes and face go hard. The red mark of her fingers growing on his cheek, he said coldly, "You're behaving like a very spoiled little girl, Samantha, and I'm getting a little sick of it. Be very careful you don't twist the tiger's tail too hard, or you're liable to find you've started something you can't finish."

Sam sat rigid as, without looking at her again, Morgan slid his body up the back of the seat to an almost standing position and stepped over and out of the car.

Although she felt rather sick, with nerves fluttering in her stomach, Sam managed a small salad at lunch, but begged off dinner, claiming a headache, promising Mary she'd have a nap before the party. In fact she did fall asleep after swallowing two aspirin and stretching out across the bed. She woke to find Morgan already showered and getting dressed. Without a word she entered the bathroom, taking an extra long time over her bath and applying her makeup until, relief washing over her, she heard the bedroom door close behind him.

She entered the now empty bedroom, stepped into lacy white briefs and gold evening sandals. She brushed her hair into deliberately wild and disordered curls around her face. She sprayed herself lavishly with a light, spicy perfume and, with more than a little trepidation, she went to her closet and removed her new gown, putting it on quickly before she could change her mind. Why had she bought it? she wondered, as she studied her reflection in the long mirror. It was not her usual style at all.

Of white lace, it contrasted perfectly with the beautiful golden glow her skin had acquired over the summer. But, she reflected, it revealed much too much skin. There was very little to the top of the dress, nothing at all to the back, being cut out like a large U from one shoulder to the other. The front had little more material as it plunged in a V from her shoulders almost to her waist. The ends of her shoulders, about an inch, and her arms were covered, the sleeves of the dress being long and full. The cut of the gown gave her waist an even smaller look, and from the waist the material fit perfectly over her hips and fell straight to the floor, giving her a long, leggy look.

Sam shook her head slowly at her reflection. No, Morgan was definitely not going to approve. Glancing at the clock, she realized she was already late, so with a small shrug of her shoulders, she straightened her back, lifted her chin, and left the room.

Morgan was the first person Sam saw as she came slowly down the broad, curving staircase. He stood talking to Mary and some of Sam's friends, and as if he sensed her there on the stairs, he looked up, then went completely still. She saw a flicker of surprise go across his face and his eyes widen for an instant before narrowing. His reaction had lasted only seconds, but Sam knew he was angry, very angry. She continued to move down the stairs, her breath catching in her throat, as she watched Morgan murmur a few words to Mary and start toward her. He had taken a few strides, then stopped short, his face going hard, as a deep, caressing voice was raised above the normal tones of the other guests. "Sam, my love, if you intended to make an entrance, you've certainly succeeded. You look positively ravishing."

Sam saw Morgan turn sharply and walk away before she turned, at the bottom of the stairs now, and smilingly placed her hands into the outstretched ones of the owner of that deep voice.

Jeffrey Hampton was as handsome as ever. Tall and fair, his light hair gleaming in the brightly lit hall, he stood smiling at her, his eyes bright with admiration. Leaning to her, he kissed her gently on the mouth and said softly,

"It's great to see you again, angel, it's been a very dull summer with you not here."

Sam laughed up at him, but said in a stern voice, "Jeffrey Hampton, that's an awful thing for you to say, in view of the fact that you became engaged this summer."

"Oh, that," he shrugged lightly. "What has that to do with the fact that I still love you madly and missed you?"

Sam frowned. "Jeff, behave yourself." But she had to smile again at the quick impish grin he gave her. She had turned down his proposal of marriage twice, but even so had continued to go around with him. He was a charming, delightful companion and they had fun together.

Now she couldn't help comparing him with the man she'd married. As always, he was elegantly dressed, tonight in midnight-blue evening clothes, with a pale-blue shirt with ruffles at the front and wrists. As Jeff cupped her elbow with his hand and led her into the large room off the hall cleared of all furniture and full of laughing, talking people, she realized she hadn't even noticed what Morgan was wearing.

She glanced around quickly and saw him across the room standing in front of the fireplace, looking completely relaxed, with one arm resting against the mantelpiece, drink in hand, looking down at the young woman speaking to him. Sam's eyes went over him and, as before, the look of him did strange things to her legs and made her breath catch in her throat. His black evening clothes were perfectly cut to his long, lithe frame and along with his dark skin and black brows and hair, gave him a slightly satanic look. His white shirt and flashing white teeth, as he suddenly smiled, looked startling against all that darkness. Her eyes shifted to the woman he'd smiled at—Jeff's newly acquired fiancée, Carolyn Henkes.

Sam had never liked Carolyn overmuch and now, as she

watched her flutter long, pale-gold lashes up at Morgan, she decided she liked her even less. That Carolyn was a beauty, Sam would not deny. With long white-gold hair that framed a beautiful pink and white heartshaped face, out of which gazed large cornflower-blue eyes, she was as lovely as an exquisite china doll and, Sam knew, just as brittle. She could be delightful and sweet, but equally biting and vicious if she thought her interests were threatened. Morgan, Sam noted with dismay, seemed captivated by her.

She heard Jeff chuckle close to her ear and knew his eyes had followed hers as he whispered, "It would seem my intended is quite taken with your somewhat overpowering husband."

A few minutes later, as the music started, Sam felt Morgan's arm slide around her waist, heard him drawl softly, "I think we're to have the first dance—darling." He led her to the cleared area at the end of the long room. His appearance was that of the happy, devoted bridegroom as he drew her into his arms and bent his smiling face to her. But Sam felt cold apprehension go through her, for every muscle in his body was tense with anger and his voice, in her ear, whispered harshly, "What the hell are you trying to prove with that dress?"

CHAPTER 7

Some six hours later Sam entered her room and stood rigid, fists at her sides, her back to the door. She knew there was an angry argument about to follow her and, sighing deeply, she moved into the room, kicking her sandals off as she went. The white shag rug felt good to her tired feet and she stood still, in the center of the room, curling her toes against the soft fibers. She felt tired and slightly lightheaded. She had eaten very little all day and had had far too much champagne, as she had seemed to acquire an almost unquenchable thirst after that first dance.

The party had been torment for her. Morgan had barely talked to her after that first dance and yet he had managed to give the impression of their being the happy newlyweds as he moved about the room meeting her friends. He had danced with all the women and stood and talked with all the men, occasionally giving her one of his devastating white smiles. But his eyes did not smile and Sam could see the fury glittering in them across the width of the room. She had not been the one at his side, making the introductions. Carolyn, smiling up at him and hanging onto his arm like a growth, had performed that duty for her, occasionally casting Sam a smug, malicious glance.

Jeff had been her shadow all evening. As she had moved

about, forcing herself to talk and laugh with her friends, he had become increasingly more familar, dropping his arm first about her shoulders, then around her waist. Each time he danced with her his hand grew more bold, caressing her exposed back. Sam had told him warningly to stop when he had slid his fingers under the material and along her side. She had given her warning softly, not wanting to draw attention to herself. Jeff had laughed at her and, taking her hand, had drawn her through the french windows into the garden. The garden had been transformed into a make-believe place of moving lights and shadows by the strings of patio lights draped from tree to tree for the party. There were couples dancing on the grass just outside the doors and Jeff kept moving deeper into the garden along the hedge-lined path away from the glow of the lights. He had stopped suddenly and, without a word, pulled her into his arms and kissed her.

Sam stood passive a few moments. Jeff's kiss, as always before, was pleasant, but it struck no response from her. When she didn't respond, Jeff's lips became more demanding and Sam pulled herself free and walked away from him, deeper into the shadows. She had walked a short distance when she stopped, then, turning quickly, hurried back to Jeff, and in a voice barely controlling her anger, told him she wanted a drink. He didn't argue, thinking her anger directed at him, but followed her quietly into the house.

Sam brought the wineglass to her lips, amazed at the intensity of her feelings. Her hands were shaking and she drained the glass quickly and put it down before anyone noticed. Pain tore through her as a picture of what she had seen flashed across her mind. Carolyn, smiling face upturned, one arm stretched out, fingers touching his cheek. Morgan, white teeth flashing in his dark face as he bent over her, his big hands closing on her shoulders. It had taken every ounce of will power Sam possessed to turn away and walk back to the house. She had wanted to scream and fly at Carolyn's face with her nails. Somehow she managed to get through what was left of the evening without giving herself away. Now, as she stood absolutely still in the middle of her room, her nails dug into her palms and she felt her back stiffen. She had been sure he saw other women when away, but to actually see him, here!

Sam froze as the door opened, then closed quietly. The long silent moment drew her nerves taut and she spun angrily at his softly grated, "Get that goddamned rag off before I do it for you."

Her mouth open to argue, the words died in Sam's throat when she looked at him. The look of him frightened her. He leaned lazily against the door, and she thought wildly that he looked like some huge cat ready to pounce on her. She had never seen him this angry and, although his voice had been soft, she could see he was fighting to control himself. His face seemed carved in stone and his eyes, which could look hard and cold as black ice, now blazed at her in fury.

Sam found her voice and even managed to keep it cool. "You have no right to speak to me like that."

His purred answer drew fingers of ice down her spine. "You have thirty seconds."

Sam stared at him. This didn't make sense. All this fury over a gown? She lifted her head even higher, cool green eyes matched her tone, giving away nothing of the unease she felt. "Morgan, I don't think I understand what this is all about."

"No?" Eyes narrowing, he moved toward her. Her pose of cool indifference seemed to unleash the heat inside him. The purr took on a very rough edge. "Then I'll tell you what it's all about. That dress is an open invitation to all comers." As she opened her mouth to protest, he snarled harshly, "Don't interrupt. You're my wife, Samantha, my woman, you use my name. And what wears my brand is mine. I don't share my wealth."

All composure gone, voice rising, Sam cried, "Wears your brand? Morgan, I'm a person, not part of your stock."

"I never said you were, but that ring you wear is my brand and as long as you wear it, you're mine." Voice low, menacing he added, "And if your pretty boyfriend ever puts his hands on you again I'll drop him. Now get that damn dress off."

Sam winced as if the words he rapped out at her actually struck her. Turning her back, she put trembling fingers to the small zipper at the back of her waist and tugged. She drew the sleeves from her arms and the dress slid from her to the floor, forming a circle around her feet. In defiance, she stepped outside that circle and kicked the garment across the room. Standing straight and stiff, the lacy panties her only covering, she heard a low humorless chuckle behind her and, eyes wide, watched his jacket, shirt and tie arch through the air and land on top of her gown.

"No," Sam whispered, her shaking hand reaching for the nightgown lying across the foot of the bed next to which she stood.

Morgan's hand closed around her wrist; his voice was a harsh whisper in her ear. "Did you enjoy the feel of pretty boy's hands and lips, Samantha?"

His words hurt. A picture of him bending over Carolyn flashed through her mind, and that hurt even more. She wanted to hurt back, and giving no thought to her nudity, she wrenched her arm from his hand and turned on him hotly. "You bloody beast. How dare you? Jeff's an old friend and he loves me. He's gentle and considerate and I should have married him when he asked me." She was lashing out blindly, not pausing to think, trying to inflict on him a small measure of the pain she had felt tear through her in the garden. "I'll see him whenever I wish and if I want to go to bed with him, I shall. He at least doesn't want my money." Pulling his rings from her finger, she threw them at his face. "And you can take your brand and you can—"

The words died on her lips for, after throwing the rings, she had tossed back her head and seen his face. Real fear crawled through her stomach as his hands gripped her shoulders painfully. "You redheaded witch," he gritted between clenched teeth. "You try and put horns on me with Hampton and I'll take him apart—slowly. Do you understand that?"

Sam nodded dumbly, unable to take her eyes from his savage face, fighting the panic growing inside. Releasing her shoulders he stepped back. "Pick your rings up and put them on. Now."

It was a command, and without question she hurried to obey. But a spark of defiance made her say as she straightened, sliding the rings into place, "May I please go to bed now?"

The grin he gave her was wicked as, cupping her chin in his hand, he bent his head to hers and said mockingly, "I thought you'd never ask."

Sam jerked her head away as his mouth touched hers. "No, Morgan, it's late and I'm very tired, I want—"

"Too bad." His words cut across hers like a steel blade. "I warned you to be careful not to twist the tiger's tail too hard. You had to see just how far you could go, didn't you, Red?" He pulled her against him, his mouth hard, demanding, hurting hers.

The sound of his voice, his unbridled rage, frightened Sam and she fought him. She kicked him, hit out with her hands balled into fists and she tore at his hair.

His face grim, set, he picked her up and dumped her onto the bed. She lay sprawled, gasping for breath, her eyes wide with shock, watching him as he stripped off the rest of his clothes. Rolling over she tried to jump from the other side of the bed, but Morgan dropped down beside her, and his arm shot out and around her waist, dragging her back against him. She fought like a wild thing, twisting and arching her body away from him, hitting, kicking. She cursed him in a raw, breathless hiss and he laughed at her. Twice she was rewarded for her efforts when she heard him grunt in pain, deep in his throat. Once when her nails raked across his cheek, again when her teeth drew blood from his shoulder. She couldn't win and she knew it, but she also knew she'd put up a good fight, for his dark skin glistened as wetly as hers and the hair around his face was as damp as her own. She lay quiet, finally, drawing great gulps of air into her lungs, her eyes still rebellious and stormy on his.

"You're really beautiful, Redhead," he whispered as he lowered his face to hers. Then, his lips brushing hers, "And a magnificent adversary, but you lose." His mouth took hers in a kiss that robbed her of all breath and all reason. It was full daylight before he moved away from her to lay on his back breathing deeply, his eyes closed.

Sam lay beside him, the back of her hand pressed against her mouth, fighting, in vain, against the tears that rolled down her temple and into her hair. She was filled with shame and disgust, but with herself, not him. That she loved him she'd faced months ago, but how deep, how intense within her that love went was borne upon her now.

His lovemaking had been almost savage, and she'd been

lost from that first kiss. She'd matched his savagery with her own, obeying his commands willingly, eagerly. There was not a spot on her body that his hands and mouth did not now know, and she'd trembled in delight at their knowing. He'd bid her own to explore him, and she'd gloried in their knowledge. Yet he'd as much as told her she was a possession, part of his property, to be used when he needed, like his house, or his plane, or his horse. She felt wounded and lacerated almost beyond endurance.

He turned his head and looked at her, then sighing deeply, in what she was sure was disgust, he left the bed and went into the bathroom. She heard the water running in the shower just before she fell asleep.

When she woke it was mid-afternoon and she was alone. She lay for some time reliving the night before, then, with a deep sigh, she got up. She wanted nothing as much as she wanted to pull the sheet over her head and never leave her bed again.

Before showering she stood and studied her nude form carefully in the mirror. Again she sighed. She was beginning to have an angular look. She had always been slim, but now, with the weight she'd lost, she looked almost skinny. But this fact she barely noticed, for all she saw were the bruises Morgan had left on her. It had been a fierce battle. Morgan had not been playing with her. Even her legs had not escaped the marks from his hands. At the thought of those hands she twisted around and went into the bathroom.

Sam had dressed in slacks and longsleeved shirt and was sitting at her dresser brushing her hair when Morgan came into the room carrying a tray. Her eyes, guarded, wary, met his in the mirror. Lifting the tray in a wry salute, he arched a brow, murmured sardonically, "From Beth, with orders to eat all of it." He walked across the room and set the tray on the table by the windows, then stretched out in the chair next to it.

"I'm really not hungry." Sam went back to her brushing.

"It's two o'clock, you've eaten practically nothing for over twenty-four hours, Samantha. Come over here and eat something." His voice held a lazy drawl. It also held an order.

Flinging the brush down, she spun around, eyes blazing, ready to argue. The sight of his face stopped the words in her throat. He lay back in the chair, eyes closed, looking incredibly tired. He had a pinched, drawn look, the welts her fingernails had made red and angry looking across his cheek.

She had seen him after weeks of working fourteen- and sixteen-hour days, and he had never looked like this. *What are we doing to each other?* she thought tiredly. All fight and anger drained out of her. She walked to the table and sat in the chair across from him. The tray held a pot of coffee, two fat mugs and a covered plate, which held bacon, eggs, and two toasted English muffins dripping with butter.

Sam filled both mugs with coffee and sat watching Morgan, gnawing on her lip. He had obviously been riding, as he wore boots, jeans, and a blue cotton shirt, the sleeves rolled up to his elbows. "Your coffee's getting cold." She said the words softly, not sure if he'd fallen asleep. At the sound of her voice he slid his body up in the chair and opened his eyes, one brow going up in question at the look on her face. She lowered her eyes, stammered "I—I'm sorry about your face."

The soft laugh had the sound of bitterness, not humor. "You're some tigress, Redhead." He nodded at the tray. "Eat something, Samantha, then I want to talk to you."

124

Reaching a hand to the tray, he murmured, "May I?" He picked up a piece of the muffin at her nod.

He sat munching the muffin, watching her as she forced down a piece of bacon and some of the eggs. When she sat back in her chair, her mug cradled in her hands, he said, "Finished?" Sam nodded, watched his fingers smooth over the welts on his cheek. "I told Mary I rode too close to a tree branch. So if anyone asks, you know what to say. Unless, of course, there's someone you'd like to tell the truth to."

"Morgan, please."

He smiled slightly at the note of reproach in her voice and went on. "Well, then, Mary tells me we've received quite a few invitations, beginning with a dinner dance at the club tonight and varied other things right through the weekend. You had remembered that this is the Labor Day weekend?" At her brief nod he continued. "I told her, for my part, she should accept any of these invitations she wished, but I'd send you to confer with her on the matter. Okay?"

"Yes, of course."

He drank his coffee, held the mug out for her to refill it, before going on. "Now the important part. I like your family very much, Samantha, and I see no reason why we should worry them with our marital difficulties. So I suggest we call a truce. At least for the remainder of our visit."

"You mean to take me with you then, when you go home?" Her voice was low, but she had managed to keep it steady.

Morgan had bent his head to his mug, but at her words his head jerked up, his eyes going hard and cold. "Are you trying to tell me you're not going with me?" Before she

125

could answer, he added, his voice very soft, "Maybe you're thinking of ending this marriage."

The last thing in the world I want is to end our marriage, her mind cried. Aloud she replied carefully, "I thought, perhaps, you were thinking along those lines."

He looked at her a long time through narrowed lids before answering shortly, "You know that's impossible under the circumstances, don't you?"

"Yes," she whispered.

He gave her a strange look, then rapped, "All right then, do you agree to a truce?" When she again whispered, "Yes," he stood and completely surprised her by bending over her and brushing his lips across hers. Straightening, he began to unbutton his shirt. "Do you have any plans for what's left of the afternoon?"

"Yes. I have a friend who runs a boutique not far from here and I thought I'd run over and do some shopping. Why? Did you have something you wanted to do?"

He threw her a wicked grin. "Yes, I'm going to take a shower and have a nap until it's time to dress for dinner. Too bad you can't join me."

"In which?" Sam retorted.

His grin widened. "In both. Are you going to be shopping for something to wear tonight?"

"Yes, why?" She eyed him warily, thinking their truce would be short-lived if he tried to tell her what to buy.

He was tugging his shirt from his jeans as he answered. "Get something in white. Although I didn't approve of your dress last night, I have to admit that with the tan you've acquired you look pretty terrific in white." Without waiting for her to comment, he turned, pulling his shirt off, toward the bathroom.

Sam's eyes widened when she saw his back, for, although they were longer, the red, angry-looking welts crisscrossing his back exactly matched those on his face. How could she have done something like that? she thought as a small gasp escaped through the fingers that had flown to her mouth.

On hearing her gasp, Morgan turned quickly. "What is it?" Sam's eyes widened even more at the ugly mark her teeth left on his shoulder.

He frowned and his voice sounded concerned. "Sam, what is wrong?"

"Oh, Lord, Morgan, your back—your shoulder. Do you think you should have a tetanus shot?"

With that he laughed aloud in real amusement. "No, I don't, my redheaded tigress, I get T shots regularly and I doused myself with antiseptic this morning and I will again after I've showered, so stop looking so scared. Run along and enjoy your shopping." Still laughing softly he turned and strode into the bathroom.

Sam did enjoy her shopping. After a short consultation with Mary, during which she agreed to all plans for the weekend, she and a very willing Deb made the short run to the small shop. She and Jean, the woman who ran the shop, spent a few minutes catching up on news of each other, Jean exclaiming over Sam's ring, then the three women got down to the serious business of clothes for Sam's slimmer figure. She bought slacks and a few skirts, tops, and three long gowns, one in white, even though she'd told herself she wouldn't. Then telling Jean they'd see her at the club, they went back to the house and right to their rooms, as it was time to get ready for dinner.

Morgan was still sprawled out on the bed asleep when Sam got back and her eyes kept straying to his sleeping face as she moved around the room quietly, hanging her clothes away. Relaxed, his face had lost the tight, drawn look and in turn seemed less grim and hard.

127

She slid silently into the bathroom and was standing in brief panties and bra in front of the bathroom mirror, some fifteen minutes later, making her face up, when the door opened and he leaned against the frame watching her.

Raising the eye shadow applicator to her lid, she lifted her eyes, caught the look on his face reflected in the mirror, and repeated his words of that afternoon. "What is it?"

He stretched out an arm and his fingertips touched gently at the large, purpling bruise on her arm. Then his hand dropped to her hip where another bruise was partially covered by her panties. Giving a light tug at the elastic, he exposed it in all its colorful size. His eyes went over her slowly, noting all the marks on her. As his eyes came back to her face, he raised his finger to her cheek, gently caressing it. His voice deep and husky with emotion, he said, "And you were concerned about me!" His other hand lifted her arm and drew her toward him as he bent his head. Pressing his lips gently to the bruise on her arm he murmured, "I'm sorry, Sam, I had no right to do this to you. You have my word that it won't happen again."

Taken completely by surprise by this gentleness he'd never shown to her before, Sam's reply sounded cold and stiff. "All right, Morgan, now we'd really better get ready as it's getting late."

"Of course." His hands dropped and he stepped back abruptly.

She noticed, for the first time, that he was already partially dressed, lacking only shirt, tie and jacket. Scooping up her makeup she slipped by him. "I'll leave you to shave."

She had finished her makeup and was struggling with the long zipper at the back of her gown when he reentered the room. Standing as if fascinated, he watched her a few seconds, until she snapped in agitation, "Don't just stand there for heaven's sake, help with this blasted thing." His lips twitching, he walked up behind her and with one tug closed the zipper. Stepping back he ordered, "Turn around."

She turned around slowly as he took in the white sheath. It was simply cut and fitted snugly, with long close-fitting sleeves and a low, square neckline, but not too low. The tight skirt was slit to the knees on both sides.

"Very nice. Now stand still," he murmured, going to the dresser and taking a case from the top drawer. As he walked back to her, he opened the case and removed a necklace from it, then, flipping the case onto the bed, he stood behind her and clasped the chain around her neck. Sam went to the mirror and stared at the large diamond-encircled emerald that hung at the end of the platinum chain.

"But why?"

"Call it a belated wedding gift." He shrugged, went to the closet, pulled out a white silk shirt, muttered brusquely, "Now say thank you and get the hell out of here, so I can get dressed." Hesitantly, she went to him, gave him a quick kiss, mumbled "thank you," and hurried from the room, not understanding him at all.

The evening passed pleasantly enough, the only sour note as far as Sam was concerned was Carolyn's obvious interest in Morgan, and the fact that Morgan seemed to return that interest. Even Deb, who had decided Morgan was just about perfect, looked from one to the other, then to Sam with raised eyebrows.

During the next few days Sam felt the admiration and respect she already had for Morgan growing steadily. She knew he worked very hard, giving little time to relaxation and games, and yet, in the company of wealthy young men who made games their vocation, he adjusted quite well. He joined Bryan and two others in a round of golf and finished with a score only slightly higher than Bryan's, who was considered by far the best golfer in the district. He played a hard, fast game of tennis, with a serve that shot across the net like a missile. Sam had once before witnessed his swimming ability, the powerful strokes propelling his body swiftly through the water. She now found he could surf well and sail a small boat expertly. But it was when he stepped into the saddle that he put them all in the shade. All of her large group of friends rode well, the women as well as the men, but with Morgan, it was a part of his life. He seemed to become one with any horse from the moment he mounted, and no matter how difficult the animal, left no doubt as to who was the master.

They went to casual luncheons and cookouts and a formal dinner party at the home of Jeff's parents. At a wild, late-night poolside party Morgan stunned Sam by cutting in on Jeff and executing perfectly some very intricate dance steps. As the days slid by, Sam found herself becoming more and more withdrawn and rigid, for every time she'd look around for Morgan, she saw Carolyn hanging on his arm, and the look of concern growing in Deb's eyes. Deb, Sam knew, might be crazy about her new brother-in-law, but she adored Sam and she was worried.

They were at the breakfast table the Thursday following Sam's birthday party when Morgan was called to the phone. He took the call in her father's study, which he had commandeered as his own, making long phone calls and doing an endless amount of paper work whenever he had a few free minutes and late into the night. As before he put in sixteen-hour days.

He was in the study about ten minutes when he came out, barked "Sam" and went up the stairs two at a time.

Sam finished her coffee, lifted her shoulders in an I-don't-know to the questions in Mary's and Deb's eyes, and followed him up the stairs. When she entered their room she stopped cold. Morgan had their cases open on the bed, and was packing his own.

"What—" she began, but he cut her off.

"Something's come up, Samantha, that needs my personal attention. We've got to leave. I've already phoned to have the plane ready. I'll take you home, grab a few things I need, and take off." He turned back to the open dresser drawer.

Sam didn't move. When he turned around, hands full of clothes, he raised his eyebrows at her.

"How long will you be gone?" she asked softly.

"A week, ten days maybe," he shrugged. "I'm not sure. Why?"

Making up her mind suddenly, she answered, "Couldn't I stay here?" Before he could protest she hurried on. "Deb's wedding isn't too many weeks off, you know, and we have gown fittings and shopping to do. Morgan, we don't even have a wedding gift for them yet. Couldn't you come back here when you've completed your business?"

He looked at her hard and long before answering. "All right, Samantha, but don't shop for a wedding gift till I get back, we'll do that together. And, Redhead, behave yourself while I'm away." He laughed at the startled look she gave him. "Now come help me pack so I can get moving." It seemed he was gone in no time, and Sam was left with a strange, empty feeling.

The following day Sam and Deb were having lunch at the club when Jeff dropped into the chair next to Sam and

131

said in mock forlornness, "Would you ladies allow a deserted man to join you for lunch?"

"Of course," Sam smiled. "But why deserted?"

His eyes danced devilishly. "My beloved left yesterday afternoon to visit with an aunt in Maine and I'm on my own for a week or so. And, as I understand you're also on your own, I was thinking, perhaps, we could be on our own together."

Sam had not missed the sharp look Deb had turned on her when Jeff said Carolyn had left so soon after Morgan and she felt slightly sick, but she managed to keep her voice light. "Sorry, Jeff, but Deb and I were just now making plans. You see, we have hours of shopping and fittings for the wedding and it's going to be a rush to get finished before Morgan gets back."

His handsome face wore a look of disappointment. "Oh, well, some days you can't win any of them."

Somehow Sam got through lunch, even managing to laugh at Jeff's mild jokes, but she drove home in silence, refusing to acknowledge Deb's worried glances. At the house she went straight to her room to pace back and forth with one thought. Had Morgan taken Carolyn with him? It seemed too much a coincidence, their leaving within a few hours of each other.

With a soft knock Deb entered, said hesitatingly, "Sam, darling—" but she got no further as Sam whispered, "Don't ask, Deb, please."

Sam was miserable. Although she went shopping and had fittings and oohed and aahed over incoming wedding gifts, one thought tormented her. Is he with her? She alternated between anger with and love for him and felt disgust with herself for her own weakness. She ate less than usual and lost more weight. She felt numb inside while maintaining an outward composure. She heard nothing from him.

Two weeks after Morgan left, Deb told her quietly that Carolyn had returned. Two days later Morgan came home.

In Mary's sitting room in front of the others, he drew her into his arms and kissed her. But once alone in the bedroom, he looked her over critically. "What kind of hours have you been keeping, Redhead?" he growled. "You look like hell."

"Thanks a lot," Sam snapped. Put out because he was looking so well, she slammed out of the room. They had almost three tense weeks together before he was gone again, not to return until the week before Deb's wedding.

Sam hadn't been feeling well since the middle of September, and when she began being sick to her stomach in the morning, then missed her second period, she faced the fact that she was pregnant. She had mixed feelings about it. She wanted Morgan's baby very badly, but she was beginning to believe he wanted out of their marriage. By the time Deb's wedding was over, they were barely on speaking terms, though they put on a good front in public.

The day after the wedding Morgan told her to pack. "We're going home. I have to go to Spain tomorrow."

"How long will you be gone?" she asked as she had weeks before.

His eyes and voice cold, he answered, "Ten days, possibly two weeks. Why? Aren't you coming with me again?"

"No, I'm not." At the look of anger that came into his face she added quickly, "I'm going home, Morgan, but I want to drive."

"Are you crazy?" he snapped. "I've seen you drive, remember? You'll come with me."

Growing angry herself now, Sam took her stand. "I do

not, as a rule, drive like that and I think you know it. I want my car."

"For God's sake why?" he grated, his eyes furious. "You have the Jag and the wagon at the ranch."

She held firm and to keep herself from shouting at him, she said through gritted teeth, "Morgan, I want my own car and I'm driving it to Nevada."

His eyes held hers a long moment, then he turned away sharply. "Do as you wish, I couldn't care less." Without another word he packed and went, this time with no pretense of tender leavetaking. It seemed to Sam that all hope went with him. She had a horrible feeling of certainty that their strange relationship was over.

CHAPTER 8

That night Sam lay wide awake, her mind working furiously. Morgan had said he'd be gone about two weeks. It would take her, at most, a few days to drive to the ranch. If she waited until next week to leave, she'd be subjected to Deb's probing, concerned glances. Yet, if she left tomorrow or the following day, she'd have a week of Sara's sharp-eyed scrutiny. Neither prospect held much appeal.

Aunt Rachael! The name sprang into her mind out of the blue. Sam had received several letters from her favorite aunt, coaxing letters, asking her when she was coming to visit. On the spur of the moment Sam decided to fly to England and stay with her mother's sister for a week. And Morgan Wade could just go hang.

Arrangements were quickly made and two days later, much to the surprise of her family, Sam was on her way to England. On the plane the thought, belatedly, struck Sam that Morgan had never told her what the Messrs. Baker had wanted. With a shrug she dismissed it, too busy concentrating on not being airsick to worry about it now.

Rachael Crinshaw, tall, elegant, her auburn hair still glowingly beautiful, was waiting for Sam at the airport. After the general confusion of luggage collection and customs, they followed Rachael's chauffeur to her Mercedes.

When she was settled into the car, Sam let her head drop back wearily against the seat.

"Are you all right, Samantha?" Rachael asked in quick concern. "You are absolutely white and, to be perfectly honest, you look like a stick with material draped around it. I realize the fashions call for slimness, but don't you think you've carried it a bit far?"

"I'm fine, Aunt Rachael." Despite the tiredness dragging at her spirit, Sam smiled. "I haven't been dieting. The summer was so hot and humid I simply had no appetite. I'm sure I'll regain the weight now that summer is finally over." *In fact,* she thought wryly, *I'm positive of it.*

"Well, I should hope so," Rachael chided gently. "Really, dear, you look absolutely haggard. I fully intend supervising your meals while you're here. I can't imagine what that husband of yours is thinking of to allow you to reach this degree of—of gauntness."

"Oh, really, Aunt Rachael," Sam laughed a little unsurely. "Morgan has no control over what I eat. You, of all people, should know how I'd react if a man tried directing my life down to the food I put into my mouth."

At least the Samantha her aunt had known would never have allowed a man to direct her life, Sam thought ruefully, memories of the number of times Morgan had done just that making her squirm with discomfort.

Sam greeted the sight of her aunt's tall, imposing house with a sigh of relief. She was so tired her eyelids felt weighted with lead. Why was she always sleepy lately?

"If you don't mind, Aunt Rachael," Sam said, the minute they stepped into the large, formal hall. "I think I'd like to go right to my room and have a nap before dinner."

"Good idea." Rachael eyed her sharply. "I want to see some color back in your cheeks, my girl. Now, go along with Claude and have a good rest. Dinner at seven, as usual."

With a wan smile Sam followed her aunt's very correct butler up the stairs. When she came down again three hours later, Rachael ran a critical eye over her, before declaring, "Much, much better. You are still pale, but the tight, pinched look is gone. Really, my dear, I had no idea they led such a wild existence in Long Island. Indeed, I understood your stepmother, Mary, was a shy, timid woman."

"Oh, Aunt Rachael!" Sam laughed. "Mary is a shy, timid woman and I love her dearly." Sam went on to briefly outline the activities that had been planned for her and Morgan. "Quite a few were held outdoors and, as I mentioned earlier, the heat really bothers me. I assure you I am fine."

Finally convinced, Rachael smiled warmly. "Good. I've been very busy since you called, Samantha. As I know how flying makes you sleepy, I planned a quiet dinner tonight, but I've invited quite a few of your friends for dinner tomorrow night."

"Oh, but Aunt Rachael—" Sam began, the idea of not only having to act well when she felt so washed out, but also appear as the happy bride, daunting.

Her aunt didn't let her finish her protest. "You haven't been over here in ages, darling, and all your friends want to see you. Several in particular." Her brows arched expressively. "I reminded them that you are now a married woman."

The dinner party turned out to be much more of an ordeal than she could have anticipated, even though it started out well. On awakening that morning she had been pleasantly surprised to find no sign of the gripping nausea or wracking sickness that had dogged her mornings for the past few weeks.

She and Rachael spent a leisurely, relaxing day, Sam wondering at times about the almost smugly self-satisfied expression that periodically played across her aunt's face. As Rachael was not forthcoming about the reason for her inner pleasure, Sam went to her room to dress for dinner in a bemused, questioning frame of mind.

Her question was answered the minute she stepped into her aunt's large drawing room, for one figure seemed to stand out from the several guests already gathered there.

"Duds!"

Sam's cry of delighted surprise brought all heads around to see her run across the room and into the outstretched arms of a tall, husky, sandy-haired man.

"Duds! How in the world did you get here? You look marvelous. I thought you were in Australia?"

The man's arms, tightening in a bear hug, cut off the overlapping string of Sam's words.

"Slow up a bit, darling." Clear blue eyes, bright with laughter, gazed into green. "One question at a time, please. But first"—his strong face split into a grin—"let me return the compliment twice over. You look delicious. Let's have a kiss."

Sam's mouth was caught in a deep, warm kiss which she returned unhesitatingly, without restraint. Dudley Haverstone, or Duds as Sam had christened him, was the only young man she had ever been able to truly relax with. From her fifth year, when her mother had married Dudley's father, Duds had been her older brother, her teacher, and her tormenter.

"Hmm, you taste delicious too," Duds murmured when he'd released her lips. Although his tone was serious, his eyes teased her as they'd always done. "And you had to go and get yourself tied to the formidable Morgan."

"You know Morgan?" Sam gasped, eyes widening.

"Doesn't everyone?" Duds drawled before adding, "well, perhaps there are a few who don't."

"But, Duds, how do—"

"Enough about the cowboy," Duds cut her off. "I want to hear about you." Taking her arm, he drew her toward the far end of the room, calling over his shoulder, "If you'll excuse us, Aunt Rachael? Sam and I will rejoin the party in a few minutes."

With an indulgent smile Rachael waved them away before turning back to her guests.

"I missed you, Sam." They were sitting close together on an elegantly covered love seat, hands clasped. All traces of his former teasing tone were gone from Duds's voice. His eyes studied Sam's face minutely. "Little sister, why are you so thin?" Real concern tinged his tone, and the beginning of anger. "Is he giving you a hard time? Or have you heard the rumors already?"

"Rumors?" Sam's throat closed with alarm, a stab of fear jabbed at her stomach. "What rumors?"

"Oh, bloody hell," Duds groaned softly. His hands tightened almost painfully on hers. "Forget I said that, love."

"What rumors, Duds?" Sam's voice had steadied, gone cold.

"Sam, don't," Duds pleaded. "It's only rumors, after all. I'm sorry. I—"

"Duds, please, tell me." Neither Sam's face, nor her tone revealed the anxiety she was feeling. "I'd rather hear it from you. I haven't talked to anyone but Aunt Rachael since I arrived yesterday and even if Aunt Rachael had heard something, she wouldn't tell me. You know all the

139

people who are going to be here tonight. You also know there will be more than one willing to enlighten me."

Duds grimaced, but before he could say anything Sam hurried on. "Duds, help me. If I know what to expect, I can handle it."

"You're right, of course," Duds sighed, then his voice went hard, frustrated. "He has been seen, several times the last week or so, with the same woman. A few times in Italy and, a couple of nights ago, here."

"Here!" Sam couldn't hide her astonishment. "Morgan is in London?"

"You didn't know?" Duds eyes sharpened on her face. "You didn't come over to join him?"

Sam's head was shaking before he'd stopped speaking. "No," she whispered, "I thought he was in Spain."

"Spain? Then what was he doing in Italy?"

"I don't know," Sam laughed shakily. "I know very little of Morgan's business, Duds." She paused, telling herself to leave it at that, but she had to ask. "Do you know who the woman is?"

"No, love," Duds answered softly. "And neither did my informant. Sam, I think I'd better also tell you that the woman seemed very sure of herself and that he was being very attentive. At least that's the story I got."

A change in the buzz of conversation at the other end of the room caught Sam's attention and, glancing up, she felt her breath catch painfully at her throat. As if their speaking about him had conjured him up, Morgan stood in the wide doorway, looking cool and relaxed and shatteringly handsome in a silver-gray hand-tailored suit that, if possible, made his hair and eyes look even blacker.

With deadly accuracy those eyes honed in on Sam, paused a moment on her hands tightly clasped in Duds's before lifting to pierce hers, black fury raging in their depths.

"Morgan, darling, you're late."

Her aunt's melodious voice reached Sam's disbelieving ears and, shock waves rippling through her, she watched in astonishment as Rachael hurried across the room to him, lifted her cheek for his kiss. Did Rachael know him too then? Apparently, for Morgan murmured something that made her laugh, brushed a becoming tinge of pink across her cheeks.

Somehow Sam managed to conceal the tension mounting wildly inside. Looking cool, almost remote, she fought down the urge to run as Morgan nodded an encompassing greeting to the others before sauntering across the long room to where she sat with Duds.

Duds was on his feet before Morgan was halfway to them, right hand extended, left hand still clasping Sam's.

"Hello, Morgan, it's been a long time." Duds's voice, though friendly, held a note of wariness. "I'd heard you were in town."

"Dudley." Morgan's hand gripped Duds briefly. "When did you escape from the bush?"

"A week ago," Duds smiled fleetingly. "Although I only actually arrived in London two days ago."

"I see. The day before Samantha did." His voice was smooth, his tone even, and yet Sam felt a chill freeze her spine. When he turned to her, Sam felt the full impact of his eyes. The width of the room had not deceived her as to his emotions. For all his cool demeanor, Morgan was in a towering rage. Bending slightly over her, he caught her chin in his hand, lifted her face to his.

"Hello, darling. Have a nice flight?" His silky tone sent a shiver feathering down her arms, momentarily closed her throat. "You're a little pale, Redhead," he jibed knowingly. "Still sleepy?" Before she could answer, he brushed her lips with his, then released her and turned back to Duds. "Flying always makes Samantha sleepy, you know." One arrogantly cocked eyebrow dared Duds to admit he did.

Claude's intoned, "Dinner is served," saved Duds from committing himself and he sighed with relief. Sam rose to slip her hand around the arm Morgan angled at her.

"I thought you said you had business in Spain," Samantha murmured as they followed the other guests to Rachael's elegant dining room.

"A last-minute change in plans," Morgan replied quietly. "The meeting was switched to London."

Meeting with whom? And what where you doing in Italy? The unspoken questions lit a flame that burned away her shock at seeing him and replaced it with anger.

"And I thought you said you were driving to the ranch." The soft, silky words were murmured close to her ear as Morgan held Sam's chair for her, giving a good impression of gallant solicitude.

"A last-minute change in plans." Sam's smile was saccharine.

"Morgan, you take the head of the table," Rachael commanded pleasantly, "and, Dudley, you sit there, next to Samantha."

Sam breathed a sigh of relief. Her aunt's order to Morgan prevented his retaliation, even though the glittering glance he gave her before moving to the end of the table warned that he was not going to forget this.

To Sam's amazement most of her friends were acquainted with Morgan. *How had he met them? When?* In growing confusion she listened to the easy flow of conversation, somehow managing to remain cool as she answered questions, while at the same time avoided the black, amused eyes.

"Why aren't you eating?" Duds murmured. "Has he upset you? I mean by showing up so unexpectedly?"

"Yes," Sam answered honestly. "Duds, I don't understand this at all. Everyone seems to know him. You know him. How?"

"As far as everyone else goes, I haven't the foggiest," Duds answered slowly. "I met him in Australia several years ago. Not long after I went out there, as a matter of fact. You didn't know he has interests out there?"

"Yes, of course I knew," Sam answered quickly. "But—why didn't he tell me he knew you?"

"Possibly because he didn't know of our relationship, love." He smiled reassuringly. "I haven't seen him since your marriage and there was never a reason to mention you before." Duds paused, then laughed softly. "You and I, being the awful correspondents we are, could probably have gone through three mates before the news caught up to us."

Sam's soft laughter mingled with his. It was true, she hated to write letters and she knew Duds hated it too. Glancing up, the laughter died on her lips as her glance was caught, held by two chips of black ice. Sam felt a chill creep along her spine as Morgan lifted his wineglass in a mocking salute to her. Lifting her chin, she forced herself to meet his cold stare until he sipped at his wine, then she deliberately turned her face to Duds.

"How ever did he meet Aunt Rachael?" she asked Duds quietly. "Do you know?"

"Yes, I do. She told me he presented himself to her several months ago, while he was on a business trip here in London." He paused, then his face lightened. "And that may answer your first question. Perhaps Aunt Rachael introduced him to your friends at that time."

Sam was convinced he was right. It was exactly the sort of thing her Aunt Rachael would do. But why hadn't she told her Morgan was in London? Sam sighed, thinking, *because she wanted to surprise me.* That was also exactly the sort of thing she'd do.

The seemingly endless dinner finally did end and they moved into the drawing room. Sam, her mind still reeling from the sudden appearance of both Morgan and Duds, felt a throbbing begin at her temples that very quickly grew into a full-scale hammering. The way every female in the room fawned over Morgan upset Sam even more. *And he loves every minute of it,* Sam thought furiously.

Loving him, hating him, Sam watched as Morgan, so effortlessly, set her so-called friends' hearts and imaginations on fire. His long, lean body propped indolently against the mantelpiece, white teeth flashing in his dark-skinned handsome face, his soft, lazy drawl tickled their ears and delighted their senses. Sam could feel the sensuous aura he exuded surround her as well and in desperation she fought against it. Head pounding, she riled against the circumstances that had brought her to this moment. At the same time she wanted to scream at Morgan that he had no right to amuse himself with other women while she carried his child. The fact that he was unaware of her pregnancy did not even penetrate her inflamed consciousness.

No one in the room, not even Duds, who knew her so well, was aware of the rage tearing at her mind. With an outward coolness that was almost tangible, Sam masked the pain and anger that seethed below the surface.

Longing for nothing more then two aspirins and a bed, Sam nearly groaned her relief when the door closed on the last of the guests. Turning back into the wide hall, Sam blinked and glanced around quickly. Morgan seemed to have vanished into thin air. Duds forestalled Sam's asking her aunt where Morgan had gone.

"Come have a nightcap with me, Sam. You look like you need one."

Sam followed Rachael and Duds back into the drawing room and accepted the drink she didn't want.

"I'm driving down to the house at the weekend." Duds sipped his brandy, his eyes studying Sam closely. "Why don't you two come with me? You look exhausted, pet, a few days in the country air would put some color back into your cheeks."

"I don't know, Duds," Sam murmured. "But I don't think—"

"Samantha, will you come up here, please?"

Morgan's voice, quiet and authoritative, cut across Sam's words. She stiffened at his tone, then shrugged, well, at least she now knew where he'd disappeared to. With a cool, "Excuse me," she left the room and went up the wide stairway. The pain in her head that had eased somewhat in the last few minutes began pounding away at her temples again as she walked into her bedroom.

Morgan stood in the middle of the room clad only in very brief shorts, his evening clothes tossed carelessly onto the bed. Her hand still clutching the doorknob, breath catching painfully in her throat, she watched as he stepped into a pair of brown brushed denims, drew them up his long, muscular legs and over his slim hips. After tugging the zipper closed, he glanced up, his eyes cold and remote.

"It seems I've said this so often I feel I should have a recording made to save time," he attacked, "but, anyway, I'm flying to Spain tonight. When are *you* going home?"

He sounded angry and fed up. The pain in Sam's head stabbed viciously.

"My return reservation is for Monday night."

"Cancel it." Morgan's tone was as cold as his eyes. "I'll be back Saturday. You can fly home with me."

Rebellion flared hot and fierce inside Sam. Arrogant devil, whom did he think he was speaking to, his girl friend?

"I can't do that," she snapped icily. "I've just accepted an invitation from Duds to go down to the house for the weekend." The decision made, Sam vowed nothing Morgan said could make her change it.

"The house?" His tone was mild, much too mild.

"Duds's house, in Kent." Somehow she matched his tone. They could have been discussing the weather. "The house I grew up in." Black brows shot up in question. "Duds is my stepbrother, Morgan." Sam answered the silent question.

For some reason Sam couldn't begin to understand, the knowledge seemed to anger Morgan even more. His eyes narrowed; his voice took on a savage edge.

"Is that why he has this protective—proprietorial—attitude about you?"

His tone and words startled Sam. He sounded jealous. Morgan? Jealous? For one brief instant hope flared wildly inside Sam. It died as quickly. No, not Morgan. But Morgan had pride in abundance. She could hear his grating voice of weeks before. *You're my wife, Samantha, my woman. I don't share what's mine.* And that was it, in a nutshell, Sam thought, defeated. She was Morgan Wade's woman. His pride demanded she remain exclusively his woman until *he* decided to change the status quo.

Pain that far superseded the throbbing in her head ripped through Sam. She went hot, then cold. What about her pride? What had become of the cool, poised Samantha Denning who had effortlessly turned away from any hint of involvement with any man? And now this one man, this—this cowboy who had sold his name, dared to question her? Searing anger mingled with the pain.

"Duds is like a brother to me," she finally snapped. "His attitude has always been protective."

"How nice for you," Morgan drawled nastily. "You can tell him to relax his guard, find his own woman to protect." His voice lowered with menace. "You have a protector."

"That's going to keep you rather busy, isn't it?" Green eyes cool, Sam faced him unflinchingly. At the question in his eyes, she smiled, purred. "I hear you have a friend."

"I have many friends." His glittering black eyes held hers evenly.

"I mean a special lady friend." A flash of irritation surged through her as his lips twitched in amusement. The beast, it had taken every ounce of composure she possessed to say that calmly and he thought she was funny.

"Samantha," he drawled, "if you want to know if I've taken a mistress, why the hell don't you ask me, instead of pussyfooting around?"

Sam's stomach lurched sickeningly. Suddenly afraid, not wanting to hear him admit it, she shrugged, turned to leave the room. Closing her eyes, she lied through her teeth. "I really couldn't care less. I'm going to spend the weekend in the country. Have fun, Morgan, *wherever* you're going."

"Samantha."

Sam's hand froze in the act of turning the knob; his deadly calm tone causing her blood to run cold. She hadn't heard him move, yet his warm breath fluttered over her hair. Her breath caught in her throat when his arm slid around her waist and drew her back against his hard body. His voice, soft and caressing, made his actual words more terrifying. "If I find out he as much as touches you, I'll kill him, pseudo-brother or not."

A picture of Duds's strong face, cold and still, robbed forever of its happy grin, rose in Sam's mind. *Dear God, he means it,* she thought sickly. A shudder passed through her too-slender body and, as if he could read her mind, Morgan underlined, "I mean it, Samantha. So be a very good girl while you're enjoying the country air and I'll expect you at the ranch within two weeks. Now get out of here so I can finish dressing."

Sam fled, first the room and two days later, the city. Her weekend in the country was not altogether successful.

Duds tried repeatedly to draw her out of the self-protective shell she'd built around herself. Again and again, obviously growing more frustrated each time, he begged her to open up. He began his assault on her defenses the afternoon they arrived at the house. Rachael had retired to her room to rest before dinner while Sam and Duds strolled through the house, reacquainting themselves with the familar objects.

"Hullo! Look at this, Sam."

They were in the playroom, so named because both Sam and Duds had disparaged the word *nursery.* Sam was perched on the broad windowsill, a sad smile on her lips, paging through a much read, dogeared book of fairy tales. Glancing up at Duds's quiet exclamation, the smile softened reminicently. Her smile was reflected on Duds's plain face as he gazed down on a scruffy rag doll.

"Carmen!"

At Sam's whispered cry he lifted his eyes to hers, his eyes growing as impish as on the day they'd christened the doll.

"Ridiculous name for such a ratty-looking thing," he teased, tossing the doll to her.

Sam caught the doll, clutched it possessively against her breasts. "But that's exactly why we gave her such an exotic name, because she was so ratty." Sam's eyes clouded over mistily. "Don't you remember, Duds?"

"Yes, love, I remember."

As he walked across the room to her, his face set in somber lines. When he stopped before her, one hand came up to smooth away a stray hair that lay over her cheek.

"Sam, my pet, you worry me." Duds's voice was low, heavily edged with concern. "You're looking almost as ratty as that doll. God, if he's hurt you—" He sighed. "Can't you tell me what the trouble is?"

"Oh, Duds, it's so good to be with you again." Sam's eyes grew wistful. "I hadn't realized how much I'd missed you until I saw you again."

"Sam, my love," he chided. "You are avoiding the question."

"I know." Sam's attempt at a laugh fell flat. "I'm a big girl now, Duds. I must solve my own problems." Jumping up, she walked quickly to the door. "Come along, big brother, we haven't seen half the house yet and Aunt Rachael will be expecting her dinner soon."

After dinner Duds declared they all needed a walk in the garden. Aunt Rachael declined, but insisted Sam join him. Even though Sam knew what was coming, she went along with him.

"Look, darling, I don't want to be a nag," Duds began the minute they'd started along the path to the rose garden. "But I can see Aunt Rachael is nearly frantic about the way you've changed. Let us help you."

"Stop badgering me, Duds," Sam scolded. "If I thought there was anything either of you could do—" She stopped,

Morgan's words clear in her mind. *I'll kill him, I mean it.* Sam shook her head. "But there isn't any way you can help me."

Sam slept very little that night, tossing and turning in the canopied bed that had been hers until she was seventeen. She longed for Morgan's wide bed beneath her, and Morgan's slim frame beside her. Duds's large, beautiful house was no longer home. Even the memories of her happy childhood here seemed hazy and unreal. With a sigh of regret Sam faced the fact that there was only one place on earth that she would ever feel at home in. And that was beside Morgan, no matter where he was. And that was the one place there was no real welcome for her.

During the following two days she spent long hours in the saddle, sedately, because of her condition, following the routes she'd ridden hundreds of times as a young girl. But now the countryside she'd so loved passed by unseen. Her mind's eye, filled with the memory of a long, lean body, along with glittering black eyes and a hard, sensuous mouth, was closed to the scenery around her.

Sam managed to avoid being alone with Duds again until Sunday evening. After dinner they went into the sitting room where a cheery fire crackled invitingly. Duds kept them entertained with stories of his life in Australia and informed them he'd be going back within the month.

"I don't know quite how it happened or when," he said softly, a faraway look in his eyes. "But suddenly I knew that I wanted to spend the rest of my life there." Then to the amazement of Sam and Rachael, he added, "I'm going to sell this house. That's one of the reasons for my being here now."

It was not yet eleven when Rachael stood up and said she was going to bed. Sam, curled up in the large chair that had been her stepfather's favorite, slid her legs to the floor with the intention of following her. Duds's hand on her arm stopped her.

"Samantha, are you pregnant?" he asked bluntly as soon as Rachael was out of hearing.

"What gave you that idea?" Sam hedged.

"Aunt Rachael." Duds eyed her seriously. "She's been observing you closely, as I'm sure you're aware of, and she told me this afternoon that she's convinced you are."

Sam's eyes shifted to the dying flames in the fireplace. For a few seconds she was tempted to lie, tell Duds her aunt was wrong. Sighing deeply, she shrugged her shoulders lightly. What was the point in denying it? Her answer whispered through stiff lips.

"Yes."

She heard an echo of her sigh, then a muttered curse.

"That bastard."

"Duds, please." Sam's eyes swung back to his pleadingly.

"But how dare he treat you like this?" Sam had to bite back the words that Morgan dared almost anything. "Why isn't he with you now?" Duds's tone held indignant fury. "He must see how frail you look."

"He doesn't care," Sam choked.

"What the bloody hell do you mean, he doesn't care?" Duds exploded. "He doesn't care about you? He doesn't care about his child? What?"

"He doesn't care about me," Sam whispered. "And he doesn't know about the child."

"Doesn't know?" Duds repeated blankly, then, decisively, "Don't tell him."

"What? But I have to tell—"

"No." He cut in firmly. "You do not have to tell him anything." He grasped her hands, held them tightly. "Divorce him—marry me."

151

"Duds!" Sam's eyes flew wide in surprise. "What are you talking about? You don't love me—at least not that way."

"No, not that way," he admitted. "But I do love you and I can't go back to Australia with you looking like this. Your eyes would haunt me." His fingers squeezed hers painfully. "Love, come with me. Let me take care of you. You and your child."

"No, Duds," Sam shook her head. "Morgan would—" She was about to say Morgan would come after them, would very likely carry out his threat. Duds's angry words cut across hers.

"Morgan would deserve to lose his child, his actions convince me of that." He frowned. "You know, I liked him. From the first day I met him, I liked him. Liked and respected." He frowned again, then shrugged. "Strange, my first impressions of people are usually correct." Again he shrugged, more strongly this time. "No matter. The hell with Wade. Come with me, Sam. I promise I'll take as much care with your baby as I did with you."

"I'm sure you would." Rising swiftly, Sam lifted her hand to caress his beloved face. "But I can't let you." When he would have protested, she slid her fingers over his lips. "Sweet, sweet Duds. Somewhere, either out in the outback or wherever, there is someone for you. You'll never find her with me and Morgan's offspring hanging around your neck. Besides, he does really have a right to know about his child. I must go back and tell him."

"And if he still doesn't care," Duds groaned around her fingers. "If he doesn't even want it. Then what? What will you do?"

"I don't know," Sam confessed tiredly. "But I can always stay with Mary. She's been very kind to me, Duds. Kinder than you'll ever know."

Not for anything would Sam ever tell Duds or her aunt the reason Morgan married her. Or Mary's offer of support on hearing the terms of her father's will.

"Sam, please." Duds's voice held real pain. "Won't you reconsider? I tell you I can't go back and leave you like this."

"Yes, darling, you can," Sam insisted. "You must. I will be all right. With or without Morgan I will be all right."

Sam only wished she felt as much conviction as her forced tone implied. Later, as she undressed for bed, she stared blankly at her trembling hands. Would it ever end? She thought despairingly. Or would the pain of loving him go on and on until all thought ceased?

Their return to London on Monday morning was made in strained silence. Rachael and Duds insisted on seeing her off and when, finally, Sam boarded the big jet, she did so with a feeling of anticlimax. What awaited her at the end of her flight? Sam was afraid even to face the question, let alone try to answer it.

CHAPTER 9

Sam's drive cross-country took much longer than it should have. She stopped to stroll around whenever a city or small town appealed to her. Although it was mid-November and much of the fall foliage was gone, there were still spots where the blaze of color was breathtaking. She wandered through big stores and small shops and even bought a few pieces of heavier clothing, for the nip that had been in the air a week ago was now more of a bite. She told herself she would be a fool not to take advantage of this opportunity to see something of the country. For although she had spent a good deal of her time traveling, it had been mainly in other countries and she'd seen very little of the States. She also knew she was lying to herself. She was putting off, to the last possible minute, her meeting with Morgan.

She longed to see him and yet she was afraid. So afraid, in fact, that she had almost decided not to go at all. She was not sure she could bear to hear the words "I want a divorce."

It hadn't been an easy decision. After returning to Long Island she told herself she must think it out calmly and unemotionally, and she had. For two days she thought of nothing else. She had decided she'd divorce Morgan, stay where she was loved, have and raise her baby alone. Mary would help her. She had found herself thirty minutes later frantically packing a suitcase, asking Mary to have everything she owned shipped to the ranch, saying hasty goodbyes to everyone, and jumping into the Stingray telling herself grimly she was going home, whether Morgan liked it or not.

All the way across country she had argued with herself. Did she have the right to use their child and her money to hold on to a man who didn't want her? But then, Morgan had told, no, ordered, her to return to the ranch, and didn't he have the right to at least know about his child, have that child born in his own home?

She arrived at the ranch mid-morning over a week after leaving Long Island. She was tired and stiff and mentally exhausted, but Sara's warm welcome helped chase some of the weariness. There was no sign of Morgan and Sam wondered if he had returned from Spain, only to leave again for someplace else.

She called Mary to let her know she had arrived safely, and then decided to call Babs. At the sound of Sam's voice Babs cried, "Sam, darling, when did you get back?" Her voice warm with affection, Sam answered, "Not much more than an hour ago. How is Benjie?"

Babs and Ben had not been able to go East for Deb's wedding, as Benjie had become ill. Now Babs laughed. "Oh! The imp's bouncing around like a kangaroo again. It turned out to be only a mild throat infection, but Sam, I just couldn't leave him."

"Of course not. How is everyone else?"

"Perfect," Babs enthused. "I'm so glad you got home in time for the party, Sam."

"What party?"

Babs's voice held a touch of exasperation. "That Morgan, didn't he leave you a message or anything?"

"Well, I don't think he knew just when I'd get here." Sam hedged. "I didn't know myself. Have you talked to Morgan?"

"Talked to him," Babs exclaimed. "He's here. Or, that is, he was here and he'll be back. He drove to Vegas to pick up a friend of ours, but he'll be back later today."

"I see," Sam said quietly.

"When are you coming down?" Babs's voice had an odd note now.

"I don't think—" Sam began.

"Well I do," Babs said firmly, then her voice grew urgent. "Sam, I think you'd better go throw a change of clothes, a nightie, and a dinner dress into a bag, get in your car, and come down here."

"Babs."

"I mean it, Sam. I'll look for you in a few hours. Bye now." Before Sam could say another word, Babs hung up.

Oh, what now? Sam thought. *And when did Morgan get back from Spain?* Deciding to find out, she went into the kitchen and asked point blank, "Sara, when did Mr. Morgan get back?"

"Why, over a week ago, Mrs. Sam," Sara answered. "He left again yesterday morning. He didn't say where he was going, never does, but he did say he'd call and let me know when he was coming home."

"He's at the Carters," Sam told her. "And I'll be leaving in a few minutes to join him, so please don't bother about lunch. And we will call and let you know when we'll be home." Without waiting for any questions from Sara, she left the kitchen and not much later, the house.

It was mid-afternoon when Sam pulled into the Carters' driveway. She was pulling her bag from the back of her car when Babs ran to meet her. "I'm glad you came," Babs panted. "I'm going to take you right to your room so we

156

can talk." With those words Sam found herself hurried through the house to the room she had slept in eight months before.

As Sam removed her jacket, she forced a light laugh into her voice. "Now then, pet, what's the mystery?" But she grew still at the look of concern on Babs's face and her exclaimed, "Sam, are you ill? You're so thin."

"No, of course I'm not ill," Sam was quick to assure her.

"But what is it then? Something's wrong with you. Is it Morgan?" At the look on Sam's face she added, "You love him, don't you?"

"Desperately," Sam whispered, then sank tiredly onto the bed.

"But I don't understand. What's the problem?" Babs demanded.

Sam sighed, maybe it would help to talk to someone and who better than Babs? "It's very simple, pet, he doesn't love me. In fact, he can hardly bear the sight of me."

"That I don't believe," Babs snorted. "And as for him not loving you, don't you think if you had a, well, a more normal relationship?"

"You mean, if I slept with him?" Sam asked softly.

"Well—yes."

"Oh, Babs, I've slept with him since two weeks after we were married. You know him. Can you imagine him having it any other way?"

Babs laughed ruefully. "No, as a matter of fact I can't. He's quite a man."

"Yes." It was a simple statement.

"And it still didn't jell?"

Sam shook her head briefly and Babs went on. "I don't understand it. I always thought you two were perfect for each other." Sam looked at her sharply and Babs shrugged. "All right, I admit it, I've been trying to get you two together for years. I could have cried when Morgan couldn't get here for the wedding. I had it all planned. Then when you told me about your father's will, oh, Sam, I never dreamed you'd be hurt like this."

"Well, it's no good crying over it now and besides which you haven't heard the worst yet." Sam hesitated just a moment. "I'm pregnant, Babs."

"And he's still cold to you?" Babs was incredulous. "Why Sam, Morgan loves kids."

"He doesn't know," Sam said quietly.

"Well, you must tell him at once," Babs replied sharply. Her voice hardening, Babs added, "That should take care of her highness."

"Her highness?" Sam asked blankly.

"Stacy Kemper," Babs offered. "That's how I always think of her—the mercenary bitch." She laughed at Sam's startled look. "I know that's not like me. But with this one, I really mean it. She's the reason I insisted you come down. She's also the reason Morgan drove to Vegas."

Sam's eyebrows went up in question, even though she wasn't quite sure she wanted to hear any more. "As you know," Babs explained, "we've all known each other forever. Well, Stacy was one of the group, and for a while there it looked as if she really had her hooks into Morgan. That is until it became apparent that Morgan intended putting everything back into the ranch and not on her back. She took off with and married the first man with money that asked her, without bothering to say a word to Morgan. All of a sudden she was gone. We heard about her marriage later from her very embarrassed parents. I don't know how deeply it affected Morgan, for as you know, he doesn't let anything show."

Sam nodded, but remained quiet, waiting. Babs lit a

cigarette, drew deeply, then went on. "We heard a few years later that she had divorced her husband and taken up with an Italian shoe merchant or some such and then, last night, out of the blue, she phones me and invites herself here for a visit. She said she'd heard we were having a party tomorrow night and that she'd love to come. Believe it or not, Sam, I was speechless for a minute. Well, what could I say? So, of course, I said we'd be glad to have her. Then she said ever so sweetly that as she was without transportation at the moment, could someone come to Vegas for her? And as Ben had to be away most of today on business, Morgan offered to go. And I don't like it, Sam, I don't like it at all." Babs sat back, punched out her cigarette, and immediately lit another.

Sam didn't like it either, although she said nothing. She lit a cigarette and sat thinking as she studied the glowing red tip. An Italian shoe merchant—and Morgan had been seen with a woman in Italy. A coincidence? It was hardly likely. Had he brought this woman, this Stacy, back with him? That seemed much more likely. Yet he had told her to come back to the ranch. What sort of game was he playing? First Carolyn, now this Stacy person. *Damn him, damn him, damn him,* Sam's mind cried furiously. Should she leave? Not wait to suffer the humiliation of being introduced to his ex, and now current, lover? Babs made the decision for her as, jumping to her feet, she picked up Sam's jacket and bag and said firmly, "Come with me." She flung the door open and marched across the hall, to fling another door open and drop Sam's things onto the bed.

Sam glanced around as she entered the room and stopped dead. Morgan's suitcase lay on a bench at the foot of the bed; his brush and comb rested on the dresser.

"Really, Babs," she began, only to be cut off by a very determined-sounding Babs.

"Honey, I don't know how Morgan feels about you. I don't know if he feels anything for her. Hell, I don't know how he feels about much of anything, the clam. But in my house husbands and wives sleep together, not husbands and friends." At the look of pain on Sam's face she added with force, "Oh, Sam, at least make a fight of it. Don't run away."

Sam stayed.

She spent the rest of the afternoon getting reacquainted with Benjie and an amazingly bigger Mark. Ben got home just in time for dinner. Morgan didn't. Ben seemed genuinely happy to see Sam and kept the conversation going throughout the meal.

A few hours later Sam sat curled into a chair in the living room. She had stopped speaking to sip sherry, and had opened her mouth to continue her description of Deb and Bryan's wedding for Babs and Ben, when she went rigid.

Babs glanced swiftly at Ben and then at Sam. They had all heard the sound of the Jaguar as it came up the drive.

Sam was well aware that Babs had filled Ben in on the situation, and she had a moment of pure panic. *I shouldn't be here,* she thought. They had all been friends in one way or other and the last thing Sam wanted in the world was to bring dissension of any kind into this obviously happy home. Before she could unfreeze herself enough to move, the door opened and Morgan strode into the room followed by a woman a few years younger than himself.

Sam barely looked at the woman, for her eyes fastened on Morgan. The night was cold and he was dressed in a heavy tan sheepskin-lined jacket, collar up. Along with black leather driving gloves, boots, and the inevitable black Andalusian hat, he looked rugged and knee-weakeningly masculine. On seeing Sam he stopped in his tracks and she thought she saw an odd look on his face, but it was gone in an instant. He reached up to pull his hat off, his face expressionless, as he moved into the room, closer to her. She was glad she was sitting down, for there was no mistaking the look in those black eyes. He was angry, very angry. As he shrugged out of his jacket, he said in a voice even and smooth as silk, "Well, Samantha, when did you get home? And how did you get here?"

Sam hated when his voice took on that silky tone. Lifting her chin, she answered coolly, "I got home this morning and I drove here in my own car. It's parked in the garage. And I'm fine, thank you," she tacked on, reminding him he hadn't asked. Very slowly she turned her head to look pointedly and haughtily at the woman who had walked up to stand beside him.

She saw the corner of his mouth twitch. In what? Amusement? Annoyance? She was too busy studying the woman to figure out which. She was, without doubt, beautiful. Hair and brows as black as Morgan's with startling red lips in a perfect matte white face. Her eyes a blue so pale as to be almost colorless. But she had, Sam thought, the look of—what? The word *predator* jumped into Sam's mind.

Morgan's smooth voice drew her attention. "Samantha, this is Stacy Kemper, an old friend. Stacy, my wife."

"Hello, Samantha." Stacy's teeth flashed white. Her voice was pure honey.

Sam did not rise or extend her hand. With only a hint of a smile touching her lips, she nodded slightly and murmured frostily, "Miss Kemper."

In a capsulized instant Sam's cool, green eyes recorded the reaction of the other four. Ben's face revealed his surprise. Babs seemed to be having a great deal of trouble keeping a straight face. Stacy withdrew her hand slowly, a look of wariness in the pale blue eyes. And Morgan? Morgan's reaction baffled her. Although he had stiffened at her arrogant iciness, his black eyes, locked on hers, glittered with an emotion she couldn't quite define. He was either extremely amused or flat-out furious. But which? Sam had a sudden overwhelming urge to run for her life. Sheer will power kept her motionless in her seat, her eyes steady on his.

After what seemed half a lifetime, but was actually only seconds, Morgan released his visual hammerlock. Turning away with a casual ease that mocked the tension his eyes had generated so easily in Sam, Morgan tossed his jacket and Stacy's coat onto a chair and grinned at Ben and Babs.

"Stacy informed me, not ten minutes ago, that she was dying for a drink." His lazy drawl shattered the stillness that had held them all motionless and galvanized Babs into action.

"Of course," she exclaimed, jumping to her feet. "What a rotten hostess I am. Ben, will you get the drinks while I hang up their coats?" As if she realized she was speaking much too fast, Babs stood stock still, looked directly at Stacy, and said slowly and distinctly, "It's been a long time, Stacy. How are you?"

Studying Stacy with an outward composure that required every ounce of will power she possessed, Sam didn't even hear her response to Babs or, for that matter, any of the ensuing conversation until a laughing remark from Stacy penetrated her concentration.

"I suddenly just could not win." The malicious gleam of satisfaction in her pale-blue eyes contradicted the rueful pout on her lush red mouth. "The dice had gone absolutely stone cold for me." Calculating eyes flickered over Sam and the rueful pout smoothed into a smug smile. "If Morgan hadn't been there to cover my losses, well, I just don't know what I'd done."

Blind fury turned Sam's eyes into chips of green ice. Whose money had he used to cover Stacy's losses with? And how had she repaid him? By allowing him to cover her as well? The questions stabbed painfully at Sam's mind and the green ice chips swung to Morgan in accusation.

One black brow arched elegantly; he returned her stare blandly, lips twitching tauntingly.

Fed up, sick to her stomach, Sam finished her drink, placed the glass carefully on the coaster on the table at her elbow and, rising with unconscious grace, excused herself and left the room. Morgan did not follow her.

She just made it to the bathroom. After her stomach had relieved itself of her dinner and the sherry she'd gulped, she cleaned her face, brushed her teeth, then stood irresolutely in the middle of the bedroom, Morgan's bedroom, wondering what to do. Surely, she finally decided, Morgan had not entertained the idea of having Stacy warm his bed while he was in his best friend's home? With a shrug she slipped between the sheets. Her last conscious thought was, what would he think when he found his wife in his bed?

Sam was not to know, for she fell into a deep, exhausted sleep. She half awoke during the night, feeling chilly, and without thinking burrowed under the covers closer to the warm body beside her. She was only vaguely, if pleasantly, aware of a feeling of warmth as Morgan's arms slid around her, drew her even closer against him. She didn't remember it in the morning, but she knew he had slept beside her, as his pillow still held the impression from his head. And she sadly decided she'd dreamed the sound of his voice, almost a groan, in the night, whispering her name.

Stacy had not yet put in an appearance, Ben had finished eating and left the table, and Sam and Babs were sipping their second cups of coffee and discussing the new fall clothes, when Morgan walked lazily into the dining room. He poured himself coffee, reached across the table to pick up a piece of bacon Sam had not eaten from her plate, cocked a brow at her, and drawled sardonically, "And how did you leave your—ah—friends, Samantha?"

Sam decided she disliked this sardonic tone as much as his silky one. Looking at him coldly, she answered in kind, "With much difficulty, I assure you." Rising slowly, she turned her back to him and left the room thinking, *and so the battle is joined—again.* The next day passed smoothly enough as Sam saw little of Morgan or Stacy.

Sam was left alone to dress for the evening, as Morgan had finished dressing and left the room while she made up her face in the bathroom. She had brought with her a gown she had bought, with the coming holidays in mind, on her drive West. After slipping the gown on, she carefully brushed her hair, then, stepping back, viewed the results critically. The gown, of deep-green velvet, was simply cut, with close-fitting long sleeves and bodice snug to her still small waist. The neckline plunged in a V to a point between her breasts. The full skirt came to an inch above the floor. She went over to the dresser, removed the black case, flipped the lid, picked out the emerald ring she'd removed before starting her trip, and slid it onto her finger. Then she lifted out the pendant and fastened the chain around her neck. The emerald, which rested just below the base of her throat, glowing warm and rich against her now pale gold skin, seemed to reflect the exact color of her eyes and the circle of diamonds glinted with light. Giving a quick nod of satisfaction, she left the room.

164

She intercepted Babs in the hallway between the dining and living rooms.

"Good grief, Sam," Babs, wide eyes fastened on the emerald pendant, whispered in an awed tone. "That's the most fantastically beautiful thing I've ever seen. Did you knock over Cartier's or something?"

"That's just the half of it, pet." Laughing softly, Sam held out her hand, moved it slightly so the light got caught in the large stone on her finger.

"Wherever did you get them?" Babs breathed hoarsely.

"The ring was a birthday present," Sam replied reluctantly. "The pendant was a belated wedding gift."

"Who from, for heaven's sake?" Babs dragged her eyes from the ring, lifted them to Sam's face, and added. "An oil-rich Arab sheikh?"

"I don't know any Arab sheikh, oil rich or otherwise," Sam murmured. She hesitated then said even more softly, "The gifts were from Morgan."

"And you, my dear peabrain, claim he doesn't care for you?" Babs's already wide eyes widened even more. "Don't you know only a man in love with his wife will buy jewelry like that for her?"

All that long evening Sam clung to Babs's words, determinedly pushing away the thought that the gems were purchased with her money.

Entering the living room, Sam came to a stop at the barrage of greetings called to her by the dozen people gathered there. Stacy, beautiful in an ice-blue sheath that gave her a deceptively fragile look, stood watchfully by the liquor cabinet, but there was no sign of Morgan. Babs laughingly joined Ben as the cry went up for a belated wedding toast and, as they refilled glasses, Sam fought a rising unease. Where was Morgan?

"We can't have a toast without the bridegroom." The

protest was registered by a tiny brunette whose name escaped Sam at the moment. "Where is Morgan, anyway?"

"Right here, Karen."

The lazy drawl, so close behind her, sent a shiver down Sam's spine. The hand that curved around her waist drew her close to his side, turning the shiver to a tongue of fire.

The toast was given, then Sam felt his fingers tighten against her side as Karen chided, "Well, for heaven's sake, Morgan, kiss the bride."

Startled, Sam glanced at him quickly, saw the devil dance in his eyes as he lowered his head to hers. His lips touched hers briefly and yet even in that fleeting instant he reasserted his ownership. With a muffled gasp of shock, Sam felt the tip of his tongue, hard as the tip of a stiletto, pierce her unwilling mouth. Her eyes shot angry green sparks at him when he lifted his head, murmuring tauntingly, "Do you still feel like a bride, Sam?"

In retaliation she let out the first thing that came into her mind. "A somewhat battered one, perhaps."

Though his facial expression didn't change, Morgan's body stiffened and his eyes turned cold and hard. His voice dropped even lower than before, and held a frightening edge of menace.

"Touché, Redhead."

Hating herself, hating him, Sam watched in amazement as his eyes went flat before he turned back to the guests, a deceptively relaxed smile on his face. Drawing her with him, he sauntered into the room, his tone languid as he responded to the renewed calls of congratulations.

When the well-wishing was finally over, the punishing hold on Sam's waist was removed and Morgan left her side. Moving casually, as though his only interest lay in refilling his glass, he joined a pouting Stacy, still standing sentinel by the liquor cabinet.

At any other time Sam would have enjoyed the party. Babs, Ben, and Morgan's friends accepted her as one of their own. They had known previously of the closeness between Sam and Babs, and the fact that she was now Morgan's wife seemed to delight them. The conversation was easy, most times amusing. The food was delicious. Sam was miserable. Although Morgan was careful not to be too blatantly attentive to Stacy, the smug, self-satisfied expression her beautiful face wore dashed all the secret hopes Sam had harbored in her heart as she'd driven West. She kept up with the chatter and badinage until shortly after three and then, unable to bear any more, she excused herself and went to her room.

Within minutes she was crawling into bed, tormenting herself with the question of whether Morgan would spend what was left of the night in their room or Stacy's. But at least the torment was short-lived, for as the night before, she was asleep as soon as her head touched down on her pillow.

CHAPTER 10

The sound of Morgan's voice nudged her awake. Forcing her eyes open, she dully registered two facts. He was fully dressed and was holding a steaming mug of coffee in his hand. He watched her silently as she sat up and rested her back against the headboard.

"I'm going home this morning, are you going with me?" His voice was flat and even as he handed her the mug.

Sam sipped gingerly at the hot brew before answering. "Yes." His next words turned her insides to ice.

"Good. We have some talking to do, Samantha, and I'd prefer to do it in private."

She gulped her coffee too quickly, the hot liquid making her cough and, reaching out swiftly, he plucked the mug from her hands. Watching her, he drank from the mug, then handed it back after she'd caught her breath, wiping her eyes with the back of her hand. "I can't actually go with you, I have my car."

"I remember." His voice held the tone of a parent talking to a dim-witted child. "I'll follow you in the Jag."

"All right. What time do you want to leave?"

She emptied the cup and he took it from her. "More?" She nodded as glancing at his watch he told her, "It's eight thirty. I'd like to be ready to go in an hour. Marie's getting breakfast now."

Sam's voice was startled. "But we can't leave without seeing Babs and Ben."

"I have no intention of doing so," he replied patiently. "But they'll probably be up by then. Now you'd better get moving. I'll get your coffee." He walked to the door and stopped, hand on the knob, when Sam said, "Morgan, I told Sara we'd call."

"I called her last night," he answered without turning. "And told her to stay home today, take the day off, as we wanted to be alone." He opened the door and went through, closing it softly behind him.

Had his voice been mocking? she asked herself, pulling her nightgown over her head as she leaped from the bed. Deciding it was, she grabbed panty hose and bra from the dresser drawer and dashed into the bathroom and under the shower.

She walked back into the bedroom ten minutes later to find Morgan sitting in the chair by the window sipping her fresh coffee. She felt suddenly shy of him seeing her in nothing but panty hose and bra and turning away quickly stepped into jeans and pulled a bulky knit sweater over her head. When she turned around to face him, he handed her the mug with a twisted smile. "Breakfast is just about ready, you'd better pack." He placed her bag on the bench at the foot of the bed and flipped the lid open as Sam collected her makeup and toiletries from the bathroom. She packed the few things she'd brought with her quickly and, as she was carefully folding her gown, Morgan said softly, "That's a lovely dress, Samantha, it suits you."

Sam stood still in shocked speechlessness a moment before answering, her voice sounding wooden to her own ears, "Thank you, I think that's everything." But she stole a glance at him as she closed the lid and was surprised to see the bleak look was quickly gone from his face.

He got her jacket and picked up her suitcase, then stood waiting at the door while she put on her boots.

As Sam left the room, she heard voices from the nursery. Telling Morgan she'd join him in a few minutes, she went in to say good-bye to the boys. She talked a few minutes with Judy, then, with a tug at her heart, gave good-bye hugs and kisses to Benjie and Mark. She left the nursery quickly and walked down the hall to the dining room noticing her suitcase sitting next to Morgan's at the front door.

Morgan was filling two plates from the covered dishes on the sideboard, so she slipped into her chair and sipped her juice. When he placed her plate in front of her she bit back the protest that rose to her lips. How in the world would she eat all that food? she thought, eyeing him warily. Nevertheless she tried.

He had finished, poured himself a second cup of coffee, and lit a cigarette, watching her steadily, when Babs and Ben joined them.

"I see you're all set to take off after you've eaten." Babs filled her plate and sat down saying lightly, "You weren't going without saying good-bye, were you?"

"Of course not," Sam cried.

"I'd have come in and tilted your bed," Morgan added dryly.

Ben laughed softly. "I don't doubt it a minute."

"Nor I," Babs teased, before adding seriously, "I hope it's not eight months before we see you two again. As a matter of fact, we'd like to have you for Christmas."

"Well, we'll see," Sam hedged, then nearly jumped as Babs gave her a kick under the table while turning a sweet smile on Morgan. "Do you think you could make it?"

"I don't see why not." Morgan's white teeth flashed in

170

a grin as he answered blandly. "Let us know what time, Babs."

"I will," came the emphatic reply.

They waited until Babs and Ben had finished eating, then made their way out. As Morgan stashed their suitcases and Ben brought Sam's car from the garage, Babs whispered, "Have you told him?" Sam shook her head. "Well, do it as soon as you get home," Babs ordered. Sam hugged Babs, whispered, "I will and thanks for being my friend." Babs kissed Sam lightly on the cheek. "Always, you know that, Sam."

Sam, feeling tears too close, nodded and slid behind the wheel. Giving a quick wave, she drove out of the driveway, the Jaguar right behind her. Halfway to the ranch Sam began to resent the short distance Morgan kept between them. *As if I can't be trusted behind the wheel,* she thought peevishly, her foot pushing the pedal to the floor. The Stingray shot ahead and in no time had put some distance between them. Her satisfaction was short-lived, however, as glancing in the rearview mirror, she saw the Jag gaining rapidly on her. *I should have known better,* she was thinking when the car hit an oil slick and went into a spin. Sam gripped the wheel, but going with the spin, not trying to halt it, and by some quirk of fate, the car didn't roll over. She finally managed to bring it to a stop facing in the same direction she'd been going. She was still clutching the wheel, shaking all over, when the door was flung open. "What kind of a stupid trick was that?" It was the closest thing to a shout she'd ever heard from Morgan. "You crazy broad, are you trying to kill yourself?"

It was the wrong side of enough. Sam refused to listen to this cowboy speak to her like this any longer. The engine was still idling, and forcing her shaking fingers from the wheel, Sam did two things at once. She reached out for the handle and slammed the door shut, seeing Morgan straighten in surprise as she did so, then she floored the pedal again. She kept it floored until she reached the road to the ranch property, thankful of the sparse traffic, and then only slowed down a fraction until reaching their driveway. She crawled along the driveway sedately, parked in front of the garage, jumped from the car, and ran to the back door of the house, rummaging in her bag for the kitchen door key.

Inside the kitchen she stood breathing deeply, shaking all over with reaction. Her body jerked when she heard the Jag purr to a stop in the drive and she ran from the room through the house to the bedroom. She flung her jacket and purse onto a chair and sat on the side of the bed fighting for control. *I must leave him, get away from here,* she was thinking wildly when he walked into the room in a cold fury. Wincing at the slam of the door, she repeated her thought aloud, "I'm going to leave you, Morgan, get a divorce."

His eyes glittered like two pieces of wet coal and his voice was icy.

"What kind of games are you playing? What the hell did you come back for?"

At the end of her rope, her voice rose. "I'm not playing games."

"No?" Morgan's eyes narrowed as he walked slowly toward her. "You didn't drive all the way out here just to see the scenery. Or to tell me you were going to divorce me. So let's have it."

"It doesn't matter." Sam had to fight to keep her voice even.

"What doesn't matter?" He stopped in front of her. "What aren't you telling me?" At Sam's helpless shrug his tone lowered threateningly. "Tell me, Samantha."

"I'm pregnant," Sam whispered starkly.

Cold eyes in a rock-hard face raked over her. "Is it mine?"

"Oh, God," Sam's whisper held pain, anguish. "Oh, *God*." Feeling nausea churn upward from her stomach to her throat, Sam brought one hand up to cover her mouth, moved to get up, away from his cold eyes. His hand grasped her shoulder, held her still as he sat down beside her.

"I'm sorry," Morgan grated harshly. "I had to know. When?"

"What?"

"When is the baby due?" he snapped.

"Late spring," Sam whispered. "The end of May."

"I see." He had finished his mental calculations; his deductions were only partly correct. "And you drove all the way out here just to watch my face when you told me?"

Sam's eyes widened. He really believed she'd come to lay some sort of guilt trip on him, torment him, because of his actions on the night she'd conceived. His opinion of her hurt unbearably. Blinking quickly against the hot sting in her eyes, Sam looked up at him. His face was set in hard, rigid lines; his eyes studied her coldly.

"You really hate me," she whispered brokenly, "don't you, Morgan?"

The hand gripping her shoulder tightened painfully while his other hand grasped the hair at the back of her head and forced her face close to his.

"Hate you?" he grated. "You redheaded witch, I love you."

His crushing mouth smothered her gasp of disbelief. Had he really said he loved her? Wild hope mingled with

173

the fire surging through her veins. The smothered gasp came out as a low moan when he lifted his head.

"Morgan."

"No." His lips teased hers. "Don't talk. You can add my scalp to all the others on your belt," he groaned against her mouth. "But don't talk. Not now. It's been so long, Sam."

In between deep, hungry kisses their clothes were abandoned and then, as their hunger grew urgent, it was the two of them that gave in to their abandon. Driven to the edge of delirium by his hands, his mouth, Sam clung to Morgan, moaning softly deep in her throat, begging him to make her a part of him.

He came to her almost hesitantly, but that hesitancy was soon lost to the need to possess and be possessed. As their shudders subsided to gentle tremors, Sam's hand lightly caressed Morgan's warm, moist back.

"Don't go, Sam." The words were muffled against her hair. "These last weeks have been hell. The idea of spending the rest of my life without you is unbearable. Stay with me. Bargain with me one more time."

"Bargain?"

Morgan sighed, then the sweet weight of his body left hers and he lay beside her, his fingers lacing through hers as if he couldn't bear the thought of breaking all physical contact.

"I want my baby," Morgan said softly. "Your baby." His fingers crushed hers. "I want you. I'll match the amount that was laid on the line last March, if you'll stay with me."

"Match the amount?" Sam repeated incredulously.

"Yes," he answered flatly. "I can't give it to you in one lump sum, but I'll put one million a year, for the next five years, in an account in your name."

"But how?"

"I don't need your money, Sam. I never have," he went on in the same flat tone. "And I haven't touched it."

"But Babs said—" Sam began uncertainly, but he cut her off.

"I know what my friends think and I've let them think it. It's kept the cats away. But I was never as broke as they thought and I've made a lot of money over the last ten years. I'm a fairly rich man, Samantha, and I worked like hell for every cent of it."

Confusion kept Sam quiet for several minutes. His tight grip on her hand was causing her ring to dig into her finger and that sparked a sudden thought.

"My jewelry and the plane and the Jag?"

"I paid for them. Your charge accounts too." His flat tone grew an edge of amusement. "That's why your lawyers wanted to see me. They couldn't understand why we hadn't drawn on the money."

"But when you bought the plane and the car you consulted me!" Sam exclaimed.

"Of course." All traces of amusement fled. "You're my wife."

"I don't understand, Morgan." Sam spoke slowly. "If you didn't need the money then why did you—"

"Marry you?" Morgan finished for her. "I wanted you," he added bluntly.

"Physically?" Sam whispered.

"Yes."

His head turned on the pillow and Sam found herself looking directly into unreadable black eyes.

"I wanted you physically," he said clearly. "From the minute I looked up and saw you framed in the doorway of Ben's living room." His eyes roamed over her face, a small fire springing to life. "I've wanted many women,

Samantha, and I had most of the ones I wanted, but I had never wanted a woman on sight as badly as I wanted you." The fire leaped a little higher in his eyes. "I had to fight the urge to tear your clothes off and throw you onto the floor."

"But you seemed to dislike me," Sam gasped, the flame in his eyes igniting a similar one inside her body.

"What I disliked was the intensity of my own feelings." His free hand came up to touch her face, his long index finger traced the outline of her upper lip. "But believe me, I'd decided there and then that I'd have you. And when Ben outlined your proposition, I agreed at once. If I hadn't fallen in love with you by the time we got married I'd have taken you a lot sooner than I did." The tip of his finger slid between her lips, brushed the edge of her teeth. "And when I did take you, it was because I could no longer control myself."

His eyes, watching the play of his finger, darkened with fresh desire. His other hand loosened, moved to caress the inside of her arm as his head moved closer to hers.

"Will you bargain one last time, Sam?" he asked huskily.

"You want to *buy* me, Morgan?" Sam murmured tremulously.

"If that's the way it must be, yes," he said bluntly. "You and our baby."

"Who was conceived in violence."

The moment the words were out, Sam wished them unsaid. Raw pain flashed in Morgan's eyes before he rolled away from her to sit up on the edge of the bed.

"Yes, who was conceived in violence," he repeated harshly, long fingers of one hand raking through his hair. Sam barely heard the whispered words that followed. "But welcomed with love."

He turned back to face her again, his hard, muscular shoulders gleaming darkly in the late afternoon sunlight slanting through the window. The golden mellow rays brought into relief the harshly defined features of his face.

"And he *will* be welcomed with love, I promise you that." His hand massaged the back of his neck and his voice grew husky again. "I've hurt you badly and I know it." He paused, his hand dropping to his side, before adding roughly, "I wanted to hurt you."

"Why, Morgan?" Sam asked softly, then wished she'd been still as she lay and watched the fire of desire explode into a blaze of fury.

"Why? Because I had been bought and paid for, that's why."

"But you just said you didn't need—"

"But you didn't know that, did you?" Morgan's harsh voice slashed across her protest. "You wore my ring and you shared my bed and then you calmly told me you'd sleep with anyone you wanted to."

"Morgan, please," Sam cried, suddenly frightened. "I never meant it. I was lashing out in jealousy."

"Jealousy?" Morgan looked completely stunned. "Jealous of whom?"

"Carolyn." At his totally blank expression, Sam cried, "I saw you with her in the garden the night of the party. I saw you take her into your arms." The anger she'd felt that night returned to jab at her. "Did you take her with you the first time you left Long Island?"

"I did not." The denial was prompt and emphatic and held the unmistakable ring of truth. "And I did not take her into my arms in the garden. She had a few suggestions along that line but I politely declined." One black brow arched sardonically. "I figured I had enough to handle with a fiery-tempered, green-eyed redhead. The last thing I needed was a doll-faced, simpering blonde."

"And what about a white-faced, black-haired, ex-mistress of an Italian shoe merchant?" Sam shot back, forgetting her nakedness as she sat up to glare at him.

"What about her?" Morgan returned easily.

"Do you deny you were with her in Italy and London?" Sam almost screamed at him. "Or that you damned near crawled all over her last night?"

The light of devilment jumping into his eyes, Morgan studied her for long moments before he dropped back onto the bed, his body shaking with laughter.

Staring at him in impotent rage, Sam was struck with two conflicting urges. The first was to slap his laughing face. The second was to caress his smooth dark skin. Trembling with anger and the longing to be in his arms, Sam snapped, "Damn you, Morgan, answer me."

With the swiftness of tightly coiled springs suddenly released, Morgan's arms shot out and his hands, grasping her shoulders, hauled her down with a jarring thud on top of him.

"No, you answer me," he demanded. "Do you love me?"

"Morgan, let me go." Sam struggled wildly, gasping softly at the sensations the feel of his hair-roughened chest against her breasts sent splintering through her body.

"Do you love me?" One hard hand released her shoulder to grip the back of her head and force her lips to within a whisper of his.

"Yes." His lips touched hers briefly. "Yes." Another touch. "Oh, yes." With a sigh Sam sought the searing brand that was his mouth.

* * *

Sam surfaced to the pearl-gray of pre-dawn, reaching for Morgan before she opened her eyes. When her searching hands found nothing but empty sheets beside her, she opened her eyes, called his name unsteadily.

"Coming." The reassuring sound of his voice and the fragrant scent of freshly brewed coffee preceded him into the room.

Sam was sitting up, covers draped around her shoulders against the chill morning air, when he sauntered into the room, a mug of coffee in each hand.

"Good morning."

A light shiver rippled over Sam's shoulder at the husky timbre of his voice, the altogether male look of him. He was freshly showered and his taut, dark-skinned cheeks gleamed with an attractive, just-shaven sheen. Dressed in tight jeans and a finely knit, longsleeved white pullover, merely looking at him did crazy things to Sam's senses.

Morgan saw her shiver and, after setting the mugs down on the nightstand beside the bed, he strode to the closet that ran the length of the far wall, pulled out a white terrycloth robe, and walked back to the bed holding the robe for her as he would a coat.

Unsure of him still, Sam hesitated, but when one black brow went up slowly in a ark she drew a deep breath, scrambled off the bed, and slid her arms into the sleeves of the robe. As her trembling fingers pulled the belt tight, his hands tightened on her shoulders then were removed.

"Drink your coffee before it gets cold."

Turning quickly, Sam took the mug he held out to her then sank onto the side of the bed, her eyes fastened on his back as he walked to the window, stood staring through the glass, his face set in brooding lines.

His strangely cool, withdrawn attitude, following so swiftly on the heels of his hot, passionate lovemaking, sent a shaft of fear through Sam's heart. Sipping the hot brew she watched him nervously, trying to steel herself for whatever he had to say.

"Do you still want to leave me, Samantha?" He did not turn his head to look at her and Sam shivered again, this time at the flat emotionless tone of his voice. "Do you still want a divorce?"

Sam's mouth went completely dry. Was he trying to tell her he wanted her to go? After the night they'd just spent together? She considered using delaying tactics in an effort to draw him out, find out exactly what he wanted. For herself, well, she knew what she wanted but, if he wanted his freedom, her pride dictated that she should give it to him, walk away from this debacle with her head still high. Her sigh of surrender could be heard across the room more clearly than the whispered words that followed it.

"No, I don't want to leave. I don't want a divorce." Sam drew a deep breath. "I love you, Morgan. I want to stay here with you."

She couldn't see his face, but she heard his breath expelled slowly, as if he'd been holding it a long time. Then he turned to face her, his knuckles white from gripping his coffee mug.

"About Stacy," he said quietly. "I was with her in Italy and London."

Panic crawled through Sam's mind. Had he deliberately waited for her to commit herself before telling her about Stacy? She was suddenly sure she didn't want to hear any more, but before she could tell him he asked, "Who told you, Dudley?"

"Yes."

"I see." His tone was so cold Sam shivered again.

"No, Morgan, you don't." Sam stared unflinchingly into those cold, black eyes. "What I told you in London

180

was true. Duds is like an older brother to me, nothing more. He is protective of me, he always has been. That's the only reason he told me you had been seen with her."

"I see," Morgan repeated, but in a different tone. "It seems I owe the both of you an apology for what I was thinking about your relationship." He finished his coffee and placed the mug on the wide windowsill behind him before going on calmly. "I ran into Stacy in Spain. She told me bluntly that she had had a violent argument with her shoe merchant friend and that, as he had acquired another to replace her, he was kicking her out."

"But what was she doing in Spain?" Sam asked in confusion.

"She said she was paying a last visit to some close friends," Morgan replied dryly. "When I mentioned that due to a change in business plans I was flying to London in two days, she begged me to take her with me." He shrugged carelessly. "We flew to Italy the next day. She collected some of her things and made arrangements for the rest to be sent to her parents' here in Nevada. We flew to London the following morning."

"Did you bring her with you when you came back to the States?" Sam asked hoarsely.

"Yes," he answered flatly. "I also gave her some money. In Spain, in London, and again, two days ago, in Vegas."

Sam closed her eyes against the sudden hot sting of tears, swallowed with difficulty against the dryness in her throat. The sharpness of his tone brought her eyelids up again.

"I did not touch her. Not in any personal way. I wasn't even tempted." His lips curved in self-derision. "Even if I had been, I doubt if I'd been able to do anything about it. She doesn't have red hair."

"Morgan." A different kind of shiver slid down Sam's

spine and her heart gave a wild double thump. "She seemed very sure of herself at Babs's," she said carefully. "Did you make any—promises?"

"Are you out of your beautiful red head?" Morgan grated. "I just finished telling you I can't see any other woman—" He broke off suddenly then added softly, "I wanted you to assume there was something between Stacy and me." His voice dropped to a ragged whisper. "I thought that if I couldn't get at you any other way, maybe I could hurt you through your pride." He laughed harshly in self-mockery. "You were so cool, so untouched, by it all. I was sure the only one I'd managed to hurt was myself, again."

"Again?" Sam repeated. "But when—?"

"The night of the party," Morgan answered her question before she'd finished asking it. "I was so damned mad. I've been mad ever since."

"But, I—"

"Not at you," he interrupted again. "At myself."

"Why?"

"Why?" He barked. "Good God, Sam, I'd never physically harmed a woman in my life and I'd savaged you." His lips twisted in a grim mockery of a smile. "And I'd done it deliberately. I walked into that bedroom knowing I was going to hurt you in some way."

"Morgan, stop."

His smile, the harsh lines of self-disgust that edged his face, clutched at Sam's heart. The punishment he had meted out to her was as nothing compared to the punishment he'd obviously inflicted on himself.

"You were so magnificent," Morgan went on as if he hadn't heard her. His black eyes grew warm with admiration. "You are some woman, Red, and I handled you badly." His smile turned self-derisive. "It was a new experience for me—the jealous lover. I'd never cared enough about any other woman to feel jealousy."

"Jealous?" Sam breathed, wide eyed. "You, Morgan?"

"Funny, isn't it?" Morgan shrugged, as if uncomfortable in a too snugly fitting coat. "Want to hear something even funnier? I was scared. Deep down gut scared."

"*That* I find impossible to believe."

"It's true all the same." Morgan's eyes caressed her face. "The scary feeling began soon after that first night we slept together. It got worse every time I had to go away. I was so damned scared that one day I'd come home and find you'd gone." He smiled ruefully. "Last summer when you first started to lose weight I grasped at the idea you might be pregnant."

"You wanted me to be pregnant?" Sam cried in disbelief. "But I was positive you'd be angry if I was."

Morgan's head moved sharply in the negative. "I was praying you'd become pregnant. I thought—I hoped that might keep you with me." Again that rueful smile curved his lips. "Stupid, I know. But, as I said, I was running scared and willing to grasp at any straw."

Wide-eyed, stunned, Sam stared at Morgan as if at a stranger. Where was the cold-eyed, unfeeling, arrogant man she had thought she'd married? A series of scenes flashed through her mind. Morgan, Benjie clasped firmly in his arms, laughing down at Mark. Morgan, his eyes soft, his voice gentle, asking Deb to be his sister. Morgan, his eyes filled with contrition, giving her his word that he'd never hurt her again. Suddenly she knew that if this man was a stranger to her, she had no one to blame but herself. Drawing a deep breath, Sam decided to get to know this stranger better.

"Of course"—Morgan's eyes skimmed her body possessively—"I dreaded that trip to Long Island. I felt sure that once you left the ranch you'd never come back. You'd been jetting around the world all your life." He waved his hand to indicate not only the room but the whole property. "After the world, what could this place offer you?"

"You."

All the harshness drained out of his face at her whispered reply. His eyes, flaring with rekindled passion, set off tiny explosions of pure joy all through Sam's body. She shivered deliciously as he walked slowly to her.

"I love you, Sam."

Cradling her head in his hands, he tilted her head back. As he lowered his head she chided, "You said I was your woman."

"I also said you're my wife." His lips brushed hers tantalizingly. "I want you to remain my wife. Tell me you love me, Sam."

"I love you, Morgan."

His mouth touched hers, the pressure increasing as he slid his body onto the bed. His arms, closing around her, drew her body alongside his. His mouth left hers, sought the tender skin behind her ear.

"I could bear not being your wife, Morgan."

"Samantha!"

Morgan's head jerked back and his black eyes pinned hers, narrowed at the teasing light he found there.

"But I don't think I could bear not being your woman."

Sam swam the length of the pool slowly, reveling in the delicious feel of the water on her body. It was the first time she'd been able to go into the pool and the July sun had quickly pinkened her pale skin. Pulling her body through the water, Sam was grateful for her renewed energy, the strength in her arms. For so many weeks after she'd left the hospital she'd been so damnably, stupidly weak.

Movement along the side of the pool caught her eye and she turned her head to see who it was. The sight of her husband's tall form sent all thoughts of her health out of her head. Dropping her feet to the floor of the pool, Sam watched as Morgan walked to the edge of the pool and stood, hands on hips, watching her. He was incredibly dusty and incredibly sweaty and incredibly beautiful.

"Come here, Red."

Sam was galvanized into action by the soft order. When she reached the side of the pool, she raised her hands for him to help her out. Ignoring her hands, Morgan bent down and caught her firmly under the arms and lifted her out of the water as he straightened. When she stood, dripping, in front of him, his hands dropped to circle her slender waist.

"Do you have permission to go in the water?"

Morgan's eyes, searching her face, warned her she'd better have.

"Yes," Sam replied softly, knowing full well the importance of her answer. "I gave the doctor a verbal report on my condition by phone this morning," she went on to explain. "He told me I could resume swimming and all normal activities."

The pressure of his hands on her waist increased. Bending his head, he brushed his lips across hers.

"*All* activities?"

The pulse in Sam's neck fluttered wildly. "Yes." She breathed softly around her excitement-tightened throat. Taking a step nearer to him, she brought her hands up to cup his face, draw him closer. His hands held her body firmly away from his.

"Sam, stop," he groaned against her lips. "I'm filthy and sweaty."

Lightly her hands slid over his taut jaw, down his neck

to the front of his cotton work shirt. Her mouth still touching his, her fingers began opening the buttons.

"What are you doing?" Morgan murmured.

"Unbuttoning your shirt."

"I *know* that," he rasped. "But why?"

"I want you to swim with me."

"Sam," Morgan groaned hoarsely. "I've got to get cleaned up."

"The chlorine in the pool will clean you," Sam said complacently, tugging the shirt from his jeans. When the shirt was free, her hands went to his belt buckle, flipped it open. When the belt hung open, she opened the snap of his jeans and, caught at the zipper pull. One hand left her waist and covered her fingers, stilling their movement.

"Sara will see."

"No, she won't," Sam denied. "Both she and Jake are at home—playing grandparents." Her teeth nipped his lower lip. "We're alone till bedtime, Morgan."

She heard his sharply indrawn breath, then her hand was brushed aside. He stepped back, shrugging out of his shirt. He glanced up at her when his hands moved to complete the job she'd started on his zipper. Eyes dancing with deviltry, he teased, "Are you prepared to yank off my boots?"

"At your service, sir." Even in a bikini Sam's curtsy was graceful. "But I'd think it would be easier if you sat down."

Abandoning the jeans, Morgan dropped to the grass and lifted a very dirty booted foot. After much tugging and exaggerated grunting the boots were removed and his socks followed swiftly. Springing to his feet, Morgan released the pants zipper and stepped out of his jeans. His thumbs slid under the elastic of his very brief Jockey shorts, then he paused, black eyes skimming her bikini.

186

"The suit's got to go," he decided, laughing at her shocked face. "If I'm skinny dipping, so are you. Will you take it off," he grinned, "or will I?"

"Mor—gan," Sam pleaded.

"Either you take it off"—he took one step toward her—"or I will."

He dropped his briefs, kicked them aside, then waited, a small smile on his lips, while Sam removed the two skimpy pieces. As soon as they were gone, he held out his hand, grasped hers, and jumped into the pool.

"God that feels good," Morgan sighed when he surfaced. "How about you amusing yourself while I do a few laps, sluice the grime off my hide?"

"Be my guest," Sam waved a hand to encompass the pool. "Just don't be gone too long."

"I won't," he promised, shooting away from her.

Doing a slow sidestroke, Sam watched as Morgan's powerful arms cut cleanly through the water. After the fourth lap he came toward her. With hardly a break in motion his one arm caught her around the waist and he drew her with him to the side of the pool. Pinning her back to the smoothly painted wall, he growled, "I want my kiss."

"What kiss?" Sam asked, her eyes innocently wide.

"The kiss you've been teasing me with ever since I got home, you witch."

Planting himself firmly in front of her, he brought his mouth crashing onto hers. His lips were cool from the water and tasted slightly of chlorine. His tongue was hot and hungry. Excitement splintered through Sam's body sending tiny, sharp shards of pleasure along her veins. Her hands moved slowly up his chest, over his shoulders, loving the feel of his cool, wet skin.

"Let's get out of here."

Moving away from her, Morgan pushed himself up and over the edge of the pool, then turned to lift her out. She was no sooner on her feet than she was off again, swept up into Morgan's arms. Holding her tightly against his body, he strode to the house, his clothes and her bikini forgotten.

Once inside the bedroom, he kicked the door closed, dripped across the carpet, tossed her, soaking wet, onto the bed, and dropped down beside her, his mouth urgently seeking hers. Sam moaned a protest when his mouth left hers, then her face was caught, held still by his hard hands.

"Is it safe, Sam?" he grated harshly.

"Morgan, please," Sam whispered, her arms tightening around his neck, trying to bring his mouth back to her.

"Is it safe?" he demanded.

"Yes," Sam sighed, then, "Morgan?"

It was all the assurance, or plea, he needed. His hand moved, slowly, arousingly, from her face to her breasts, to her hips and back again to her breasts where they lingered, his fingers gentle, but exciting. His mouth demanded, his tongue searched, until she cried out with her need for him.

Their union, after so many weeks of abstinence, was wild and sweet and totally satisfying.

Her breathing returned to normal, and Sam lay in Morgan's arms, unmindful of the damp sheets. A soft sigh, almost a purr, escaped her lips at the delightful sensations Morgan's hand, stroking her thigh between hip and knee, created in her. Shifting his body, Morgan buried his face in the curve of her neck.

"You don't like taking those pills, do you?" he asked quietly.

"Morgan."

"Do you?" he insisted.

"No, I don't," Sam admitted reluctantly. "But it's all right, really, I—"

"Goddamnit, Sam," he grated roughly. "You should have let me have the vas—"

"No." Sam's tone was soft, but sharp with finality. "You'll change your mind some day, you'll see." She felt the movement of his forehead against her jaw as he shook his head.

"I need you, Sam," Morgan whispered close to her ear. "Not just for times like this, but all the time. I need to know you're mine, that you're here, that you're alive."

"Morgan, don't," Sam urged. "Don't talk about—"

"I must," he cut across her plea, "I must talk about it. Dear God, Sam," he groaned. "If it hadn't been for Babs and Ben, I'd have torn that hospital apart."

"Morgan, stop."

"I was so damned scared," he went on as if he hadn't heard her. "I felt that I had to get to you, help you, hold on to you to keep you from slipping away from me."

His arms jerked convulsively, crushing her to him so tightly Sam had to bite her lip to keep from crying out in pain. Her own arms held him fiercely, protectively, her hands smoothing over his tension-bunched muscles.

"I know, darling," she soothed softly when he shuddered. "I know."

I know now that this is some kind of man I married, she mused wonderingly. The gentle way he'd taken care of her through the long winter, into the spring, had amazed her. If Sara had fussed and clucked over her like a mother hen, Morgan had guarded her like a watchdog. In March, when she had cried and stormed at him that she was enormous and ugly, he had teased her out of her bad mood by declaring he liked the round, full look. And it had been such a bad winter. And he had worked such terribly long hours.

From their first meeting she'd thought he was unfeeling and hard. Over the winter she'd found out she'd been right on one count. He was hard. Hard and tough. The amount of hard, physical work he did appalled her. And as if that wasn't enough, he'd had to make several business trips. Each time he'd come home looking exhausted, and she'd found out, through Ben, by way of Babs, that he drove himself tirelessly in an effort to get home to her sooner.

The knowledge had induced feelings of guilt and she'd stared morosely at her steadily growing, increasingly clumsy body.

Who could have known? Even her doctor had not suspected. Had never, he admitted later, thought of ordering x rays.

When she'd gone into labor four weeks before her due date, Sam had panicked, Morgan had not. Talking to her quietly to calm her down, he'd made her comfortable in the Jag and driven at his usual high speed to the hospital. It was later, Sam learned from Babs, after they realized there were problems, that Morgan began pacing like a caged animal.

She had come very close, too close, to dying and although Sam was beyond the point of caring at the time, Babs later told her that they all knew and what the news did to Morgan was terrible to watch.

His eyes, Babs had said, were frightening and on several occasions he'd actually snarled in reply to what anyone said, even Ben. His long, rangy frame had measured the room countless times before the door had opened to admit Sam's doctor. And that poor man, Babs had laughed afterwards, had looked terrified when Morgan's head had snapped around to him, his eyes narrowed dangerously, his teeth bared like a hungry dog's.

That, to Sam, was all hearsay. All she knew of those long hours was of crying out in agony for Morgan, and hanging on to life with all the will she possessed. When it was finally over, and she lay in a bed in a private room, her body spent, but her mind strangely alert, Morgan came to her.

The door opened and he stood there staring at her for long seconds. The same Morgan who was capable of endless hours of hard, physical work. The same Morgan who had promised to "drop" Jeff and would have. The same Morgan who had threatened to kill Duds and could have. That same Morgan stood staring at her, then walked to the bed, dropped to his knees beside it, lay his head on her breast, and wept. Wept with the release of bottled-up fear, as only a man, strong in himself, can weep.

"Have you seen them?" Sam's hands, looking white and fragile, smoothed his hair.

"No." His head moved from side to side in her hands.

"Go see," she urged softly. "They were worth it."

His head jerked up, his eyes luminous, but fiery, pinned hers.

"Nothing was worth it."

"They were."

Now Sam trembled in Morgan's crushing grip. Her convalescence had been so long, how good it felt to be with him like this again. Loosening his hold, Morgan lifted his head, his eyes, sharp with concern, studying her face.

"What's the matter? Are you cold?"

"No, I'm not cold." A becoming pink tinged her cheeks. "In fact just the opposite. Oh, Morgan, I want you to make love to me again before Sara brings the boys back."

"Our boys," Morgan chided softly, an enticing smile on his lips. "Our redheaded twins," he murmured. The smile twisted. "I love them so much, Sam. And they nearly killed you getting into the world."

"But they didn't," Sam whispered, the tip of her tongue teasing the corner of his mouth. "I'm alive, I'm here, and I'm yours."

Her words were stilled by the pressure of his mouth, her tongue was caught, entwined with his. When his tough, hard body moved against, then over, hers, she moaned in surrender. His mouth left hers to seek, tantalize, the gem-hard tip of her breast and she gasped, crying, "Yes, please, Morgan, make me your woman again."

Leona Karr

Colorado's Romance Writer of the Year!

FORBIDDEN TREASURE. Beautiful and unconsciously alluring, young Alysha had resigned herself to the dreary life of a seamstress. Then a carriage accident left her stranded at a lavish French castle, and Alysha was lured into a world of seduction and danger by darkly handsome Raoul de Lamareau, master of the chateau.

_____2707-0 $3.95US/$4.95CAN